To my Brother ~
'Nuff said !

Tony J Argosi

george avgoustis

NEVERKING

PRINCE OF THE ELVES

Neverking

Published by Armida Publications 2009

Copyright © George Avgoustis 2009

George Avgoustis asserts the moral right
to be identified as the author of this work

Cover: Dripping blood © Sean Gladwell - Fotolia.com

Original back cover artwork and map (page 8) © Leigh Donovan 2009
www.visionality.deviantart.com

Page 5 artwork: sword © Bertold Werkmann - Fotolia.com

This publication was partially funded by the Ministry of Education
and Culture of the Republic of Cyprus. Funding of this publication
does not imply endorsement by the Ministry of Education and
Culture of the contents or views expressed by the writer.

Printed and bound by
Kailas Printers and Lithographers Ltd, Nicosia, Cyprus

ISBN 978-9963-620-71-5

Armida Publications
P.O.Box 27717, 2432, Engomi, Nicosia, Cyprus

www.armidapublications.com

george avgoustis

NEVERKING

PRINCE OF THE ELVES

an epic novel

armida | 2009

for my brothers
Jim and Mario
and my buddy Leo
who patiently read my book as it was written,
my private editors.
(how much do I owe you Jimmy, 14 bucks?)

for my buddy Chad
without you there would be no protagonist
(what were we, twelve?)

for Shawn Speakman, Web Druid for Terry Brooks
you provided me some helpful advise, thank you

for my baby boys
who contributed the letters C and V
while sitting on my lap

for my mom
who gave me life and love

and most of all... Pops.
You unwittingly wrote this book

prologue
11

cursed 13   176 ...... north

the pupil 16   199 ...... land's end

three sticks 21   210 ...... abyss

servant 32   221 ...... coming to terms

the unknown 36   234 ...... gogatha

evil dispatched 47   240 ...... tension

night flight 53   249 ...... foreign soil

mount skala 58   263 ...... less than human

descent 66   284 ...... vyn-turion

grandalimus 76   294 ...... sovereign's reach

cutthroat city 88   306 ...... failure

feo-dosia 98   319 ...... too far

leader 126   332 ...... confrontation

integrity 142   348 ...... legend

charisma 151   376 ...... home

one stick 162

381
epilogue

"I will take blood from my very heart
and use it to sign my name!"

Avador Andor, Prince of the Elves

Prologue

The lake was liquid sapphire. Gentle moonbeams bounced and glittered off its silky surface. The water itself seemed to breathe, radiate life, though no life dwelt below its gleaming surface. One soul watched. A living, breathing, restless being stood anxiously at its edge, lost in reflection… and waited.

A new life this very moment was about to breathe its first breath of the world's air. One that he hoped would mirror his own, a life of honor and trust, one that described the soul of integrity and goodness. A life of leadership and respect was what this man could only hope for. The man standing at the edge of this miraculous lake was called Andor, Grandalimus Andor. Grandalimus was the King of Elvenkind.

His green eyes sparkled with a curious hue of violet as he looked up high towards the moon. Tears streamed unwittingly down his scarred cheeks; the first cry of his newborn son resounded across the land and into his heart… where it will stay forever.

Chapter 1 - Cursed

Moons descended and moons have risen. It was never anything the people (save for the rare magic-users or abundant thieves) took very seriously. But this night, this icy turbulent night, the moon seemed to alter and warp itself into something unrecognizable. Murky clouds danced around it in an incomprehensible rage. An illusion. It must have been a trick that the eyes were playing. This was unnatural. Sadly, unnatural or not, it was real and happening that very moment.

Twenty years have passed since his son was born. Grandalimus was attacked countless times but each time, he and the Elves resisted the assaults of innumerable foes. Men, Ogres, and even Dark Dwarves driven by lunacy, have coveted the 'throne' that the Elven King now keeps.

Grandalimus never wanted this charge of being ruler of the Elves for it meant more than ruling Elvenkind... much more. His was a kingdom that signified something to its people, a kingdom with real power that made a difference. Even other races began to show their respects to the Elven King. It started with a handful of Humans and Dwarves pledging their allegiance to him that brought on a major disorder to the natural rhythm of life.

To look at Grandalimus and follow his everyday moves, one would never guess he was a ruler of nations. He blended in as a commoner, mingled with his people and never accepted superior treatment. Maybe it was because he never wanted to be a king, especially one with his position. Or maybe he believed all men are equal no matter what blood dwells within their veins. Regardless, this title was thrust upon him and it was bitter like an unripe lemon and sweet as a sugared berry leaf. When it came to war, or a quest of great peril, or even keeping the peace, Grandalimus was recognized as a king of greatness. 'A good captain can not be judged when the seas are tranquil.'

*The Elf king gazed thoughtfully at the new site before him. The wind lashed at him menacingly, his honey-blonde hair whipping savagely at his cheeks. What was happening? What was this spectacle that was occurring before his and the nations very eyes? A war he understood. A quest of great importance he acknowledged. But what was **this**?*

Abruptly, without warning, a light so intense that it overwhelmed the land with its brilliance, blinded the Elven King and forced him to lunge to the ground clutching his head in pain. Where did it come from? Who or what was doing this?

A thought pierced him like a blade. His family. Where was his family and what was happening to them? With more power than he thought he had, Grandalimus stood to his feet. He wanted to scream. He wanted to die. His senses were frayed but he must get to his family.

Though he could not see, he moved ahead, one excruciating step at a time. He clutched the trees, felt their texture. He recognized them. He felt the ground beneath his feet. The terrain was his and he advanced across it. Was it hours? Was it days? He did not know. Time was unrecognizable. Miraculously, he heard a sound he could make out: A lamb within the blinding light cried a few meters before him. He found the village. Pelendria, the village that reared the Elven King stood around him; he heard others. They were screaming in panic, fearing the unknown. His family. Where was his family?

Then, without warning everything stopped. The pain, the evil light, it all went away. A wicked laugh took its place. A laugh that froze the blood as it surged in its veins. It took an extensive moment for Grandalimus or anybody to come to their senses. When he did, he realized the village looked exactly as he knew it. Exactly except for one thing: Surrounding the village was the murky cloud that swirled around the misshapen moon and now haunted the outskirts of the generally quiet township.

The Elf King looked uneasily up at the silver disk that hovered silently over the land. It was the moon he had always known. Was this a nightmare slowly coming to an end? No. It was not. People remained frozen where they stood not knowing what to do. Instinctively, they looked towards their leader for some kind of enlightenment. Grandalimus positioned himself between them and the eerie murkiness that was slowly creeping closer. All suddenly felt a cold presence. The Elf King, without warning or weapon, slumped unexpectedly to his knees... everything went black.

Chapter 2 - The Pupil

"Avador! Avador Andor! Where is your brain tonight?" An imposing voice resonated into the lads pointed ears. The youngster, still trying to breathe, gazed up from where he lay and found a thick quarterstaff pointing right between his violet colored eyes. Slowly he moved a tuft of honey-blond hair that fell over his face and stood pathetically before a menacing mentor who looked back at him in disgust.

"Master Wylme," Avador faltered nervously, "I... I don't know what is wrong with me tonight. Something feels odd..."

"Never mind the excuses!" Wylme shot back, "you are officially dead because your mind is not here or anywhere nearby!" Without another word, Combat Master Wylme Tagom turned his beefy back (a back that often made Avador think of a wall), and marched off to another student.

Avador remained where he stood. His mind was truly somewhere else. It wasn't enough that tonight was the eve of Commencement and tomorrow he takes his final Trial, something else gnawed at his mind. Something unnatural happened and he was certain of it. A few minutes ago his heart took a jolt that made his limbs go numb and fall lifelessly at his sides. It certainly was not the blow he took from Master Wylme (one he could have easily avoided). The young Elf glanced around him. Man, Dwarf and Elf students were doing their best to win the pride of Master Wylme. The rest of the village slept soundlessly.

~****~

Moonlight filtered through the large window of Grandalimus' bedroom. The humble king sat in bed looking intently at the brilliant sphere that floated high in the starlit sky. Moments earlier he was asleep... or at least he *thought* he was asleep. Now he sat sweating and uneasy next to his wife, his life-mate Simetra. He gently brushed a curl of crimson hair away from her soft cheek. She stirred next to him and instinctively took her husbands hand in her own. Once everything felt right and in place, she drifted back into sleep. The Elf King tried to make sense of something that was completely alien to him. A mere moment separated one event from the other. It shuddered his very bones. It *must* have been a nightmare. What else could it have been?

"Beloved," a soft and silky voice glided through the moonlit room, "is something disquieting you?"

"My sweet Simetra," responded Grandalimus soothingly, "all is well." With that they both drifted into a deep, dreamless sleep.

~****~

The day took on the night and morning finally approached the Village of Pelendria. The luminous sun now took its watch high above the hills that represented the ceremony grounds. People of every race began to fill its usually empty area. Master Wylme was busily going through the motions of this Day of Commencement seeing that everyone was seated and taken care of in the way of refreshments. After all, this day was as much a test for him as it was for all his pupils. Finally he took his place in front of all that were present. The hills before him gradually elevated forming a natural amphitheatre. His voice resonated effortlessly to all that were seated.

"I bid you all greetings and gratitude for attending this

significant ceremony. A ritual which takes place only once
every ten long, and for some, agonizing years," his husky voice
naturally brought everyone's ears to attention. Master Wylme
continued with his speech and everyone remained silent and
attentive. Even the other Masters who sat to the side of Master
Wylme bestowed him their undivided attention as he spoke.

"So how did everything go last night, Son?" Grandalimus
whispered to Avador. They were seated at the very back behind
all who were present. Avador paused before answering. He
really didn't know what to tell his father but there appeared to
be a mutual understanding between the two. Avador took in a
long breath. Then exhaled.

"Everything *was* going well, Father. I was on top for the
entire sequence with Master Wylme. Then the most perplexing thing happened to me." Grandalimus listened patiently to
his son somehow knowing what he was trying to explain, " I
don't know what it was, but I lost absolute control, I felt a jolt
in my heart and in that instant, Master Wylme defeated me in
combat." Avador was shaking his head at the thought.

"Do not think too much of it young Avador," Grandalimus
consoled, "somewhere, an explanation exists." Avador looked
at his father.

"Do you know anything of this, Father?" Avador asked with
extreme curiosity.

"I can not say I understand what happened to you last
night, my son, but I know that something transpired that was
beyond our control. What happened to you was a mere taste
of what I felt last night." Grandalimus watched as his son's
eyes widened. "Yes Avador. Something happened to me as
well." Avador started to speak but Grandalimus was already
waving his hand. "Put aside your questions my son, we could
speak of this at another time. Now we... especially you, have

other matters to attend to." Avador's forehead furrowed in disappointment but he said nothing.

~****~

Master Wylme raised a great quarterstaff high above his head.

"Avador Andor, son of King Grandalimus! My pupil of ten years! Before this great observance of our fellow people, do you acknowledge that your final trial is to defeat me, your mentor, in a hand-to-hand combat that is to take place here on these chosen grounds, the Elven forests of Gwynfell?" Avador took one last look at the audience that stood behind him. No one defeated Master Wylme in hand-to hand-combat.

"I acknowledge!" exclaimed Avador, his eyes now fixed on the smirking face of Master Wylme. Wylme was of no doubt one of the biggest men Avador has ever seen. He had the word 'battle-hardened' written all over his muscular body.

The young Elf's parents stood in the shadows of the trees watching in silence not allowing their faces to exhibit their worries. Grandalimus was puzzled. Why after so many final tests, has Master Wylme, for the first time chosen *himself* as a contender? The other Masters also seemed perplexed but have said nothing. The Elf King fixed his concentration on the melee about to take place between Avador and his mentor.

"You are afraid young Avador," Wylme said quietly with a mocking sneer. The people drew a step closer. They didn't want to miss any of the action between the two combatants. "You have the guise of a timid rabbit. Do not show fear Avador. It gives your opponent conviction." Avador couldn't believe Master Wylme was honestly giving him last-minute lessons.

He began to resent him. But there was no time for any more thought. Wylme's quarterstaff was swinging wildly and within seconds struck the staff that the young Elf carried sending it flying somewhere into the dense undergrowth of the forest. For a Human, Wylme was fast; there was no uncertainty about that. Avador was faster. Before his staff struck ground, Avador whirled, landed on one hand, and propelled his legs with unbelievable momentum in an arc that struck hard. Wylme's legs were taken out from under him. There was a crash and the people watching took in a harmonized breath.

Avador paused, completely astonished. Wylme, though red in the face, took that pause to his advantage. With a grip of steel the mentor took a hold of Avador's ankle and jerked upwards. The Elf fell hard on his face. Simetra Andor buried her face into Grandalimus' chest.

"I was a fool to think you would be a worthy opponent Elfling," Wylme stood now to his full height and cast a colossal shadow over Avador, " do you admit def..." Master Wylme never got to finish what he was saying. Avador was on his feet and took hold of a low branch off the nearest tree and snapped it off with one quick heave. With the same energy he let the branch fly striking Wylme full on the mouth. It was the Master's turn to be in shock. The young Elf lunged into the trees known to him since childhood and swung himself up and whirling straight towards the dumbfounded Wylme. Grasping his mentor just underneath the chin with his forearm, Avador's momentum and full body weight took him down hard. The next instant, Wylme found himself with a young Elf's boot pressing down firmly on his throat. The people roared as Avador stared down triumphantly at the man who was once his master.

Chapter 3 - Three Sticks

The Andor house was an unpretentious home built by Grandalimus more than fifty years ago just on the outer edge of the village boundaries. It was put together with stone and timber with a terrace that went all the way around it. The house merged rather well with its thickly forested surroundings.

Inside, Avador was busy choosing something to wear for the evening's dinner, as was tradition after the Day of Commencement. It would be held in the village's largest building, the Kentro, standing just on the outskirts, it was the hall that held many events such as community dinners or celebrations.

The young Elf stood in his room staring at himself in a full-length mirror. He wore beige coloured tight fitting pants with black leather Elven-made boots and was left choosing what to wear on top. He was slim but well built for an Elf as young as he was. Before he had time to reach into his garment chest, there was a knock at the door. Grandalimus barely waited for a response when he entered Avador's room carrying a small wooden box with intricate engravings. His face veiled no pride for his son; he had a smile that beamed brighter than the stars.

"Son," the Elf King said barely holding back the tears of joy and sat on the bed with the chest on his lap, "come sit next to me." The young Elf stood momentarily wordless.

"Father, are you okay? I have never seen you this thrilled in all my life." Avador face had a quizzical, almost suspicious look. Grandalimus remained with his smile and patted the spot on the bed next to him. His son did as he was told and sat down.

"What happened today," Grandalimus took in a long breath, "what you accomplished today signifies more than you have realized. Throughout the years of your education, I have sensed something immense within you, Avador. Throughout the years of your life, something exceptional has been guiding you in the way you are, the way you carry yourself." The Elf King gave his head a quick shake suddenly remembering the small box that was waiting patiently on his lap. He opened it and gazed inside.

"Avador. As you know, I, as a king have been through many trials." Grandalimus spoke softly now hinting the importance of what he was about to say, "most I have not asked for or even wanted. Most say I am a formidable king. As a father, only you have the right to judge," Avador began to speak but was cut short with a wave of a hand.

"Since your birth, and for many years before, there have been countless unforgettable events and wars. Wars fought with steel and flame and wars that brought good people to the limits of their capabilities. You have seen none of those wars. Each time I kept you and your mother as far away from the bloodshed as possible." Avador shifted uneasily next to his father but let him continue.

"I have observed much of our enormous lands, seen many wonders both good and evil. Scores of kings have deemed me as their ally on one hand and held a knife for me in the other. These kingships only operate through their own high councils and ministers whereas the king himself leads no one." Avador just *now* began to understand the reality of how Grandalimus earned his respect. It wasn't only the virtues that his father carried deep within his heart. It was also the fact that he, one man alone led a vast amount of followers that stood at his side even if their death was imminent. He has no high council to sway any of his decisions or ministers to squabble between themselves trying to figure out the correct next move. The only man who has never wanted to be king was the only man that proved worthy of the title.

Grandalimus reached into the small, intricately imprinted box and withdrew articles of clothing that shimmered in the waning light. Covering a gleaming silver chain-mail shirt that sparkled with hints of green when light touched it a certain way, was a hooded sleeveless tunic violet in colour that ended in a V a foot below the waist-line's front and back. A pair of matching chain-mail pants were folded neatly at the bottom of the wooden box. Avador remained flabbergasted not ever seeing these clothes before now. His father wore an identical set throughout his reign that was now tattered and worn during the course of many hard-fought battles.

"Son," said Grandalimus holding the soft textured tunic before Avador revealing a large black 'A' that ran the length of its front, "I had this made along with mine the day you were born. Mine is now well worn while this, after twenty years, is just now being taken out of its box. I was saving it for when I felt it would be worn with merit and pride... by *you* young Avador." The Elven King allowed the tears to flow down his cheeks, "Tonight, you will wear it at the dinner. Tonight..." he let his words end abruptly and embraced his son, who was also choked up. After a moment, he salvaged his composure and stood up. With a smile and a friendly jab on the chin, Grandalimus was out the door.

~****~

The Kentro was convulsing with activity. Tables were set up in long stretches within the hall and outside on the balcony, which overlooked the wild Cerulean River that flowed relentlessly within a deep gorge. Masters at all levels took their places at their designated places next to their pupils. Cooks worked hastily to finish and send out the last of the evening's meal. Wine and ale were distributed among each table and the people felt looser and at ease as the night progressed.

Tonight there was no moon for it was shrouded in murky patches of cloud. Though the wind howled through the distant trees as though weeping in disdain, tonight no one seemed to discern the disturbing atmosphere of the surrounding background.

Outside on the balcony, bamboo poles that held torches were set up all around the outer edge to illuminate the otherwise gloom of the outdoors. Small groups of friends joked and laughed between themselves. Others walked around congratulating each other and enjoying the celebration.

Avador stood alone at one corner of the balcony. His hands gripped the outer railing as he gazed at the black depths below where he can faintly hear the gushing resonance of the river. The air was cool and sent his long hair fluttering softly about his cheeks. His Elven eyes scanned across the chasm penetrating the darkness and making out the outline of the impressive peaks of the Trood Mountains, home of the burly Pike Dwarves. He frequently visited the foot of those mountains with his father but never ventured further. The Dwarves he met there were kind enough, always ready with a good joke or a funny story. They took a liking to young Avador from the moment they met. 'Charismatic lad' they had called him and with a wink told him to take care of his father.

Someone slamming a powerful hand on his shoulder abruptly interrupted the young Elf's thoughts.

"Hey!" a familiar voice broke through the noise made by the festive crowd. "What's the matter with you tonight my pointed-eared comrade?" It was Tigran Eviathane, Avador's companion throughout combat training. He was a Human, well built and tall, nearly seven feet at his full height. He wore his thick black hair long. It ended at his waist and tied back with a leather band. Black eyes caught behind a fallen tuft of hair twinkled in cheerfulness that complimented an ever-warm smile. The clothing he wore showed that he wasn't one for being 'appropriate' and 'proper'. He was who he was no matter what he wore or where he presented himself. This evening's attire was a simple leather vest and his standard worn out hunting pants.

"You're the evening's luminary famous person and you're moping around here like your dad's *not* the King of the Elves or something." Tigran pulled on Avador's ear making him smile for the first time this evening.

"You're right my friend," Avador looked up at him ruefully, "tonight I should be rejoicing. It's not every day you graduate from the most difficult academy in all the land and have the fortune to do it with the greatest friends anyone could ever ask…"

"What *is* this?" Avador was interrupted again. This time by a slender dark bearded chap in blue robes, "ignore-Falstaff-and-have-your-own-private-party-night?"

"Falstaff!" Exclaimed Avador startled by all the suddenness. " No, we were…I don't know…um…Tigran, what were we doing?" The young Elf ran out of words but the trio laughed and with their arms around each other's shoulders went inside, found a table and began to relish the moment with large glasses of ale.

Simetra Andor was dwelling in her own little world. She was sitting near the stone fireplace at a table with her husband. She wore her crimson hair in a thick braid and was dressed in creamy white. Grandalimus couldn't help but smile at how radiant she looked, especially with the fire intensifying her features. Though he did not know it, Simetra was also admiring *him*. She noted all the changes in his characteristics and at how handsome he remained throughout the years. His jaw, square and firm always held high with dignity and honour. She observed tiredness in his green eyes masked only by a misleading smile, which only she cannot be fooled by. She noticed his honey-blonde hair greying slightly at the temples bringing the word 'eminent' to mind. He looked every bit the King he was.

Tonight though, his mind was divided. Simetra mentioned this to him but he quickly dismissed it as just her mind's eye. Instead of persisting in her thought, knowing she wasn't going to go anywhere with it, she glanced over at her son's table. He was sitting with two of his closest friends whom he had known since childhood and now graduated together. The bond between them was unquestionably genuine - an authentic link between three very different yet distinctive individuals. She smiled at their merriment and at the same time wondered where all these years have been consumed. She watched Avador all grown and developing into manhood, he shone brilliantly in his pristine outfit. Grandalimus, she noticed, did nothing to suppress his show of pride either. His smile was ear-to-ear as he too stared at their son giving Simetra's hand an acknowledging squeeze.

"This evening is faultless," he said almost inaudibly. Simetra wasn't sure if he was talking to her or just thinking out loud, but she agreed anyway.

Then, without warning, a severe looking knife flew threw the crowded hall and lodged itself into the edge of Avador's wooden table. Somebody shouted and the hall instantly went silent. A large bulky figure of a man silhouetted in the rear entryway stood shaking and breathing heavily. After seeming content with the reaction of the silenced crowed, he took a step into the hall and into the dim light. It was Master Wylme, enraged and very drunk.

"Andor!" He screamed at the top of his lungs, his voice penetrating through the silence in a thunderous boom. He took another pace towards the table of the young companions his eyes fixed on Avador. Simetra began to move to her son's side but was quickly stopped by her husband's grip.

Avador was on his feet with the dexterity of a cat. His friends were instantly at his sides. Wylme charged blindly, rushing towards them like an enraged bull. The three friends scattered at once and Wylme slammed both fists onto the table, splitting it in two. As the glasses and ale jugs sprayed their contents, the companions were all over Master Wylme. Avador swept his legs out from under him while Tigran Eviathane smashed a powerful elbow into Wylme's unsuspecting jaw. The big man went down with a resounding crash. Knowing this only made Wylme even madder, Falstaff raised a wooden chair high over his head and brought it down hard breaking three of the big man's ribs. Master Wylme went limp and remained where he was in a broken heap on the floor. Avador kneeled at the large man's side and checked if he was still breathing. Finding there were short ragged breaths, he stood slowly to his feet.

"Someone get Master Wylme to a healer." Avador said still half stunned by what had just taken place.

~****~

The King of the Elves stood out on the balcony with his hands placed loosely on the outer railing; the cooled steel felt relaxing on his calloused palms. He faced the Trood

Mountains that loomed out of the darkness beyond. The Kentro was empty now. The people of Pelendria eventually withdrew from the night's ceremonies and retired to their homes, the nearby village a brisk walk in the gloomy night.

Simetra, accompanied by her son and his two friends, made the short trek through the opaque forest that surround her home. Grandalimus chose to stay alone; his mind grew increasingly elsewhere. One torch was kept alight and he stood by it letting its glow envelope him. It was hours later. The wind increased and he subconsciously pulled his cloak about his shoulders when he heard someone approaching from the entrance of the hall. The serene silence was disturbed by laughter advancing through the darkness of the empty building. It was Avador, Tigran, and Falstaff. They had decided to come back to the Kentro to meet Grandalimus for he was the only other person awake in the village.

"Evening Father." Avador said with unconcealed delight, "do you mind if we join you out here on the terrace?" Grandalimus, though weary, smiled and motioned the three to a small table away from the torchlight.

"What's the matter my young conquerors? Can't sleep tonight?" Grandalimus was sarcastic knowing the reason they were awake was from all the adrenalin invoked by tonight's occurrence.

The four sat at the table after Falstaff obtained a jug of ale with accompanying cups and set them down in front of everybody. Soon, the veranda was once again alive with high spirits and gaiety. The company of four had their own private party that excluded the rest of the world. Stories of the past were once again brought to life and ignited laughter. Tales of each other's lives as they matured together, some humorous and some that provoked embarrassment were replayed tonight on the terrace.

This went on until the sky began to fight off the dusk and change into a feverish orange. The four were now silhouettes against their mountain background. In the growing silence, the resonance of the Cerulean River rushed passionately in the canyon below. Grandalimus sat with his feet fixed firmly on the wooden decking, his back to the mountains, he faced the three friends. His expression became stern and serious which caused everyone to become silent and attentive.

"Boys," The Elven King said quietly as they sat in the peculiar period between night and day. "Over the years, I've had three sons, not one. I have watched you all grow from infants to become the men that you are today. Not once have you lied or cheated each other. You have done only the contrary." Grandalimus' eyes fixed on the eyes of the companions each in turn. They fidgeted uneasily under the scrutiny of the Elf King.

"If I were to take only three people with me in a war," Grandalimus continued, "it would be you three. Trust and friendship such as yours are the elements required not only in warfare, but also in life. Contrary to what Wylme has taught, combat is more than just a series of parries, blocks, retreats and advances. It is heart. It is passion for your people. It's taking what is right and turning it into a fighting force so strong that it can shield you and everybody you love from anything trying to harm you." Grandalimus stood now and walked around the table to be with the boys.

"If you take a stick, a fair sized stick, you can break it. It does not take much. But if you put a second stick with the first and try to break them, you *might*, but with more difficulty." His face grew more intense and the youngsters gave him their undivided attention. " Find a third stick and put it together with the other two... you will *never* break them." He gave them all a wink and turned his back.

"Tigran Eviathane. You have been Avador's ever-faithful friend since the beginning of your time together. You have looked out for each other for as long as I can remember." Images of the two boys helping one another growing up came to the Elf King in a lucid rush. "I trust you with his life." Avador was starting to not like where this conversation was heading.

"Falstaff." Grandalimus continued without facing them. "You and my son have studied together about legends and lore, languages and races. You have researched cultures and history... but that is not what you are after." Falstaff swallowed hard as Grandalimus turned now and faced him. "You want to be a wielder of *magic* though you have never *seen* such a thing. None of you have. Not everyone can be a magic user. You have to want it to be a part of you. You have to *believe* you can use it. I have seen magic in my travels and believe me, it can be the most wondrous thing in the right hands. But it can also be the most horrifying entity in the hands of wickedness." He strode now to where Falstaff was sitting and put a strong hand on the young man's slender shoulder. Falstaff looked up at him with intense blue eyes.

"You have it within you, young mage-to-be. I have seen the nearly non-existent art being used and believe me...you are one of the rare people that can bring it to life. But take heed when I tell you this: power is *nothing* without control."

In the silence that followed, there was a growing uneasiness, yet a feeling of mutual understanding between the men standing on the Kentro's terrace. Grandalimus took his seat next to his son and put his arm around his shoulders.

"Son," he said with the pride returning to his face, "the time has come for you to lead." An icy chill seized Avador's heart so abruptly that it froze him where he sat. He began to speak but words were lost somewhere in his throat. "Fear is not an option for you Elven Prince." His words were a mere whisper, "we have both felt a surge within us that we do not comprehend. I will do my best to try and recognize what had happened exactly. The only thing I truly know is that I am running out of time…"

"But you have many years left within you Father." Avador's voice returned to him in a sudden rush, "Why are you saying all this to me?" Grandalimus was shaking his head and squeezing the young Elf's shoulders trying to relax him.

"I have one more mission I have to set out for. I must go alone and I am not sure how long it will be before I return." The Elf king was now blunt with his words, his green eyes potent, "you must stay here and watch what I cannot. You are a man now, my Son. Do what is right."

And with that, the King of the Elves bolted so quickly from the balcony and out through the hall's entrance that none of the companions had time to react. Avador rose to his feet to give chase but two sets of strong hands held him back firmly.

"Father!" Avador screamed as the first fragments of light seeped through the apex of the Trood Mountains. The echo of the young Elf's voice resonated across the valley below with such force that it might have shattered the mountain peaks.

Chapter 4 - Servant

The chamber was nothing as it used to be. Nor was the courtyard for that matter. In fact, the entire castle stronghold looked nothing as it once was. Yes, it is still set up on a colossal mountain on an island across a vast body of water. But what it once was and what it is now are utterly two different things.

Where flourishing green and gold vegetation formerly gave the fortress splendor and exquisiteness, the setting altered to an unsightly view from afar. Those who approached regretted it the moment they drew close to the eeriness of what it had become. The once high-polished gray stonewalls and pillars were now distorted to charred black, dripping with grime from years of neglect. The desolate stronghold, monstrous in size, used to flare with activity. Now only a small number lingered within, most of which wondered why they still remained. Brightly colored banners and flags once upon a time, donned the vast castle walls. Now torn down or burnt years ago, their remnants flutter silently like spider webbing across dusty walls. The sun, in the past, used to shine high overhead above incredible towers and illuminated the whole countryside. Now even that is gone. All that is left is a dull, misshapen moon that hangs gloomily somewhere to the east of the once vibrant stronghold.

"Skneeba!" The name hissed through the chamber for the third time. A man in dark robes was hobbling as fast as he could through corridors dimly lit by torches, some burning, some long burnt out in their brackets. A deformed man, tall, twisted and gaunt, almost skeletal under his dark robes, ran with quick jerky movements. He had the appearance of someone running with one leg a good deal shorter than the other. He ran to heed the beckoning of his master. If he were too slow, he would be disciplined once more.

The dark robed character reached the entrance of the chamber just as his name was called the fourth time. He clenched the hood of his robes with bony fingers panting heavily and sweating profusely under the heavy clothing.

"You summoned, Master?" His voice was ragged and raspy and he barely got the words out past the hood that concealed his face. He paused and tried again. "You called for me your Highness?"

The chamber was vast with marble floors and pillars. A once exquisite fountain now emptied of its water and collecting dust, sat in the precise center of the chamber. Broad, spacious flights of steps occupied the left and right sides of the rectangular hall giving the look of bleachers in a games arena. A giant crystal chandelier clung, if barely, to a tall ceiling exactly above the fountain. A higher, steeper flight of steps were set opposite the corridor entrance of which the man called Skneeba now stood waiting to be commanded.

"Come closer." The voice came from a powerful looking man sitting on a granite throne that rested on the pinnacle of the far steps. A thick mane of curly hair, gray with hints of rusty red, flowed from under a golden crown. He had a bushy unruly beard that reached his bulky, yet solid chest. Thick forearms protruded from the sleeves of a disheveled kingsrobe. One hand securely seized a slender scepter three meters in length. On the scepter's tip, copious green vapor emitted from a small black sphere flanked by two crescents.

Skneeba took slow uneasy steps forward like a child that knows he is to be punished. He stopped deliberately at the fountain hoping *this* distance would suffice. Putting one gnarled hand on the cold stone of the fountain, he steadied himself as he watched and waited for what his master would ask of him.

"Did you do the magic?" The master asked so abruptly that it made Skneeba jump as the words echoed within the chamber.

"I did." Skneeba said after finding the ability to speak again.

"Come closer." The man on the throne commanded once again. Skneeba twitched uncomfortably but did as he was told. As he approached the base of the high steps to the throne, the big man deliberately raised the scepter a few inches higher above his head. Skneeba cringed at the motion and with gritted teeth shrank back a few paces.

"Is he out of my way?" He asked, his gaze never leaving the broken man below.

"He is, King Aonas," Skneeba replied with a hint of remorse in his raspy voice. "The Elf King has met a fate worse than death." There was a time-consuming silence.

"Why haven't I heard from you today, Skneeba?" The man stood now, menacing at his full height. The robed man at the bottom of the stairs lowered his head and wished he could disappear from existence.

"I was resting," he lied.

"*Think* before you act, Skneeba." The burly man warned glaring at the other who stood humbled beneath him and asked again, "Why have I not heard from you today?" Skneeba knew there was nothing left for him to do but to tell the truth.

"I was mourning the death of King Jadonas." The words exited his mouth in an acidic sigh. Aonas took one step down from his throne, the color drained entirely from his face.

"I have warned you never again mention my brother's name." King Aonas was suddenly overcome by fury so severe that Skneeba shrank away in terror. He began to run in the opposite direction but was stopped short by Aonas' commanding voice.

"Stop!" Aonas was shaking with rage, the scepter raised high above his head.

"Master." Skneeba was whimpering, "Master, please."

"Come forth! I order you!" The words oozed through clenched teeth. The tall, broken man twisted ever so slowly to face his master. He was compelled, without the ability to do otherwise, to obey his master no matter what the command. Nothing good could become of what was to follow.

Chapter 5 - The Unknown

"Where do we go from here?" Eviathane was looking over his shoulder with Avador and Falstaff leading the way. The town of Pathen began to grow sleepy with the approach of nightfall. They were miles from home and deep in the Trood Mountains when they arrived at the Dwarven village.

Avador stopped short and scanned the area with his keen Elven eyes. The village was not on level ground. Built in the mountains, the houses and structures were situated on all kinds of points and altitudes. The roads barely levelled off, usually winding upwards or downwards, twisting between the stone-built buildings and disappearing into the darkness.

"The only thing I am completely sure of Eviathane is that we need to get some rest." Avador answered noting the darkness overcoming the village.

"He's right," Falstaff agreed, "we've been travelling since last night without rest and it is night again. Frankly, I could use a hot bath and a solid drink." He scratched at his short black beard and looked around uncomfortably.

The events after the disappearance of Grandalimus were a whirlwind of haste. Avador, after finding the strength to calm himself down and suppress his anger at his friends for holding him back, decided that they were right. The Elf King had his reasons for doing what he did. He always had his reasons and no one questioned him, regardless at how illogical everything seemed.

Avador had returned home. He briefly relayed the disastrous events to his mother and told her he had to leave. It was all a complete shock to Simetra Andor and she protested in utter disbelief. Her husband disappeared and now her son was leaving too?

The young Elf remained firm to his actions and packed whatever he could for food in a leather travelling sack and slung it over his shoulder. He went to his parent's room and retrieved his longbow and quiver of arrows, which he had originally used for hunting. What he found bizarre was that his father's battle clothes were missing. Everything else the Elf King used remained where he had left them. The near weightless shield with the Andor insignia of a black tree on a deep blue background, still hung on the bedroom wall above the bed. The long, jagged dagger and the broadsword that he used in battle were also left behind. The *sword*. The sword that his father admiringly called the *Kingblade* was still in the room. Avador buckled it, still in it's scabbard, to his waist along with the dagger.

After a moment, and a long exhale, the young Elf exited his parent's bedroom and faced his mother once again. He dropped everything he held and embraced her. She did not want to let go. With an excruciating effort, he took his things and left the house promising he will return. He did not look back knowing that if he did, he would stay. Instead he looked ahead to where his two friends, stubborn as they were against his protests, waited for him to go along.

Avador took his companions around a corner of a stone building where they crouched in silence and merged with the shadows. The owners of the home were asleep so they moved ahead silently to avoid any unnecessary attention. The road ahead led to a building alive with lights and commotion. Dwarves entered and exited periodically, some laughing and some quietly minding their business. The three, wrapped in their traveling cloaks gave the impression of wraiths as they navigated the darkening night. They approached and read the wooden sign that dangled on a pole over the entrance: *The Spider's Web.*

Grandalimus had spoken of this place in the past to Avador. A tavern, doubled as an inn for travellers exploring the Trood Mountains. *'A place to rest, but keep your wits sharp.'*

The three remained fixed at the base of the wooden porch before the entrance. A drunken Dwarf poured out the door and nearly plunged headfirst down the steps. Eviathane instinctively caught the man as he fell.

"Pardon me, m'lady." The Dwarf said looking up with a grin and glossy eyes. Then he stumbled off mumbling something about how big they make women nowadays. Tigran Eviathane didn't know whether to be insulted or to just laugh.

"I think it's safe to go in." He said turning a little red in colour.

The tavern was seedy-looking at first appearance. In one corner, two burly Dwarves were locked in an arm-wrestling match with a handful of spectators holding out pouches of coin and placing bets. The interior was designed mostly with wood and timbered planks for the flooring. Dim lanterns hung here and there, illuminated the tavern with their soft glow. People were chattering amongst themselves in loud voices. A Dwarf barmaid, short and stocky like the men, but with a cheerful smile, skittered from table to table to serve drinks. A second barmaid was getting ready to start work for the tavern would get busier as the night progressed.

A balding barman with a huge red beard paused at cleaning an ale mug when the three strangers walked through the door and waited watchfully at the entrance. Abruptly, everything stopped. The usual disorder of the tavern, the noise, the chatter, it all came to a sudden halt and everyone's attention fell to the three cloaked figures standing uncomfortably at the entrance.

"Why are they watching us like that?" Falstaff whispered out of the corner of his mouth.

"Maybe it's because we are armed to the teeth." Tigran Eviathane answered back adjusting a large bulky shield strapped to his back.

Without another word, Avador found an empty table in the middle of the bar and sat down. The companions did the same looking around smiling. This made the Dwarves gawk even harder with open mouths.

"I think you should have found a table where we could put our backs to the wall, I don't think they trust us." Eviathane said quietly still smiling at the curious patrons.

The barman then broke from his curiosity trance and gave the barmaid a gentle shove towards their direction. Hesitantly, but with a newly formed smile, she approached the companion's table.

"Um, we'll have a large pitcher of ale, please." Avador said politely. The barmaid's smile broadened and without a word went to get the order. Eventually, the noise level rose back to it's usual height and things were back to normal.

"We'll stay here for the night." Avador said to his friends. "I'll try and get some information before we leave."

"Leave to *where*?" Falstaff asked abruptly. "How do you even know where we have to go?"

"Avador knows." Tigran intercepted the conversation. "Somehow he knows. We are here to support him, not question him." The three stopped talking when the barmaid returned with a large pitcher of ale and three tin mugs.

"So boys," she said sweetly, "is there a war going on that we don't know about?" The companions smiled politely.

"No, no." Avador replied swiftly, "we just finished some combat training and now we're heading home." The lie was obvious and the young Elf cringed to himself. The barmaid remained smiling and placed the ale and mugs in front of the young travellers. Avador took some copper coins from his pouch and paid her. She left them alone to their drinks and went about her business.

Eventually, the bar became smoky and packed as the night moved on. Avador stood up and walked to the barman as soon as he noticed he had a moment to talk.

"Respects and good wishes." He said to the barman and was greeted with a smile. "Is it possible to get a room for tonight?" The barman looked the young Elf up and down before answering.

"We have a room up the stairs. The third one on the right." His voice was gruff but friendly. "It's a little small for three big fellows such as yourselves, but it's the last one left."

Avador was about to reply when he saw the barman's eyes widen into the size of teacup saucers. Without a moment's hesitation, the young Elf whirled and took a defensive stance and realized that *he* wasn't in danger.

Falstaff had been pulled from his chair. He was half crouching half standing, and firmly held back by a very irate Dwarf. There was a flash of steel and Avador caught site of a knife held against his friend's throat dangerously cutting into his skin.

"This is an outrage!" The Dwarf roared thrusting Falstaff's chin upward like a lamb to be slaughtered. "Why do we allow evil such as *this* into our village? He is here to throw a foul curse at our feet!" He was clearly inebriated and judging by the work clothes he still wore, he had been in the tavern all day.

Something large and heavy suddenly flew across the crowded room and the drunken dwarf was struck down. Falstaff was immediately on his feet holding his throat. His attacker lay motionless on the floor with a hefty war-hammer on his chest. His teeth were smashed out and he bled freely from his mouth. The tavern went still as if petrified in time.

"I *told* him to go home hours ago." A single Dwarf, brawny in a black vest, sauntered through the mass of people. His arms swelled with muscle, his stride solid and sure. The people made way for him as he passed. Without acknowledging anybody, he picked up the heavy hammer and left the way he had come from somewhere behind the bar.

Tigran and Avador sat a few moments with Falstaff. Somewhat shaken, the young companions waited as the patrons, losing their appetite for drinking any more, cleared out of the smoky tavern.

"Are you all right, Falstaff?" Tigran asked the young scholar.

"Nothing hurt but my pride." He retorted.

~****~

Avador and his companions spent the night in the little room that the barkeep had offered. The rest of the night was uneventful and they slept undisturbed until morning. The first signs of daylight trickled into the room from behind a thick curtain. Dust hovered not quite motionless in the air, exposed only where light was shed. The little room became stuffy and dank not having the proper ventilation with the closed window.

Tigran and Falstaff awoke to find Avador missing from the spot on the floor he had slept on. But within minutes the door opened and he had returned.

"How are you guys?" The young Elf seemed well rested and perky.

"I *told* you we should have made camp in the mountains," Falstaff answered rubbing the back of his neck. "These beds are made for Dwarves, and you two taking the floor didn't help *my* situation at *all*!"

"We were just trying to be gentlemen, Falstaff." Tigran

41

replied with a smirk and a wink to Avador. "After all, you had a traumatizing night last night, we couldn't let you take the floor."

Avador began packing his gear and the two companions did the same. Within moments they were down below and into an empty tavern. The red-bearded barman was the sole person downstairs and he was busy fixing the leg of a broken chair.

"Hello again, Norscio." Avador greeted him merrily.

"Greetings lad," the Dwarf replied without looking up from his work. "There are eggs and smoked pork waiting for you and your friends in the kitchen behind the bar."

They ate eagerly, famished from the meagre meals they rationed for the trip to the Dwarven village. Avador pulled out six silver pieces and handed them to Norscio. The Dwarf gave the young Elf a look of warning and shoved the coins back into Avador's hand.

"I told you young Elfling, you will pay nothing more for your stay here." His eyes were serious and Avador knew there was no arguing with him. "Now you remember the directions I gave you?"

"I do."

"Take the pack I have set for you from the bar counter. There are provisions for all of you for at least a few weeks… *if* you are careful, that is." The red-bearded Dwarf rested two stout hands on the Elf's shoulders. "Sorry I cannot offer more…"

"You have offered more than I could ever ask of you, Norscio." The young Elf shook hands with the barkeep and handed the leather pack with the replenished supplies to Tigran. The rest of the party were half in shock not knowing how Avador managed to win so much favour from the burly barkeep.

Outside, the air was fresh with sharpness to it. Avador looked around and concluded that the weather was changing. The sun was lower in the horizon and the surrounding mountain peeks hid it from view.

He led his friends down twisty cobblestone streets that wounded up and down between the stone-built homes. The villagers were mostly away in the fields situated just on the outskirts of the now quiet hamlet. He came to a T-intersection and chose the road that went right. Few Dwarves that remained gave them curious glances but nothing more as they carried on with their daily routines. The road led out of the village and eventually turned into a dirt pathway.

"What happened back at the inn?" Falstaff's curiosity got the better of him.

"Norscio recognized me." Avador answered frankly. "He knew my father during his travels through these mountains and remembered me as his son that came with him. I remembered him as well early this morning when I awoke and went downstairs. It's been many years since I came with my father to the foot of these mountains. He admitted at first he wasn't sure who I was but this morning he had no doubt I was the son of King Grandalimus."

Avador took them off the path and into a wooded patch that offered some cover. They sat under a large pine and drank from their water flasks. The Elf waited a few moments before speaking again.

"I will tell you now what we are here to do." He said without looking away from his feet. Falstaff and Tigran watched their friend patiently until he continued.

"I am not sure how to begin to tell you this, so I guess straightforward is the best way." He took a deep inhale before carrying on. "Last night, before the sun came up, I had left our room for the *first* time." His friends gave him a perplexed look but he continued without pausing.

43

"My father speaks to me," he said bluntly ignoring the looks of surprise. "Sometimes, during the time between night and day, he beckons me. I do not know where he is for he never reveals his location. But I *feel* him calling to me rather than *hear* him." He paused now looking up to meet his companion's eyes. To his surprise, he found absolutely no disbelief, only curiosity.

"How does he talk with you?"

"Why only during *those* strange hours?"

Avador smiled at the utter loyalty his friends had for him. There was a sound of steel sliding against steel. Avador had unsheathed the *Kingblade* and held it before his friends. The broad blade gleamed sheer white in the daylight. The polished dark blue hilt held effortlessly in both hands and felt warm to Avador's touch.

"*This* sword is *magic*." Avador glanced over at Falstaff and gave him a wink. Tigran Eviathane began to laugh but Avador put a finger to his lips cutting him short.

"With *this*," Avador said waving the blade in a short arc, "my father finds me." The two humans stared at each other, not sure of what to think.

"How?" Tigran asked. None of the company has ever seen any magic and the possibility of it being in their presence was somewhat bewildering.

"I don't know how it works Eviathane," Avador answered, "but I know what it does. Somehow, through the sword, the *Kingblade* as my father calls it; he summons me during the small hours before night turns to day. I go outside and I hear his voice in my mind as I hold the sword before me. He tells me where to go. He *wants* us to find him. My father has fled for reasons no one understands but I am *sure* it's because of something against his will."

"But if he wants us to find him, why hasn't he told you where he is?" Falstaff asked.

"He's preparing me by sending us to certain places to obtain help along the way. That's how I know where we have to go. For now anyways, he tells me where we must go before giving me *his* location." The young Elf stood up and gathered his things. "That is all I know for the moment, my friends."

"Where do we have to go now?" Tigran asked, both wanting to know.

"That way!" Avador pointed and they continued down the dirt path leading away from the village.

~****~

The trail went on for another hour. The sun was higher in the horizon and directly in front of them, which made it difficult, to see past it's powerful glare. There were patches of trees on either side of the trail in periodic stages as they advanced down the slender dirt road. Their leaves were beginning to transform from their original green to brilliant reds and golds.

The terrain before them took an almost dramatic change. It sloped significantly giving a magnificent view of a hilly landscape that coursed downwards for miles before turning into another mountainous backdrop. They continued for a few more minutes when Avador found what he was looking for.

The cottage was in a bit of a mess and in bad need of arrangement for all the clutter that littered the grounds around it. It was a small stone structure with a brick chimney that spouted thick grey smoke. A broken wagon with a missing wheel lay on its side near a heap of lumber. Tools lay scattered everywhere in an indiscernible pattern for what the owner had in mind.

Approaching the dwelling, the companions heard the sound of hammering coming from behind the overturned wagon.

They walked cautiously not to alarm whoever was working and found a very strongly built Dwarf with his bare back turned to them, hammering at a spike in the belly of the wagon.

"If you's are here for a cup of tea, you can go elsewhere." The burly Dwarf said startling the three travellers. Immediately they recognized him as the Dwarf with the battle-hammer back at the Spider's Web. He stood and looked up at them waiting for some kind of reply.

"Greetings," Avador spoke up instantly. "We were directed here from Norscio, the bar-keep of the Spider's Web..." The young Elf never finished what he had to say when the taciturn Dwarf's eyes widened and he suddenly dropped to one knee bowing his head.

"You are the son of the King of the Elves," the stocky Dwarf whispered, "my life is yours." The three companions stood there not knowing what to do.

"I am Stone Warhelm, soldier and right hand of Grandalimus, *my* king and the king of all Elvenkind."

Chapter 6 - Evil Dispatched

Dark foreboding clouds moved like sleek spectres around a warped moon. As if daring *anyone* to approach, they wisped slightly towards the earth and back up to their nocturnal domain. A rain released itself from its murky prison and plummeted savagely towards the earth. A rain so cold it became ice upon touching ground; a black ice that looked merely like wetness on the streets below, deceiving all who dared venture outside.

The fortress now possessed by King Aonas loomed above its island nest. Sitting at the summit of its towering mountain, it seemed unreachable. An entire city encircled the stronghold in a perfect ring. The mountain city built hundreds of years ago and once under the regime of a powerful king, thrived exceptionally, regardless of its solitude.

People always had work. The land was cultivatable. Industries flourished within the city and markets were plentiful with much to gain. No one was left in deprivation.

That was when the city was under rule of the late King Jadonas. Now the people starved. From the hundreds of thousands of its population, only a few thousand remained for they lacked the means to leave. Without the leadership of their true king, they were in desperate need of guidance. Jadonas was a decent and moral king made superior by the collaboration of another great king: Grandalimus, who advised him of what to do in order to govern a city as great as his.

King Grandalimus and Jadonas met infrequently, for the

distance between them was too great. But the quality of their visits outweighed the need of frequent ones.

No one expected the death of the great king. There were suspicions that it was the king's own brother, Aonas, that assumed the guilt of murdering him. No one spoke a word of it out in the open. Only if they were safely hidden behind closed doors would anyone attain the nerve to *whisper* the accusation.

Now the people of the ancient city known as *Sovereign's Reach*, were virtually slaves behind the very walls that encircled and once protected them. The walls, a massive last defence from wars hundreds of years forgotten, embraced an entire city. Guard posts were set at strategic points at the top of the wall that spanned the circumference of the upper ring. Soldiers were able to scan for miles for any ships approaching from all directions.

Once, in the time of King Jadonas, rare was the need to descend the great mountain for *anything*. Now the people must sneak away in secrecy to trek the island below for much needed supplies. Many never returned.

Rumours whisper of a great evil that guards the mountain. A beast formed of magic that allows nothing to live, attacking quickly and silently in the darkness. The *Gali-gunzaro*, as it was known in the native tongue of the island people, means "creature of night", unidentified in size and relentless in it's pursuit to kill. Cursed days lay ahead for the people of the island.

Aonas stood alone in his bedchamber. An oval window overlooked the dark ocean that expanded as far as the eye could see... that is, if darkness hadn't permanently shrouded the island and only a dull, misshapen moon was left to light the outdoors.

He was gazing thoughtfully out his window, his hands held loosely behind his back when there was a knock at his door. Immediately he walked to his sceptre that was left on his bed, it's black sphere emitting the green vapour.

"Who calls?" He demanded in his commanding voice.

"It is I your Highness, Gan-Potou." It was Aonas' head of his private guard. Originally a resident of the island below, he was once a great soldier who fought by Jadonas' side now forced to serve his malevolent brother. "I have the prisoner you requested."

Aonas squeezed the sceptre until his knuckles went white. "Bring him in," he said after a moment's pause. The door opened and a dark skinned soldier in full body armour and in obviously great form, escorted a slouching robed character into the bedchambers. "Leave us." The king demanded.

Upon further thought he added, "but wait by the door, I have need of you." With a bow, the soldier exited and took a stance outside the door. The slouching robed figure inched his head upward to face his king. The dim light revealed a tormented Skneeba. Dried blood encrusted his face around his mouth. His steely grey eyes looked hopelessly at his master. At this distance, King Aonas studied his dark complexion, each wrinkle of worry, and the way his mouth moved mechanically up and down.

Also a native of the island below, the *Isle of Gogatha*, once known by its inhabitants, he had studied the art of *Lun-Kara*, or Moon Magic in the translation of Man. He excelled in it, and wielded the power as if it were an extension of himself. Once, seemingly eons ago, he had used it for the purpose of good. Now, under the control of Aonas and his terrible sceptre, he is forced to perform ungodly duties of magic. The *Sceptre*. How could a tyrant such as *this* obtain the Sceptre of Kara-Toh? Those who brandish it have the power to control

49

those who wield magic. Skneeba sighed at the thought. His contemplation was interrupted soon enough.

"Skneeba," Aonas whispered with a sneer, "have you eaten today?" The broken man before him nodded "yes".

"Did you have the smoked fish?"

Again, he nodded.

"How did it *taste?*" The king roughly grabbed Skneeba by the cheeks and squeezed until the remnants of a tongue protruded slightly from his lips. "Next time you lie to me, you are going to want to *die!*" He then shouted for the guard to enter. Gan-Potou obeyed and closed the door behind him.

"You and this *worm* are from the same township, is that correct?" Aonas asked without taking his eyes off of Skneeba.

"Yes your Highness," the captain of the guard answered with a bit of an accent.

"Then you can translate to me what he writes down." It wasn't a question but a demand.

"Yes your Highness." Gan-Potou knew that Skneeba only spoke the Human tongue but read or wrote none of it.

Aonas, walked over to a large wooden desk. "Bring him here," he said pointing to the chair. Gan-Potou directed him towards the desk where Skneeba sat grudgingly on the chair. Yellowed parchment was placed in front of him along with quill and ink.

"Now, Skneeba," Aonas' voice was cynical, "write down your answers to my questions and Gan-Potou will translate for me... do you understand?" Skneeba nodded.

"Why hasn't the sun emerged for days?" The words were venomous and spoken with obvious anger. Skneeba paused. Then, ever so slowly, he dipped the quill into the black ink. He wrote lethargically. The sound of the quill scratching against the parchment was the only sound in the dusty bedchamber. After a moment he stopped writing.

Aonas snatched the parchment and handed it to the captain of the guard who read it and swallowed hard upon finishing.

"What does it *say*?" The king barked.

"It says *all magic used with that magnitude has a consequence. It is a result of the type of magic used, a reaction to the power of the curse.*" The guard looked up at Aonas questioningly but said nothing.

"How can we restore everything to how it was?" Aonas was getting increasingly impatient. "I am tired of looking at that ghastly moon and the lack of day." Skneeba began scratching at the yellowed parchment once again. When he finished, Gan-Potou read from it.

"*The residue of the curse lasts for all eternity.*" The stalwart guard read on silently before translating, ignoring the irritated look from his king. "*The only other way to bring everything back to the way it was is if the origin of the curse... dies!*"

Aonas shot a glance at Skneeba and was surprised to see him staring back with poison in his eyes. He thought he saw the hint of a smile on his bloodied lips. Gripping the sceptre with both hands he stomped over to the oval window and glared at the horizon.

"Leave us!" The king ordered Gan-Potou with a hiss. The guard left without question. When the door was shut again and he was alone with Skneeba, he walked slowly to the mage pointing the sceptre directly at him.

Skneeba's face illuminated green with the power of the sceptre. He was under the complete control of Aonas.

"There is something you are not telling me, is that correct?" Skneeba nodded, unable to do otherwise. The malicious king paced back and forth for a few minutes before stopping dead in his tracks. He moved swiftly towards Skneeba causing the helpless magic-user to cringe in the chair.

"The King of the Elves has an *offspring*!" The words flowed effortlessly. "Of course he does… but not for long." He shot another glance over at Skneeba who sat in utter misery.

"Send the Ecliptic Wraiths to find this *child* of Grandalimus and slay it. I will not have anything else stand in my way!" The order was spoken as if it were nothing more than a greeting to a friend.

Skneeba slouched helplessly in the chair; sorrow overcame him completely…

S tone Warhelm placed another chunk of wood into the fireplace. It was late in the afternoon and the sun disappeared behind a huge bank of cloud. Fresh winds coming off the northern slopes of the great Trood Mountains chilled the hilly regions that surrounded the Dwarf's home.

Inside his humble cottage, the companions sat at his table drinking warm spiced ale as they contemplated what they were to do next. Pulling their heavy travel cloaks tighter, they marvelled at how Stone remained comfortable wearing nothing but black leather pants and a thin vest.

"I'm a Pike Dwarf," Stone Warhelm had stated noticing their stares, "we're built tougher than most'a you's." Pike Dwarves are reared on the highest slopes of the coldest mountains and are known for their tolerance of cold weather.

Avador had inquired about the seasoned Dwarf's adventures with Grandalimus and was told simply there were many. Grandalimus, he had said, is the greatest man he has ever met and would gladly die fighting by him for *any* cause. They survived countless battles, most by raw grit and strength of mind, the rest by mere luck. The Elf King *knows* how to put the right company together for the right quest. He knows when to act and how to attack a situation. He is a true leader whose ethics guide him without fault. For that alone, Stone Warhelm has placed himself next to the King of the Elves. That same commitment trickled down to Avador.

Falstaff had moved over by the fire and was sitting alone

on the warm planked flooring. With legs crossed under his robes, he sipped thoughtfully at his ale. He held open a large worn book on his lap and stared at the pages as if they were mesmerizing.

"What do you think he's reading?" Tigran whispered to Avador. They were sitting with Stone at his table drinking the strange tasting ale that the Dwarf had offered. Eventually, they acquired its taste and it began to go down smoother than the first cup.

"I am not completely sure but I think it has something to do with magic judging by the way it looks."

"You mean like *spells* and things like that?" Tigran asked but Stone had already risen and walked over to find out.

"What've you got there, Shortbeard?" Falstaff pulled himself away from the pages and found Stone staring down at him where he sat.

"Um, it's a book my grandfather gave me before he left our village many years ago. It explains how to test magic."

"Was your grandfather a magic-user?"

"I'm not sure, I never met him… but people claim he was." Falstaff noticed a smirk developing under Stone's bushy black beard.

"Why's it so damn big? You like carrying the extra load?" Stone was getting irritating.

"It fits nicely in my pack," Falstaff answered, "it doesn't bother me at all."

"Time will tell," said the burly Dwarf, "time *will* tell." With that, Falstaff replaced the book in its pack and swallowed the last of his ale.

The company spent the night at the cottage. Stone slept in his only sleeping quarters (he had offered the bed to Avador but it was politely, yet sternly refused) and the three laid out blankets by the fire.

The hours moved on and the party slept soundlessly. It was far past midnight when Avador awoke with a start. The deep night shifted in a way that made even his skin feel uncomfortable. He scanned the cottage through the gloom, his Elven eyes piercing the night. There was nothing. Yet something disturbed his sleep. His companions were still asleep near the dwindling fire, all accounted for.

He inched to his feet, slowly unsheathing the *Kingblade* from its scabbard. Moving like a spectre in the darkened room, he crept towards an open window keeping to the shadows. He stopped at the wall beside the window and listened intensely. Something was out there, he was sure of it. The only thing that remained was deciding what to do.

He dared a quick glance to where his friends were sleeping trying to steady his breath. Sweat beaded his forehead in spite of the night's chill. The sound of Stone's deep snoring coming from the other room threatened to disturb the young Elf's concentration.

Moonlight flickered dimly through the curtain-less window. A sudden break in the flow of light brought Avador to greater attention. The break came and went as if something skittered in front of the window and was gone again. Without another instant of delay, the agile Elf bound through the open window and landed soundlessly on the dirt outside.

Gripping the *Kingblade* tighter with both hands, he scanned the surrounding darkness. His heart was throbbing in his ears and a sudden terror threatened to overwhelm him. His breathing became short and ragged and his vision blurred. The hands gripping the sword began to tremble and the enchanted blade began to lower as if to drop to the ground. Avador was gritting his teeth trying to fight off the panic as tears flooded his cheeks. A cold numbing sensation plagued within his chest. *Why* did he come out here? *Why* did he feel so alone?

Suddenly a voice whispered sharply in his mind, a voice that unexpectedly brought him back to attention. *Fear is not an option for you Elven Prince, fear is not an option...* it echoed inside his head and he shot open his eyes.

As Avador gained back his senses, something peeled itself from the shadows behind the overturned wagon. Something darker than the night moved silently yet with unbelievable speed towards the unsuspecting Elf.

If not for his acute reflexes it would have had him. The blade flashed in a wicked arc slicing through something inconceivable. The thing was fluid night, tall and stick-thin with elongated ghoulish limbs. Cut in half by the *Kingblade*, it was left writhing on the ground, it's fanged mouth gaping in a silent scream, lidless eyes opened wide. As quickly as it had came, it disappeared with the passing of the bitter night wind. Then, the Elf caught a glimpse of a second one running in frenzy towards him from the murky distance, elongated arms flailing above its head. Avador raised his sword ready for the attack when someone propelled into it from the side knocking it into the dirt. The thing and its attacker thrashed fiercely on the ground sending dirt and debris flying everywhere.

It was Stone Warhelm and he had it by its throat repeatedly thrusting a deadly dagger into it. Avador was rushing to his side when the night creature gained the upper hand and flung the hefty Dwarf on his back and started tearing at his naked torso with lethal claws. A resounding battle cry penetrated the night air. Avador was off the ground swinging the *Kingblade* in a deadly sweep separating the creature's head from its body. It too vanished silently with the night air.

The next instant, Tigran Eviathane was next to Avador

brandishing a long-sword with both hands, his face in utter shock.

"What the hell *happened* out here?" Tigran was talking without realizing it, standing back-to-back with Avador and searching for signs of any more danger. Falstaff was kneeling next to the fallen Dwarf who rudely pushed him aside.

"Grab your things," Stone was shouting, "we're not waiting around here a moment longer!"

There were no arguments.

The hilly terrain that surrounds the home of Stone Warhelm was far behind the companions. Their trek persisted throughout the rest of the night with uneasy glances behind them. Consistent gloom threatened to swallow them. Each noise was the sound of something hideous coming at them from the dark; each movement was a ghastly assailant reaching out for them as they passed. Their weapons held always at the ready, their grip on them never loosening.

Stone, in stride alongside Avador kept them at an insistent pace, unyielding to the terrain growing rockier and steeper with every step. Falstaff followed, always half a tread behind with Tigran Eviathane taking the rear, a horrifying chill licking at their spines. Fear kept them moving unwaveringly. Fear drove them on past their natural capability with the feeling that if they stop, they die.

They marched until the muscles in their legs burned under the stress and their chests heaved as though they would split open at any moment. They advanced through the night climbing higher as the mountain under their feet inclined to loftier altitudes. Oxygen was gradually reducing making it increasingly more difficult to take in a full breath. The air became cooler, stinging their lungs.

Falstaff faltered for the first time. He slumped forward only to be caught by the strong Eviathane and dragged back to his feet. The slender scholar valiantly collected his robes once more and focused only on forcing one foot in front of the other. He took quick glances at his companions who were only a few paces ahead, mere shadows in the darkness.

But the darkness waned. The impenetrable blackness, assaulted finally by a rising sun, began to lose its authority. What was once pitch black became a lighter grey. Daylight pierced through the rocky peaks above in brilliant beams forcing the incessant night to bow down.

The party found itself somewhere on the tallest mountain they had ever seen. The advancing daylight revealed a rocky terrain with patches of green shrubbery scattered here and there. Only evergreens were present at this elevation of the mountain. Sharp edged and cold grey, the mountain levelled off sporadically without pattern. A chorus of their heavy breathing was the only sounds save for the chirping of awakening birds. The wind increased slightly at this height biting at any exposed skin.

Clinging tightly to their heavy cloaks, the group took a moment to look the way they had come. An overwhelming view loomed before them. Far off into the distance, the hills separating two mountain ranges still half covered in shadow, spread out like giant cushions. Somewhere in those hills rests the humble home of Stone Warhelm. Further still in utter darkness, was the beginnings of the Trood Mountains nestling the Dwarven village of Pathen.

"Nice view 'ey?" Stone was crouching in a large crevice already building a fire using the dry green shrubbery for kindling and branches off a fallen tree. The wood began to pop and crackle as the fire strengthened, it's heat intensifying. The four companions collapsed heavily and sat around its comforting warmth.

They sat in silence for a lengthy hour, nobody really knowing what to say. Avador was the first to speak, agitated by the quiet knowing there must be an explanation for the things that attacked them in the night.

"Have you seen anything like those creatures before, Stone?" He looked at the Dwarf who accepted a small copper bowl filled with a yellowish cream from Falstaff.

"What is this, Shortbeard," he asked Falstaff momentarily ignoring Avador's question.

"Spread it on your wounds, it will help stop the bleeding." Falstaff explained.

Stone looked down at his wounded chest for the first time since the flight from his home.

"I've bled before," he said stubbornly but dipped his hand into the bowl and did as he was told realizing his strength was fading. "No, Avador." The taciturn Dwarf turned his attention to the waiting Elf. "I have *never* seen anything like those creatures. But I have learned something about them from our encounter." The young Elf was attentive. "That sword of yours is our only defence against them. I stabbed at the one with my dagger and I swear it was laughing at me." Stone glanced over at the weapon Avador laid across his lap. "Your father used it in war and not *once* did I see it do what it did for you." He let Avador to his contemplations and looked over at Falstaff.

"Still want to carry around that useless book, young Falstaff?" Stone was obviously annoyed with the youngster. "Almost didn't keep up back there." Falstaff said nothing in reply. Instead he unbuckled the flap to the pack that contained the book and pulled it out. He opened the worn book to somewhere in the middle and read intensely from its aged pages.

Abruptly, the fire that flared between them detached from the wood that it was burning and began to swirl above their heads. Then, faster than their eyes could follow, the ball of flame shot through the crevice and into a large boulder outside shattering it into a million fragments. The company flinched at the noisy *boom* then stared with their mouths open at Falstaff.

"Build another fire, Stone." Falstaff's grin was ear-to-ear.

~****~

Adrenaline ran with the strongest of currents within the small company. Though in desperate need of rest, they were huddled around the small fire that Stone rebuilt and ate from the roasted grouse that Avador hunted earlier in the afternoon.

The conversation grew increasingly more enthusiastic as the hours progressed. The young travellers learned more about the usually taciturn Dwarf and what he does on his own time. Apparently the drunken Dwarf that got his teeth knocked out back at the Spider's Web was once a soldier of Grandalimus' ever-growing army. He had slowly lost his mind after a bad encounter with a magic-user. Stone did not provide all the details and received a round of groans.

"So if he was a fellow soldier," Eviathane asked," why did you attack him?"

"In the Spider's Web, I offer my services to keep the peace, y'know, for a bit of coin... I figured it was better that he was severely hurt than Falstaff severely *dead*, y'know what I mean?" The company could not help but to agree.

The late afternoon sun drifted slowly across the horizon heading for the mountains directly across from them. Knowing that night was not far away, Avador delegated shifts for keeping watch during the night, the young Eviathane taking the first watch.

They learned from Stone that they were at a high southern point somewhere on Mount Skala, the tallest mountain in the great Trood mountain range. Spending a night in the wilderness did not appeal much to the companions; the thought alone of those night creatures returning was enough to chill the blood in its veins.

Tigran Eviathane stood ten feet away from the crevice's entrance. Night had finally overcome the day and he was an hour into his watch when he unsheathed the *Kingblade*. Not because there was any sign of danger or he felt threatened (in the dark that feeling was constant), but because he was more curious than anything. There was no moon and the only reason he could see anything at all was because his eyes merely attuned to the dark. Yet the sword's broad blade showed reflection. Eviathane admired it's burnished steel, it's perfect form despite it's many years of hard battle. Where did its power come from? 'Hopefully tonight we won't need it,' Tigran reflected the words spoken to him by Avador as he handed him the enchanted weapon.

Returning the sword to its scabbard, he gazed around the gloom as the night's chill enveloped him. White breath emitted from his mouth as he exhaled. Twice he checked over the ridge to see a scattering of lights in the valley below showing small settlements. All was at peace. He patrolled at slightly higher and lower elevations but always kept sight of the large fissure where his companions slept by the burning fire.

Another hour crept by. With a long yawn Tigran entered the crevice and woke Stone Warhelm. The Dwarf stirred with a deep grunt and accepted the *Kingblade*. The two exchanged a few words before Stone disappeared through the opening and into the night beyond. Tigran stared after him with admiration. The man nearly died in a duel with one of those *things* (Eviathane could only imagine what one even *looked* like), yet there he was; without question ready to face them again.

~****~

"My Prince." The voice came from Stone Warhelm, a deep whisper in the darkness. The Elf arose quickly, his silver chainmail glimmering faintly from the diminishing fire. He faced the Dwarf and asked how everything went.

"All at peace," said Stone handing over Avador's sword, "but that is not to say things will remain that way." He gave Avador a look that said to take heed. The young Elf glanced at Tigran and Falstaff who slept wrapped in their travel blankets. Putting a hand on Stone's shoulder, they looked at each other with understanding. Avador threw his cloak over his shoulders and left.

A thin silvery crescent moon was struggling amidst a swift current of cloud patches. The clouds were toying with it. One moment they were allowing it to breathe and the next swallowing it whole, and snuffing its feeble light. Avador smelled the air. Rain was coming soon. He stood exactly in front of the crevice entrance and the weather changed significantly. The winds lashed at him with savage outbursts threatening to take him with them. But the Elf stood firmly, legs apart and his heavy cloak embraced tightly around him.

Avador glanced behind him with envy where Stone rekindled the fire. He wanted to be with them, asleep and warm. But he knew he would stand his ground out here in the freezing cold. If anything attacked tonight, he would *not* be to blame for their deaths as they slept.

The valiant Elf forced his mind to stay away from the fire. He held the *Kingblade* tightly in his hand and observed how right it felt in his grip. He shifted positions to fight off the cold and allowed his thinking to drift elsewhere. He considered where he was: Mount Skala. He let the name linger in his mind for a moment. He thought of Falstaff and Eviathane and how they used to talk about travelling to places they had never been. In their fantasies, it was not like this. A journey to distant lands was supposed to be planned. They were to leave home with a hearty wave to their parents and a promise to return soon. They certainly were not to leave like thieves in the night with very little explanation to search for a father that disappeared without warning.

Avador moved slowly, a phantom melting into the night's shadows. His keen eyes scrutinized all around the area of the crevice they chose for shelter. He listened through the normal sounds of his surroundings, his ears trying to pick up anything unnatural. All he wanted was for the night to end and the sun to rise. Midnight went by hours ago; to Avador it seemed as though it had not even arrived. The minutes skulked by slowly as if wanting to taunt him a little longer than usual. He felt the cold tingling numbness of fear pass though him and forced his nerve to remain. The Elf was crouched under a thick evergreen fighting off the bitter wind when his father called to him.

With the hilt of the *Kingblade* held firmly, both hands squeezing its black leather grip, its blade dug into the rocky terrain beneath his feet. Avador shut his eyes so he could see nothing.

"*Son.*" Grandalimus' voice was hollow, an echo with no source. "*Tonight you and your friends have nothing to fear. You are safe for the moment and J am very proud of you Avador.*"

"Father," Avador sounded desperate, "why do you not reveal everything to us? My friends follow me blindly and faithfully not knowing where we are going. Tell me now

Father... are you *dead?*" Avador was a lot more blunt than he wanted to be.

"*Son. Your patience must match your courage.*" The Elf King's voice, though empty, became soothing. "*No I am not dead. Soon we will meet and all will be revealed.*" Avador listened to his father, eyes held tightly closed with tears of relief escaping through his eyelids. "*Tell Stone Warhelm to guide you to Lord's Lair. There you will find me and I shall explain everything... I promise.*" The resonance of his voice faded into the heavy winds and Avador knew that he had left once again. He felt the first of the chilling drops of rain. When he opened his eyes, the sun had taken over the horizon but surrounding them as if it were a personal vendetta, were storm clouds preparing to unleash their wrath.

Chapter 9 - Descent

The north-eastern horizon radiated brilliant red and orange streams that reached out like giant's fingers towards the Trood's northern peaks. Miles below the summit, the horizon over-looked enormous foothills, rivers and luscious forests. The sun revealed a vast body of water in the far distance as it carried out its daily ascent.

The south-western face of the Trood Mountains was the exact opposite of the horizon's clear skies. Blanketed in menacing black clouds, everything was pummelled with chilling rain... few had the fortune to be at the right altitude and the correct part of the mountain range to be able to witness both extremes at once.

"Bogdan. Bogdan, wake up." The Gnome was shaking his companion as he slept near a small fire, a thin line of grey smoke rising skyward. The morning air was fresh within the small wooded area they chose to camp in during the night, mist hovering in streams all about them. The Gnome, short and stumpy with patches of a dark beard and a nose as long as his thumbs, decided to give up trying to wake his friend. He slumped down by the fire taking in the scenery and sniffing the air with huge nostrils. He was quite disappointed that he had to experience two dramatically different weather scenes at once by himself.

Grazing twenty feet away near the clearing was a small brown mule. A clutter of pots and pans and all kinds of utensils and large sacks filled with practically anything lay near the mule's feet. It's white mouth chewed mechanically at the tall dew-coated grass.

The Gnome was beginning to get bored when he spotted his friend's left eye open and close abruptly.

"You're awake!" He screamed causing the mule's ears to spring upwards. "You've been awake this whole *time!*" Bogdan stayed motionless under a torn blanket.

"Are you still mad at me for lending my mule to Losha?" That did it. The other Gnome threw his blanket in the air and sat straight up.

"Badom you're an idiot!" He said bluntly. "You can't lend your mule to *anybody*! It's better to lend your *wife!*"

Badom was aghast. "What! *Why?*"

"Because at least your wife can *tell* you what happened… even if you have to torture it out of her. How's a *mule* going to tell you if he was treated properly?" Bogdan's fat nose was flaring with annoyance. "Now mine has to carry *twice* the load."

Badom scratched at his patchy beard pondering Bogdan's logic. Just by habit, he began stuffing tobacco into a large curvy pipe when Bogdan smacked it out of his hands.

"And I thought I told you to quit smoking that thing, it'll kill you."

Badom and Bogdan were friends for as long as they could remember. Bogdan, thought to be the older of the two (neither of them know their ages), took it upon himself to be the acting father figure to Badom (who apparently 'couldn't find his way out of a hollow log').

Gnomes generally had no certain place they call "home"-especially these two. Each day they travelled and every morning they awoke somewhere new. As far as personal hygiene, they hated water. They were perfectly at home in the dirt.

The two friends had a quick breakfast of dried pork and

bread. They drank wine from their flasks to help fight off the cool weather. Badom helped Bogdan, whose grumpiness seemed to have faded somewhat, to load his mule. The animal was soon piled with sacks and clanging metal objects until it looked as though everything could fall at any moment.

"That *is* quite the weather," Bogdan muttered to his companion. They were sitting by the fire looking at the dark clouds encircling the mountains south-west from where they sat. "It looks like the storm is heading west," he added.

"It's strange. We can even see the rain falling from here." Badom was enthusiastic. Bogdan's reply was a grunt and he stood and stretched to his full height of four feet.

The Gnomes packed the rest of their things and put out their little fire. Slowly they trudged down a small path that declined gradually eastward. The mule followed behind them with its freight swaying back and forth as it walked.

~ **** ~

Lord's Lair?" Stone was perplexed. "Why would he be *there*? Not like him at all." He was leaning on the cool rock of the crevice's entrance shaking his head and pursing his lips. The rain continued to beat down the outdoors; it's sound so monotonous it became a steady hum.

No one seemed to have heard him. Tigran was talking with Falstaff about the magic his friend conjured and Avador was deciding on their next move.

"Magic weaves the things of dreams into fabrics of reality." Falstaff was still giddy from the spell he cast, the dismal weather doing nothing to douse his excitement.

"I realize that Falstaff... but can *I* do it?" Tigran was particularly curious.

"Here, try it," Falstaff said handing him the large book. But when Tigran tried reading from the archaic pages, the ancient language meant nothing to him.

"I think I'll stick with *this*," Eviathane said putting a hand on the hilt of his sword and handed the book back to Falstaff.

Stone turned from his contemplation and hefted the huge battle-hammer over his shoulder. He walked to where Avador was crouching by the fire noting rain seeping through openings in the fissure.

"Are you thinking what I'm thinking my Prince?" The burly Dwarf spoke quietly regardless of the overpowering rain.

"We must move out." Avador said getting every one's attention.

"You're right. The crevice could collapse at any moment under this heavy rainfall." Stone was already packing to leave knowing that it was not the crevice that Avador was thinking about. Falstaff and Tigran paused at the suddenness but did the same and wondered where were they going to go in these conditions.

Falstaff wrapped his book with a heavy blanket and shoved it in his pack. Throwing a thick grey cloak over his robes he looked outside and swore the rain was beating down even harder. Eviathane strapped all his armour and adjusted his shield to his back. The big man stooped slightly so he could put on a steel helmet. Tightening a heavy cape about him, he stepped towards the entrance and listened to the rain pound like a thousand drums and the wind scream it's lament through the thrashing evergreens.

Avador stood with his back to the exit, his own cloak flapping wildly about him, one hand gripping the cowl to keep his head covered. He looked at the eyes that shone with life staring back at him and waiting for his command. The Elf smiled. With a nod to Stone Warhelm, the four vanished into the pulsating downpour.

Instantly drenched and momentarily stunned, the companions fought to find their bearings. Stone, familiar with the land shouted above the incredible winds with Avador anxiously keeping everyone together. The violent rain was an overwhelming distraction. Direction was lost, so blind faith in the seasoned Dwarf was unavoidable. Avador did not want to travel aimlessly. Somewhat, the cowl of his cloak helped keep the rain from his sharp eyes allowing him to help Stone with direction.

Abruptly the terrain sloped downwards, the Dwarf screaming for them to brace for a difficult descent. Driving rain beat at them and their surroundings as if it were alive and angry. Rainwater formed small channels beneath their feet and they felt the rivulets trying to take them down by their ankles. The small party struggled to stay balanced as they skidded blindly downward with the sharp ground biting into the soles of their boots.

The terrain rarely levelled off. Falstaff had the most difficulties with his wet robes restraining his movements. He cursed to himself and the thought of giving up came to him more than once. Desperately he tried to keep his footing and to keep himself from falling into Tigran who was half a tread in front and pushing ahead relentlessly. Barbed undergrowth clutched and tugged at his loose clothing as if trying to hold him back. He felt his momentum becoming too fast for him as their descent became dangerously steeper.

Avador was suddenly at his side. Falstaff did not see how he got there but did not protest when he stopped him short. There were flashes of steel in the driving rain. He heard unrecognizable shouts from Stone. Tigran Eviathane climbed back to where Falstaff stood confused, his heavy shield held out before him and his long-sword released from its scabbard. With a sudden jolt, Falstaff realized they were under attack and was thrown roughly to the ground by Avador.

There was an unexpected surge of spears that embedded themselves into the trees around them, some missing the group by mere inches. Falstaff caught a glimpse of Eviathane deflect one with his shield and propel himself up the slippery rise. He released a thunderous battle cry swinging his sword and striking down an attacker. Avador was in the trees, his longbow creaking as he drew an arrow to his chin. Finding a target he let it fly and with a dull thud, struck someone in the chest.

Everything was distorted. How were they supposed to make out *anything* in this rainstorm? Falstaff was growing increasingly frustrated. From the ground where his head lay, he saw Stone's boots trampling the wet earth next to him, his battle-hammer swinging in a great arc. He heard a loud *crack* and something fell next to him. It looked like a Dwarf, bearded and dark complexioned, lifeless eyes staring at him. Blood was oozing out of his skull and mixing with the rainwater. He heard more shouts and looked up, his eyes squinting to ward off the rain. Avador thrust himself from the tree above his head. A blurred figure, quick and deadly, the *Kingblade* held in one hand. The agile Elf dropped fifteen feet before lunging the enchanted blade into an assailant and rolling with a crash into the soaked bushes. Falstaff failed to see any more movement from Avador. He saw instead a handful of indistinct silhouettes closing in on where his intrepid friend lay motionless.

With desperate glances all around him, he saw that they were greatly outnumbered. Dark stocky figures with lethal weapons moved relentlessly in wild advances towards the small party. Fasltaff felt the surge of helplessness begin to overwhelm him. He lost all sight of his companions. Were they still alive? Were they still struggling? Why did he come with them? He felt useless. They acted instinctively when all he did was cower on the ground like a beaten puppy.

An overpowering rage prevented the rush of hopelessness from taking over. This was real. *This* was the time he was supposed to act. These attackers were trying to *kill* them; they were not going to let them go unharmed. With a desperate decision and a frantic clutch at his own will, he recalled words of ancient lore. He forced his mind to stray elsewhere trying to focus only on one thing. He delved into his memory searching for the correct words, the right pronunciation and the proper accent in which to say them. His lips moved unconsciously, phrases escaping deliberately from them. He must stay centred and keep his focus away from the death that was approaching.

Falstaff stood slowly, the wind sweeping at his robes and wild rain stinging at his exposed skin. He released the ancient words into the maelstrom fighting to remember them, eyes held tightly closed. An attacker spotted him and ran with full force, a lethal battle-axe raised to strike him down.

That attacker was the next to die. Blue lightning sparked from Falstaff's raised fingers. It arced skyward into the ferocious rain and back down striking his assailant with unbelievable speed. He died instantly. The lightning spread and crackled into the others where they stood in disbelief and they too met the same fate as their cohort. Stone Warhelm recoiled from the blinding electricity releasing his grip he had on one of the attackers. He stared in disbelief. The man before him convulsed as lightning surged through his body; he collapsed in a lifeless heap.

Tigran saw the whole thing and stood dumbfounded as the rain beat down all around him. The screams of their attackers silenced abruptly. For the moment, only the sound of the constant downpour was heard.

Avador crawled from where he landed in the thick shrubbery and found four attackers laying dead and steaming, mouths gaping in soundless screams. He lurched to his feet and gazed around mystified. Eviathane moved to him just as bewildered.

"Are you alright, Avador?" Tigran found he had difficulty recovering his voice, his heart pounding frantically in his ears. "You saved my life." He added between gasps for air.

"*He* saved all of us." Warhelm scaled the rise to where they were standing and pointed down to Falstaff; at least twenty bodies lay steaming all around them. The young mage was still standing by the tree that Avador propelled himself from not one minute ago.

The three fighters declined the mountainside to stand beside Falstaff who was trying to contain the adrenalin that surged through him like the blue lightning that he invoked.

"Not *bad* Shortbeard." Stone slapped a large hand on Falstaff's back.

"Are you okay, Falstaff?" Avador was trying to make his voice heard above the howling winds.

"Are *you*?" The young mage turned to face Avador. Despite the miserable weather the three friends all at once embraced each other and danced like children.

Stone allowed them to have their moment. Then he walked over to them with his hammer slung over his shoulder, rainwater pouring down his face.

"Hate breaking up yer celebration, but we have to leave… *now!*" The burly Dwarf was right and they knew it. Without another word, the four continued their risky descent down the treacherous mountainside.

~****~

Two excruciating hours later, the company finally found themselves on level ground and the storm behind them. A small wooded area stood before them, dry and untouched by the rain. They entered it slowly and cautiously, fanning out slightly as they warily swept the area.

Once satisfied that the danger was also behind them, they removed their wet cloaks and laid them out under the midday sun. The small group assembled together and before long, a fire crackled and popped before them. It was not until Avador opened his pack and removed some rations that the rest realised they could use some food.

Stone sniffed the air. "Gnomes," he said disgustedly and spit on the ground.

"What's a Gnome?" Eviathane asked the revolted Dwarf.

"They're nuthin' but stinking midgets who want to be Dwarfs." Stone answered bluntly. Then he turned to face the three who were gathered around him looking for answers.

"War had just broken out." He said knowing what they were thinking. "Those attackers up the mountain were Dark Dwarves, the only creatures I despise more than Gnomes. They are in allegiance only with money."

"How do you know that war broke out, Stone?" Asked Avador beginning to get even more concerned.

"It's usually the first sign of war. Dark Dwarves only attack if they are paid too. They *love* war. And during a war, if you are not one of them, you're an enemy; they don't care *who* you are."

"Who sent them?" Avador continued.

"How the hell should *I* know?" Stone was getting agitated. "I was with *you* the whole time, remember?" Then he turned with an apologetic expression knowing that the young Elf must be more curious than he had ever been. "Anyway lads, we're going to camp here for the night. Tomorrow we reach Lord's Lair and we'll need rest. And who knows? We might find ourselves chin deep in the first war I know nothing about."

Chapter 10 - Grandalimus

Stone found he had trouble sleeping. Something was disquieting him. His mind was filling up with thoughts, all of which were not good. Sure he was getting increasingly anxious to meet with his old friend Grandalimus again. But something was gnawing at him. Who could have sent these revolting beings that call themselves 'Dwarves'? How long ago did war break out and why? What plan does the Elven King have? The burly Dwarf sat up and rested a thick forearm on one knee. The stars were all showing tonight. Stone could pick out the entire gathering of stars and their formations without any hindrance of cloud.

"Can't sleep Stone?" Avador came up behind the troubled Dwarf and crouched next to him.

"Aye Elfling." Stone was scratching at his thick beard. "How's the watch going?" He asked with somewhat indifference.

"All is quiet... but I guess if it wasn't, you would know." Avador put his hand on Stone's shoulder and sat next to him. The companions remained without fire this evening for fear of more dark Dwarves discovering them. A cool breeze swept by them and they reflexively tightened their cloaks about themselves.

"Where are we exactly?" Avador asked yawning.

"We are nearly at the eastern foot of the Trood Mountains. In the morning we will continue our descent and reach the Foothills of Larnaka." Stone paused noticing Falstaff and Tigran sit up from where they were laying under thick blankets and listen to the conversation.

"You's can't sleep either 'ey?" The Dwarf asked with a wry grin. Then he continued. "From the foothills we head west and we find Lord's Lair... *and* your father," he gave Avador an intense look. Avador's heart began to tingle at the thought.

"Then maybe we can get some answers," Stone finished before lying back down and covering himself with his blanket. Avador glanced over at his friends and smiled. They smiled in return, happy for their friend. Maybe something will finally go *right* on this perilous quest. The thought was inviting. They had enough of this adventure and they wanted to go home.

The sky remained cloudless throughout the night. The shifts were carried out within the small company without any threats and soon the sun was peeking over the horizon. A small fire was built to cook the morning meal. Falstaff sat by it and read from his hefty book, concentrating and with great interest. The thought of spell casting made his heart gallop. Grandalimus was right. He *did* have it within himself to be a magic-user and that alone excited him.

Soon everything was packed and the small party set out with a little more enthusiasm. They followed a small path that declined steadily eastward. The panorama before them was breathtaking. From this position of the Trood mountain range, lakes and forests and lengthy rivers could be seen with great clarity. Even the Foothills of Larnaka that were laid out miles below them were exposed with an unhindered view. The four followed the path that progressed gradually downward. The amount of trees decreased and the air grew less chilly as they declined the frigid mountains. Within a few hours, they found themselves at the bottom and staring at the foothills before them.

The group stopped and ate briefly from their rations before Stone led them westward. The afternoon sun took its stance high above them yet it did nothing to ward off the cool weather. They advanced across the hilly terrain and gradually headed north. There was no one around for as far as the eye could see. The hours moved on and the group travelled with little conversation. They grew increasingly eager to find Grandalimus and hopefully go home. The thought of a war currently under way swayed them from their hopes. Where was it taking place? Who was under attack and who was attacking? The questions were innumerable. Before any more contemplation, Stone stopped them short when they found themselves facing a scattering of strange white structures that stood on a tall rise and seemed to have appeared out of nowhere.

"Lord's Lair." Stone whispered to no one in particular looking at the columned buildings that stood before them.

~****~

Avador, Falstaff and Eviathane stood in awe in front of the strangely designed buildings. They were off-white in colour and all one level. Thin, almost stick-like columns surrounded each building as if caging the structures to the ground they were built on. There were no windows to be found anywhere on the rectangular shaped buildings. The entire area smelled of dust and decay countless of years old.

Avador walked cautiously to the closest building and put his fingers on one of the columns. He instantly pulled his hand away as a sudden horror chilled his blood, his skin creeping in fear.... *bone.*

"Where is my father?" He asked at once backing up to where his friends stood waiting.

"Lord's Lair to be precise young Elfling, is that building in the centre of all the rest." Stone stepped beside Avador and pointed with his hammer. A building slightly larger than the others but with the exact shape except for a second level, stood in the precise centre, encircled by five others.

"Stone." Avador said keeping his gaze on the bizarre buildings. "What *is* this place?"

"No one truly knows, my young prince. The only thing we have for answers are the myths told by all of the races, each twisting the tale to suit their purpose." Stone found a large white rock and sat down. "I don't believe *any* of them. The only way to find out for sure is to go inside."

"Have you ever been inside?" Falstaff crouched next to Stone, his curiosity beginning to get the better of him. He took note of a single large entrance that accommodated no door or gate.

"No." The seasoned Dwarf gazed uneasily at the large square access in the front of the building, the darkness within impenetrable. "But I *will* today."

Avador was getting frustrated. His father had told him he was here. But all he could see are sand-covered bone buildings and no trace of the Elf King. The thought that his father might not be here came to his mind and panic began to creep up on him. He began to sweat in spite of the cold breeze. The Elf looked at his friends who stood near him. The look they returned him said they were ready for his next move, eager and dedicated.

"I am going inside," Avador said before realizing he was even talking.

"And we're going *with* you." Eviathane stepped forward and tightened his mouth in stubborn objection before the Elf could protest. Avador's gaze went to Eviathane, then to Falstaff. There was no winning of any arguments here. Stone Warhelm turned his head to hide his grin.

The entrance to Lord's Lair shed no light. It stood before the company like a sinister darkness daring them to enter. Avador accepted a torch that Stone took out of his small pack and lit. The Elf's ears strained to hear any sounds coming from inside. There was absolutely nothing, which is what worried him. Why would his father make him come here and not show himself? Was he deceived into thinking his father was alive by some evil sorcery, and tricked into a trap? He was beginning to second-guess his decisions to come here. Did he bring himself and his friends into an ambush that could cost them their lives?

There was no turning back. He glanced behind him to where everyone was standing. Steel slid against steel as the *Kingblade* was released from its scabbard shattering the silence. He must have confidence in the enchanted weapon. It was not mere chance that Grandalimus left it behind and Avador had brought it with him. Then, releasing all doubt, he stepped inside Lord's Lair.

~ **** ~

Aonas stood at the entrance of his father's bedchamber. He could vaguely hear the voice of the ruler of Sovereign's Reach through the thick wooden door. The young man rolled his eyes when he realized his father was mourning the death of his mother. He knocked hard against the wood of the door. There was a silent pause.

"Yes?" A deep voice trying to find composure came from inside the room.

"Father, it is I, Aonas. May I have a moment with you?" His father shook his head at his son's thoughtlessness. He always had a lack of consideration.

"Enter." The King of Sovereign's Reach spoke half-heartedly.

Aonas opened the door and walked inside and past his father to a large oval window. His father sighed and sat in a cushioned chair behind a polished oak desk.

"Father, I've been thinking." Aonas spoke without turning from the window, his large muscular back to the King. "Jadonas is to be made ruler after you." He almost hissed the words.

"That is correct my son." Aonas' father became stern knowing there was going to be an argument here.

"But why? I am your firstborn. I should be the one next in line!" Tears of rage flowed down Aonas' clean-shaven cheeks. "Why Father?"

"Son. Do you wish to have a title and nothing more? Your brother Jadonas is simply more suited to rule a kingdom. I am not going to let details such as who is the rightful heir get in the way of doing what is right." The King stood up and walked over to his son. "Please try to understand Aonas, your brother had shown interest in what I do. He accompanied me to countless meetings. He took initiative and proposed ideas in many serious discussions. He even led the quest to seize the Sceptre of Karah-Toh from that evil island dweller Mungus, who we both know tried controlling the dark magic-users into doing his bidding." Aonas' Father stopped and waited for a reply. When there was no response he walked closer to his son. They were interrupted by a knock at the door.

"Your Lordship." A gentle voice came from behind the door.

"Skneeba," the king said with a smile, "enter."

A tall and thin man entered wearing grey robes and carrying a leather-bound book. His dark skin showed that he came from the island below the mountain, Gogatha.

"I have brought the book you have requested."

"Thank you Skneeba," said the king and directed him to put it on his desk. He did so and with a bow, left father and son to

be alone once more. Aonas' face was serious as he waited for his father to continue.

"My dear Aonas. I have signed already my kingship to Jadonas. The papers have been sent to the Authority of Sovereignty... and that's where they will stay."

A fury overcame Aonas and pushed him to the verge of lunacy. "Let his reign begin today," he whispered through clenched teeth. Without warning the young man snatched his father and launched him out the large oval window. The King of Sovereign's Reach released a horrible scream that ended many stories below where he died instantly in the streets of a great city. "You should always watch where you put your signature." Aonas left the room and slammed the door behind him.

The merciless ruler awoke with a start, sweating profusely under his blankets. He rubbed at his thick beard and instinctively reached for the sceptre, which lay next to him. He managed a glance over at the oval window that overlooked nothing but an incessant night that refused to go away. He lost track of the days. For all he knew he was sleeping and there should have been daylight coming through the window.

His mind began to warp into something foreign to him, a twisted maelstrom of past events. His own past became outlandish and imaginary; his present perverse, wicked... and he liked it. The future? He saw it unmistakably clear. So clear that he could almost live it as if it were happening right now: The Elves were dead. The Dwarves were slaves, and the Humans his faithful servants. And *magic.* Magic was his to control. The magic-users had given it to him. It was all *his.*

A smile formed underneath his greying beard. He thought of the war he had just begun, an unasked for surprise to the rest of the world. He thought of the Dark Dwarves who became exceptionally loyal to his cause. It was a large price to pay but the damage they cause makes it all worthwhile. 'You have to spend money to make money.' Aonas laughed out loud. Money? He did not want it now anyway. When the lands are cowering under his heel... *that* will be his greatest reward.

The King of Sovereign's Reach pulled the sceptre of Kara-Toh closer to his face, the green vapour slithering around the bed as if it had a life of its own. With *this*, he thought, I will have control of all magic and its source. The thought delighted him to no end as he imagined vulnerable magic-users bowing to his every command. And with that, he sunk his head into his pillow and drifted off into a very soothing sleep.

~****~

Avador's heart throbbed inside his chest. The corridor that he and his friends stood in just inside the entrance of Lord's Lair was soaked with dankness. His torch cast ginger light into the gloom. The passage was narrow and long and the meagre light could not reach the end of it. Even the Elf's eyes, sharp as they were, could not penetrate the obscurity beyond.

Eviathane was at the rear of the group, a walking arsenal and an intimidating defence in case someone or some*thing* attacked them from behind. He noted the crowded narrow halls and slid a short-sword out of a leather sheath strapped to his back. He walked with his shield held out finding it difficult to see anything.

Stone was a pace behind the young Elf. Avador refused to let him or any of them take the front. This was *his* desire to go after the King of the Elves and if he was the first to die and they had a chance to escape, so be it.

The four inched stealthily down the murky passageway, silent figures within the mysterious walls. Avador's breath puffed into the light of his torch showing a sudden drop in temperature. The minutes seemed never-ending as they advanced deeper down the corridor. Every now and then the company paused to make sure everyone was present and okay.

At last the torch's feeble light found an arched metal door at the end of the passageway. The group bunched together at the find, adrenalin rushing within them. Avador put a finger to his lips touching the latch that opened the door. To his surprise it slid open easily. He took a cautious step inside the entryway. The gloom was impenetrable. Four hearts beat so hard that they thudded painfully within their chests. The brave Elf swung the torch left and right until he spotted something on the wall behind the doorway. It was an unlit torch still wedged into its bracket. Avador touched his own torch to it and it flared immediately to life. Next to it, about two metres apart was another, and then another. The torches ran around a large rectangular room and Avador lit them all.

The small company stood together, back-to-back in the centre of the room, their breaths steaming in the frigid air. Something came to their attention in a sudden rush. A skeleton lay on a small platform situated on each of the four walls. Each skeleton held a sword to their chests. A broad staircase led to a darkened landing where a fifth skeleton lay with a black shield resting against its platform.

The small party took a moment to take in the scene. They shivered at their situation. This was not what any of them expected of Lord's Lair.

"This place is more than just a monument in the middle of nowhere." Stone was the first to dare speak. The rest of the company followed his gaze to a skeleton that was seconds ago lying down, standing with a sword in its bony hand. The shock went straight to their hearts and they froze instantly.

Abruptly the other three began to stir on their platforms,

climbing down with an unnatural scraping sound. Each skeleton moved slowly at first but their pace hastened as they approached the small group huddled together in harmonized terror.

Avador's mind raced, the *Kingblade* held tightly in a frozen hand. This cannot be *it*. His father is not here. Why would his father send him to his death? It was a deception after all. What a fool he had been. And now his friends will die with him.

A cry of rage escaped the Elf's lips, his teeth clenching. With a vicious snarl he raised the enchanted blade and attacked the nearest skeletal being. Eviathane, shaken from his state of shock thrust himself into another, swinging his sword. The sound of metal clanging on metal reverberated in the large cold room. The skeletons fought with unexpected skill deflecting blow after blow, their counterattacks sending the party back into surprise.

Falstaff suddenly felt cold steel tearing into his robes and into the flesh of his leg. He heard the valiant Stone curse, for it was he who deflected the skeleton man's sword trying to defend the young mage. Falstaff went down scarcely avoiding another attack as a dull blade swished above his head. He saw Eviathane spring over him, the sound of his armour chiming in his ears. He saw the skeleton fall in a crumpled stack when Tigran rammed it with his shield and ended its resistance with repeated strikes with his sword.

Avador felt his strength begin to falter and yet the skeleton man fought without any signs of fatigue. He began to tire. The *Kingblade* started to waver in his hands. Instantly Stone was at his side, beads of sweat forming on his forehead. Together they retreated to where Falstaff lay wounded and formed a small circle around him along with Eviathane. Reassembled with his friends, Avador felt his strength return to him in a sudden rush of vitality. He howled in frenzy trying to keep his movements under control. The *Kingblade* swung in a great arc decapitating a skeleton man that went in for a killing blow.

Falstaff's lips were moving, cryptic words seeping through them. He ignored the searing pain in his leg. From where he lay, his fingers curled and a flaming ball appeared within them instantly increasing the light in the room. He heaved himself to his knees and with an agonized scream threw the ball of flame. It launched into a skeleton and splintered it into innumerable fragments. Everyone recoiled at the thunderous noise and shielded themselves from the flying fragments.

Stone squandered no time. The hardened Dwarf leaped to one side and sprung with powerful legs towards the fourth skeleton. His great battle-hammer swung low crushing into its legs at the knee taking it down to the cold floor. With a mighty pounce he brought the hammer down into its skull pounding at it until nothing was left but ground dust.

Then suddenly the companions spotted Avador bounding up the broad staircase as if an animal possessed. He was attacking the fifth skeleton that stood alone with the black shield in hand. As the enraged Elf drew nearer to the skeleton man standing behind its raised shield he caught a glimpse of something familiar. A fragment of a violet tunic hung from its bony shoulders. Avador stopped short near the top of the staircase. He looked at his own tunic... the same violet colour. This *thing* killed his father.

"No!" Avador felt his knees buckle. A rush of dizziness swirled in his head. His father... *dead*. Enraged anew he brought the *Kingblade* up high above his head and sent it crashing into the black shield. The sound was deafening and resonated throughout the entire room like a warped church bell. Time and time again he savagely attacked the skeleton man but each time the incessant black shield deflected his strikes.

Avador faltered and fell to one knee. The skeleton did nothing. It stood there waiting for another blow. The Elf breathed heavily with fatigue. He brought his sword up again but this time he paused, a frozen figure in a painted scene. He caught the face of his *father* in the blade's refection. His heart missed a beat. Completely taken aback, Avador brought the *Kingblade* closer to the skeletal creature that stood before him. In the blade's silvery reflection, where a skull should have been, was Grandalimus' face.

Avador's fingers lost all control and dropped the enchanted sword where it clanged on the stone staircase. He looked up at the skeleton and it bowed its head in silent sorrow.

"Father." Avador whispered to the cursed creature that stood before him.

igran Eviathane inched up the broad staircase where Avador was slumped on his knees at the landing above him. The Elf's shoulders were heaving involuntarily as he sobbed, grief and anguish overtaking him completely.

Eviathane's own heart grew heavy for his friend. He stopped scaling the steps when he saw the *Kingblade* lying on the rung before him. He picked it up and held it tightly in his gloved hand. Slowly he removed his helmet, his black hair draped about his shoulders and down his back, sweat dripping down his face in small rivulets. Drawing closer to Avador, he knelt next to him and bowed his head, the *Kingblade* reflecting the face of Grandalimus as it once was.

Stone Warhelm had helped Falstaff up the staircase without Avador or Eviathane realizing it until they too stood before the skeleton man and kneeled next to the grief-struck Elf. The four knelt in a half circle before the skeletal form of the King of the Elves. Grandalimus stood tall and straight, his head bowed, his stance still showing the pride of the Elven King.

Avador silenced abruptly his sobs and dared to look up at his father, tears still pouring down his face. The Elf King bent slightly and took the *Kingblade* from Tigran who handed it to him wordlessly. He raised it to his face showing a smiling Grandalimus in the blade's reflection, a fatherly smirk that the young Elf grew to love affectionately.

Grandalimus' voice suddenly came to life in the dank chamber. The skeletal mouth moved up and down but the lips in the reflection formed the words. *"Do not lose all hope my brave Avador. J know this is too much for you to bear without your essence changing forever."* Grandalimus was fixed to where he stood, careful not to approach his son any more than he had to. *"The time has come for an explanation for all of this."* Even in this appearance Grandalimus' gaze felt scrutinizing as he looked from one man to the next. The four remained frozen on their knees, speechless and waiting for the Elf King to clarify to them what exactly is happening.

"J have been attacked in a way that no one has ever attacked me before. For years the attacks were predictable. By sword. By spear. By great armies and huge juggernauts. No one succeeded to take me down from the throne J command." The Elf King paused as he too knelt by the small company before him; even now he showed his belief in equality. *"But this time J was assaulted in a different way."* His eyes, if whole, would have narrowed. *"A man who calls himself a 'King' has obtained a power so mighty that if he takes full control, he will extinguish the lands of everything they are today. This man called Aonas, many years ago, had slain his own father coveting his throne. Aonas had aloud his brother Jadonas to reign in his place, all the while loathing him and planning his demise. One wicked night, that moment had come. Jt was when Jadonas, a man J have respected throughout the years had been sleeping in his chambers, peacefully believing he was loved by all, when he was murdered as he slept. Aonas still carries the smear of his brother's blood on his hands."*

No one spoke as Grandalimus continued, still completely in awe by the Elf King's skeletal presence.

"Aonas immediately took control of a powerful artefact that Jadonas had previously used for the sake of good, an artefact that in the wrong hands, like it is now, can initiate undreamt of chaos. He who wields it has the power to govern all magic-users, lawful or evil. Fortunately there are not

many in these lands that are magic-users. Unfortunately, it does not take more than one to cause the damage Aonas is intending. This one that Aonas took control of is named Skneeba.

"Skneeba was a wise and clever user of magic. His power was drawn from the moon and he had used it to help in times of need or war. He was ever faithful to Jadonas and to this day mourns his death. After the murder, Aonas seized this artefact called the Sceptre of Kara-Toh, ancient and powered by archaic mystery. He used it to take over the humbled Skneeba and attack me with a power J have never expected." Grandalimus took note of the expression of comprehension from Avador. "Yes, my son. Jt was that night you felt that surge pass through your heart as you were in combat with Master Wylme. That moment J was cursed to become what J am now. Aonas knew that if he were to succeed in his deceitful plans, he must first get rid of me by means that no one had ever attempted. Later he learned that J have a son and in turn attacked you as well. Those things that were sent are called Ecliptic Wraiths, shades stolen from a lunar eclipse by the forced Skneeba. They exist now only to obey Aonas. Aonas, for the moment believes you dead, my son. That is why you have not encountered another.

"But do not be deceived to think they attack only at night. Wherever there is darkness or shade, they may be present, lingering in obscurity ready to attack by orders of Aonas." Grandalimus silenced and raised the broad sword a little higher. "This sword, a weapon J call Kingblade, unbeknown to me at the time, was enchanted by Skneeba. He foresaw Aonas' misdeeds and charmed the blade to have the power to destroy Ecliptic Wraiths while J was visiting my dear friend Jadonas. Aonas to this day knows nothing of the weapon." Stone Warhelm looked up slowly and nodded his head in understanding.

"Father." Avador finally spoke, his voice sticking to his throat as he did so. "What must we do now?"

"Aonas, without declaring any war, is attacking our lands. He wants all races that denounce him to perish. He must be prevented in doing so. My son, you must go where I cannot. His realm is found on a mystifying island called Gogatha. You will succeed if you go without his knowledge that you are still alive. Remove him of the Sceptre of Kara-Toh and he will lose all power he holds on Skneeba. His armies, which are forced into his allegiance, must then be freed. That task as well, must be yours."

"But what of *you*, Father? Will you be free?" Avador looked at his father's skeletal face and fought to keep his composure.

"I do not know, my son. But even if I am not, Aonas' plan to be rid of the Elven King had failed. I will be animate forever in these four walls, and never truly die." Grandalimus handed the Kingblade to his son. *"I will forever be with you Avador. Know that, and you can do anything!"*

~****~

Stone finished wrapping Falstaff's leg with a soft cotton cloth after spreading that same concoction that the young mage had given him. Tigran Eviathane was strapped and ready to go and growing increasingly more impatient.

"He's been up there for a while," he said for what must have been the tenth time. He was referring to Avador staying at the top of the landing with his father. "Does he not want to eat?"

"Tigran, give him some room," Falstaff remarked to the big man. "It can't be easy learning that your father has been turned into an abomination." Tigran stopped with the complaints knowing that the young mage was right and turned his attention to the burly Dwarf.

91

"Where do you think we will go from here?" Eviathane asked trying to keep his mind away from the cold chamber and the skeleton men.

"There's a city just north from here called *Vor*." Stone's eyes were thoughtful. "It's only about a day's walk from Lord's Lair. In a way we are lucky to be near its vicinity. If we can find the right people, we can get any information from that city." The sound of steps descending the wide staircase interrupted Stone. Avador slowly stepped towards them, exhaustion marked all over his usually alert features, the *Kingblade* held loosely in a fatigued hand. "Let's move out of here," was all he said.

The small company followed Avador down the dark corridor until they reached the entrance once again. Upon exiting, they discovered that night had taken over the land. They left the grounds of Lord's Lair trying to distance themselves from the feeling that they were in an uncomfortable tomb-like atmosphere. Keeping the torch lit until wood had been gathered, they built a fire to fight off the escalating chill.

The four sat around the fire; none of them felt like sleeping. Avador stared at the flames as if there was something in them that could provide more answers to his growing amount of uncertainties. Stone Warhelm told him of his suggestion to go to Vor and all he did was nod in agreement, his eyes never leaving the fire. No one spoke a word to the young Elf of what had just taken place within those dank chambers. Their thoughts must stay on the road ahead if they want to progress in their quest.

At last Avador looked up from his contemplations and rose soundlessly. Without a word, he began a short patrol of the area before returning to his friends.

"I want to thank you all for standing by me." Avador's face shone a soft orange from the burning fire; a tear had slid down his cheek. No one spoke. Instead they all rose from the fire to stand next to the grief-struck Elf.

"What is understood," Stone Warhelm began, "need not be discussed."

The hours of darkness crept by the company like silent thieves. Avador slept a deep dreamless sleep. It was as if, for a few hours at least, he did not exist and everything was tranquil. But when the sun rose, he awoke with his recollections of last night's events rushing back to him like a tidal wave. His heart began to hurt and he wanted to fall back into that same sleep.

"My Prince, we must move out." No such luck.

The small party ate in silence before packing up and heading north. Though it was a chilly morning, the rising of the dazzling sun and the cloudless sky helped warm the atmosphere. Avador fought to keep his senses acute. He must stay focused. He *needs* to keep his mind on the quest that must be accomplished.

The young Elf kept the group at a steady pace, hopes of returning home fading with each step he made. Tigran and Falstaff, he knew, wanted what he wanted: to travel homeward and to return to the life they knew before taking on this expedition. As he stared at the cold hilly landscape ahead, he also understood that his direction is chosen for him. '*The path you take must always be determined by what is right.*'

~****~

"Hey!" Bogdan was once again irritated with Badom.

"What in Hell's Hynie do you think you're doing?" The Gnome's face was redder than an over-ripe tomato.

"I'm packing." Badom's expression showed a 'what did I do now?' look.

"Well stop packing." Bogdan snatched a metal pan that Badom was stuffing in one of the mule's sacks and tossed it on the ground. "You can't see what's coming over the horizon?"

The hills just south of where they camped were wild with tall yellowing grass that leaned to one side, the wind forcing it to bow in its presence. Obscure figures were slowly approaching from those hills and heading towards them. Bogdan counted four but wasn't sure if there would be more coming after.

"We'll wait until they get close, see what they are up to, and maybe we can sell them something." Badom was nodding in agreement even before the other Gnome finished relating his plan.

It must have been half an hour later when the four travellers approached the little camp of the Gnomes. Bogdan took inventory: Two Humans, an Elf, and a Dwarf... strange combination.

"Told you's I smelled Gnome." The Dwarf (the strongest looking Dwarf either of them had ever seen), said in disgust. Neither of the Gnomes seemed insulted or bothered by the statement.

"I must rest," said the slender Human in torn blue robes and was helped to sit and given water. Bogdan wasted no time and introduced himself.

"Good people," his smile showed all three of his yellowed teeth and he was reaching into the mule's packs, "can I interest you in some garments acquired from the legendary peaks of the Ruk Mountains?" Bogdan pulled out some brightly coloured clothing that resembled something from a children's festival.

"Put your garbage aside Gnome," the Dwarf spit, "what we need is a service of a different kind." Avador gave Stone a questioning look but said nothing. Tigran waited, curious to see what would happen.

"If we are able, we will provide," Bogdan said keeping his grin secured to his face. Badom stood beside his friend nodding quickly up and down.

"I suspect you are heading to Cutthroat City," Stone continued.

"Yes," Bogdan replied, "how did you know?"

"Your trail was obvious all the way here. And it's obvious where you are heading." Stone's glare penetrated right through the Gnome's smile and turned it into an expression of full attention. Once satisfied, he pulled from the tunic within his leather armour a small pouch clinking with silver coin. "We need some information from that city. A war broke out and I want you's to get every detail you can on it... but do *not* let on who the information is for, you understand?" The muscular Dwarf emptied about half the contents of the pouch into Bogdan's shaky hands. "The rest of the purse will be yours when you get the information." Bogdan quickly stuffed the silver coin into his own pouch and nodded hastily as he did so.

"In two day's time as soon as the sun sets, we will meet at the Statue of Elemn in front of the Thieves Guild." Bogdan wasted no time and shoved the brightly coloured clothing into Badom's hands. Then as if they had not even met, the Gnomes led the mule northward toward Vor.

"How can you trust them so easily?" Avador was the first to speak after the departure of the Gnomes.

"I despise the little stinks but one thing for certain about Gnomes: they are *loyal* little stinks." Stone's gaze remained on the Gnomes until they were out of sight, then he turned to Avador. "Once you pay them, they carry out the task until it's completed. I never met anyone that can get information better than a Gnome. They'll move into the city without stirring suspicions, and with their own way get information from someone without them knowing they even gave it out."

It took the company the rest of the day to reach Vor. The two Gnomes had arrived at the outskirts two hours before and entered. Stone kept the group at a distance until the skies began to darken, Avador never losing sight of the Gnomes until they disappeared within the tall dismal looking buildings.

"Cutthroat City." Stone Warhelm whispered almost to himself. "Never liked the city much but sometimes it pays to venture inside that filthy place." The four were looking down at the growing number of lights from a tall ridge. The lights of the city spanned a great distance left and right and twinkled north as far as the eye could see. Avador, Tigran and Falstaff remained fascinated at the largest populated area they had ever seen.

"Amazing huh?" The Dwarf smirked at the three friends who were still in awe just from the utter size of the place. "Wait 'til you's see it from the *inside*."

The moon was an ethereal creature, full and balanced perfectly against its midnight setting. Waves of melancholy cloud grazed at it as it hung above the steady rise of Vor's nightly noise. Avador stood alone on the ridge. He stared down at the place known as 'Cutthroat City', Stone's words still resonating in his ears: 'We go in keeping our faces covered and weapons showing. We want the people of Cutthroat City to trust us as less as possible; that way they'll keep their distance.'

The young Elf grasped at his cloak trying to keep it from billowing in the wind. Then he turned to face his companions.

"Show us the way Stone." Avador spoke with a face so grim they thought he didn't care what happens anymore.

Chapter 12 - Feo-Dosia

The tavern screamed with commotion. Blue smoke, fog-like and thick, drifted above each rickety table converging with the lies and half-truths spoken by the patrons. Wenches and barmaids wearing virtually nothing moved and served as best they could throughout the crowded tavern. A whore, not easily spotted but never mistaken, lurked with distorted appeal within every corner. Rogues, scoundrels, plague infested wretches, it seemed as though every foul being imaginable loitered this vile tavern in the centre of Cutthroat City.

In one section, as far away from the turmoil as possible, a Dark Dwarf, heavily armoured, was engaged in a curious drinking game with a Gnome that was clearly losing.

"… Because you are obvioushly a man of battle," Bogdan was slurring his words and waving his head back and forth, "but ansher me this… how long has it been since the lasht war?"

"Stupid Gnome." The Dark Dwarf stuck out his chest trying to intimidate the drunken Gnome, crazy black hair melded into a fuzzy beard. "I *fought* in the last war and got the scars to prove it." He abruptly unbuckled a grey plate from his armour and showed Bogdan his chest. A maze of disfigurements lined his broad torso. "And I'm fighting in *this* one too." He added. Bogdan shook his head smiling and took another swig from his ale glass.

"Guess I lose again." He reached clumsily for the pitcher on the table and filled their glasses, some of the contents poured on the table as he did so. The Dwarf grabbed his mug with a grunt and emptied it down his throat. Then he wiped his beard with the back of his hand showing his yellowed teeth with an arrogant grin.

Bogdan laughed, "why are you in a tavern if you're in a war? Did you abandon your post?" The Dark Dwarf went silent, his black eyes bulging as they pierced into Bogdan. Then he reached at the Gnome and slapped him on the back of his neck.

"Tolstyak *never* abandons!" He screamed the words and they disappeared into the crowd. No one seemed to be affected by the outburst. Then he sat down and reclined his chair. He rocked slowly as he waited for Bogdan to counter him with another question.

"Alright," Bogdan was rubbing behind his neck but still smiling, "I would be foolish to doubt a war-hardened man such as you. In fact, I would like to stop this game, it's getting painful." Tolstyak landed his chair on all four legs and quicker than the Gnome expected, a deadly dagger was at his throat.

"Go and get that pitcher of ale you owe me and *then* we'll talk about stopping the game." All Bogdan could do was hastily nod his head. Backing slowly away from the blade, he stood up and staggered into a few patrons before reaching the barkeep. Moments later he rematerialized through the smoke to the waiting Dwarf with two more flagons filled with ale.

"Okay.... *Told-yu-suk*, was it?" Bogdan slumped heavily in his chair across the Dark Dwarf.

"*Tolstyak!*" The waged soldier corrected angrily slamming a gloved fist onto the wobbly table. The Gnome was trying to shake off his drunkenness as he poured erratically from the flagon.

"You *scare* me Tolstyak." Bogdan was swallowing hard trying to stay calm. "I can't imagine being in a war."

"Gnomes have *never* fought in a war. Your race is nothing but cowards." Tolstyak was blunt but Bogdan playing on his arrogance kept him in check.

"Yes, you're right," Bogdan looked at the Dark Dwarf as if he admired him, "if there *was* war I would wish I could fight like you, but instead I'd be running to the hills with the rest of my kind."

"What do you mean *if?*" The armoured Dwarf chuckled with amusement. "If I were you, you pathetic Gnome, I'd stay away from *Feo-Dosia*... unless you want to come and see what a *real* warrior fights like."

Bogdan swallowed the last of his ale. He was swaying a little more than usual in his chair. "I'm shtaying as far away from Feo-Doshia as posssible." With that he stood up slowly trying to keep his balance as the Dark Dwarf laughed horrendously in his chair. Bogdan left him to be alone with the two pitchers and worked his way through the hazy room until he found the exit. With a sly grin he strolled out sober as can be. Seconds later Badom ambled out after him.

~****~

The arches loomed before them. Three stone-built arcs gaped skywards like maws of some mythical beast. Avador stared within; the city defied them to enter. The moon had glided eastward creating an ominous appearance over the city's dismal buildings.

The young Elf's thoughts went to Pelendria. The village would be asleep at this hour. Vor was still active and noisy. Disorder reigned here. This was a home for turmoil and confusion. People were scattered along broad filthy streets, some walking and some sprawled against the building's walls. Avador could not tell if they were dead or simply overwhelmed by the chaos.

Instinctively, Avador's senses began to probe what was not immediately evident. He laboured to keep his perception sharp in these foreign surroundings and directed his concentration to cut through the noise. Somewhere deep within the dreary streets, frantic echoes of futile screams resonated off the cold stone-built walls. Suspicious eyes watched everyone's every move as the people made their way trying to keep to their own business.

Avador and Stone passed through the arches and into the turmoil with Falstaff and Eviathane flanking them; their faces veiled within the darkness of their cowls. The youngster's immediate reaction was trying to keep their eyes from revealing how strange they felt within these surroundings. Their second was letting their fingers touch the hilts of their weapons as they entered the overwhelmingly huge city of Vor.

Stone Warhelm kept the small company as comfortable as possible telling stories and laughing loudly. They were trying to follow his instructions to look like they know where they are going. Taverns overflowing with people were found on every street; most made the Spider's Web look like a child's playpen. The grey-stone buildings, for the most part four or five floors tall, bordered the streets with their gothic exteriors, some stretching for half a mile before ending into a shady alleyway.

The moon illuminated the city with it's silvery light. Each crevice revealed; each road made visible. Avador's mind swayed from the present to the past when he and his father were still together learning and living. He felt a swift tingling ache rush through his heart when he recalled the last moment with his father in Lord's Lair: *Grandalimus'* *skeletal form stood slowly before the kneeling Avador. He took his hand in his own and returned the hilt of the **Kingblade** to his son's palm. It was almost as if a silent ceremony had taken place between them, a ceremony that put a world of responsibility on the young Elf's shoulders.*

The sound of a stringed instrument jolted Avador from his recollections. Up ahead where a large circular fountain with a statue of a hooded toad tipping a pitcher, a man dressed in loose-fitting ivory coloured clothes, was playing a lute. A handful of people had circled around him as he played.

The company listened from a distance for a minute then decided to keep moving. Before they got too far, the music stopped abruptly and a commotion took its place. Women screamed and scattered with their men in different directions. Two leather-armoured brutes holding large spiked maces remained with the stylish musician. One thug had suddenly backhanded the man while the other laughed hysterically. The small party kept their distance following Stone's orders by not involving themselves in *anything*.

Surprisingly, the man calmly stroked his sandy blonde hair and placed his lute in a brown leather case. Then with a lightning quick motion, a scimitar was in his hand and gleaming in the moonlight. The instrumentalist was pouncing back and forth with smooth fluid-like movements. He looked as though he was trying to intimidate the two brutes that had taken a surprised step backwards. They wondered what it was exactly he was doing. Eviathane nearly went into an uncontrollable laughter but contained himself when Stone squeezed his arm.

Suddenly the two brutes attacked the man at once. Incredibly, he did not retreat. Instead he continued with his peculiar stances and unusual parries. This seemed to anger the attackers even more. One sidestepped his curved blade and grabbed him by the face. With a grunt he threw the man to the ground and prepared to strike him with his mace.

Eviathane could stand no more. He shook free of Stone's grip and broke into a dead run.

"No, you *fool!*" Stone's words were pointless. Tigran Eviathane, at full momentum, rammed into the man with the raised weapon using his shield and sent him splashing into the large fountain. He then turned to the other and smashed a gloved fist into his mouth breaking his front teeth. The man in the fountain poured himself out and looked around in shock. When Eviathane unsheathed his sword and stood in an intimidating stance, the two panicked and ran in separate directions. Once satisfied, he turned to the man on the ground and helped him up.

"You can't fight *nicely,*" he said to him, "that was a *fight* not a *dance.*" Before any more conversation, Stone was at his side with the rest of the group. Eviathane understood the dangers he might have caused and they all rushed away into the mysterious shadows of Cutthroat City. The graceful musician quickly gathered all his things and raced after them.

~****~

Bogdan was quite proud of himself as he ventured deeper into an abandoned alleyway with Badom two steps behind him. They moved stealthily between large stacked wooden crates until they found what they were looking for. Four of the crates were placed purposefully horizontally in the alleyway in order to impede anyone from passing. The two Gnomes heaved at one and it slid away with a dull scraping sound. They passed through the newly made opening and slid it back to its original position. Behind the crates waited their devoted mule chewing mindlessly at some food they had left for him.

Sitting down on a couple of small boxes, they chanced at building a small fire to ward off the cold conditions of the deserted alley.

"Did you learn anything?" Bogdan was whispering to Badom after the fire was built. A nod was Badom's only answer. He proceeded to stuff tobacco into his pipe, then recalled Bogdan's reaction to it and replaced it into one of his many pockets. He sighed and reached for a piece of meat that Bogdan dangled over the fire.

"Tomorrow," Bogdan spoke while chewing loudly on a rubbery chunk of mutton, "just after the sun drops below the city walls, we must be ready at Elemn." He took a large swallow of wine from his flask then added, "So don't do anything stupid." Badom squinted at his friend but said nothing as he ate.

The Gnomes let the fire dwindle as the effects of the wine began to warm them sufficiently. Eventually they coasted into a quiet slumber while the city around the little alley hummed with activity.

~****~

Falstaff was in the dark, cloaked within the deepest shadows that night had to offer. His book lay in his lap as he crouched just outside a small wooden shed undisturbed by the moon's touch. Concealed within were Eviathane and Stone, restless and rather annoyed at the inactivity. Avador flanked the opposite side of the shed, his fingers caressing the hilt of his jagged dagger; he scanned through the darkness as if waiting for an unexpected visitor. Sweat trickled down his cheek as the uneasiness became almost unbearable... until the silence broke. At least a dozen men dressed in their black capes and leather armour poured into the narrow street wielding their large deadly maces and hunting for the hidden party; they were moving steadily towards them.

Stone heard them from inside the shed and gripped his battle-hammer tightly in his hand. He and Tigran felt the same rage wild animals feel when they are caged and away from where they want to be.

"They are on this street." He heard one shout. It was just as he figured. The guards of Vor would now be after them... and he let Eviathane know what he had done by saving the musician. The two men he attacked were among the corrupt guards of Cutthroat City and the small group was in *their* territory.

"They can't get away from us." Another almost laughed as he spoke. Avador took a swift glance around his situation. There was no way around the guards; the streets were too narrow and cluttered. Behind the shed was a wall too tall to climb. To the left and right were strange housings interconnected throughout the continual exterior walls. The guards could not see them yet but if they get closer they will.

Falstaff felt naked and exposed within the dark crevice of his shade as he watched the guards creep closer. Ever so slowly he inched to his feet awaiting Avador's signal. In a sudden quiet he heard the low creak of the young Elf's bow. The pause was nerve racking as the patrol inched towards them. The silence was worse than any noise Falstaff could remember hearing.

"Now!" Falstaff's fingers sprang forth as he was jerked out of his fear. Searing flame shot from them in perfectly straight lines. Avador's arrow flew through the darkness embedding itself into the throat of one of the guards. Two others went down enveloped in flames as they screamed in utter agony. Avador notched another arrow as Stone and Eviathane burst through the shed's doors and into the action. Eviathane sliced through a guard before the sentinel knew what was happening, Stone already crushing the skull of another with his hammer. The element of surprise was theirs.

Eight of the guards stood momentarily dazed but soon surrounded the small company, maces swinging viciously. Avador released his arrow and it pierced easily through the armour of one of the guards. Dropping his bow, he unsheathed the *Kingblade* and readied himself for close combat. A mace swung so close it tore at his cloak nearly dragging the Elf with it. With a desperate retaliation, he slammed the hilt of his sword into the guard's temple causing him to buckle over by the stunning hit.

Next to Avador, Eviathane repelled an attack with his shield and drove his long-sword through the attacker, yanking it free just in time to deflect another guard's mace. Stone was suddenly there with his hammer arcing upwards striking the guard under his jaw forcing him clear off his feet and into a motionless heap.

A guard, unseen as he stole around the struggling party, tightened his grip on his weapon and crept breathlessly towards Falstaff, the young mage's back to him as he neared. Falstaff heard his approach and whirled to meet him but he was too late; the mace was already raised to strike him down. Falstaff flinched but the hit never came. Instead he saw the guard's unshaven face stare blankly in disbelief as he fell to his knees. In his place stood the musician brandishing his gleaming scimitar soiled with the guard's blood.

In a sudden rush of panic, the remaining four attackers scrambled away from the small party and back the way they had come. The companions had no time to allow the adrenalin to settle when the thunderous sound of countless hoof beats reached their ears...

A cloud of dust rose into the night air as innumerable horsemen galloped savagely into the street each swinging deadly morning-stars. Falstaff wasted no time as he threw himself between his friends and the oncoming horsemen. He probed his mind searching for the lightning spell, their only chance to best this new onslaught for there were too many to take on... nothing came. Neither word nor citation appeared to him. His mind was bare of anything to do with the lightning spell. His eyes went wide as a horrible realization soaked in...

I am a fool!

"Run!" He screamed backing into his friends. Avador steadied him before shouting his order.

"This way," his words reached his companion's ears with unmistakable resonance and they followed without a second's hesitation. Avador raced crossways in the street and thrust himself through one of the darkened windows. Following a resounding crash, the frightened screams of the residents inside echoed into the street. The rest of the group followed him through the newly made entry and together they scrambled through the peculiar stretch of housing.

More blind than not, they raced through the darkness clambering over unknown obstacles and breaking things as they passed. Doors were rammed and taken off their hinges with people shrieking at the unexpected invasion. They pressed deeper into the building searching for some kind of escape.

Avador felt his heart pound in frustration. Anger began to develop within him as he silently cursed himself for getting everyone trapped in an unfamiliar maze. He felt a thousand little stings as sweat coated his body and into the cuts made by the shattered window. He was clinging on to hope when his eyes pierced the darkness and found their escape. In a larger room that seemed connected to all the housing, a wooden staircase led upwards to a small platform. Above the platform he could make out a closed hatch in the ceiling.

No time was squandered. The young Elf led the group up the stairs to where the hatch waited above them. He motioned to Eviathane who took Stone's heavy hammer and shattered the wooden hatch into a million fragments. Then he hefted everyone upwards and through the opening. Night air passed through their hair and into their lungs. It chilled their damp skin as they found themselves on a long stretch of roof that spanned before them in two directions. Avador chose one and led the company away from the opened hatch and away from the bewildered horsemen that were shouting in aggravation in the streets below.

~****~

The sun's light intruded the sleeping city of Vor, climbing over its walls and seeping into its streets like an unwanted trespasser. The orange radiance revealed the cracked, uncared-for walls and the filthy streets with their scattering of broken, dispirited people that lay unmoving in their own self-asserted space.

Jono Guvlundor was among the rare awake to see the first light. The Commander of the Sentinel sat at his desk sipping quietly at warm spice tea, his brow furrowing at his silent contemplation. He stood and walked to a small window holding a large stack of parchment, the daily logs of his guard, and looked out at his city with an interest that faded long ago. He could not fathom at how much his frame of mind had changed since the day he was selected to take on this responsibility. At one time it was called an honour to have a title such as his.

But the city had changed all that. Vor was in critical need

of regulation and enforcement. He actually believed he could make a difference when Grandalimus Andor, the King of the Elves *himself* recommended him for the designation. The reverence he held for Grandalimus was immeasurable and he accepted without hesitation.

How was he to know that the city would overwhelm him? His guards, easily contaminated by the influence of the golden coin, corrupt beyond repair. The people, taking delight at the way they could buy their restrictions away. Jono's thoughts went to the Elf King. He has failed him. He walked slowly to a stone fireplace and stared at the flames, the glow shining off his leather armour and revealed the uniform he once admired. Then, with an angry grunt, the Commander of the Sentinel thrust the stack of parchment into the flames and stamped out the door and into the city streets.

~****~

Bogdan was spitting incessantly in the little alleyway. It was all he could do to quench the annoyance that overcame him the moment he awoke and found Badom missing. He *knows* where he has to be when it gets dark. He *knows* they were to not separate, and most of all, he knows not to do *anything stupid*! But does he listen? No!

"You are the most *stupidest* stupid creature ever to live, you thick stupid *stupid*!" Bogdan was trembling as he shouted to a Badom that was not there, the mule's ears springing straight up at the abrupt noise.

The agitated Gnome spit one more time when he heard a scuffing noise behind him.

"Badom. You're an *idiot*! Where..." Bogdan's words froze to his lips when he turned to face his friend and discovered someone else standing there, someone holding a knife and looking right at him. The mule began to stomp uneasily at the approach of this stranger and swayed its head back and forth. Bogdan shot a glance at his mule and back to the intruder.

"Since you are going to kill me and take my money, why don't I *give* you my money and you could *say* you killed me." Bogdan was already holding out the small pouch he put Stone's silver coins in. For a moment nothing happened. Bogdan began to sweat despite the morning chill.

Then the stranger stepped from between the crates and into the light. He was unshaven, his clothes were torn and he smelled of last night's ale flagon. His dark glossy eyes stared directly at the frightened Gnome as he approached him. Then, with a quick swipe, he grabbed the pouch from Bogdan's hand and raised the knife to kill him.

The Gnome moved quicker than the thief expected side-stepping away and pouncing onto a crate behind him. The intruder stood dumbfounded for half a moment. It was all Bogdan needed. All he had to do was turn around and run... but the little Gnome did not do that. Instead, he pulled out his own little blade, seemingly out of nowhere, and leaped onto the thief's back. With a surprisingly swift movement, the Gnome's tiny blade sliced easily through the still intoxicated thief's throat. A sickening gurgling sound was all Bogdan heard as his attacker slumped forward taking the Gnome with him as he fell.

He died slowly and violently as he thrashed about struggling to remain alive, Bogdan sitting on his back the entire time. A pool of blood began to expand underneath the dieing man until finally, all movement stopped. Without another moment's hesitation, the Gnome returned the pouch to his pocket, untied the mule and hurried out of the alley to search for Badom.

~****~

"Keep walkin'!" Stone shouted at the sandy haired musician who stood there offended holding his lute case.

"Stone, he saved my *life*." Falstaff was trying to reason with the frustrated Dwarf.

"I don't care if he shoots rainbows out his rear end, he ain't comin' with us!" Stone Warhelm was adamant.

The company camped the night under a low bridge that extended over a dried out river once flowing within the city.

"Where are we?" Avador interrupted the argument.

"We're in one of the city's parks." Stone kept his glare on the musician while the others looked around the once green, forest-like area. The park was anything but cared for: statues and fountains once splendid to the eye were now cracked and falling apart. Benches used to be found scattered here and there for families to lounge on and rest during walks. Now they were ripped from their supports and cast aside never to be used again. The only thing that kept the place somewhat pleasant, Avador thought, was the natural reds and golds of the trees with their brilliant leaves carpeting the dried earth.

"Give the man a chance, Stone." Avador ignored the Dwarf's reddening face and walked over to the musician. "What's your name, friend?" The Elf noticed he was probably the best-groomed and well-dressed man he had ever met.

"My name is Nectario, a bard of vast aptitude and talent." The man bowed at his own introduction but showed offence when Eviathane chuckled in the background.

"Avador, I slept with one eye on *him* the entire night, I don't trust him." Stone growled the words.

"Has he given you a reason not to trust him, Stone?" The

Elf's gaze seemed to pierce right through the angry Dwarf, "a man should never be judged because of where you found him."

Stone Warhelm turned his back knowing he was going to lose the argument. "You're still *fresh* Elfling... but then, you're also a lot like your father."

Nectario wanted to leave the city of Vor just as much, if not more than the small party. He tolerated more than a week of the vile metropolis losing all his money and most of his belongings. Stone for the most part ignored him while the others asked him questions of his travels and his song-writing ability, Nectario more than pleased to *indulge* them with his answers. For him, the group was an escape from the tedious daily life *and* Cutthroat City. For the group, he was an interesting storyteller and a fresh face. For Stone, he was a hindrance, another person to protect without the *need* to; they had a duty to perform and this was just folly allowing him to come along.

Soon the afternoon sun coasted across a sea of dark cloud. The company ate from their provisions and drank from their flasks, talking quietly and always staying on guard. They were waiting for nightfall to gain the information and hopefully leave before night ends.

Not knowing their next move was a strain on Avador. Aonas must be stopped. But to do that they need to know what he is planning, where he will attack next and most of all, how to get to him. The possibility alone of accomplishing this undertaking was a gamble, with all odds against the small group.

How can they stay one step ahead of him if they do not

even know what he is scheming? What did they expect to do, this little group of friends, against Aonas' armies and his powerful control of magic?

Avador found himself wishing he had his father with him. The Elf King would know what to do, and he would not hesitate. The young Elf, in clear contrast, felt the hand of despair reach out and strangle him.

~****~

Bogdan abruptly stopped running. He let himself collapse onto a wall as he tried to control his breathing, the mule's reins still held tightly in his hand. Sweat trickled down his face and onto his patchy beard as he looked around the streets. He was safe... for the moment.

It was already mid afternoon and he had no idea what happened to Badom. He felt his anger alter itself to worry. This was not like his friend. He *never* abandons Bogdan, no matter what happened between them. The grumpy Gnome began to feel ashamed of himself. How could he treat his friend like that? Insulting him with every chance he got. Calling him 'stupid' all the time.

Bogdan began to walk away when he caught a glimpse of something moving from around a corner. It was a small stream of blue smoke. He approached the corner in a wide arc keeping his distance and looked. There was Badom, holding a lit pipe, his eyes staring back at him bulging from the shock of being caught. Bogdan screamed making Badom jump and drop his pipe.

"What in Hell's Hynie do you think you're doing!" Bogdan's anger resurfaced and Badom remained speechless. The 'older' Gnome reached out and tugged roughly at Badom's nose.

"I'm sorry Bogdan," was Badom's only reply for lack of a better one.

"Why did you leave the way you did?" Bogdan was insistent on discovering what happened to his friend.

"I wanted to light my pipe but I didn't want you to see me," Badom was feeling ashamed and somewhat like a child. "I went too far, I got lost, and I couldn't find my way back to you." Bogdan should not have been, but he was surprised.

"Do you know that by nightfall we have to... ah never mind." Bogdan was suddenly exhausted and wanted to change the subject.

Before any more words were spoken, Badom was unexpectedly snatched from behind by a powerful hand and roughly thrown to the ground. Bogdan froze at the suddenness and watched his friend get kicked in the ribs by a member of the Sentinel. Before he could react, a second member approached from around the corner holding his mace and headed straight for him. But Bogdan was surprised once more: A third figure, tall and muscular and wearing the same leather uniform intercepted his attacker and struck him down with his own mace. He did not finish him off. Instead the attacker stood up, obviously in great pain and limped backwards onto a wall trying to support himself. The one who attacked Badom froze where he stood.

"C-Commander," the member of the Sentinel was gasping for breath and mercy, his weapon on the ground, his hands showing surrender. Jono Guvlundor grabbed the man just under the chin.

"It's poisoned worms like you who destroyed this city." Jono said through clenched teeth as he gripped the man's jaw tighter. "I will clean it up starting with you." The Commander of the Sentinel closed a gloved hand over the city's emblem on the man's chest and ripped it off him. Then he looked over at the other man who had already torn off his leather armour and dropped his mace. Without the need of words, the scoundrel hid his face and left at once.

Bogdan immediately ran to the fallen Badom who lay motionless where he was assaulted.

"Badom. Talk to me... please." The reality of losing his friend hit the Gnome with immeasurable force. He touched Badom gently on the shoulder but the fallen Gnome did not stir.

"I'm sorry for all the names I've called you. You're *not* stupid, there *are* no stupid people... just *lazy* people." To his surprise, tears actually developed under his lids and threatened to seep out. Bogdan began to yank at his own hair and finally, the tears fell. A minute went by when Bogdan noticed movement: Badom's left eye opened and closed abruptly. Bogdan gasped at the unexpected motion.

"You're alive!" Bogdan stood straight up wiping at his cheeks. "You were okay this whole *time*?" Badom sat up with an enormous gratifying grin but rubbed at his ribs where the guard kicked him.

"You stupid... *ass!*" Bogdan lost his temper (although relieved on the *inside*). "How could you hoax me like that?"

The two Gnomes then retrieved their mule and trudged slowly down the dusty, darkening streets. Jono Guvlundor stood watching with his arms crossed and a smile... a smile that was missing for quite a few years.

~****~

Stone gazed at the skies. The clouds had bronzed as the sun began to sink behind the city's walls. The moon appeared even before daylight fully retreated giving it a wraithlike appearance within the clouds. The Dwarf knew it was time to make their way to the meeting point. The others stood ready for him to lead them to the Thieves Guild.

The company of five kept to the shadows and stayed close to one another. Stone Warhelm navigated the streets easily taking them into alleys and back-roads. At times he moved them quickly through the busier streets, occasionally he merely sauntered through emptier ones, but the pace was always steady. Noise began to increase the deeper into the city they went. The crowds became dense until they were nearly touching shoulders with everybody.

Finally they found themselves in the core of the giant city where everything was lively, even at this darkened hour. The Dwarf stopped them short and motioned for them to draw closer.

"Be on guard," he whispered, "more than ever." He took a quick glance around. "And stay close at all times."

The city's core was a sight on its own. The buildings were noticeably taller than the others that encased them. The people moved quicker and were somewhat livelier. Entertainers with monkeys and other animals performed on the streets, some doing unimaginable things with blades and fire. The small group did their best to stay focused and not show that they were in utter awe at what was going on around them.

Eventually they approached a lower building with black marble pillars all along its front. The same marble was used to construct the wide steps that led to massive double doors. Directly across the building was a surprisingly tall statue, also formed of marble, of a blindfolded man with his arms and legs in chains.

"The Statue of Elemn" whispered Stone, "the *Master of Thieves*." They approached the statue cautiously, searching for the Gnomes who were supposed to be there.

"Um, Stone?" Whispered Avador, "you don't think maybe our little friends tricked you?" The Dwarf said nothing, his eyes scanning the area. The minutes went by and the group began to get anxious... all except Stone, his face remaining calm, eyes searching the shadows.

Then, two Gnomes, practically in a dead run and dragging a mule behind them, surfaced from the crowd and were headed in their direction. Relief showed on the small party's faces when they realized who was coming. Stone turned to Avador and gave him a wry wink that was accompanied by a mocking smile.

The seven, plus the mule, moved without speaking away from the Thieves Guild and the statue of its Master. Once again, Stone was leading the way. The streets became increasingly bare as they moved steadily from one to the next. Eviathane, Falstaff and Avador were amazed at how the Dwarf could navigate such a labyrinth of lanes and avenues; Nectario simply tagged along with his curiosity building dramatically as they travelled.

At last Stone stopped them at an archway that was nearly in ruins. Beyond the arch was a scattering of dried-up fountains on a raised plateau long forgotten by the people of Vor. Once satisfied that no one had followed, they stepped through the archway and onto the dark plateau amidst the waterless fountains.

For a moment, everyone merely stared at nothing from the awkwardness of the situation, until Avador broke the silence.

"Did you get the information?" His eyes were fixed on Bogdan.

"Yes, yes we did." The Gnome took a triumphant stance. Then his voice went to a low whisper, "The Dark Dwarves are setting out to attack *Feo-Dosia.*" Bogdan's near-toothless smile showed his pride at getting the information. But the smile quickly turned into a look of surprise when he realized they were waiting for the rest. He soon understood with horror, that's all he had… until he remembered Badom. Without hesitation, the Gnome grabbed Badom by the wrist, pulled him forward, and prayed to as many gods as he could think of, that Badom didn't screw up again.

Badom cleared his throat. He was clearly uncomfortable with having all the attention, but began to speak anyways.

"Aonas, whoever *that* is, is awaiting all the leaders of the lands to bow down to him. He wants them to hand over their armies and their rights as leaders. He threatens to take them by a force that is undeniably more powerful than any of them has ever seen. A handful of these leaders have agreed under the impression that the lives of their people will be spared. Some, like Feo-Dosia, have refused. That is why Feo-Dosia will undoubtedly be under attack. Rumours say that Governor Feo-Dosia *himself* has already fallen and the people are in need of a leader." Badom finished and blinked his eyes innocently at Avador. Bogdan stared at his friend in disbelief, his mouth wide open. He never even noticed that Stone Warhelm was reaching out with the rest of the silver coin.

~****~

Before the moon reached its apex, Stone led the party to Vor's northern exit and wasted no time walking out. 'One road leads into the city and one leads out. It's up to you to decide which is which… in the end they're both just exits.'

The five marched north as suggested by Stone. Feo-Dosia was a good five or six days away and time was not on their side. The night deepened and the terrain began to smooth down to an almost flat ground refusing them any form of shelter. Continuous winds, wild, cold, and ever changing, swept at them and hindered their progress. Each man, though lost within their own thoughts, felt it a wonder they were all still alive and still together after endeavouring Cutthroat City. Travelling to the unknown was better than staying within its fraudulent walls for the rest of the night.

After a few arduous hours, the trek proved demanding to the small band of travellers. But the new sound of rushing water penetrated the ceaseless winds and broke the tediousness of the march. They moved ahead at a quickened pace, the sound of the water increasing steadily. The Dwarf led the way until they found themselves before a ferocious river at least half a mile wide, its current hastening towards the eastern darkness.

Stone Warhelm knelt on one knee and removed a glove from one hand. He traced the earth with his fingers as if searching for something small and lost. Then he stood and guided the group westward until they found a large concave embankment that shielded the wind; everyone was silently happy that it was a place to camp the night.

A fire was quickly built and everyone huddled appreciatively around it. Nectario seemed a bit out of place with his lute strapped to his back as he hunched within his thick grey cloak. He was also the first to speak.

"Is this what you guys *do* every night, travel until you're ready to collapse and sit around a fire and try not to freeze to death?" Stone shot him a look of disgust but said nothing.

"You wanted to come with us." Eviathane muttered as he broke a chunk of bread and handed it to Falstaff. "You just never thought to ask where we are going."

We don't even know where we are going. Falstaff nearly laughed at the thought.

119

Avador was smiling to himself as he prodded the fire with a long stick. He knew what Stone was thinking: he can leave any time if he doesn't like what they do.

"What exactly *is* Feo-Dosia?" He turned his attention to Stone knowing he had to get the Dwarf's mind onto other things. Stone almost didn't hear the Elf he was so deep-rooted into his thoughts.

"Feo-Dosia." Stone's thick black hair waved slightly as a bit of wind trespassed over the embankment and brushed by them, his dark eyes shining in the firelight. "How do I explain '*Feo-Dosia*'?" The young Elf's curiosity instantly raised to a new level at the way Stone made the statement.

"It is probably the most attractive piece of territory I have ever gazed at; a forest paradise, visible from Mount Skala, but far more beautiful up close. A thousand different greens when the weather is warm, and *now*... now is the time to experience Feo-Dosia, when the lands are transforming its brilliant colours." The Dwarf paused to note Avador's attentiveness.

"Feo-Dosia is governed by a good man, Governor Leorren Feo-Dosia. And if what the Gnome said is true, and pray that it is not, a good man has fallen."

"Which is why we must make haste." Avador interrupted.

"More than you know, Elfling. Leorren Feo-Dosia was... *is* a good friend of your father's. He is the ruler of the Wood Elves that inhabit the great forest. He comes from a long line of descendants that have reigned for centuries."

Wood Elves. The name sparked greater interest within Avador. An entire region named after a lineage. This should be interesting.

"What are you two talking about?" Tigran Eviathane slumped next to Avador rubbing his hands together trying to keep them warm. Before they could reply, a melodic tune from a stringed instrument abruptly pierced the night air interrupting the silent conversation.

"Shut it!" Hissed the Dwarf immediately silencing Nectario's playing. The bard gave him a hurt look but returned the lute to its case. "You want all the creatures of the night to come after us, you imbecile?" He turned an annoyed face to Avador, "when morning comes, he leaves."

Nectario moved closer to Falstaff who was the only person at the time giving him any attention.

"What's the matter with the Dwarf? What quandary does he have against me?"

"You must forgive him, friend, he has an issue with trusting people." Falstaff looked up from his book and gave the bard a reassuring smile. "His defence will break... eventually."

"What's that book you are reading?" Nectario changed the subject trying not to really think of Stone's problem with him.

"It's just a book my grandfather gave me when I was merely a boy." Falstaff closed the ancient book and looked at Nectario innocently.

"You're a magic-user." Nectario looked at the young mage with a smirk. Falstaff said nothing. "I *saw* what you did to those guards back in Vor. It caught me by total surprise, I mean... I never saw magic before. I've *heard* of it, but never imagined I would ever live to actually *see* it."

"Well... I am *learning*." Falstaff handed the bard his flask of wine seeing that the musician began to shiver at the increasing cold. He took a swig and winced, then gave Falstaff a look of gratitude.

"What were you doing in Vor anyway?" The young mage was enquiring about Nectario's intentions.

"Like I said, my newly found friend, I am a bard of great talent." Nectario's look of pride showed clearly from the fire's orange glow. "I earn my living by performing songs of lore, legends, and great adventure... only, I've never been on an actual adventure - unless you want to count my experience in Vor. I've been assaulted, stolen from and cheated practically every day I spent in that deceitful city. I don't think they really appreciated my aptitude." The bard's gaze drifted towards the night sky.

"Why did you escape with *us*?" Falstaff's interest in the bard's intentions grew. "You could have fled after Eviathane saved your life."

"You mean the big fellow?" Nectario pointed his chin towards Tigran's direction. "He didn't actually *save* me per say, I had everything under control... okay maybe he *did* save me and I am grateful." Nectario looked ashamed and stared down at his cream coloured boots. "You and your company were the only decent thing that I encountered the complete time I was in Vor. I travelled all the way from Metridad, my home, and played in many places earning quite a good wage. I thought Vor wouldn't be any different from what I have already seen. I was greatly mistaken. When I was about to meet my fate, your friend risked everything just to save me. Now I will do the same for all of you." Falstaff paused before replying.

"Do you know what you are asking of yourself? Of *us*?" Falstaff's expression went solemn emphasizing the seriousness of the question.

"I do not care what I am asking of myself. I only wish your Dwarf friend learns to accept me. It seems as though every one else has."

"Do not haste in assuming we are all okay with you coming with us Nectario. We are happy you are safe but we can't guarantee you will stay that way... *especially* if you come with us."

Eviathane, Avador, and Stone were huddled in their own discussion. The night advanced steadily, the sound of the wind gradually subsided as the hours moved ahead.

"Where will the Gnomes go now?" Tigran asked Stone.

"Not even *they* know the answer to that question. The Gnomes were born without homes; they roam the lands from birth 'til death. I used to despise the little rodents, but these two... I don't know, maybe the world's changin'." Stone gripped the handle of his battle-hammer as if to say it hasn't changed enough yet.

"We must set watch." Avador's voice was low as he subconsciously scanned the night's setting. "We need to rest."

"What about *him*?" Stone pointed his bearded chin towards Nectario who was sitting with Falstaff and in their own conversation. Avador eyed the bard a moment before answering.

"He wants to help us. It's more like he feels a *need* to."

"He cannot help us Elfling." Stone's frustration began to rekindle. "You know that as much as I."

"One thing I've learned from my father, Stone, is that you cannot make certain of something unless you come into contact with it." There was an uncomfortable pause. The burly Dwarf in the end could not refuse the loyalty that lingered in his heart for the young Elf.

"Fine! But he's *your* responsibility. Don't expect me to guard his back if it's going to hinder our own duty." Avador smiled and shook his head. This was a *very* stubborn Dwarf indeed. Then he patted his shoulder and stood.

"I'll take first watch. You get some rest."

The night went deathly silent, skulking by like an animal nearing its prey. The feeling of uneasiness returned to each member of the group as they took their watch alone. What awaited them tomorrow? What might happen *tonight?* Every question was deprived of an answer. The little party had only each other for guidance and for them... that was good enough.

Four gruelling days and four arduous nights in steadily declining temperatures awaited the group after Stone lead them across a long wooden bridge just west of their first campsite. The bridge reached over the Cerulean River and Avador found it interesting, so far from home, that he arrived at another part of the same river that flowed by Pelendria.

Before the sun's light had the chance to seep into the lands on the fifth morning, Avador woke Stone Warhelm from his slumber. The Dwarf came fully awake when he saw the worry in the Elf's eyes.

"Something is happening." Avador whispered and pointed to the northward skies. Stone's first thought was the sun was rising in the wrong direction. Then his eyes went wide when he realized the orange glow flickering onto the cloudy horizon was not the sun at all.

"We have to move." The Dwarf said loudly waking everyone as he did. "Now!"

They took flight and never stopped for hours. They ate nothing until at least midday. They trekked northward until their muscles throbbed. Stone kept them moving relentlessly until finally, they approached an embankment, stopped and dropped to their knees.

"We're too late." Stone panted the words with difficulty. Thick horrifying smoke billowed skyward. A putrid smell along with the smoke reached their nostrils. They looked over the embankment and saw the charred remains of a vast forest that used to span north and east as far as the eye could see.

"Feo-Dosia." Stone Warhelm whispered through clenched teeth.

Pain was unmistakable on Stone's face. The Dwarf stood alone staring over the embankment, the wind carrying the rancid smell of burnt flesh to his nostrils. Avador was at a loss. He looked at the rest of the company as if to find an answer, but the bewildered looks they returned denied him of any.

The scene below them was the most tragic they had ever experienced, so much to absorb that their minds were defeated. The forest was indeed vast. It was hard to visualize it the way Stone had described it, eyes shining with admiration as he spoke. The picture before them was not of the entrancing woods he had illustrated. It was of black skinny sticks that stretched for miles, steaming in the aftermath of what must have been the biggest fire in all history.

Avador examined the setting below with a heavy heart. The sun's light began to weaken. Shadows grew longer and stretched across the remains of the forest as if to blanket it's death. The air seemed to cool with each passing moment. The Elf was ready to turn away when something caught his attention. Someone was moving within the charred trees. At first he thought the fading light was playing tricks with his eyes. But when he looked again, he saw the movement and it was unmistakable. He dashed to where Stone and the others were huddled.

"Someone is *alive* down there." Avador's voice, though a whisper, was excited.

"What?" Stone's eyes went wide and hurried over to the embankment, the others on his heels. They looked and saw nothing. It was too far for them and the darkness thickened. "Are you *sure* Elfling?" Stone wanted no doubts in Avador's statement.

"Yes." Avador looked at the Dwarf who stood there astonished. How could someone be alive in *that*? Without another word, Avador motioned the group to follow him over the mound and down the embankment. He was their sight as the night began its march over the lands. They moved silently trying to avoid detection in case they were not alone in the area, a small band of brigands stealing across the terrain. Avador, though weary, sighed and moved ahead... They were not yet meant to rest.

~****~

The scathing smell of the holocaust below became stronger with each step they took. Nectario, as he grudgingly pushed ahead, pulled a small cloth from his tunic and held it to his nose. His eyes began to tear until everything became a blur. Falstaff found himself trying not to retch, a task that eventually grew impossible. He dropped to his knees unwillingly forcing the others to stop. They waited tolerantly as Falstaff's heaving stopped and forced their march forward.

Ultimately they reached level ground and the edges of the once marvellous forest. Avador gritted his teeth and pushed the company deeper into the desolation. The wind played with the remains of the horrible smoke whipping it this way and that. The stench of death became nearly unbearable. A full moon escaped from behind thick black clouds giving off an eerie luminosity to the wooded graveyard. The company found it easier to see with its bluish light touching their surroundings. After a few moments, they began to wish the moon stayed hidden.

A burnt body appeared on their path. Curled on the still steaming ground, its mouth gaped in what must have been its final scream. Its hands still clutched the earth as if trying to bear the ungodly pain of getting burned alive. Even in death, its now charred features were unmistakably Elfish. Avador's heart began to hurt enormously and his tears flowed freely down his cheeks. He looked around helplessly and saw others. A scattering of pitiable Elves, their flesh burned and misshapen, refused an escape of the burning forest. The bodies of women, men, and small children lay in every direction, some still holding on to each other even after death.

Stone dropped to his knees letting his battle hammer fall to the scorched earth. With raised arms he released the foulest curse he knew skyward, the scream resounding everywhere. What did these people do to merit a death such as this? Live in peace? Respect their surroundings? Show consideration for the people of other races? *Refuse to be taken?*

Avador took a stance next to the kneeling Stone, his thoughts parallel to those of the outraged Dwarf. He put a hand on a trembling shoulder, letting him know he was right to feel this way... letting him know that time is once again opposing them. Stone jerked from his trance of grief and snatched the heavy battle-hammer from the ground... *Duty above all.* He stood to find the others gathered around him in a semi-circle, grim-faced and determined anew. Even Nectario fixed his eyes into a resolute stare, a gloved hand gripping the hilt of his scimitar. Avador gave the Dwarf's shoulder a tight squeeze and received a determined nod. Without another thought, the Elf turned to the direction of where he saw the movement and began to scout ahead. The others, digging deep within themselves, found the necessary will and pushed after the intrepid Avador.

Embers glowed wickedly around the small group as they trudged guardedly through the night; thin streams of whipping smoke ridiculed them like scornful ghosts. Avador struggled to hear any sound outside the crackling of the cinders and found it strenuous to hear anything through the steady sound of the monotonous wind. He tried in vain to pierce the incessant smoke that licked at his eyes and burned them to a painful sting. Only the navigation taught to him by Grandalimus during many hunting expeditions as they tracked a boar through the Elven forests of Gwynfell helped him to stay on course. But those forests were lush and green with sounds and smells of its nature. The added difficulty of a fire leaving it's scorched wrath to navigate through became more and more aggravating to the young Elf.

Stone strode next to Avador noting the frustration on his face. He stopped him with a hand on his wrist and crouched to the blackened earth. Eviathane towered above the kneeling Dwarf as he watched with curiosity at what he was doing. Falstaff and Nectario moved in closer. Stone grabbed a handful of steaming soil and filtered it through his fingers. He repeated the motion but this time bringing it to his nose looking ahead with his eyes.

"We're close Elfling," said the Dwarf standing and moving forward. "You did a good job bringing us this far, now let me do the rest."

The small group began to feel sick within the burnt forest. Nausea crept up on them like a stalker in the timbered graveyard. How long were they in here? How much longer can they cope inside the shroud of smog and death? Every pace increased the sickening feeling that threatened to overtake them. The sensation they felt knowing that lifeless Elves scattered all around them, some in their very path, began to become too much to endure. Even the seasoned Dwarf faltered with the struggle and stopped more than once to find his composure.

Avador scanned ahead of where Stone was guiding them trying frantically to see through the impenetrable smog. He took quick glances behind to see if everyone was all right and found them, though struggling, present and pushing ahead. It was during one of these backward glances when he nearly walked into Stone as the Dwarf stopped dead in his tracks.

"There he is." Stone's whisper was the hiss within smoke. Everyone halted abruptly, eager to find whoever it was in here and get out. Sure enough, a silhouette of a thin figure moved with great effort through the bluish haze, the moonlight trying desperately to penetrate the murk. Their next steps developed into cautious strides… what was to say that this was not an enemy waiting to spring his trap?

They stopped in unison when the figure dropped suddenly to the blackened ground. Then with an effort of sheer will, it rose to its feet and pushed ahead. But after a few agonizing paces the figure dropped as if the last of its strength had just abandoned it to die alone in this merciless nightmare.

With caution thrown away, Avador bound to its side with only the hopes for this feeble person's survival. He kneeled silently and gently reached to touch its shoulders. He recoiled his hand when it gave out a sudden fit of horrific coughing. The others were instantly at Avador's side looking guardedly over his shoulder. The wretch on the ground, black and greased in soot seemed to reach for something at its hip… a dagger. He released it with great exertion and pointed the shiny blade at Avador. Uncontrollable coughs denied him of any protection and dropped the weapon next to the kneeling Elf who snatched it at once. *This poor soul is delirious*, Avador thought, *he must think we were a part of all this mayhem.*

With a gentle attempt, Avador slid his hands under the fallen figure and lifted it off the ground. To his surprise, it did not attempt to struggle, but when he was almost at his full height; something loosened from within his soot-covered cloak and dropped to the burnt ground. It was something wrapped in a damp blanket and it began to twitch where it lay. Stone kneeled next to it and pulled a corner of the blanket. It was a boy, no older than two and he looked back at the just-as-shocked Dwarf with teary brown eyes. Stone shot a glance at Avador who looked back with understanding.

"Which way out of here Stone?" Avador asked without waiting for a reply. Stone strapped his battle-hammer to his back and snatched the boy into his arms. With a last look at the rest of the group, and the smoky nightmare that encircled them, the valiant Dwarf, Elfling in his arms, vanished into the haze and sprinted in a direction familiar only to him. Avador held the now motionless figure protectively in his arms. He was a short step after Stone and everyone else followed behind; blind to which way they were headed, yet understanding it was away from this smoke-flooded death trap.

A minute might have been an hour during the westward slog Stone Warhelm was leading them through. The relentless Dwarf wasted no time resting. He knew: to rest was to die. Avador, strong as he was, began to breathe heavily, the dense smoke coating his heaving lungs and the extra weight in his arms hindered him greatly. Yet he moved forward, steadfast and solid, trying to keep the burning in his arms and legs away from his thoughts, trying to disregard the raw heaving inside his chest.

Abruptly, Eviathane emerged at Avador's side. The big

Human reached at the drooping figure in Avador's arms and effortlessly took over the burden. With a thankful expression, he motioned Tigran that he was okay and they continued their flight through the once striking forestland.

Falstaff and Nectario kept each other pacing throughout the escape. They knew that if they stayed any longer, *escape* would be unattainable... neither for them nor the newly found survivors. Falstaff's mind raced. He coughed loudly and sometimes uncontrollably. More than once he faltered amidst the steaming trees, more than once he nearly lost the group. Each time Nectario was at his side to help him stand and run, and together they found their way.

Just as they thought the burnt forest would never end and all hope began to weaken, something new appeared before them; something different than the recurring turmoil of the fire's aftermath came to view. The once dignified trees began to lessen in their path. Stone pushed ahead unceasingly, knowing the trees would soon diminish completely. Just ahead, the exhausted company saw an increase in light through persistent smog. The moon's glow seeped easier through the film of darkness; it showed the relieved group that they had neared the edge of the fuming woods.

Stone paused momentarily at the rim of the forest; Avador whirled and glanced quickly behind him, saw the others appear through the smoke and beckoned Stone to continue. Eviathane, unswerving and self-assured, took a position behind the Dwarf who began to slow in his pace. He waited only to see where he would bring them to a halt before laying the figure he had carried for what seemed hours, to the soft soil untouched by the rampant fire.

The company collapsed breathlessly to the earth, their hearts beating in their ears, their lungs stinging from the combination of chilling winds and brutal smoke. Stone lay the child who was crying frantically, gently in front of him and wrapped it in his thick cloak. He held the damp blanket in his fist... *clever*, he thought and tossed it aside. Avador crouched a few feet away, the near lifeless figure before him; pulse fading fast. He called to Falstaff who forced himself to forget his own exhaustion and hurried over. The young Elf gave him a look that asked if there was anything he could do. The young mage froze momentarily desperately trying to think within this trying situation. Hastily he opened his pack and pulled out a small wooden bowl. He then poured water from his flask into it and reached back inside the pack retrieving a small pouch. He untied the string around it's closed top and poured the contents (which looked like black powder) into the bowl. He reached for a thin stick and used it to blend the mixture with quick rigorous stirring motions. The result was a black syrupy substance that left a putrid smell.

"Our friend has to drink this... *all* of it." Falstaff gave Avador a stern look and handed the bowl to him. The Elf looked down at the soot and grime covered figure that lay in his lap. *How unrecognizable this poor person had become,* Avador thought and tilted the head back gently so he can begin to pour the glutinous contents of the bowl down its throat.

At first, the thick liquid flowed easily causing Avador to think in fact, this person is dead. But after a moment, he gave an abrupt cough, spraying Avador's face with what was poured in his throat. Avador looked questioningly at Falstaff who returned him a look that said to keep going. He did so, and tears began to streak down the wretch's blackened cheeks smudging the soot as they streamed downwards. Suddenly, he convulsed out of Avador's lap and onto the ground. Black liquid seeped out of his mouth, first slowly then in massive heaves as he retched for what seemed a lifetime. Falstaff judged the questioning look in the Elf's eyes.

"He is clearing the filth he breathed into his lungs and everything else that entered his stomach. I'm surprised he even survived, judging by what he's excreting.

Finally, the vomiting stopped and the thin figure slumped forward, weak but breathing easier. Avador covered him with his cloak and made sure his breathing grew steadier. The group went silent leaving the loud weeping of the little Wood Elf as the only sound. Avador stood and walked slowly to the little boy. Crouching down, he opened his arms to him and waited for a reaction. The lad looked up at him and must have found Avador's features rather familiar for he immediately stopped crying. After an apprehensive pause, he reached his little arms up and Avador took him in a warm Elven embrace where the little boy buried himself and sobbed freely.

~****~

Showing mercy for the small company that huddled protectively around the soot-covered Wood Elf, the hostile winds steadily vanished with each passing moment. Even the ghostly moon took its haunt further into the horizon showing the promise of night's end.

Avador sat with the little boy who slept wrapped in Stone's warm travel cloak, his head resting against the Elf's lap. Avador stroked the lad's cheek, happy that the little guy was, at least for the moment, feeling safe and at peace. Falstaff stood periodically from his rest to check on the ailing Wood Elf who seemed to be in stable condition. He concluded though that he would not be able to travel just yet.

Nectario decided it was time to become acquainted with his rescuer. Seeing as how Tigran Eviathane has yet to grow weary, he slumped himself next to the big man and held out his hand.

"I haven't had the chance to thank you, good man." Tigran hesitated at the unexpectedness of the bard's approach and simply stared at him.

"Back in Vor?" Nectario pressed. Eviathane's smile told the bard he need not think about it and he clamped his big hand over the other's smaller, more delicate one.

"Why did you do it?" Nectario continued. Tigran remained looking at Falstaff as he tended to his patient.

"Because right is *right*." Tigran said after a silent pause. He added nothing else leaving Nectario waiting for more. The bard realized soon enough that *that* was his answer and decided it was a satisfying one. They resumed their company with each other in silence until Falstaff walked over to them and sat at Eviathane's other side. The young mage instinctively opened his book in his lap and began to turn pages.

"How is our friend?" Eviathane asked without looking at Falstaff.

"He'll live. Tomorrow I will wash him and attempt to give him something to eat." Falstaff said without moving his eyes from the turning pages.

"What happened back there in the streets of Vor when the riders attacked us?" Eviathane was painfully blunt and referred to Falstaff's failed attempt at magic. The magic-user's face began to heat up with embarrassment and gave himself a temporary break before answering.

"I was foolish." He said finally. "What I am doing now is making sure it won't happen again."

"How's that?" Eviathane persisted with his playful torment and looked away smiling to himself.

Falstaff let out a long exhale. "Once a spell is cast, it is washed from memory and must be re-studied before casting it again... I kind of forgot that in the heat of the moment and

tried casting the same spell I used back on Mount Skala."
Falstaff glowered at his friend as if to say 'no more questions,
okay?' Eviathane took the intimation and gave his friend a
gentle nudge with his elbow. His attention soon fell on the
taciturn Dwarf sitting next to Avador who was just a few feet
away. He stood up and swaggered deliberately next to Stone
Warhelm, breaking the arc the group had formed around the
fallen Wood Elf. At first he thought the Dwarf was asleep
because he did not make any moves at his approach but
soon learned that he was just sitting in his own silent contemplation.

Eviathane sat next to Stone and removed his helmet, his
long black hair, damp and messy, fell about his shoulders and
down his chest. He was not a man who worried about his appearance but he tried to remember when the last time he had
a bath was.

"So the Elf will make it eh?" Stone asked so suddenly that
Tigran was a little startled by the abruptness.

"Yes," said Eviathane, "but I'm not sure what will happen
when he awakes."

"No one is sure lad. What can you tell someone who lost
his entire homeland in one night?" Stone's voice grew hoarse
with the seriousness of his remark. Eviathane's brain switched
off at the thought. What *can* you say? He concluded there
was no answer.

Avador stared at the members of the little group huddled
together. No one slept this night. Everyone seemed to take
comfort with the fact they were all still together and alive. It
was as if they thought that if they slept, someone would be
lost. He glanced over at Tigran Eviathane just as a thin line
of blood- red severed the sky from the horizon. The coming
of the sun cast its red light onto his face. His strong sharp
features seemed to have changed. His usually smooth face had

suddenly developed lines of worry. Unshaven and in serious need of rest, the young man appeared to have aged during this quest.

The Elf's gaze went to Falstaff. Fatigue had not been evaded by the young mage either. His face had lost a bit of his usual boyish mischievousness. In reality, Avador thought, they have been travelling for only a fortnight. Somehow, it seemed to the young Elf, it felt like years. But there they were... marching valiantly at his side without complaint. Avador felt his heart tingle with pride. Then there was Stone. Stone looked hurt most of all. Something about Feo-Dosia's destruction troubled him in particular, almost as if there was a connection that had just been detached between the two. Avador's first reaction was to talk to him about it but the Elf knew he would not get an answer from Stone tonight. He will enquire at another time, or the answer will come without invitation.

The blackened Wood Elf stirred with the coming of the new day but made no attempt to awaken. Falstaff dampened a cloth and began to gently cleanse the grime from his unrecognizable face. He removed the cowl of his soot-covered and partially scorched cloak. Long, matted hair, greasy and stuck to his neck and face, slithered down his tunic like oily weeds.

Stone had built a small fire and everyone sat around it eating a breakfast of smoked meat, cheese and dried figs. The little boy, who until now has not said a word to anybody, remained huddled within the safety of Avador's arms and ate whatever Avador gave him. The company spoke little during these early hours for none had slept throughout the night and conversation seemed to be unwanted.

But at least the coming of the sun also brought its warmth. Gone were the chill winds and the frosty climate seemed to have somewhat broken. Avador stood with the little Wood

Elf holding his hand. He was a handsome little guy, Avador thought, short wavy brown hair and big brown eyes that glimmered when he looked at him. The boy kept glancing over at the fallen Wood Elf where Falstaff was doing his best to minister to. There was a very long silence that followed. No one spoke or uttered a word until...

"Avador." Falstaff stood suddenly from where he was kneeling before his patient. "Come here and see." Avador picked up the boy and sprinted over to Falstaff. The others rose at the suddenness and followed after hoping there has been a change of events. They looked down at the fallen figure before them. Falstaff did a very good job at cleaning the Wood Elf; the person they saw before them was among the most beautiful women any of them had ever seen.

~****~

Falstaff waited for the sun to rise a little higher so that it's warmth could increase before removing the woman's filthy cloak. Concealed beneath, the mage discovered, was a large quiver filled with arrows and a curiously shaped wooden bow that seemed to be merely two branches entwined together as if it were just taken from a tree, but a bow nonetheless. Her clothing, though stained and torn, was of good quality hunting attire. She had begun to rouse more often and the mage thought she would soon awaken.

"What do we do now, Avador?" Stone Warhelm asked the Elf for the first time. Avador was rather taken aback by the question... or closer to the truth, by *who* asked it.

"When our mysterious Wood Elf awakens," Avador said after a brief pause, "she should be able to tell us some of the events that happened here. Judging by the trampled earth, it looks like the Dark Dwarves headed west... and there are many of them." Avador looked at Stone who spit at the sound of 'Dark Dwarf' and gave him a look of mutual understanding.

"The *Dark Dwarves* are headed west." Stone agreed with Avador, "Which can only mean one thing..."

"We're going west." Avador finished.

The young Wood Elf remained fixed to Avador's side. He has not said a word since his rescue from his destroyed homeland but it seemed that Avador was the only one he trusted. He ate and drank only from what Avador had offered paying attention to nothing anybody else said to him. He shied away clinging to the back of Avador's boot whenever Stone drew near. There was no misunderstanding and it did not offend the Dwarf. After all, the boy was a mere child and creatures that resembled Stone Warhelm *did* destroy his native land. But everything will get straightened out in due time, Stone thought.

The boy ventured from time to time (holding Avador's hand) to his fallen mother. He kneeled by her side just as if he was her protector and waited for her to awaken. When she did not, he moved back to Avador keeping a wary eye on everybody else. Even the brawny Eviathane tried to win the little guy's heart by being playful and mischievous. But all that did was send him pouncing into Avador's arms pushing his face into the Elf's chest until Tigran went away.

The sun was high in the azure sky and Falstaff was immersed in his book when the Wood Elf awakened. At first no one noticed, busy with planning and adjusting their next moves. But when she made a small groaning sound, everybody froze and all eyes fell to her. She tried to stand but immediately fell to one knee. When she saw that she was surrounded by the strangest people she has ever seen grouped together, she withdrew a step and reached for her weapons. But Falstaff had already removed them so that she could rest comfortably and she discovered with horror, she was unarmed.

The small Wood Elf wriggled free from Avador and sprinted with delight towards her. When she saw him she opened her arms and took him into her embrace sobbing openly and holding him tightly. The small group remained where they were in the hopes not to alarm her more than she already was. She looked from one man to the next wondering what they wanted from her.

"We do not mean you any harm." Avador was the first to speak. He took a step closer to her holding his hands in front of him to show that he held no weapons. The Wood Elf instinctively tightened her grip on the boy.

"W-Who are you?" Her voice was hoarse and she found it difficult to speak.

"My name is Avador Andor and we are all here to help." Avador tried to keep his voice calm and everyone else kept their distance.

Andor. The woman mouthed the name, her chestnut eyes staring right through Avador as if he wasn't really there. She looked from Avador to the others. For an instant, she was in a dream. She shook her head and tears began to flow down her cheeks as the memory of what had befallen her and her family rushed back to her like a river's mighty current. With an impressive effort, she regained her composure and stood up.

"Just give me back my weapons and leave us be if you want to help."

"You will not survive." Stone growled, frustration beginning to invade his own self-control. Avador held a hand up to silence the Dwarf.

"Easy Stone, we can't expect her to trust us after what she's been through." The lady Elf never felt so confused in all her life.

"What is happening?" She asked, tears threatening to fall once again. No one really knew what to say.

"We were hoping you could tell *us*." Avador dared another step closer. This time she remained fixed to where she stood with the boy in her embrace. She stood there for a long time before she spoke.

"I have to find my people." Her eyes were pleading.

"I have to find them." The words were a mere sigh but they injured Avador's heart.

Chapter 14 - Integrity

N othing moved within the Plains of Paladin. The wind itself seemed suspicious and passed through in quick watchful spurts. Tall yellowing grass forced into a hunched position from once continual winds, remained bowing as if afraid to anger an unseen god. Nothing stirred and nothing made a sound. The inactivity was beginning to get unsettling... and the Dark Dwarves were getting restless.

"Why are we waiting?" A Dwarf with exceptionally dark skin in the fading sunlight broke the unremitting silence. "I want blood." He finished with a hiss.

"The spineless Elves won't come out until night falls." Tolstyak did his best to keep his speech at a whisper. "Now shut your mouth and keep waiting." He gave the other a slap across his face making him recoil at the unexpected strike but do nothing else.

"Yes commander," he responded rubbing his reddening cheek.

The Dark Dwarves, one hundred and fifty strong, had surrounded the Forlorn Catacombs for two days. The surviving Wood Elves, and there were not many, fled from their burning homeland pursued by the merciless black-skinned Dwarves and took shelter within the underground caves.

Just outside one of the openings that descended into the catacombs, hung the heads of Governor Leorren Feo-Dosia and his son Dalowynn on crude spikes. They met their fate the night before when they tried to sneak out to search for food and water for the rest of the survivors. They crept within the shadows for a mere ten metres before being discovered by the waiting Dark Dwarves. Now they hung as grotesque martyrs, an admonition to others who might try and escape.

Tolstyak stood alone, the other left with his insulted pride. The commander of the onslaught gazed around the plains with amusement. The catacombs were beneath his feet and he knew it was only a matter of time when he will get his chance to crush the remaining Wood Elves. Then he could collect the rest of his pay and move on to other things.

How the pitiful cower, he thought. The last of the sunlight valiantly clung to the departing day but the Dark Dwarf knew that night was mere moments away. He took a last look at his men. Handfuls were positioned at each opening of the underground caves with orders to kill anything that attempted to exit. The rest encircled the catacombs creating an armed blockade. Battle-axes held at the ready, they knew there would be no sleep yet again tonight. Tolstyak's grin split his bearded face like an open wound. *Let them lick the moisture off the walls for water*, he thought with gratification. *Let them eat their own... they cannot stay down there forever.*

A hundred yards east of the encircling Dark Dwarves, Avador crouched within the tall grasses, arrow nocked and ready to fire. His Elven eyes penetrated easily through the deepening gloom... he was waiting for movement. Before the sun disappeared completely into the horizon, the movement came. A Dark Dwarf gone astray from the rest of his clan, crept in his exact direction. Avador kept his poise and drew the arrow closer to his cheek. The Dwarf neared without slowing. Avador waited until he was almost on top of him and slackened his bow.

"Did you learn anything?" Avador's words were less than a whisper.

"The scum bastard slapped me." Stone Warhelm said, a hint of a growl in his voice. "I don't know how I let you talk me into this fool plan." He then proceeded to wipe the dark syrupy concoction off his face. *If we don't get ourselves killed*, the Dwarf thought to himself, *that son-of-a-bitch is going to taste my hammer.*

The two fell into a crouch and noiselessly moved east to where the others were hidden within a shadowy grove. It was time for the second phase of Avador's plan.

"Falstaff are you ready?" Avador asked, his voice almost inaudible.

"*Yes.*" The young mage took in a deep breath.

"Are you sure?" Eviathane looked right into Falstaff's eyes, his lips almost smirking.

"Yes." He repeated with mild annoyance.

Avador moved to the crouching Wood Elf who held the little boy as if it were her last time. Her eyes were glistening though the sun stretched itself into a lean crimson streak that detached the darkening sky from the earth. The woman, who revealed her name to no one, caressed the fine wood of her bow with her free hand and gazed directly into Avador's eyes. Avador felt her willingness before she acknowledged anything to him. *What more has she got to lose?* The young Elf thought darkly.

Eviathane stared out at the Plains, his expression shifting from his customary light-heartedness to all seriousness. He sized up their situation just as Avador had already done a hundred times. It was critical. There were simply too many Dark Dwarves. He felt the spasm of reality begin to prevail; the once childlike grandeur had abandoned him. Eviathane dug deep within his heart to unearth his burrowing nerve, sweat beginning to moisten his apprehensive brow.

Sudden thoughts of home harassed his mind. He saw his father, strong and proud, watching him leave home for the first time and into the care of Master Wylme. His mother stood next to him with a brave face, hiding the worry that threatened to reveal itself. He thought of Falstaff and Avador. They were with him throughout his childhood, throughout his adolescence, and they are with him now... he must also be with *them*. His thoughts diminished all at once and he gripped his long-sword so tight his knuckles went white. He was ready.

Nectario was holding the Elf-child who was sleeping peacefully in his arms. They were a few meters further east of the rest of the group. He was not happy. He was to wait within the grove until this was all over. If the group survives, he would join with them. If they die, he was to take care of the boy as best he could. He did not like his role in the plan but he understood it was the most logical. Avador had told him if the latter occurred to take the child to Pelendria where he would be taken care of. The Elf did not take 'no' for an answer and the bard knew better than to disagree.

Avador inched closer to the Wood Elf so that his mouth nearly touched her ear.

"Keep them safe." His voice a smooth whisper in the night. She bowed her head to show acknowledgement. Then he moved to Stone Warhelm and Eviathane who were crouching and staring in the direction of the Dark Dwarves. "You can do this." It was a statement of fact. "I am with you." The two warriors clamped each of the Elf's hands.

"I trust you Avador." Eviathane was smiling once again.

145

"My life is yours, my prince." Stone bowed his head.

Falstaff stood from his stolen moment of meditation and looked to Avador for his signal. The Elf gave Falstaff a look of understanding. An immense amount of pressure lay on the shoulders of the young mage and Avador knew this. Falstaff seemed to accept it, a look of utter commitment gleaming off his face.

Avador waited only a moment before speaking.

"Go." Falstaff wrapped his robes around himself and vanished into the shadows without looking behind him.

The Elf took a last look at the remaining members of his little group, then turned his attention to the Dark Dwarves who waited with impatient recklessness. The first of the campfires were lit creating a sinister red glow within the confines of the Dark Dwarf encampment. Scores of silhouettes materialized within like ominous wraiths, fidgety and pulsating by the fires. The sun abandoned the land completely now, its valiant effort to stay was given up to the overshadowing night. Avador withdrew a long arrow from his quiver.

The Wood Elf tightened her own quiver to her hip and with a last agonized look in the direction of the sleeping child; she too disappeared into the night. Stone and Eviathane like thirsty hounds moved stealthily towards the encampment. After a few yards, they suddenly separated in opposite directions and vanished into the shroud of blackness. Avador waited until he approximated the Wood Elf's position. His heart wrenched as his plan went into action. *Can you see me, Father? I wish you were here.*

His arrow flew like an invisible bolt of lightning in the night. It found a target and sent it gurgling to its knees. The others barely reacted when another struck from the opposite direction. Stone burst in from the southernmost side of the Dark Dwarf camp, howling like an enraged killer. Eviathane saw the signal and with the instincts of a colossal lion, he thrust in from the northern side swiping at anything that stood there astonished. The two warriors killed half a dozen dumbfounded Dwarves before the rest could respond in any way. They were surrounded in seconds, lost in a torrent of infuriated Dark Dwarves. But their weapons were ceaseless striking out and keeping them at bay.

Avador moved quickly and silently around the outskirts of the camp and away from the fire's glow. The Wood Elf exactly opposite him moved as one with him like two hands of a giant clock. Their arrows were unrelenting, striking the Dark Dwarves that threatened to kill their friends as they fought alone inside the hellish turmoil. Tigran and Stone, also opposite each other fought on their own private battleground killing those they could and scarcely avoiding death as an Elven arrow struck the ones closing in for the kill. The exasperated Dwarves thought an army surrounded them and panic began to creep in.

"Stand your ground!" Tolstyak was screaming above the chaos. "Stand your ground or you will die before you regret it!"

Handfuls of Dwarves were dieing at the hands of the little group working together as one fighting mechanism. Avador and the Wood Elf continued their movement in a giant arc letting their arrows fly, persistently stunning the Dark Dwarves and protecting Eviathane and Stone as they fought within.

The Wood Elf shot her last arrow, striking a Dwarf that raised his battle-axe to strike down Eviathane from behind. From the shadows outside the fire's reach, Avador saw that Eviathane was suddenly unprotected, the big man depending more on his shield and his raw determination. The Dwarves closed in to kill this incessant pain. Avador fired a last arrow killing one of Stone's would-be assassins. There was utterly no time left. He grabbed his last arrow that he had wrapped in an oil-soaked cloth and bounded inside the encampment. Dwarves grabbed at him from all sides but the Elf was too fast dodging them by mere inches. The turmoil shifted in his direction with Dark Dwarves howling in rage. With a last frantic pounce, Avador reached the nearest campfire and thrust his arrow into it, the heat scorching his exposed hand. The arrow's tip ignited at once and he nocked it into his bow. With the speed of a cornered python, the Elf sent the arrow skyward where it lit the night air with a great flaming arc.

Falstaff's cryptic words released at Avador's signal and the skies exploded with blue lightning. Electric death rained onto the Plains of Paladin like the wrath of an infuriated god. Falstaff's arms were raised above his head as he shouted incomprehensible words above the sonic booms and crackling of lightning. His voice was drowned by the screams of dieing Dwarves, their lives taken by the deafening lightning surge. Dozens convulsed on the ground while others stood there in utter disbelief only to be cut down by Eviathane and Stone. Many fled in every direction as fast as their legs could take them leaving Tolstyak, their commander, in a frantic loss.

The leader of the Dark Dwarves shook off his mass confusion, desperately trying to focus on this unbelievable confrontation. Avador came into his sight, the Elf's back to him. Tolstyak, himself an impressive war machine, gripped his own battle-axe and bolted towards Avador in a dead run. Seconds away from striking the unsuspecting Elf, Stone appeared out of nowhere and rammed into the attacking Dark Dwarf with his brawny shoulder. Tolstyak fell to his knees but pounced to his feet with incredible speed. Avador unsheathed the *King-blade* but Stone was already on top of him swinging his great hammer. The Dark Dwarf dodged it feeling the stream of air on his sweating forehead. Indeed, Tolstyak was a seasoned soldier. His battle-axe came down where Stone stood only to dig itself into the dirt with Stone sidestepping the deadly blade. With both hands clutching the handle of his battle-hammer and a resounding battle cry, Stone brought his heavy hammer down on the Dark Dwarf's blade. It shattered it into countless pieces and sent a shockwave up Tolstyak's arms. He dropped the useless handle on the ground as if it were on fire and met another blow from Stone's hammer that caught him full on the mouth. That was the last thing he saw before passing out flat on his back in a toothless yawn.

Leaderless and bursting with panic, the remaining Dark Dwarves took flight as the last of the crackling lightning faded within it's own thunder. There was nothing left for them here but to run as fast and as far away as possible into the cursed night; their consequences can be paid later.

~****~

Nectario watched the melee with a mixture of shock and admiration. For the most part he stood there in awe. But at one point a rush of adrenalin nearly took over his self-control. He almost forgot his position and abandon his role just to leap into the action. The child amazingly remained asleep. The bard looked down at him as he slept in his arms, then towards the plains where the battle had just ended.

He saw the silhouette of the child's mother heading in his direction, her thick wavy hair bouncing as she strode. He walked smoothly towards her and they met somewhere near the battlefield.

"Thank you." She whispered and he thought he saw the beginnings of a smile on her lips. Handing the child over to her, he repaid her with a large grin he could not contain.

"It was naught but a duty," he said and together they walked back to where Avador and the rest of the group waited within the still-smoking encampment.

The face of Stone Warhelm was grim as he returned from a short sweep of the camp. With glazed eyes he looked at each member of the group and took in a deep inhale until his lungs filled completely. Then, ever so slowly, he released what seemed to be the greater part of stress and sorrow in the form of his very breath.

"The Wood Elves are still beneath our feet." He said in a softened voice, "but the governor and his son are dead."

Chapter 15 - Charisma

Quiet shadows crept uneasily from their peculiar refuge of the Forlorn Catacombs. One by one they surfaced onto the darkened Plains of Paladin like zombies with no emotion and staring at nothing in particular. The Wood Elves, bereft of everything, had nothing to act as a guide... unsure even with what to do with their own emotions. The plains were hushed as though every bit of sound was buried into the cold earth, exiled to never resurface.

Then, a wail escaped the mouth of one of the surviving females and disrupted the silence, inaudible at first but gradually intensified to an almost deafening magnitude. Not long after, another joined in unison with the first, and then a third creating an ominous chorus of grief and sorrow. Men, half caked in soot and mud dropped to their knees clutching their temples in despair. Others, barely strong enough to restrain their emotions put their arms around the women and wept bitterly beside them.

The female Elf that accompanied the little group emerged from one of the dark stone-carved entrances of the catacombs holding the hands of two children, her chestnut eyes flowing with tears as she climbed the eerie steps to the surface. She found herself wishing she had not gone down; the witnessing of what her people suffered below the earth strangled her heart. It physically hurt inside her chest. The hands of the two children slid away from her grip and they ran to a familiar face. Was it a relative? A mother? She was not certain. Her contemplation soon ended when her knees lost all feeling and buckled beneath her. The little boy she rescued from their burning home was at her side instantly... together they wept.

Stone Warhelm kept his distance from everything. He watched the sombre setting with a troubled spirit; the lamentation before him was among the gravest he had ever seen. How much did they lose? Did they even know what family they had left? Who among them died? --- Ah, they have suffered. He watched Avador as he struggled to gather the Elves together, Falstaff and Eviathane helping the wounded and sick. Were they *really* out of danger? Or were they to suffer another attack? What more can they do if the latter occurred?

At a loss, Stone stared down at the ground before him. A fallen Dark Dwarf lay inches away from his feet, it's mouth opened to reveal a swollen purple tongue. An arrow was pierced right through his neck with blood slowly trickling from the two unnatural holes. He was about to look away when something caught his attention: Moonlight glinted off the arrow's tip. He looked again, this time more closely. The arrowhead was of a dark blue colour and where it wasn't stained with blood, flashed with tiny white sparkles. Stone nocked an eyebrow and yanked the arrow free from the dead man's neck. *Sapphire.* The Dwarf took in a sharp breath triggered by abrupt recognition. Sapphire tipped arrows were the markings of Leorren Feo-Dosia's family lineage.

The female Wood Elf looked up when a shadow blocked the light of the moon. Stone Warhelm kneeled next to her holding the arrow in a fisted glove, the muscles of his arms tensed with veins snaking under the skin like tiny rivulets.

"Do'ya remember me, girl?" Stone's voice seemed chafed, yet soft. She stared at him blankly.

"N-No." Her voice was a mere whisper.

"I don't expect that you do, you were only this tall when we met." Stone held his hand three feet off the ground.

He waited only a moment for a reaction. When he saw her blank face staring uncomprehendingly, a quick smile came and left from his lips. "Leorren Feo-Dosia was my friend, ally to Grandalimus Andor. I have travelled to your homeland with the Elven king visiting the governor on more than one occasion." Now the Wood Elf raised a slender eyebrow in curiosity, thin salty lines left over on her cheeks revealed by the moonlight. "He had a son... *and* a daughter." Stone said nothing more, instead he lifted the sapphire tipped arrow to eye level where the moons light touched it once more. Tears formed in the Elf's eyes again and this time she buried her face in Stone's massive chest waiting for the feeling of sorrow to recede. The Dwarf put a strong hand to her shoulder as if to say she at least, was safe.

Avador, with great effort and with the help of Eviathane and Falstaff, got the remaining Wood Elves into the best orderly fashion they could. The Elves knew only that this small group had somehow defeated the bloodthirsty Dark Dwarves and saved them from the cold dark prison of the catacombs.

The young Elf shifted his now empty quiver over his shoulder noticing the lack of weight and walked to where Stone sat with the Wood Elf.

"We have to make a move." He said almost regretting the decision. Stone looked up at Avador and gritted his teeth. He knew he was right.

"Avador Andor," Stone's familiar gruff voice had returned, "this is Myia Feo-Dosia, daughter of Governor Leorren." The Dwarf watched as Avador's eyes widened.

"Myia Feo-Dosia." The young Elf whispered and kneeled next to her. His violet eyes met her chestnut coloured ones. She looked at him with an almost guilty expression and turned away.

"Yes," she said after a moments pause, then turned her attention to her kinfolk waiting by a burning fire. There was a mere forty or fifty remaining from the once strong nation. Myia clenched her jaw and summoned all the courage she could muster, "where will you go now?" Her lips trembled as she spoke. Avador looked at Stone who returned him a determined expression. Tigran and Falstaff appeared behind the Elf and Avador knew he was the focus of everyone's attention.

"Is he alive?" Avador's question was directed to Stone.

"Scarcely." The Dwarf stood and disappeared momentarily into the darkness beyond the fire only to re-emerge with a half struggling Dark Dwarf. Myia gasped. It was Tolstyak, swaying as if drunken in Stone's steel grip, his mouth bleeding and emptied of teeth. Stone threw him roughly on the ground and stepped on him.

"Quit moving you bastard's-excuse-of-a-Dwarf!" Stone had no pity whatsoever. The Dark Dwarf struggled feebly but his body soon slackened under Stone's foot. Was that a smile forming on his bloodied mouth?

Tolstyak's feet were tied and his hands bound tightly with his own rope. He lay before the group, broken yet defiant. Eviathane watched him. He had absolutely no trust for this revolting character, even though Stone had tied him before bringing him over. The big man stood over him with his long-sword held ready for any sudden moves.

Myia moved away from the group to join her people. Avador watched her as she neared them; her movements were fluid and seemed to add to her beauty. He watched as the cluster of Wood Elves opened and swallowed her into its embrace.

"The little boy is not her son." Stone seemed to have read Avador's thoughts. "She has not taken a mate young Elfling." Avador didn't move or show expression. "Governor Leorren's son is… *was* the boy's father. He is her nephew, last in line to inherit Feo-Dosia." A snicker escaped from Tolstyak as he lay between them. Eviathane lost his temper. He reached down with both hands, yanked the Dark Dwarf roughly to his feet, and jabbed his neck with the point of his sword. The voices from the nearby Wood Elves hushed at the act and looked over. Tigran Eviathane trembled with anger and everyone expected him to kill Tolstyak right then. But with a snarl, the big man swung his unarmed hand and slapped Tolstyak on the back of his head knocking his horned helmet to the ground.

"Next time it won't be your *horns* I take off you!" Eviathane's words were a near-shout and he thrust Tolstyak back to the cold ground.

Avador crouched next to the fallen Dark Dwarf and kneeled onto his bound wrists. Slowly the Elf unsheathed his father's jagged dagger from its slender scabbard and put the deadly blade to the Dwarf's filthy fingers.

"I think we all have seen enough blood today." Avador whispered with a hiss and put pressure on the dagger just enough to penetrate Tolstyak's skin. The Dark Dwarf flinched at the stinging pain but knew if he moved any more, he would lose a finger entirely. "Why did you do this?" Avador swept his free hand across the plains. Tolstyak spit on the Elf's face. Avador clenched his jaw and stayed Eviathane and Stone from a fit of rage. He then dug the dagger's blade until it ripped through nerves and meat. The Elf felt the resistance of bone and stopped as Tolstyak lay howling in pain.

"I was paid!" Tolstyak's voice developed into that of a snarling beast. He remained on his side huffing from the searing pain.

"You were *paid?*" Avador was appalled; the thought entered his mind to finish what he started with his dagger. "By *who?*"

"A henchman of some king!" The pressure remained on Tolstyak's thick finger.

"Who?" Avador screamed the word pressing the blade a little more.

"Aaaah! You cursed Elf! Let me free so I could rip out your insides." Avador hated this just as much as Tolstyak. Forcing the hand flat on the ground, he sliced through the rest of Tolstyak's finger. The Dwarf screamed until he nearly lost consciousness. He forced his breath out in quick white puffs and felt the cold steel of the Elf's blade touch a second finger.

"Avador." Falstaff was suddenly at his side. He saw the rage developing on the Elf's face and put his hand on his shoulder.

"Tell me everything you know." Avador was speaking through clenched teeth ignoring his friend's touch.

"Aonas... King Aonas of Gogatha..." Tolstyak's breathing was laboured, "... is preparing an army to attack your lands. We, the Dark Dwarves were only a warning... that fire was only a spark..." the company listened as the Dark Dwarf seeped the information from his bloodied lips, "the Elf King is dead and Aonas has somehow taken a vast amount of his followers into his control along with an army that once followed Aonas' dead brother." Tolstyak took a moment to steady his breathing. "The army is immeasurable, greater than any of us will ever see while we live." A sudden remembrance came to Avador that this Dwarf does not know who he is.

"Where is this army?"

"*That*, I do not know." Avador snuck a quick glance at Stone who nodded in return.

"Who is this henchman?" The Elf was unrelenting now that he secured Tolstyak's cooperation.

"Some dark-skinned man in robes...*Skneeba* his name was.

He is voiceless; he cannot speak. In my pouch... there is the letter... he gave me from Aonas." Tolstyak slumped his head to the earth, exhaustion overtaking him. Stone rummaged through the leathers of his armour and found a brown fur pouch. In it was a folded yellowed parchment. Stone flattened it and read:

Tolstyak of the Dark Dwarves, commander of the Black Army of Scithe. Your allegiance is requested upon the reading of this letter. I have sent my subject Skneeba with the offer of three hundred gold pieces to all who follow you in the task you will perform. Once it is completed, another three hundred will be arranged to all who survive. To you, Tolstyak of the Dark Dwarves, thrice the amount for leading the assault... Destroy the sacred forest land of Feo-Dosia and its inhabitants, a forewarning to what I will do with my newly acquired armies once loyal to Grandalimus Andor and my deceased brother Jadonas. Once your task is performed, tryst at the Harbour of Land's End where Skneeba will await with your disbursement. The Dark Dwarves, your obedience attained, will remain untouched by my impending onslaught.

The burly Pike Dwarf crumpled the parchment slowly into his gloved fist. "Aonas." He whispered staring at nothing.

"Skneeba," said Avador, "the magic-user my father told us about." Eviathane and Falstaff were filled with sudden eagerness. Nectario stood there at a complete loss. What was going on? Then, without another word, Avador strode to the Wood Elves signalling Tigran and Falstaff with him. Nectario noticed he stood alone with the sour-faced Stone and felt immensely uncomfortable. He left after the others in an awkward haste.

Stone Warhelm waited until the others were buried in the huddle of Wood Elves. He looked at Tolstyak who lay at his feet. *You betrayed your master.* The Dwarf thought, *you'll betray us.* Then with a great heave, the battle-hammer rose above his head and crashed into Tolstyak's exposed skull killing him instantly.

~****~

Eviathane stood with Nectario and Falstaff. Together they watched as Avador met with Myia and a few of the men of the Wood Elves. Stone had been scouting their vicinity for nearly an hour making sure no Dark Dwarves (or anyone else) had returned. Tigran offered to accompany him but the Dwarf refused mumbling something about all his armour clammering so loud it would wake dead people twenty miles away.

"Myia." Avador was giving the Wood Elf a stern look. "You *must* lead your people away from here." Myia was not disagreeing whatsoever. The only problem she had was *not* being able to bury her father and brother appropriately on the sanctified burial grounds of Faeble, the heart of the Feo-Dosia woodlands. Instead, she watched her people build makeshift stretchers out of long lengths of the Dark Dwarves firewood and remnants of their sturdy leathers. Their bodies were already resting on them, covered with blankets and coiled with rope. The crude apparatus' made her disgusted that their final journey will be on these disrespectful *things* built from the very implements of the ones that killed them. The thought of the irony brought acid to her throat. But she knew that Avador was right. They were to travel south, clinging to every bit of cover they could find. Some of the men were armed with longbows and knives. They would hunt for food and protect the old and the young. The young women, strong and full of fortitude would look after the sick and sustain their Elflings.

Together, they would find the Gwynfell Forest and build new homes around the village of Pelendria. They were to send word to the village that its sons are still alive and *will* return. The Wood Elves were determined to not let everything Avador and his men have risked for them be a complete waste... they would survive and prevail.

The western horizon brought two things as time continued its march through the night: The first was the promise of dawn's approach with great lines of red, purple and violet cutting through the lower part of the sky as if a giant slashed at it with uneven strokes of his enormous blade. The second was Stone Warhelm. The Dwarf returned finally from his scouting of the area with news that they were *momentarily* safe. A few of the Dark Dwarves were scattered in the northern exterior of the plains but they showed no interest in returning to the Forlorn Catacombs any time soon.

The morning allowed a fresh gentle breeze to pass through the Plains of Paladin. Avador stoked the fire as most of the Wood Elves awakened from a much-needed slumber. Though nothing moved and all was calm, the little group had remained awake through what was left of the dark hours. For a while nothing could be heard but the soothing snapping and crackling of the wood burning in the fire.

Myia had awakened among the first and gathered what little belongings she carried. She found Avador by the opposite side of the fire.

"You must be tired." Her voice was small within these sleepy morning hours; the whites of Avador's eyes had turned glossy pink.

"I am." Avador's smile curled up at one corner. A quick breeze blew past them and Myia's wavy brown hair fluttered away from her face. Her childlike features made Avador shake his head at how deceiving looks were. This woman was a lot stronger than she appeared. Facing the opposite direction as Myia, his own hair had toppled about his brow and cheeks. Myia reached up and tucked a honey-blond tangle behind his ear.

"Thank you for saving us." She said and looked down at her soft brown boots. Avador stared stupidly at her. He couldn't comprehend 'thousands lost' as *saving them*.

"Are your people good hunters?" Avador asked deciding to avoid his issue. Myia half smiled and gave her head a tiny nod.

"Yes," she responded giving Avador a quizzical look. "Why do you ask?" The young Elf took in a deep breath before responding.

"We do not have enough food to provide for everybody," Avador thought of the last of their rations that he gave to the surviving children. "When you make your way south, there might not be any game until you cross the shallow river before the northern reaches of Gwynfell Forest. Perhaps you could send a few of your hunters to trek ahead and fish from that river." A rapid memory of the river he used to venture to with his father shot in and out of his mind. There were many silvery fish of various sizes that swam in that river. He remembered how the sun reflected off their backs as they moved along faster than the river's current. "Once you cross the river, Gwynfell will become visible. There you will find good game."

The Wood Elf could not help but to gaze at Avador in admiration. All this weight on his shoulders and it seems he was trying to add to it. With a regretful smile she moved away from Avador and made her way between her kinfolk. She stopped where the body of her father lay and kneeled next to him. Tears were attempting once again to free themselves but she kept them at bay. Reaching down next to her dead father, she picked up his full quiver of the distinctive sapphire-tipped arrows and adjusted it to her hip. Her brother lay next to him and she moved slowly over to pick up his quiver, that in which she slung over her shoulder. Without another word she began to group her people together for the long march south.

Stone was at the Wood Elf's side, appearing seemingly out of nowhere.

"Remember," he began, "keep to as much cover as possible." She looked and found the rest of the little group standing near her with looks of both determination and encouragement. Avador pulled in close.

"When you reach the Village of Pelendria, find my mother, Simetra..." it seemed for a moment he lost the will to speak, "tell her... tell her it hurt my heart to leave her the way I did and for that alone, I will return unharmed." Myia nodded and they shared a short silence together. She then removed her brother's quiver from around her shoulder and handed it to Avador. The Elf stared at the dark redwood quiver; his mind went completely blank.

"If I am not to come with you... at least take these." Avador knew he had no chance of *not* accepting the arrows. *He would also be a fool*, he thought gravely; and it was a bitter thought.

With no more words shared between the two groups, they parted ways. The larger group began their voyage south towards the shelter of Gwynfell Forest. The smaller marched northward to where the unknown awaited them.

Chapter 16 - One Stick

Empty plains stared back at the little group as they faced northward. The yellowed grass stretched out before them like a giant carpet of swaying limbs. The sun kept them company on their western flank; its touch was a warm kiss on their cheeks, though it did nothing to increase the group's low morale.

After a few long hours of cautious marching, the company began to feel the effects of not sleeping or eating. Their stomachs wrenched inside them and they began to feel light-headed. Their movements grew less confident until they forced themselves to focus on putting one foot in front of the other.

The grasslands seemed to go on forever, its ends dipping over the four horizons and falling off the world itself. The five travellers began to feel smaller and smaller, five specks in a yellow sea. Avador looked back at his companions, desperately in need of rest but with the spark of determination still in their eyes. Every now and then they would remove their water flasks and sip sparingly at the little contents they had. The wind picked up its pace and brushed by them in quick sweeps. They travelled a few yards more when Avador stopped short and put up a hand.

"What's..." Stone began.

"Ssh." Avador put a finger to his lips. There was something in the wind very familiar to the Elf. A smell carried by the current of air came to his nostrils and left just as fast as it came. But there was no mistake... it was there nonetheless. Everyone stood frozen to the ground not knowing what was happening. Avador made a motion with his hand for everyone to crouch low. They did. Then, ever so slowly the Elf slid an arrow from his new quiver and nocked it to his bow. He stretched the bowstring until it reached his chin, the blue arrowhead gleaming in the sunlight. The arrow shot and dug somewhere in the tall grass and away from view. Then, with a motion so swift it seemed as though a second arrow simply appeared ready in Avador's bow, Avador took aim as something jumped out of the tall grass on the opposite side of where he shot the first arrow. The Elf released the arrow before anyone really knew what he was shooting at and it found the thing that bolted into the air and forced it back to the ground.

"I am guessing Elfling, that you found us some food?" Stone said as Avador walked to where he shot the first arrow. The Elf reached down and heaved the long shaft from the ground and displayed a large grey hare that hung limply from it. Stone walked over to where Avador shot the second arrow and found that it too pierced through what might have been the hare's mate. "You're good, Elfling." Stone was shaking his head, "real good."

~****~

The company ate eagerly after Stone cleared away some of the tall grass and dared a small fire. Their spirits rose significantly after eating and regaining their lost strength. Sitting in a circle around the tiny fire, cloaks wrapped tightly around them, they began to talk with renewed enthusiasm. Tigran returned to his usual self teasing Falstaff and Avador and throwing rude jokes into the conversation. Even Stone seemed to loosen up as Nectario portrayed illustrious stories and fables. The bard appeared to have blended into the group rather nicely, almost as if he too had been with them since childhood.

"If I may," Nectario's cheeks were burning from the continuous smiling, "I would assume we are heading to Land's End." Silence followed abruptly as everyone was brought back to reality.

"We are." Stone said plainly and tossed a thin greasy bone into the fire. "You don't have to come, you *know* that."

"And miss stopping an all out war? Imagine the songs I will write from this adventure."

"This is not a game, *bard*!" Stone's frustration was rekindled. Nectario could do nothing more than stare at his feet trying to avoid the Dwarf's gaze.

"I never said..."

"Good! Keep it that way." Stone stood and began throwing things back into his pack.

"Do you two always have to be in conflict with each other?" Avador, once again the mediator, stood and stretched his legs. Then he walked over to the fuming Dwarf. "Stone, he is not as seasoned as you, I don't think he understands quite as much as you about what is at stake here."

"He doesn't understand even half of *this*." Stone made a gesture with his thumb and forefinger almost touching.

"Neither did *we*," Avador swept his arm in the direction of Falstaff and Tigran who were still sitting by the fire watching the argument, "but look at what we accomplished." The Elf waited for a comeback. When it didn't come, he walked back to the others and told them to pack their things. They did wordlessly.

The sun swayed over to the west as it continued its great arc above the endless plains. The company knew that they would look for a place to camp when night approached, but for now the glowing sphere that hung over their eastern flank did nothing to radiate the heat they knew it was capable of.

"How far do these plains go?" Avador broke the ongoing monotony of the wind.

"A few days longer." Stone's gruff voice penetrated the wind easily. "I suggest we set camp over there." Avador squinted against the sun's light at the direction Stone was pointing with his hammer. He saw a section where the grass seemed taller.

"Now's a good time." Avador advised. He waited as Stone contemplated.

"Now *is* a good time," he agreed, "we'll sleep through the rest of the day and travel at night." Avador knew that everyone needed sleep more than anything. He couldn't remember when it was the last time they slept.

"There is also something else." Stone reached out and grasped Avador by the wrist. The Elf looked at him questioningly. "The northern plains are inhabited."

"They are? By *who*?" Avador looked around at the endless sea of ashen grassland and saw no houses or any type of dwelling.

"Ogres." The young Elf looked at Stone to see if he was serious. Stone looked back as if to say, 'do I joke?'

"I have only *heard* of them by my father."

"I know first-hand of them Elfling. Your father and I encountered a few during our travels." Stone looked up at the sky and released a sigh. "They're huge, eight to nine feet in height and strong like oxen in their prime. But they're also *stupid*. We didn't kill any; we merely escaped by tricking them." By now everyone gathered around the Dwarf to listen.

"If they live here," Eviathane interrupted, "why don't we see any?"

"They are *north* of here, about a day's march. But that is not to say they won't venture into this area." Stone replied.

"Yes." Said Falstaff. "Look at *us*. We are not from around here either, what stopped us from coming?"

"The difference between us and them, Shortbeard, is that if they see *us*, they'll want our blood." Stone watched as Falstaff nodded and withdrew from the conversation. "That's why we decided to travel at night. Our little lack of sleep was a blessing in disguise."

Avador led the group to the area where the taller patches waved in the rushing winds.

"We'll sleep here," he said and dropped his pack into the grass that stood just above his hips. Sleep... it was reaching at him like ghostly tendrils, there was nothing he wanted more. "I'll take first watch."

The little group made no arguments as they laid out their blankets and prepared themselves for the much-awaited slumber. Avador watched as each man surrendered one by one to the long-needed and relieving sleep. *They could not stay awake even if they wanted to.* The Elf smiled and rubbed his face with both hands. Fighting the urge to sleep, he imagined, was harder than fighting an Ogre.

It was two hours later when Avador awakened Stone to relieve him of his watch. The sun was still hours away from disappearing under the eastern horizon. The Dwarf rose with the discipline of the soldier he was, but his eyes were red and stinging with the need of more sleep. Stone reached for his flask to splash water on his face but thought better of it recalling their water supply was scarce. Instead he nodded to Avador and the Elf wrapped himself in his cloak, sleep taking him almost at once.

Falstaff's eyes were sticky and burning. Why did he tell Eviathane that it was okay and that he would take the watch *for* him? *He* never stood guard before. What was he *thinking*? He took a glance over at the big man as he snored quietly under his travel blanket. *Oh well,* he thought, *might as well let him enjoy his rest. I can sleep again later.* The young mage narrowed his eyes at the all-too-brilliant sun. It had moved further across the sky showing him that he *must* have slept a few hours at least. He decided to take out his book and study. But after a minute, the words became distorted and muddled. Falstaff shook his head and replaced the large volume back in its pack deciding that it was not a good idea to read himself to sleep.

The wind had died down, Falstaff noticed. It became a light breeze, soft and soothing. The mage felt a slight pain in his spine from hunching too much as he sat amidst his slumbering friends. He laid flat on his back to stretch his sore spine. He heard a tiny *snap*; it felt nice. The last thing he remembered seeing was the tall grass swaying rhythmically in the gentle breeze...

The bottom half of a crimson sun was embedded into the western horizon when the Ogres discovered the slumbering party. They wasted no time taking advantage of this unbeliev-able stroke of luck. Five sleeping little peoples, *that* is enough to feed ten hungry Ogres.... isn't it?

With scarcely a sound, the Ogres seized upon the sleeping companions by throwing crude nets over them. They awoke but were able to do nothing as they were immediately entangled. They were screaming things in their strange language that the Ogres found to be nothing but gibberish. It didn't re-ally matter. Their weapons were seized in moments and soon they will be food.

The short plump hairy one was tangled in one net with a taller more slender little person. A thin one was put together with another slightly thinner one. One, larger than the rest was fixed into his own net. Without a doubt, this was a great stroke of luck... and just as the day was ending too.

"Avador!" Stone was trying to ignore the pain of having the Elf's knee pushing into his ribs. "Elfling! Can you hear me?"

"Yes." Avador was also feeling pain. His hair was being pulled tight around his temples. It was caught into the nets fastened opening and they were being carried roughly into darkness.

"If you struggle they will kill you. The Dwarf's voice was laboured. "*These* are Ogres."

Avador instinctively reached for a dagger that wasn't there. "Where are they taking us?" The Elf didn't get an answer. Instead he heard the unnerved screaming of Nectario somewhere to his right. "Don't fight!" Avador shouted. "Don't fight or they will kill you." He didn't know what else to say... or if he was even heard. The only thing he knew is that he had just experienced the most violent awakening of his life. It was all a blur of movements and silhouetted attackers in near darkness. Whatever these Ogres were, they were fast... fast and silent.

Tigran Eviathane was enraged. He did not like being in a net and half dragged half carried into obscurity. *Especially* after experiencing the sweetest sleep he's ever had. What he liked even less was being stripped of his weapons and manhandled. Whoever these *things* are, they are going to pay terribly. Just as he tried shaking himself free he felt a sudden jolt and a swift moment of midair suspension. The next thing he felt was being rammed onto the ground as something screamed at him in the most unattractive tongue he has ever heard. A hot pain shot at him from his hip and he went limp. It became immediately harder to breathe as he felt his side scraping against the ground. Then, everything went completely black and he simply didn't feel anymore.

~****~

The hours were incessantly endless. The little group, cramped into unsophisticated nets and suffering the continual bobbing and jerking of the Ogre's uneven paces, were in agony like never before. Darkness was all they could see. Direction was lost. Every now and again they would hear an Ogre speak to another in an unrefined tongue. They were getting the sense of what they looked like just by their coarse, ugly speech.

Falstaff's head was throbbing. Even when Nectario's frantic screaming developed into light whimpering, the dull ache remained. If there was ever a moment he wanted to be dead, it was right now. How could he have been so *stupid* to fall asleep? How could he have done this to his friends? He was just beginning to pray for a cliff for the Ogres to throw him off when his net was suddenly dropped harshly onto the ground. He saw stars when one of Nectario's heels struck him in the eye.

Avador's eyes were piercing through the night. He could make out the Ogre's figures as they left the nets where they were dropped and began to move about. They *were* huge. The young Elf stretched his neck from the odd angle it was in to get a better view. *What were they doing?* Suddenly he saw a spark. They were setting camp. Within moments a fire was made. He saw trees. They were leafless and black, eerie gnarled things. Where had they been taken?

"Stone…. Stone answer me." Avador dared an almost inaudible whisper.

"Here Elfling." The Dwarf breathlessly replied with difficulty.

"Any ideas?"

"Can you see our weapons?" Avador strained to lift his head off the ground. He saw a total of eight Ogres sitting next to the fire. To the right of them near one of the twisted trees was a small bundle or a pile of something. The firelight caught something metal and it reflected into Avador's eyes.

"I think so. But I can't be sure."

"Then pray we'll have a chance to reach them." Stone's voice trailed off and Avador knew he was hurt. He quit talking trying to give the Dwarf a chance to regain his strength.

The Elf looked around desperately. He saw Falstaff and Nectario huddled together in their net, their chests moving as they breathed. He was relieved they were still alive. He then proceeded to look for Tigran. The big man wasn't near the others. He must be around his other side where he hadn't looked yet. It crossed his mind to ask Stone to check his blind side but thought better of it. With great effort Avador shifted his body so he could look over Stone's chest, which was blocking his view. Nothing. There was no one on his other side. He couldn't have been that bundle he saw by the tree; it was too small. Then with a sickening realization, he discovered that Eviathane was not with them.

~****~

The first things Tigran felt was a searing pain in his right hip and numbness from his ankles and wrists. The blackness had now become a light so bright that it hurt to open his eyes. When he finally felt the ability to blink them open, the stinging sensation he experienced forced him to close them even tighter. The sun had returned. How long was he unconscious? *What is happening?* His mind was racing and it felt like a thousand galloping horses were inside his head. Regardless, he needed to know his situation and decided to bear the pain and open his eyes.

The first thing he saw when his vision recovered was the ground. It was about ten feet below him. A deep red blotch stained the earth underneath him and red drops were slowly being added to it... blood. It was *his* blood. The realization jerked him into greater attention. He looked up and found his wrists and ankles tied to long lengths of rope that dangled from knots firmly tied to thick branches of a black gnarled tree. He had been stripped of all his clothes. Blood was leaking slowly from a wound in his abdomen and trickled down his ribs and over his chest. He felt the warm wetness of his blood running down his throat and off his ear. His hair was tangled and sticky with his own blood, the long black length of it waved below him like the dark standard of death. *The bastards are bleeding me*, Tigran thought gravely. Panic was a heartbeat away.

The big man looked around frantically. He was alone, alone with the gnarled tree. How did he get separated from everybody? Where were his attackers? He tried desperately to find his bearings but the world was literally upside down. *Calm yourself, Tigran.* Eviathane was at a loss. He never felt so much fear. Even diving into an entire camp of Dark Dwarves was preferable.

The wind picked up from a direction Eviathane was unsure of. Its cool touch was somewhat relaxing, considering his predicament. Through the keen glare of the rising sun, Tigran could make out the plains in which they had been travelling. How far was he carried and to what direction? He was beginning to get light-headed and more than a little dizzy. The pain in his abdomen flared with the increasing winds. He retched abruptly and involuntarily. He felt the veins in his forehead pulsating and his throat burning as he choked and gasped for air. The sounds of the wind and his ragged breathing were the only things he could hear. He did *not* want to die like this.

The minutes turned to hours. His shadow had moved from one place to the next as time tortured him slowly and crept mockingly by his hanging body. Tigran tried for what must have been the millionth time to free himself; each time was an agonizing attempt that grew weaker with every effort. Frustration grew intense within him and the tears finally burst from his eyes.

"Damn you!" His scream sailed into the wind reaching nothing. "Damn you all, you sons of whores!" Eviathane wept as he dangled, a helpless swinging piece of meat drying in the sun. His tongue seemed too large for his mouth; the need for water was unbearable. *Where are you all?* The thought of his friends seemed to stab his heart. *Please do not be suffering like this.* His head felt like it was about to burst.

Suddenly, he heard a sound. It was a noise like an animal grunting. Where did it come from? Was it real or just his burning imagination? Hysterically he swung himself and tried to see what it was. At first he saw nothing, just the endless plains that spread all around him. But when he turned his head again, his heart stopped in his chest. He was almost face to face with an Ogre that stood mere inches below his head. Eviathane froze at the unexpected terror. The thing was all muscle. Its huge round head bare of any hair with only two slits for a nose and tiny pointed ears. Two long fangs protruded from its lower jaw and flanked its thin curling upper lip. Its skin had a yellowish tinge with light brown spots without pattern.

Tigran saw a giant wooden cudgel resting on one of its

hunching shoulders and a long makeshift spear in its strong, clawed hand. At first it did nothing, simply staring at Evia-thane as if sizing him up. Its breath was rotten and did nothing to help Tigran's feeling of nausea. But eventually it placed a giant hand behind Eviathane's head and pulled him close. It sniffed at him causing the big man to cringe with disgust. Then it turned his head and barked out its horrible language. Eviathane, with added dread, saw that it was speaking to another of its kind. He hadn't noticed it before; his attention was utterly on this one that was evaluating him. Its partner snarled something back at it and stomped off over a ridge and disappeared.

The Ogre took a pace backward and raised its sight to Tigran's wounded abdomen. It seemed to have been thinking about something. Then, with an abrupt jab with his long spear, he prodded Tigran's crusting wound and the blood trickled faster. Eviathane's scream resounded across the plains.

~****~

"Did you hear that?" Avador whispered sharply under his net that now seemed to have increased in weight.

"Hear what?" Stone's voice was ragged and dry.

"I heard a scream coming from the distance."

"No, Elfling. I heard nothing." Stone spoke quickly now noting the Ogre turning its grotesque head away from its huddled company and glare at them in warning. "You think its Eviathane?" He said hushing his words. Avador hoped it wasn't.

"We have to find a way out of here." The Elf spoke softly and glanced over to where Falstaff and Nectario still lay under there thick net.

"Sooner than you think Elfling." They won't leave us here forever, shortly they will decide how to divide us and then it will all be over." Stone's face was grim in the fading light.

"What is...?" Avador didn't finish his question. An Ogre snuck up beside his net and gave him a rough kick to his ribs. He and Stone rolled from the impact nearer to Falstaff and Nectario in a tangled heap. Avador was struggling to regain his breath.

"Shades!" Falstaff hissed. "Are you okay Avador?" The Elf allowed himself a brief pause to recover. Then he merely nodded and winced in pain as he put a finger to his lips and a hand to his ribs.

I must find a way to get us out of this hell trap. Avador thought. *I can't let them die like this. Eviathane, please be alive.* The pain in his ribs forced tears to seep from his eyes.

The sun had left Eviathane abandoned to hang in darkness with his life draining slowly from his body. He began to believe that his fate had crept up on him and threatened to come to pass as a lifeless dangling piece of meat for the Ogres to feast on. The moon skulked in and out of swiftly moving clouds providing him quick dismal glances of what has become of him. Hope deserted him completely. Or closer to the truth, *he* has deserted hope.

It had become increasingly difficult to even breathe, something Tigran has been doing since birth. The scarlet puddle below him, revealed from time to time by the evil moon as it broke free from its cloudy prison, grew in size with each passing. Tigran Eviathane, strong as he was, became limp as he swayed involuntarily, the thick branches above creaking as he did so. The clouds were gone now, leaving in their absence the moons eerie light to reign over Eviathane.

His eyes were open, or at least he *thought* they were. Everything was hazy. Sometimes he would blink and dark grey spots would glide before his eyes like sailboats moving smoothly in distant waters. The low creaking above him had become incessant yet calming in a strange sort of way. He was so tired... so very tired. Why not just let go of everything and stop breathing altogether? The flashes of grey continued their games that they were playing on his hallucinating eyes. Things seemed to move in the far off distance. What was once upside down had become natural to him now. This is how things have *always* been... was it not?

Eviathane felt a hysterical laughter brewing inside him. There were too many visions moving before him. All pain had gone now, but his sight was there. He wished he had lost his sight along with the pain. Even his own mind was taunting him. The laughter came now. He reasoned: if he was to die, he might as well die with a smile. Another apparition had come. This one last vision increased his amusement: two little dots were heading his way... and, was that a *mule* floating between them?

I t hurt them when the Ogres strung the little group upside down. It hurt them even more when they struggled. They never *imagined* such strength. They were played with as if they were lifeless dolls jostled by horrible children.

It wasn't enough that they were violently ensnared while sleeping and carried off to wallow in a pool of their own fear. It also wasn't enough that they were forced into silence under heavy nets that seemed to gain weight with every passing hour. They were furthermore subjected to watch as the Ogres feasted on what remained of a poor wretched traveller that must have lost his way and stumbled into Ogre territory. The companions observed in horror at the way they ignored the blondish hairs that were still left on the scalp and how they crunched on the bones that made their skin crawl with every bite the Ogres took. It didn't take long to realize that *this* meal would not suffice all the Ogres; they would need more food soon.

Now they were hanging upside down from the branches of these black trees, stripped of all their clothing and jabbed in the stomach with long sharp spikes so that they could bleed freely. They saw their fate. It was devoured within minutes. Soon, they ceased to struggle; it hurt more when they moved. At times, when the wind picked up they would sway helplessly, listening to each other's gasps as they separately fought to breathe.

Avador felt the stings on his blistering wrists and ankles as they sweat under the coarse rope. If the Ogres, he thought, were indeed stupid, they still knew how to hang a person in such a way that they could not struggle for long. The only thing he could do was frantically look around and realized how vulnerable they all were. He caught glimpses of all his friends and felt the added pain of failing them. *Tigran, where are you? I have failed you too, my brother. I am sorry.* The tears flowed and streamed from the corners of his eyes and down his forehead blurring his vision. He blinked them away and saw their things scattered everywhere. The Ogres had left but he did not see which direction they took.

He was sure they would return.

His blood trickled over his torso, as did the others, and dripped slowly onto the ground below them. The feeling was sickening. How much longer can they hang like this and stay alive? Everything was going numb. Soon it felt as if he had no legs. He knew that he did but still looked up every now and then just to make sure.

Falstaff's mind was racing. There was an immense pain in his lower abdomen and hot blood was seeping from it. The young mage, stripped of literally everything, pride included, wished for the death that was coming too slowly. It was *him* that allowed all this to happen. *He* was to blame and he could not take it. He refused to look at the other's faces, even when they were stuck under the Ogre's nets. He was afraid of the looks they would surely return him. How could he make this right again? A spell? Would that save them? It might if one would ever enter his memory. All those years of studying that confounded book were reduced to nothing. His shame is held accountable for that. His pride had been peeled away only to reveal that disgusting shame that glowed like a thousand candles and threatened to burn him until he died.

So why was he struggling to breathe if he wanted his life to end? Hope? Hope that he could found a way to save his friends and restore his dignity? No. Something more made him struggle. No one else stopped. Why should *he*? Is that what he really wanted? To die willingly just so he no longer feels his disgrace? That would only immortalize his shame. He would stay alive for as long as he could and help his friends get out of this predicament. *Magic*, he thought, a passage from his book reaching out to him, *magic, like water, trickles through crevices until it finds a place to settle...*

Suddenly, the Ogres returned seemingly out of nowhere. How many were there? It seemed like half were missing but it was difficult to tell from their position. Fear had returned anew. Was this *it*? Would they finish them off *now*? The Ogres were tramping the ground like maddened beasts. Suddenly one struck another with a clawed hand and they all burst into hysteria at once. Dust and grass was thrown in the air, the sound of their fighting was unbearable; it made the feeling of helplessness double in magnitude. The feeble company *saw* now what the Ogres can do if they are angered. Merciless were their attacks and with unbelievable strength. One would throw another to the ground with a force that would instantly kill a human. But the Ogres would return to their feet only to counter with another strike.

The group watched with horror from where they dangled mere inches above the battling Ogres. At times one would be thrown on his back and forced to use his feet to fight off his attacker. They felt the putrid breath of the Ogres as they wailed in frustration just below their heads only to return to the fight so as not to get struck by a massive cudgel or clawed from behind.

What caused all this? Why did they turn on each other? Were they also to take out their frustrations on *them*? Falstaff lost all the concentration that he managed to muster. He was struck by blows that went astray, as did the others. They were forced to painfully sway like pendulums in the wind. The screams of the Ogres became deafening and the sound of their grotesque language chilled their blood.

Just as the party thought the skirmish increased in enormity and their end was near, the fighting stopped. The dust settled and the companions noticed that the Ogre's attention turned somewhere else. The sound of a galloping horse reached their ears and it was getting louder as it neared. Abruptly two arrows struck an Ogre in the chest. And then another flew into a second. The Ogres screamed in rage and pulled the arrows out and flung them away as if they were mere sticks.

The horse was in sight now and so was its rider. The archer nocked another arrow as the horse carried him closer to the enraged Ogres. Avador strained to see as a thick trail of dust thrashed into the wind behind the galloping horse. Its rider fired the arrow and led the horse to run in a great circle around the scattering of gnarled trees.

The Ogres went immediately into action. Gone now was the reason they fought each other. The only thing that mattered was that more food was running around them in a blur of brown and dark green. The only problem was that it was shooting things at them and they did not like it. With a movement quicker than anyone expected, one of the Ogres threw himself at the horse as it tried to run by him. It didn't make it as the Ogre heaved its great shoulder and sent the horse off its stride and caused it to stumble onto its lower jaw. The horse nearly folded in half and its rider flew off rolling into its dust.

There was a sound of steel sliding on steel. Without warning the rider appeared through the dust brandishing a sword and dagger, its cloak billowing in the wind. The companions saw who it was.

"*Myia.*" Avador breathed, astonishment showing unmistakably on his face.

Stone was struggling once again. His muscles strained as he pulled at the taut ropes that kept him suspended in mid air. He saw what was happening down below: Myia Feo-Dosia had somehow returned to the Plains of Paladin and found them. Now she was going to get herself killed trying to rescue them. She might have bought them some time but that was *all*. Sooner or later the Ogres will catch her and she'll be in the same predicament. Fury welled up inside Stone Warhelm like molten lava ready to burst from every crevice. His scream echoed loudly into everyone's ears. The Ogres stopped moving at the suddenness. Myia was in a tree faster than anyone can react, her dagger already cutting through the ropes that held Avador Andor.

The young Elf was suddenly free. Myia bound from one tree to the next, her blade relentlessly slicing the coarse ropes. Avador was on the ground, naked and taunting the Ogres.

*See if you can catch me **now** you bastards!* Avador ignored the searing pain in his gut and unbelievably shook off the deadness in his limbs. The chance to undo his friend's death sentence propelled him into an adrenalin rush that sent him in miraculous motion. He moved between the flabbergasted Ogres with the agility of a wild cheetah. In turn they dove and reached for the nimble Elf finding emptiness and air as they grabbed at nothing. They howled in frustration. All they wanted was the incessant Elf who wouldn't let them catch him. Myia had freed the rest of the group noting that Eviathane was missing. Quickly they gathered their weapons and proceeded to move to Avador's side when something stopped them: The Ogres had once again started fighting each other. They all wanted to be the one who caught the Elf. *This* was their chance.

"Avador!" Stone screamed as he gathered his things from the ground. The Elf was already dashing towards the assembling group. Before the Ogres realized what had happened, the little group had taken back their clothes and weapons and disappeared over a ridge and into the hills.

~****~

"Why is he hanging up there?" Badom asked Bogdan.

"Ssh." Bogdan hissed to silence his friend. "You don't recognize him?" He asked in a hushed tone. The other looked up again.

"No." He said plainly. Bogdan gave Badom a look and shook his head.

"That's the big human who was with the group that paid us in Vor!" He said with decreasing patience. Badom wrinkled his high forehead and closed one eye.

"Ah, never mind." Bogdan was exasperated. "Let's just get him down."

"Is he dead?" Badom asked.

"I don't think so, his chest is moving a little… see?" Badom thought he was wrong and that it was *not* moving but after a moment he saw that he was right.

"How are we going to get him down?"

"Unload the mule. I'll climb up there and cut the ropes."

"But isn't he just going to fall on his head?" Badom was inquiring more than Bogdan had wanted.

"Just do it!" Bogdan snapped. Badom began unloading without another word as Bogdan climbed the gnarled tree and took out his little knife. "Hmm. This is quite the trap, isn't it?"

Bogdan scratched at his patchy beard as he evaluated how he was to cut the big man down. He noted his legs were tied with individual ropes that stretched higher in the taller branches. His arms were tied in the same way but to the lower branches of the black tree. Each rope was as taut as a bowstring. He looked down to see if Badom finished unloading the mule.

"Why are we unloading? We're not staying here." Badom shouted up to his friend in the tree.

"Are *you* going to catch this guy when he drops or am I?" Bogdan was about to speak once again when something caught his attention. Something moved on the plains east of where they were. Two yellowish creatures a lot bigger than Eviathane were moving at a quick pace in the Gnome's direction.

"Ogres." Bogdan hissed to his friend below.

"Where?" Badom couldn't see over the ridge.

"Unburden the mule *now* Badom or I'll make you regret you ever knowing me." Badom moved now with a lot more haste while Bogdan cut frantically at the ropes attached to Tigran's legs. With an abrupt lurch, the big man fell like dead weight only to swing from his arms that were still tied to the coarse ropes.

Bogdan dared a quick glance at where he saw the Ogres. They were a lot closer now climbing up towards the ridge; their awful voices were now audible. Badom (with the miracle of some god) understood what Bogdan was planning and positioned the mule under the hanging Eviathane. The mule's back rested perfectly between Tigran's dangling legs. Bogdan was moving now. He was trying to reach the lower branches without falling off the tree. His knife reached the remaining ropes and he cut them loose. The little Gnome heard the big man slump onto the mule, which took a few side steps at the sudden weight. Somehow Tigran remained on the mule, his arms and legs hanging on either side of the animal.

Bogdan was off the tree and throwing his newly acquired

length of rope around Eviathane's back and under the mule's belly.

"Get his things." He whispered to Badom frantically tying Tigran as best he could with the little time he had. Bogdan heard the sound of large feet scraping the ground just on the other side of the ridge. "Never mind, let's go!"

The Ogres arrived eagerly at their new catch only to find long lengths of rope hanging off their branches and swaying gently in the light breeze. Their minds literally stopped working when they saw a large mound of pots and sacks scattered under the tree. One actually had the thought of following their food's trail but the idea left when the other slapped him on the back of the head which prompted an all-out brawl between them.

~****~

Nectario flinched at the tightening of his bandages. Myia Feo-Dosia looked at his face. His once gleaming eyes have lost their lustre. That was the *first* thing she noticed. She looked around at the others that were huddled within a concave section embedded under a bowed ridge in the plains terrain. The wind sang above them, at least helping to drown out their voices. Their faces were dark and grim, which was normal. How else were they supposed to look after staring at the face of a horrible death and then cheating it by mere moments?

Avador's head was bowed, his chin touching his bare chest as he sat with his back to the soft hollow of the ridge. His fingers brushed gingerly at the hilt of the sword he nearly lost. Everything had happened too fast. He looked at the group as they chanced this much-needed rest. Unlike his body, his mind was moving: Somewhere, out there in the fading light, was Eviathane. Should he leave the group here and scout for him *now*? Should he wait for them to rest and head out together? No. It can't be safe for them to be here forever. Sooner or later they would be discovered. The Elf was at a loss. Slowly, quietly, Avador pulled his dirt covered mailed tunic over his bandaged torso, the glimmering violet barely noticeable. Then he reached for his thick travelling cloak and wrapped it about his shoulders. Myia saw the movement and walked over on her knees to him not wanting to stand, as it would risk showing her head above the low ridge.

"How are you feeling?" Her voice was quiet and sweet. Avador could not put the voice to the intrepid Wood Elf that sprang not too long ago from tree to gnarled tree after crashing into the Ogres' death trap on horseback.

"How did you find us?" Avador asked ignoring her question. Myia smiled before answering.

"You have a lot to learn about Wood Elves, brave Andor." She sat next to him. "We arrived to Pelendria, just as you directed. Everything you said had come to pass: The river, the forest. My people survived because of your guidance. We were welcomed to your village the moment we arrived." Myia saw the Elf's eyes light up with the mention of her being there. She noted this. "All is at peace there, Avador. All rejoiced at the news of your survival." Avador's heart was about to erupt.

"My mother..."

"Is a beautiful woman." Myia finished for him smiling like a child. "I told her what you said. She loves you very much young Andor." Myia's eyes matched Avador's in brightness. "She gave me this to give to you." Her hand came up holding something that dangled from a silver chain. Avador recognized it at once.

"*Andor.*" Avador breathed, his eyes widening at a circular amulet held before him. Tears built up under his lids, ready to overflow. He reached up and took it in his hand. The amulet was deep blue with a black tree in its centre. Grandalimus wore it in times of war, he had once told Avador. He used it to bring his men to attention. The Elf turned it to see its profile. It had an indent at either side like tiny channels entering the amulet. Avador trembled as he placed it over his head letting it dangle just below his chest. This wasn't meant for him, he thought, this was his *father's*.

"I had said to the others that I was leaving in search for you the same day we arrived." Myia continued. "They wanted me to stay, afraid for my safety. But they knew I was not changing my mind. Others offered to come with me but I knew that speed and stealth was what I needed to get to you."

"So you didn't rest either." Avador looked at her with admiration.

"I am resting *now*." Myia said and let her head drop back against the ridge wall. "The people of your village gave me supplies for my journey. Someone named *Wylme* gave me the horse." Avador thought that no matter what else happens, *nothing* would have surprised him more than Myia's last statement.

"What? *Wylme* gave you his horse?" Avador was shocked. Myia's look showed that she expected this reaction.

"He said that this act is his apology to you. It was indeed a good horse, Avador. It travelled quickly and with little rest. Without it, I would not have reached you in time." Avador was staring at nothing. *Wylme helped save their lives.* He looked at the others. Finally they began to stir.

"Tigran." The Elf said abruptly. "We must find him." Myia did not dispute this. Instead she gathered her travel pack and began putting things back in. Avador stopped her

185

momentarily by putting a hand to her wrist. "Thank you for coming back to us." Myia smiled and continued to pack the replenished food and other supplies. Soon, the others had stood from their resting places with renewed energy and morale.

"We have a brother to find, Elfling." Stone's voice had returned to him out of nowhere. Avador grinned and put a thankful hand on the Dwarf's shoulder. He glanced at Falstaff and Nectario who nodded back to him with rekindled spirits. Together they emptied out of the concealing ridge and into the deepening gloom to find Tigran Eviathane.

~****~

The Gnomes were in their own predicament. They were miles from where they left the Ogres to quarrel amongst themselves, safe for the moment. But that only meant that they were miles from their food and supplies. Bogdan stared at the tiny fire that burned between him and Badom. Tigran lay a few feet to his left. Both Gnomes had removed their cloaks to cover the big man and so they huddled a little closer to the feeble heat of the tiny flames. Bogdan dripped a little water from his flask onto a torn piece of cloth. At least the flasks had straps, he thought, and they had them on themselves when they fled. He dabbed the cloth on Eviathane's cracked lips letting a little moisture enter his dry mouth. His breathing seemed to have grown a little steadier.

"How is he now?" Badom's voice was a whisper in the night.

"He lost a lot of blood," Bogdan answered, "but he is strong... *very* strong to have survived the Ogres."

"He needs his clothes." Badom said straightforwardly. Bogdan merely nodded. "I'll go and get them."

186

"Stay right where you are." Bogdan's voice rose to a higher pitch. "You feel like getting killed?"

"But you said Ogres don't travel at night." Badom was insistent.

"I said they *hate* travelling at night, now stop talking." Bogdan thought the argument was over but he soon realized when Badom was moving to the mule that he had in fact *lost* the dispute.

"It's not *that* far. I will return before night's end. You stay here with the man." With that, the little Gnome tugged slightly at the mule's reins making a clucking sound with his mouth. The mule hesitated a moment but then took its first steps behind the already moving Badom. Moments later they merged into the dark and the sound of their footfalls disappeared altogether. Bogdan sighed and reached over to dab the damp cloth at Eviathane's lips.

~****~

Avador led the group through the darkness. They stayed close to each other feeling the open air hit them on their exposed sides. Most of them could see nothing but blackness and depended on the sound of the Elf's footfalls to guide them. Avador secretly favoured the fact that the moon had not come out of the thick clouds that hung stagnant above the Plains of Paladin. The Ogres couldn't see them. He and Myia could at least pierce the night's darkness with the others following closely.

The young Elf led them as close as he would dare to where they left the Ogres. There he found their tracks. Quickly he moved over to Stone.

"Somewhere nearby is where the Ogres parted with Tigran."

Avador watched as the Dwarf squinted in the darkness. "I am trying to decipher from the direction they were heading..."

"North, Elfling. They took us north." Stone interrupted. "Far in the distant northwest, when the clouds parted briefly, I saw a glimpse of the tips of the Ruk Mountains. They were far ahead but to our left side. The Ogres must have parted with Eviathane further back." The Dwarf pointed with his hammer in a southern direction. Avador kneeled and studied the trampled grass, and then turned the group in the direction the tracks were coming from. *He was far away.* The Elf was thinking. *I just barely heard his scream. But I **will** find him.*

They headed south for nearly two hours when Avador stopped them abruptly. Again he kneeled to study the earth. Another set of tracks indeed separated from the ones they had been following; there were fewer Ogres, Avador determined. They branched off from the original northern course to take on a more northwestern route. Avador was on his feet and once again the little group followed. His pace quickened and the blood seemed to flow faster in his veins. *At the end of this trail... we'll find Eviathane.* The rest of his thought, that he might be dead, was pushed aside by gritted teeth.

Badom led the little mule as fast as he would dare towards the area that enclosed the black gnarled trees. The darkness hindered his progress but determination became his guide. He was getting closer. He and the loyal animal moved without making a sound through the gloomy plains, his thoughts were constantly on the likelihood that the Ogres might still be there. Their flight *from* that ghastly place was at a much faster pace; he tried to estimate how much longer before he arrives. Before he could calculate, he saw the horizon curve slightly upwards when the moon's feeble light filtered faintly through the thick clouds. The twisted trees appeared before him as silhouettes on a dark grey background.

The Gnome froze in his tracks, the mule imitating him a moment after. Nothing moved ahead. Was it because there was no one there or because they were sleeping under the trees? Badom left the mule to stand motionless where it halted. Ever so slowly he crept over the remaining distance towards the trees all the while listening for any sounds that might warn him of any threat. He found it difficult to hear anything above the heartbeats in his ears but he made it to the top of the rise without incident. No Ogres seemed to be in the area but his fear kept him as quiet as possible.

The Human's weapons and clothing were scattered over the darkened ridge, which made it frustrating for the Gnome as he tried to decipher which was most important to take back with him. He did *not* want to be here any longer than he had to. He decided he should only take the weapons, clothing and food.

With somewhat of a plan laid out, Badom began to carry things back to the mule. He found the sack with their rations and slumped it as quietly as he could over the mules drooped back. Eviathane's sword was, remarkably, still near the tree where he was hung and that too went into the large bag. Badom cursed to himself at the deep gloom that hindered his progress, his imagination bringing Ogre breath on the back of his neck. He thought he saw Tigran's large shield and other forms of armour but decided against carrying anything cumbersome. He then collected what he could, or at least what he *thought* was Tigran's clothes, and decided to take no more risks... it was time to leave.

As Badom took his first step to exit the grounds, he kicked a tin pot that he never noticed before. To him, the clanging sound it made was deafening in contrast to the silence he tried so hard to keep.

"Shah's Beard," he cursed impulsively.

~****~

Something brought Avador to a halt. The sound was unmistakable. Even the others heard it.

"Someone is there," he whispered scanning the area ahead. The trees stood unmoving not fifty yards before them. But something else *was* in motion. The Elf penetrated the darkness with his keen eyes. A small figure was hustling towards an unmoving animal. *Is that a donkey?* Avador spotted two creatures that greatly dwarfed the smaller one... and they were giving chase. Avador's bow was nocked in an instant. "Let's move!" He shouted and pulled back the string.

The arrow flew and found its target. The Ogre grasped at his neck and staggered, losing a few paces. It screamed in fury. Myia had already drawn her arrow and sent it soaring into the second creature. It too howled as it watched its would-be catch gain some distance between them. There was a sound of ringing steel in the night as Avador released the *Kingblade* from its scabbard and ran full on towards the Ogres. Stone Warhelm was at his heels, his mind void of anything save for the borderline insanity of attacking these Ogres. Nectario followed, scimitar in his hand and fear rushing through him like a surge of fire.

Avador was the first to reach the enraged Ogres, his blade slicing at the leg of the nearest. The beast wailed as blood sprayed everywhere. Stone's hammer was swinging in a great sweep smashing into the other's knee. A loud *crack* was heard as the Ogre doubled over in unexpected pain. The Ogres were caught unawares by attackers that came out of nowhere in a rush of pain and shock. Avador leapt high in the air plunging the *Kingblade* deep into the Ogre's stomach. It toppled where it stood. Nectario, renewed with courage, moved behind the Ogre that was struck by Stone swinging his scimitar in deadly swipes to the Ogre's exposed back. The cuts would have killed a lesser being instantly. But the Ogre was no lesser being. It reached at the attacking bard and grabbed him by the throat and proceeded to squeeze the life out of him. Nectario dropped his blade and dangled helplessly in the creature's steel grip.

Stone Warhelm saw the bard's dilemma and with a battle cry that resonated across the plains, he leapt towards the kneeling Ogre that held Nectario. Holding his hammer with both hands above his head and still in mid air, the powerful Dwarf brought it down on the Ogre's thick neck. There was a crunching of spine and the beast slumped forward dropping the bard on the ground. Nectario gasped and crawled backwards away from the creature as Stone smashed his hammer repeatedly into the Ogre's head until it stopped moving altogether.

Avador jerked the *Kingblade* free of the Ogre's belly and bound to one side, a clawed hand missing the agile Elf by inches. The Ogre limped after him reaching with both hands. Blood was spouting from his mouth but anger was still on its revolting face. Avador was about to retreat but threw himself back towards the hobbling Ogre once again surprising it with the unexpected movement. The *Kingblade* found its belly once again burying itself to the hilt. The Ogre's blood showered Avador in a spray of hot liquid as the beast collapsed on top of him. It shuddered momentarily and then stopped moving completely.

Falstaff reached the battleground just as the fighting ended. He was kneeling by the fallen Ogre that pinned Avador to the ground. Thrusting his hands underneath the dead creature, he tried in vain to relieve some of the weight from the young Elf. Stone and Nectario were instantly at his side pulling and tugging at the Ogre's enormous shoulder. Together it lifted enough for Avador to squirm free dragging a bloodied *Kingblade* with him. The three fighters slumped onto the ground next to each other breathing heavily.

"Y-you, you saved my life." Nectario said to Stone nearly out of breath. The Dwarf said nothing for a moment catching a look from Avador. Was that a smile on his face?

"Even *you* are a part of my duty, bard." Stone found it difficult not to grin, as did the others. There was a moment of silence until the others understood Stone's discomfort.

"What better way to learn how to use a sword then in battle?" Avador added in Nectario's defence and patted the burly Dwarf on the shoulder. Strangely, this brought on an unanticipated laughter from everyone. Then, Avador turned his attention to the bewildered Gnome who stood by his mule; he was still in shock that he was even alive. He walked over to them, Eviathane's clothes draped in his folded arms.

"Your friend is with us," Badom said almost inaudibly. Together they gathered the rest of Tigran's and the Gnomes things and loaded them onto the mule. Without another word, the little group followed the Gnome towards Tigran Eviathane.

~****~

Tigran awoke to see the face of Avador Andor looking worriedly down at him. At first he thought he was in a dream. Then with an abrupt movement, he reached up and grabbed the Elf by the collar of his cloak.

"Avador!" The big man managed to shout in utter shock.

"Easy, my friend," Avador said quietly, the smile on his face stretching across his cheeks, "you need to rest." Eviathane ignored the last statement and sat up fighting off a swirl of wooziness.

"What happened?" The big man noticed his clothes lying next to him; his own travel blanket fell from his muscular torso and covered him only from the waist down.

"Lie back down, big man," Avador pushed him gently onto his back and re-covered his chest. The young Elf knew that Tigran must have wondered how they were all back together again. "The Gnomes had found you hanging on the Ogre's trees, you were near death. And if that wasn't fortune enough, Myia had returned and rescued the rest of us."

"Myia?" Eviathane's surprise had just been amplified. He turned until he saw her smiling face in the firelight. He returned the smile and put his head back down. "This is all unbelievable."

"Don't be runnin' to celebrate just yet young fighter." The voice was Stone Warhelm's. The Dwarf waited for Eviathane to look over. "I am guessing that whoever is waiting at Land's End for the Dark Dwarf leader to return with news of his completed mission..."

"Skneeba." Falstaff added, partly to show Tigran that he was there too.

"Right, Skneeba, whatever. Anyway, I am speculating that he won't be waiting for much longer. We have lost costly time with the Ogres, time we can't afford." Stone let out a long sigh as if to emphasize the continuing burden of racing time. "If he returns to his master, our chances of discovery will be too great."

"We'll move towards the harbour as soon as we are *all* rested," said Avador.

"I agree Elfling, but keep in mind, we are still days away

from the coast. We have no idea how long Skneeba is permitted to linger at the docks. Were any of the other Dark Dwarves besides the leader informed of where their money waits? I do not think they would have gone to collect a pay for a job they did not complete, but how can we be sure if they didn't flee to at least give an excuse?"

Everyone knew that Stone was right. All they could do was gather up their courage so they could awaken in the morning to take on another day. A watch was set.

No one slept during the shifts.

The morning produced a gleaming sun and the smell of frying fish. Badom had awoken early and cooked for everyone before they once again parted ways. Stone and Avador watched the little Gnomes from a distance. Tigran was standing in front of them. The Gnomes heads reached just above the big man's waist, they were looking up at him. Eviathane kneeled on both knees. He bowed his head as if in prayer and then reached for Badom and pulled him in close. After a moment he did the same with Bogdan holding them both against his chest; his shoulders seemed to be trembling.

"I was wrong about Gnomes." Stone broke the momentary silence between Dwarf and Elf. Avador listened without taking his eyes off Eviathane's rescuers. "These little rodents gained my respect." Stone smirked at his last statement and looked at Avador with a little shine in his eyes.

"I guess we learn more with every passing day." The Elf smiled back and together they walked to where Falstaff was sitting near the Gnomes but far enough away to give Tigran the moment he needed. Myia and Nectario were busy with packing the supplies into a sturdy rucksack given to them by the Gnomes.

Stone waited a few moments before walking somewhat awkwardly towards the Gnomes. He too kneeled next to Eviathane. He said nothing. He merely gazed hard at Badom, then to Bogdan. They nodded slightly showing the Dwarf they understood. They smiled. He smiled back. Avador was the only one standing, arms across his chest. He seemed unaffected. But the fact that his eyes were wet betrayed any attempt to hide his emotions...

"Can you travel"? Falstaff was asking Eviathane.

"Of course I can travel." Tigran was trying to stand. No one had stopped him, partly so they could see just how stable he was. The big man stood to his full height. If he felt any dizziness, he had done a great job of covering it up. Eviathane was already adjusting his shield and sword when Avador moved next to him.

"Tigran... Brother," Avador's face was expressive, "do you know that I was half expecting to find you... to find..."

"We are *all* still together." Tigran had read the Elf's face perfectly, "and shouldn't we be moving ahead?" His smile stretched across his unshaven face. Avador shook his head and threw his arms around Tigran's broad frame clattering his still unstrapped armour.

The group once again parted ways with the Gnomes, both parties eager to leave these Ogre-infested territories. Stone Warhelm chose the direction needed to find Land's End and with a last farewell and good hopes, the company left the Gnomes to continue with their life-long journey.

"Land's End is half a day's travel beyond the last village before the shoreline. The village is simply called, 'North'." Stone spoke as he trudged beside Avador.

"How clever." Eviathane smirked as he interrupted the Dwarf, his eyes moving constantly for any signs of Ogre.

Stone ignored Tigran. "There, we can replenish any supplies and with a bit of luck, acquire some helpful information."

The hours went on without incident. The group stopped only for brief rests only to set out once again towards their goal. They did not know whether Skneeba will still be at Land's End, but there was no other choice than to push forward clinging on to a bare hope.

"East of here is the Timberline." Myia was the first to speak as they sat down for one of their short stops. "*If* it still remains," she added.

"What's the Timberline?" Tigran asked curiously.

"It's a thin column of trees protecting the entire northern edge of Feo-Dosia." It was Stone who answered. "There are cleverly hidden guard towers nestled in sporadic locations along the line." The Dwarf's face went grim. "How the Dwarven *dogs* managed to creep past unnoticed, is a bloody mystery."

No one spoke for long minutes. Eviathane sat near Stone and Myia and watched Falstaff rob a few precious moments to study from his big book. Tigran's heart swelled. *He wants to help as much as he could*, the big man thought. Avador was standing beside Nectario. They both had their swords drawn and it seemed the young Elf was giving the bard points on how to hold the hilt. "He *is* a good lad." Eviathane said finally.

"Aye," Stone agreed, "but I wish he wouldn't learn to shave on *our* faces."

Myia released a small chuckle. She stood and brushed off dry grass that clung to her pant legs and walked towards the large rucksack. Once again the short rest came to another end.

Eviathane stared after her, his mouth forming a stupid smile. Stone gave him a cuff on the back of his helmet.

"Wh- what was *that* for?" Eviathane was in shock.

"She's an *Elf*!"

"Yes, so?"

"You're... *not*!" Stone stood and walked away leaving Eviathane to readjust his helmet and laugh... it was all he could do, the Dwarf made sense from his own world of logic.

~****~

It was well into the evening when the companions could see the village of North. The plains were distinctly behind them and the terrain changed drastically to an earthier surface. The hamlet was built at a considerably lower elevation from where they stood, little yellow lights twinkling in its midst. It was small and it seemed as though the little structures could easily be counted.

"With any luck," Avador said still gazing at the village below, "we'll find good lodging there before we continue towards the sea."

"With any luck we'll get to have a good *bath*." Falstaff added wryly. With that, they began the short descent to where the village waited.

The structures were small and built of wood. Most of the inhabitants were indoors; those who were still outside gave the travellers suspicious looks and hurried away. The streets were narrow, some mere dirt pathways developed from the trampling of the townspeople. The only road that seemed wide enough for two wagons to pass was the road that led in and out of the village; one of its ends could be seen from the other.

The haggard group moved quietly down the main road that ran south to north in search for an inn. After a few moments of walking, it seemed that one did not exist here. But Stone kept moving, the others following quickly behind him. He turned right down one of the dirt pathways, at the end of which was a slightly taller building with weak amber lights in windows that ran two levels. The front entrance was set at the end of the trail, an unbalanced wooden sign hung over the opened door: '*The Pass*'. Stone entered first, the others a step behind.

The tiny tavern was badly lit by few candles set on three of its five empty tables. A barkeep, balding and broad chested watched as they entered and sat at one of the tables. He seemed unsure of what to do with this diverse looking crew.

Around a hidden corner, behind a thick wooden beam, a smaller table was set. At that table sat the bar's sole patron.

Skneeba was watching the newcomers from under narrowed eyelids.

B efore anyone decided to order, a round of ale was brought to the table by the wordless barkeep. The stout man simply placed the jug with six tin mugs onto the companion's table and disappeared through a curtained entryway behind the bar. No one said anything for a moment, stunned by the bartender's strange behaviour. Stone raised a full mug to his nose and sniffed. With a shrug he drained half its contents down his throat and wiped the foam from his thick moustache.

"Not *bad*." He said after noticing the stares from the rest of the group, "almost as good as the brew we mix in Pathen." The others decided that they would find out what is going on soon enough. For now, they just went with the current and drank what was given to them.

A full hour went by and the barkeep did not re-emerge. The flagon of ale had been drained but the company didn't seem to give it much attention. The conversation was spoken in hushed tones; their eyes moved mechanically for any signs of uninvited ears. Their plan seemed simple: get to the harbour of Land's End with the hopes of intercepting Skneeba. They would have to find him before he leaves to return to his master with news that may betray them. Then, they would improvise. After all, none of them know what the man even looks like. The *plan* was simple... *executing* it was the problem.

The voice came from nowhere. Their hands went instinctively to their weapons. *"You found the snake and you're **still** looking for its tracks?"* A tall hunched man, thin and robed in a black that made night seem pale was standing next to their table. His skin was dark beneath the cowl of his robes, his features impossible to make out. Slowly, a gaunt, twisted hand grasped the cowl's opening and removed it. The man gazed at the group with eyes that gave the impression of steel.

No one moved. They just sat staring dumbfounded at the robed man that must have simply materialized at their table. He reached for an empty chair and sat uninvited.

"*Avador Andor,* **Prince** *of the Elves.*" His lips never moved once. "*Ah, how you resemble the Elf King.*"

"Skneeba," Avador whispered, his eyes revealed an increasing shock. Venturing further with boldness he thought he didn't have, he kept his gaze fixed on the dark mage. "How long have you been with us?"

"*Believe if you like, my prince, but our paths have not met until now.*" Skneeba's mouth had yet to open.

My prince? Avador gave the others a quick glance. Can *they* hear him too? Their uneasy looks told him 'yes'.

"*But I have been in the presence of your great father.*" Skneeba continued with his telepathy.

Everything was returning to Avador like a slow, gradual trickle of memory. "What will become of...."?

"*Easy, young Andor. Speak to me with your mind. I have cleared this tavern but one never knows what can reach unsought ears.*" It seemed as though Avador's brain switched off. He was unaccustomed to such things.

"What trickery *is* this?" Stone was suddenly heated.

"*If this was deception, you would all be dead.*" Skneeba's face remained cool but his gaze towards the Dwarf was as sharp as a blade. Once again, no one spoke, but their hands remained on the hilt of their weapons. There was a long difficult silence until Skneeba's voice re-entered their minds.

"*You have all been attempting to intercept my leaving but it seems I have done what you sought.*" The group remained bewildered. Skneeba knew there were many unanswered questions. His eyes dropped to Avador's sword, a hint of a smile forming on his lips. "*Your father's blade.*" It was not a question.

"How did..." the Elf never finished.

"*It was **I** who enchanted it many years ago. No weapon in this world can do what **it** can.*" Everyone decided it was better to just listen. "*Through it, you have a connection to the Elf King, **that** you already know. But I also have a connection to it. That is how I knew you still lived, my prince. If you die, I lose that link.*" The dark mage let his eyes slide around the table. "*It was **I** who put the curse on Grandalimus Andor by no will of my own. I am but a tool employed in a hideous plan. I too have endangered my life to come here. In the morning, I am compelled to leave... commanded by my master. He too has the power to know if I use my magic. I pray that he cannot detect this telepathy, this mere thought transference. Of you, he knows naught.*" He gave them a severe look, "*if he did, I would have killed you all by now.*"

"*What are we to do now?*" Falstaff attempted excitedly to use Skneeba's telepathic current.

"*Ah, we have a young mage in our midst.*" Falstaff blushed at Skneeba's words. "*I am to leave now to make the journey to the docks before sunrise where a ship awaits me. I have arranged a second, much smaller schooner called 'The Matheia'. **That** one, along with a guide awaits you. Tell the guide it was I that sent you. He will transport you to the island of Gogatha.*" Skneeba paused as if to stress the importance of his next words. "*You are what is left of the world's hope.*"

My master...Aonas, believes he has covered every detail for his plan: the Elf King's armies are his along with the armies of his deceased brother. Combined, no other army could stand against its vastness." Skneeba gazed suddenly through the open window across the room. Then he hastened his words. *"My time here has ended. Once you get to Gogatha, find the city called Sovereign's Reach and breach my master's stronghold. You must destroy the staff he holds, the staff in which he has the power to control magic-users."* The dark mage gave Falstaff a quick glance. *"We do not want him to learn of you, young mage, gods forbid it...or any of you."* Skneeba stood suddenly, fear betraying his dark features. *"I will do whatever I can to help, and I know I leave many questions unanswered. We were lucky to have even this short-lived meeting. You have survived this far,"* Skneeba looked at everyone as if it were his last time, *"you can see this quest to its end."* With that, the dark mage replaced his cowl and limped awkwardly through the exit leaving everyone with the same surprise as when they met. No one spoke for long minutes. Their simple plan was made suddenly more complicated.

~****~

The next morning was different from all the others before it. The sun had barely risen and the shadows of North were long and morbid. Melancholia seemed to drape over the tiny village like oppressive webbing. Those of the Village of North that had awakened began to clatter about, the sounds heard easily from any point of the hamlet. A church bell tolled suddenly, it seemed as though it swung on its hinge just beyond the walls of the inn.

The companions, all in the same room, were already awake and dressed for travelling. They sat in silence waiting for the bell to stop its rhythmic swaying. Unsure but determined; they gave each other long comprehensive looks. The inn had provided them all with food and bath. Refreshed were their bodies but their minds were strained.

"Skneeba may now be on his master's ship." Nectario spoke as the bell's final strike still resonated in the air.

"Highly possible." Stone's face was the epitome of gloom. "On his way to his *death*."

North was soon a village left behind, a mere stepping-stone during this long, hard journey. The little group had paid for the night's lodgings and left without speaking to anybody. They were gone as if they never were; the small settlement carried on with its daily routine.

Stone Warhelm took the group northwest, Land's End awaiting their arrival. Once more they hadn't a clue of what to expect but they moved ahead with an unavoidable reckless-ness. The burly Dwarf had told them they would arrive by mid-morning when they stopped once to eat from their ra-tions. A new scent reached them as they sat in a semi-circle and unwrapped their provisions. It came and went sporadi-cally, salty yet fresh.

"The sea air." Stone said, his expression unreadable. "We are not far." The Dwarf gazed northward to where the land dropped abruptly. Nothing can be seen but sky beyond high cliffs. After the few moments of rest, the companions set out once again.

The wind intensified gradually until they reached the edge of the cliffs where it hit them with surprising force. With the same abruptness, the blue sky melded with a deeper blue... the ocean loomed before them, glimmering under the midday sun. The salty smell was unmistakable now; it was everywhere. The group of six stood in a row and gazed far below in sheer wonder, their cloaks held tightly about them as if they feared the wind would take them with it.

The far edges of the ocean seemed to arc from edge to edge only to disappear into emptiness. From this height, the companions thought they could see the ocean in its entirety. Little boats were scattered in all directions, silhouettes but distinguishable. They floated within the midst of sparkles in the shimmering water. Below the group was the shoreline. It ran without pattern from west to east as far as the eye could see. Here and there were the docks, scattered in uneven distances between each other. Avador found himself wondering which ship was the *Matheia*.

Abruptly, Stone motioned for them to follow. The Dwarf led them westward where the cliffs declined and turned right ramping naturally towards sea level. The company followed wordlessly until they reached the bottom. The noise level was far greater down here than from the tops of the cliffs. Port workers, sailors and fishermen were going about their business, most talking loudly with each other with their own lingo. They cursed and demeaned each other but no one seemed to mind.

The little group stared at the harbour and its organized chaos. Masts were erected and lines were drawn. The sound of mechanisms grinding and creaking was everywhere amongst the shouts of the many people along the shoreline. Ships large and small entered and exited the waterfront as naturally as someone would enter and leave a tavern. It was indeed a wonder to behold.

"Once we leave this soil," Stone had stopped and turned towards the group who stopped when he did, "my task as guide ends." His eyes were intense. They realized he had never travelled beyond the shore.

"We'll be on our own," responded Avador, "but as luck would have it, we will still be together."

No one gave any attention to the little band of travellers as they made their way along the shoreline. The commotion, a mixture of shouts, the flapping of sails, and the ocean's own slapping as it struck the sides of the larger ships, drowned out everything but the very wind that whistled past the group's ears. No one knew where to start searching for the *Matheia* so they decided simply to choose one direction and follow it until they found the vessel.

A good hour went by and it seemed the line of piers and quaysides would never end. Finally, after another half hour, the end of the harbour came to view. The little company began to wish they chose the other direction. The *Matheia* was nowhere in sight. The last of the bigger ships was behind them about a hundred yards. All that remained along the end of the harbour were smaller vessels that seemed mainly for the purpose of near-shore travel. The company sighed and began to turn around.

"Wait," said Avador and put a hand on Stone's wrist, "there she is." Everyone turned to look at the direction the Elf was pointing. At first they thought he was mistaken. But when they squinted past the sun's glare, a sleek midsize schooner had the charred inscription on its starboard flank... *Matheia.*

"*That* is to cross the *ocean?*" Stone Warhelm seemed appalled. The ship appeared to be predominantly constructed of wood, most of which was creaking as it lobbed up and down above its shallow ocean bed. The round iron portholes streaked with rust along with the iron edging along the bow. The shrouds stretching from both of its sides to the three mastheads were, for the most part, frayed, and the long tapered spar extending forward from the ships bow was completely disconnected from the front sails.

Avador's eyes ran along the *Matheia's* long slender length. The wood's cobalt paint must have been peeling for some time, its bluish colour fading almost completely.

Stone stared at the ship without a word. He glanced from the other ships that gleamed in the sunlight in near perfect condition and back to the *Matheia*. He released a snort and turned uncomfortably to Avador.

"Shall we go and meet the captain?"

Finding the schooner's captain was not a difficult task. He was the only person standing aboard the ship. The man was tall and trim with dark skin, almost as if trying to imitate his own ship. His thick white hair was badly wind-blown as he stood with palms against the iron railings. He seemed at first not to notice the strange lot that walked the narrow ramp way and onto the ships deck. He turned only when they approached him completely, his eyes so grey they might have been forged.

"Good day," said Avador awkwardly. The man did not respond. "We have been sent by Skneeba." The Elf decided to take the direct tactic.

"I know." The captain's lip curled on one side in the form of a smile, "I am Man-Poda, your guide to Gogatha." The man's voice was raspy and he spoke in a strange enunciation. He shook hands with Avador.

"Why does this ship have no crew?" Stone's eyes were searching left and right noting the lack of the usual commotion.

"Oh, the ship has a crew, my good Dwarf," Man-Poda's lips held the sardonic smile, "a crew that no other can match."

Falstaff and the others were standing behind Stone and Avador; their faces donned both excitement and confusion.

"How long will it take to get there?" Avador asked. The captain of the *Matheia* paused as if to ponder his answer.

"If the sea allows us," he answered finally in his raspy voice, "and the winds fill our sails... about a fortnight."

"A *fortnight?*" Stone was aghast, "we don't *have* a fortnight!"

"Stay yourself Dwarven warrior," Man-Poda's face remained calm, "if Skneeba arranged our meeting as such, then you still have a chance... and please, keep your voices low." The steely eyes swept from one member to the other. "Now, shall I show you around the ship?"

~****~

The schooner seemed a lot bigger when the company had the chance to explore it. The masts loomed above them like three tall towers, each with its own crow's nest, the mainmast curiously towards the ships stern. The upper deck was also surprisingly spacious though the hull seemed more slender when looking at it from the docks. The sails were all lowered in complicated bundles along booms cradled on even more complex rigging. Pulleys, hooks, mechanisms, lines...they were everywhere, but where were the men to operate these things? Stone counted a total of at least thirteen canvases, some larger than others, and noted the many sails the ship uses.

Avador was sitting at a bench bolted alongside the schooners bridge. The wheel inside was unmanned along with the other controls. The Elf was taking in the odd feeling of the ships movements when Stone and Eviathane sat next to him on the bench. Falstaff, Myia and Nectario were gazing over

207

the ships side at the land they were about to leave. Were they ever to see it again? They sighed and moved towards the centre of the ship where Avador sat with the others.

"All this waiting is poisoning my mind," Stone was irritated and more than a little edgy. Before anybody could reply, they caught sight of Man-Poda's slender form as he rose above deck and headed their way.

"Are you all ready for the journey across the sea?" The captain asked as he approached.

"Is there any *ale* on board?" Stone asked.

"Below deck, master Dwarf," Man-Poda replied, his expression almost curious, "we have many kegs in the galley's stock room."

"Then we're ready."

Before anyone else could speak, a sudden rumbling could be heard. Underneath their feet, the companions could feel a slight tremor. They looked at one another questioningly.

"Ah, the crew has awakened." Man-Poda's face had a pleased expression.

After a few minutes of marching in perfect tempo, the chanting had begun. The ships crew in a double file line emerged from below deck and into the open air. The language they used was completely foreign to the little group who stared dumbfounded at the bizarre crew that based their movements on their chanting. Tall and hunched, their skin an almost grey colour, they made their way around the ships deck in a deep chorus of unfamiliar rhythmic words. Little by little the grey-skinned scantly clad crew reached their posts and allowed those that had not, to carry on. The marching was noisy yet revitalizing. It made the group excited whether they wanted to be or not and the chanting, though unfamiliar, was aggressive making the blood seem to flow faster. Eventually all of the schooner's posts were filled, from the tallest crow's nest, down each crossbeam and netting, to the hoists and sails and pulleys that decorated the old schooner.

Abruptly the marching and chanting stopped all at once leaving a dead ring in the group's ears. The silence sounded strange. Man-Poda stood amidst the stillness with his arms crossed against his chest and a proud look on his dark features.

"Aweigh!" He shouted after a few heartbeats. In unison the chanting began again but this time sails were lifted and the anchor rose. The sound of winding chain could be heard from all sides. The crosstrees groaned way up high in their masts as the many different sized sails cloaked the dark ship from the bright sunlight. The sound of a creaking rudder pierced the air as it turned on its hinges against the sternpost. The sails were filled instantly and the schooner reeled as if a giant pulled on its reins. The chanting continued and blended with the rhythm of the sea. Every crewmember moved in a mechanical pace working the ship with total control. The little group stared in disbelief as the *Matheia* pulled away from shore and pointed towards the deep blue white-capped ocean that seemed to be waiting without patience.

Chapter 19 - Abyss

Eventually the driving chant decreased in intensity. Soon the long line of land was completely out of sight, left behind a haze of mist until it disappeared completely. The open water was astounding. The *Matheia* had pulled away from the rest of the ocean ships and took a course only *she* was familiar with. The schooner was a mere point on a backdrop of shimmering blue.

Avador Andor was standing at the bow watching the strange crew working mechanically with the rhythm of their chant, now a low hum as the ship sailed itself. The wind was strong and it was ruffling his wavy hair, as it was the unattached halyard lines along the bowsprit. He looked at the crew with the peculiar skin colour as they moved as one with their ship. They wore almost nothing and voiced only the chant in unison never speaking directly to one another. Their ears were short and sharp and their hair was long and white. The look in their eyes was one of utter concentration. Nothing seemed to draw their attention away from their work.

"Graylings." A voice came from behind the Elf. Avador whirled in surprise and found Man-Poda standing behind him holding two tin mugs of steaming liquid. He handed one to Avador and leaned against the railing next to him. The Elf took it without question and looked at the milky contents lifting an eyebrow to show he has never seen this drink before.

"Thank you," Avador said and sipped at the hot fluid. It had a sweet almond taste, strange at first but he decided he liked it.

"The crew are called *Graylings*, Gogatha's oldest inhabitants, born sailors. Aonas had distaste for them and attempted genocide on their race. I managed to save my crew, they are the only ones left...as far as we know."

"Why are we heading to Gogatha if Aonas wants them dead?" Avador was curious. Man-Poda raised a corner of his thin lips.

"Skneeba has us magically cloaked from the islands king. It was long ago before Aonas could finish with his mass destruction of the Graylings." Man-Poda could barely hide the disgust that flanged off his raspy voice. "When we get there, you and your men will be the only ones able to see us." Avador seemed to relax at the captain's last statement. They finished the rest of their drinks in silence. The drink warmed the Elf from inside out, keeping the cool wind' s harshness at bay. Sooner than Avador expected, Man-Poda excused himself taking the Elf's empty mug and went back below deck.

The Elf noticed Stone Warhelm sitting on the bolted down bench, his back against the bridge's rough wooden exterior wall. The Dwarf never moved from that spot since the *Matheia* left the port over an hour ago. Something was not right, Avador concluded. When he walked over to sit next to him, that *something* hit him like a runaway wave slapping against the ships hull. That *something* came in the form of short breaths and a white-knuckled grip of steel on the bench's thin armrest. Avador took a quick glance around their perimeter. Everyone else was preoccupied, their attention elsewhere. He turned back to the Dwarf, who might have been a statue.

"Stone?" The Dwarf's gaze remained locked to his booted feet. "Stone, are you well?" Avador wanted to panic; this was unlike the valiant Dwarf he grew to love as his own blood.

"I am fine, Elfling." The words left no room for argument.

"Do you have something that you want to tell me?"

"I told you I am fine." Stone looked at Avador now, his

face softening, "I am just a little more at ease if my feet are on solid ground." Avador knew now exactly why Stone has never travelled beyond Land's End.

"I am sure you have faced greater dangers than being out to sea." Avador smirked fanning a hand toward the water.

"Yes," Stone said quietly in his gruff voice, "but my feet were on *solid ground*." He stomped one foot against the boards below it. Avador could not think of one thing to say to him. He looked up and spotted Myia. She stood alone peering over the side and noting the way the deep blue of the ocean turned white where the schooner was cutting through it. Stone followed his gaze.

"Go." The Dwarf said and his eyes found his feet once again. Avador sighed, patted Stone's knee and strutted over to Myia.

Avador and the Wood Elf stared at the deep blue expanse of the immense waters. For a while they said nothing. Every now and then a cool spray would gently coat their skin leaving the taste of salt on their lips. The wind tousled their hair. Avador noticed that Myia had wrapped a blue, like the colour of sapphire, bandana about her head. It helped her thick brown hair stay behind her ears and away from her face. The two extra lengths where she had tied the wrapped cloth flapped wildly behind her.

"You didn't have to come with us." Avador broke the quiet, though silently, he was glad that she had. Myia kept her gaze toward the wind. For a moment, the sounds of flapping sail and groaning plywood were the only things audible. The chant of the Graylings had died completely.

"Yes." She said finally. "Yes, I did." She turned now and faced Avador. The Elf squinted his violet eyes at her as if to protest but she stopped him before he could. "I cannot, as much as I would yearn the peace of my forestland, stay behind and allow Aonas to finish what he has started. If you lost anything in your life, you have not lost as much as I." Avador could not argue. His head bowed involuntarily.

"I cannot say you are wrong to feel what you are feeling." Avador looked up now, directly into her eyes. "But you have one thing that I do not." Myia raised a slender eyebrow. "Closure," Avador answered her quizzical gaze. She listened. "You will, and I pray for it to end quickly, mourn for your loss. What Aonas had done to you and your people is unforgivable. I will not dispute you being here, but I will not say that I do not want you safe."

"What I risk is my own choice." Myia Feo-Dosia narrowed her eyes. "What closure are you speaking of?" Avador paused before replying and took a deep breath.

"The King of the Elves is *not* dead." The Elf's voice dropped to a whisper. Myia stared blankly at him. Did she hear correctly? "He is neither alive." Now she was really confused and it showed on her face. Avador told her all he knew and saw of his father. He told her that having him in this form is torment enough without the *option* of closure. Myia had gasped at this. She felt as though her very breath would never return. She felt her limbs grow numb.

"Young Andor," she managed to say to him, "I am so very sorry." The new pain in her heart mixed with anger so overwhelming caused the tears to flow involuntarily... Aonas *will* pay.

~****~

Tigran Eviathane and Nectario stood near Falstaff where

he was sitting with his back to the railings around the stern. His hands were resting on his knees and his robes pulled at his body as the wind forced against them. His face showed a hue of green and his friends were there to comfort him. In reality, he was not at all pleased that they were there. He was embarrassed. In fact he came up from below deck in the hopes to be alone with the fresh air. He was convinced they were enjoying this.

"Do you two have nowhere *else* to go?" Falstaff did not care if he sounded rude.

"But Falstaff," said Tigran, "you do not look well... are you feeling ill?" Nectario was trying his best not to let a chuckle escape. It seemed that his friend could not handle the gentle swaying of the schooner as it skimmed over the swelling ocean.

"I am *fine!*" The young mage was doing his best to show a healthy front. He even stood up to add substance to his claim. What he wanted to do, what he *really* wanted, was to hang over the rails and vomit everything in his stomach. But he would not give these two jesters the satisfaction. It seemed that they would stay here with him until the inevitable came to pass. But somehow, someway, a compassionate god smiled down at him. Avador approached and said he needed the help of the two stronger men. Falstaff was standing as straight as a board now, a smile wide across his bearded face. The Elf nodded to him and led the others away. When they were out of sight, he slumped back and leaned hard against the railings, the wind on his face helping his situation slightly. But he wasn't sure how much longer he could suppress the acidy sickness that swirled like a storm inside his guts.

~****~

The little group had finally gathered together. The captain of the *Matheia* called them all below deck after the Graylings of the ship's mess hall seemingly subconsciously prepared the meals for them and the crew. Everything on the nailed-down table before them was foreign; a mixture of exotic plantation apparently edible and meats covered in unfamiliar sauces offered a surprisingly pleasant aroma. They did not know where the crew ate for none were at their table or any of the others that surrounded it. The dining area was simple. Oil lamps that bore no flame lighted it. A doorway led to what everyone assumed was the kitchen. Another entry showed nothing but blackness within and the third was the one they came through. Man-Poda had sat with them.

"You must get accustomed to the sea life." The captain spoke as he ate. All ate hungrily, Stone and Falstaff picked at their food and ate slowly and mainly out of necessity. "Our journey across the ocean has only begun. Until now our progress has been fine. Our vessel is now on a course that extremely few have taken; do not expect to see others any time soon."

"Do you expect any danger?" Avador was unsure if he sounded stupid.

"When you travel across your lands," Man-Poda began, "do *you* expect danger?" The Elf paused, now he *felt* stupid. Everyone stopped eating. "I will not lie to you. The *Matheia* and its crew have seen much trouble whether it came from within the ship or from without. Unfortunately, that is why this course is rarely taken." The others listened intently. "We have at least found a route where most of the threats lurk elsewhere." Avador thought of his father travelling to Gogatha. Stone fidgeted in his seat. A pot clanged from the galley. Everyone jumped to their feet as if they had just *spoken* the danger to appear. Man-Poda's laugh was uncontrollable.

The sun was pushing itself into the western horizon. The effect was dreamlike. The waters grew blacker with each passing moment as the giant crimson ball gathered its radiance of amber-orange into itself. Eventually it left nothing for the world, taking it all with it as it vanished below the water line.

"Our first day on the ocean has just ended." Avador was saying to his companions. The long narrow bench seemed to have become the centre of their world. They could see the helmsman from the open window of the bridge. The Grayling stood almost soldier-like as he held the big wheel in place. The flameless lamps shone in even rows along the deck, the effect was eerie. The wind seemed to behave itself as night took its watch over the world.

"The world, though beautiful," Nectario began, "is an unstable place." The lute was in his hands now his fingers working the tuning pegs. The wood of its large rounded body gleamed against the pale glow of the lamps, twelve strings two by two ran along its short neck and over the bulky body. Three holes, each one a different size sat below the taut strings.

"Why do we do what we do?" Eviathane's voice entered the momentary silence. "Others betray, others steal. Many *kill*. Some just want to be left alone and do nothing as their world is taken over. Is it okay with them? Why are *we* acting out while others stand against us?" No one answered. They all sat in silence until Stone raised one hand in front of them all. He wiggled his fingers.

"Are they all the same?" The reply was so simple they almost missed its meaning. The taciturn Dwarf released a tremendous sigh and looked away. The night air, calm now, was suddenly made full by the resonance of perfectly tuned strings. Stars sprouted over the *Matheia's* starboard flank. Wispy clouds streamed against their blue-black setting. No one knew what awaited them within or beyond these waters, but when Nectario released his voice into the music, even the fidgety Dwarf seemed to relax the threads of tension that almost strangled him.

~****~

"Nectario truly *is* talented." Myia Feo-Dosia spoke quietly trying not to wake Falstaff and Stone. The *Matheia's* upper level housed a quarterdeck, an area slightly more elevated near the ships stern. Instead of individual cabins, the company favoured this area as their choice of lodgings. It had a low ceiling but the only one that needed to slouch slightly was Eviathane. He did not mind because they planned for using this room for sleeping; it was large, warm and kept the elements away from them. Inside was bare save for a row of cupboards attached to the far wall. The windows were narrow and ran along the lengths of all four walls, if they wanted to see anything outside they needed to be close to the windows, likewise from outside in.

"His talent surprised me," whispered Eviathane listening to the muffled music. Nectario remained outside, alone with his lute. He claimed that he has spent enough time without playing and he was probably right; a bard after all makes his living with his instrument.

"If magic had not existed," said Avador quietly, "music would be its substitute. Look what it has done to Stone and Falstaff." He raised a hand towards his sleeping companions. The others smiled. But there was a lot of truth to the Elf's thought. Music existed. It was something from nothing. It comes and leaves at will, moving everything it touches. Small children experiencing it even for the first time rocked and swayed at its enchanting melodies.

Crash!

The ship jolted rearward. The cupboards doors shot open with a simultaneous *slap*. They cracked as they hit the backs of the others. The sudden jerk was heart stopping. Avador was on his feet and glaring through the narrow windows. Nectario shot through the single door, his eyes wide with terror. Stone, though shaken, was already standing next to Avador, his battle-hammer gripped for attack. If he remembered being on a ship, he did not show it.

Swiftly the little company burst outside just as the *Matheia's* bow pitched forward. They braced themselves, forced into a crouch as the once even decking angled suddenly forward. It was not steep enough to topple them but they could feel the dip under their boots inching dangerously to a greater slant.

A booming chant resounded into the air. The Graylings were above deck almost at once. Many took their typical posts but the captain's thunderous voice divided the others wielding hand held harpoons into a battle formation. The world became strange; the ocean's angle was completely off-centre. The chanting continued and blood was pumping. The armed Graylings were fixed along the bow's outer rim each with a long quiver filled with the sleek harpoons. The chant thundered to a higher magnitude, all at once the Graylings released a rain of deadly steel. There was a blood-chilling shriek from the ocean's depths that sent a tremor throughout the ships hull.

Avador's party gripped onto anything that was bolted to the floor as their feet began to skid forward. The chant's level rose again and another wave of harpoons pierced the roiling water. Abruptly the ship's nose shot skyward and everyone felt their stomachs lurch into their solar plexus. For a split second they hung suspended a few feet above the floorboards only to land roughly onto the thick wooden decking. The ships front end dug deep into the ocean and for a moment it seemed as though it would bury itself nose-first. Salty water burst overhead from both of the ships flanks and rained onto the shocked company soaking them to the bone. The *Matheia* pitched upwards and the world straightened once again.

"It released us!" Man-Poda was screaming above the rhythmic chanting. "Now!" Another wave of harpoons sunk into whatever it was that wanted the *Matheia* so badly.

What released us? Avador was thinking as he pounced back onto his agile feet. He made sure everyone was accounted for. Stone now had both his arms wrapped around the base of a wooden pillar, his hammer dangling uselessly in his right hand. The look in his eyes reflected unimaginable terror. Falstaff's robes were wet and weighed down, his lips were moving, and his arms were raised. He was trying to cast a spell. Good. Eviathane, Myia and Nectario rushed to Avador's side and together they reached the shouting captain.

"What is happening?" Avador asked above the turmoil. The captain did not answer. Instead he thrust a handful of roping into the Elf's hands.

"Hook these to yourselves and to any railing you could find. Now!" Man-Poda had already turned his attention elsewhere.

Avador did not hesitate. He ran towards Stone, Eviathane and Myia one step behind. Nectario stumbled after, eyes blank with fright. The roping Avador held was designed in such a way that at first confused the Elf. He handed one to Tigran and another to Myia and Nectario. Instead of a spell that could help the situation, the nearby Falstaff lost the power to contain his queasy insides. He retched violently on the *Matheia's* decking. Avador thrust a line into the mage's hands. He then single coiled an end around the panicked Dwarf's waist. That end had a loop. He shoved the other end that was fitted with some kind of clamp through the loop. Quickly he looked around for something to attach it to. A rounded bar encircled a vertical rod near Stone's pillar. The fastener clamped with a dull *snap*. Myia, Eviathane and Falstaff had done the same for themselves. Nectario stood frozen with the clamped end of the roping in his hand. He was merely staring at it.

Then, again without warning, something pushed upwards against the ships underbelly and the *Matheia* seemed to have levitated above the water. That *something* gave out a cry so shrill that it seemed to pierce right through the eardrums. Avador felt the pain in his ears; he thought they would bleed. Everyone wanted to cover their ears but from the sudden heave, they instinctively grabbed onto their roping, their hearts missing a beat.

Nectario and Avador, along with everyone else came off the floor when the ship dropped back into the water. Only *they* weren't connected to their lines, and the *Matheia* was threatening to capsize. It landed on a treacherous angle along its starboard side. Avador grabbed onto a wrought iron grate and swung his free arm towards the petrified bard. He grasped his wrist just as Nectario's body fell towards the ships slant. The Elf's shoulders snapped at the strain and he felt the heat of pain run along his arms. Another spray of heavy water surged into them, many Graylings fell over the side and into the swirling abyss. The chanting never seized or missed a beat. Instead it surged to a higher level. The sails and booms were close hauled but many poles and blocks became useless splinters. Somehow, miraculously, the *Matheia* straightened once again but not before Avador lost his grip on Nectario, the sudden weight too much for him. The abrupt levelling of the ship is the only thing that saved Nectario from a fatal plummet over the edge. Instead he rolled hard into the inner railing and remained there motionless.

Chapter 20 - Coming to Terms

Skneeba's eyes were focused intently into the very night. The remains of his tongue clucked above the opening to his throat, an acquired nervous reflex when he was in deep thought. A day behind his deep grey ship aptly christened '*Stormcloud*', the *Matheia* sailed the same waters... he later thought grimly, he *hoped* that it still sailed.

His mind raced, poisoned with the fact that someone still controls his every move. How much longer can he go on like this? How much more can his mind endure? His only hopes originate from a small company aboard a ship in treacherous waters and whose quest appears ill fated; success hanging on a frayed line. How much longer can the little group be kept a secret from the cunning Aonas with Skneeba having little or no room to move?

Stormcloud sailed the waters with a forbidding presence. Much bigger and more intimidating than the *Matheia*, it journeyed unscathed. Where it lacked in speed, it made up for in strength. The ancient ship was used exclusively for the King's own purposes and supplies: from spices and clothing to war mechanisms and siege engines, there was nothing the vessel could not carry. At present, another consignment of easily corrupted soldiers filled the ship, eager to join forces with the well-paying Aonas. *How many others were brought to Gogatha before this wave?* Skneeba thought miserably shaking his head. *Do they not know it is to their doom they travel? Ah, the selfish are blinded once again.*

~****~

The calm was nerve-racking and the added darkness encircling the *Matheia* made it nearly unbearable. Every remaining Grayling was a statue on board the ship. Avador could do nothing but listen to the sound of his own heart beating in his ears. Everything seemed to be moving slower than what nature intended. Eviathane was at the Elf's side, long-sword drawn though he wasn't sure what to do with it.

"Are we to *do* something?" Tigran whispered to Avador, his eyes moving from his friend to the dark waters. The Elf merely shook his head.

"Stay attached to the ship," he said finally. He then glanced over to Man-Poda who was walking backwards towards him, his attention elsewhere.

"Master Elf," Man-Poda said in a low voice, "are you hurt?"

"No." Avador was waiting for some kind of explanation as Nectario came into view limping towards them. Quickly Man-Poda retrieved the bard's dropped line and clamped him to a railing.

"It is not over." The captain's face was stern. He understood that they wanted to know what was happening. He also knew they had little time for explanations. "Below us lurks a *'Fythi'*." His voice was leaving his mouth in quick spurts, his grey eyes severe and constantly darting from one shaken member to the other. "Sea-farers call it a 'beast'... I call it 'intelligent'." The others remained silent, listening within the few precious moments of stillness. "It is one of *many*. They claimed the Western Fathoms, creatures nearly the size of this ship. I made the mistake to explore their unfamiliar waters months ago." Man-Poda pointed a clean-shaven chin towards the west signifying that beyond the endless blue is *their* territory. We managed to escape the cluster of its kind but this one, well... this one *hunts* us." A low rumbling from below forced the captain to silence.

"What is that?" Myia Feo-Dosia broke from her moment of immobility.

Man-Poda actually smiled. "We hurt it." The ship shook from a feeble hit to its underbelly.

"What does it want?" Avador's voice squeezed out between clenched teeth. He wasn't sure why he even asked such a question. "How can it be stopped?"

"The Fythi bleeds." Man-Poda said solemnly. "Until now the Graylings harpoons have been our only *defence*. Stopping it is a problem we haven't solved. At best we have only delayed its attacks." The Elf couldn't comprehend more than one attack from this creature.

The moon escaped the veil of dark cloud that was snuffing its bluish light. A small rounded edge was missing from the once-full disc. Avador saw now the movement within the shimmering black waters. Something bulged just below the ocean's liquid skin, moving slowly away from them. It was dark and massive; the Elf could almost feel the skin along his spine shiver just by sighting the creature's indistinct form. He did not like being in the middle of nowhere with this thing sharing the same waters. He could only imagine what Stone was feeling. He glanced over at the Dwarf. He too was staring after the Fythi; his face was unreadable.

It seemed like forever had just come and gone, but the night had finally ended. The group had continued with their accustomed nightly watch, but no one had actually slept soundly. The waters were blue once again, gleaming with the coming of the sun. Breakfast was eaten with no enthusiasm. The Graylings were all above deck, stern and ever ready. The ones posted high above in their crow's nest stood silently like statues with their arms folded across their bare chests. The helmsman stood within the undersized bridge, face grim as he held the *Matheia's* course.

Avador Andor felt the salt-laced breeze cool his sweating brow. He was atop the rigging that housed the sails of the foremast doing what he could to help the Graylings with repairs on the damaged shrouds. Some of the roping dangled uselessly but most he managed to help reattach to the masthead. The sound of the captain's scratchy voice came from below and drew his attention.

"Master Elf. Come down, quickly."

Avador was back on the deck in moments, everything going through his already pessimistic mind.

"Captain." The Elf said, eager to know what is happening.

"Not to cause any panic, Master Elf, but assemble your friends. Make sure they have their safety lines." Man-Poda watched Avador as he moved without hesitation to gather his group.

The Fythi attacked again shortly after the Grayling atop the mizzenmast spotted the creature approaching the *Matheia* from the rear.

"Dead Astern!" Shouted Man-Poda. The rear of the ship filled at once with defending Graylings. Once again a moment of unbearable silence encircled the ocean before the *Matheia* suffered another clash with the incessant Fythi.

The ship shook with the likeness of a devastating earthquake. But they were not on unyielding ground. They were in the middle of an unfathomable ocean that waited impatiently to swallow them. The *Matheia* splintered and creaked as the Grayling's thunderous chant rose above the turmoil. The burnished steel of the harpoons reflected the sun's light as they pierced the air and dug into the uneasy waters. But this time the creature's scream did not reply to the Grayling's attack. Instead, the *Matheia's* stern heaved to one side, the hinged rudder creaking its defiance on its sternpost.

The powerful Fythi forced the ship into a one hundred and eighty degree spin; the *Matheia* now faced the direction it had come from. The creature knew the defenders were now all on the opposite side where they could do it no harm. *Intelligent.*

Avador and his group struggled to no avail to stay on their feet, their safety lines stretching against the sudden jolt. The Graylings had taken flight towards the *Matheia's* bow but they were too late. The Fythi was already pulling the front end of the ship into the agitated ocean. The Elf could hear the indistinct shouts of Man-Poda. His friends were lying down across the slanting deck, their safety lines taut and holding them in place. The seasoned Graylings were having difficulty keeping their balance as they raced across the deck.

Avador caught a glimpse of the Fythi. It was scaly and blue-black. It shimmered as it emerged slowly to meet the sun's light. Peering over the bow's upper railing was a single yellow eye twice the size of a man. Below the eye, Avador caught sight of a cavernous mouth curling to reveal a row of knife-like teeth. The Fythi released a triumphant howl and submerged once again below the ship dragging its front end further into the sea. Waves of salty water could now leap into the ships bow. It was too late for the *Matheia*.

Avador was *not* going to wait for a miracle. He didn't need to be a veteran sailor to understand the ship stood no chance. His final thought of his friends dieing because they wanted to help *him* sent him into action. Avador's jagged dagger was in his hand. With a quick swipe, he cut his safety line that held him to the ship and pounced to his feet. Instantly he bound towards the ships front end easily overtaking the staggering Graylings. The nimble Elf darted to either side avoiding irritating obstacles before running straight for the bow. He heard the faint screaming of his friends who were struggling helplessly near the rear of the ship before pouncing over the railing and into the ocean's deathtrap.

The shock of the sea's frigidness nearly made the Elf lose his ability to act as he pierced through the chilly water. Almost at once he was face to face with the Fythi. The creature did not react, or so it seemed. The turmoil was overwhelming to the young Elf but he knew that he must take action now. Frightened and half blind, Avador thrust his dagger into the yellow blur only inches away. The scream that followed erased the Elf's senses; a shockwave went through his body. The next instant, he was floating motionless within the salty waters…

The *Matheia's* bow pitched upwards and somewhat levelled. The entire crew heard the high-pitched wail that came from the turbulent waters beneath the ships hull. Stone and the others released themselves from their safety lines and ran to where Avador dove out of the ship. They looked over the railing in utter disbelief. Dark red blood was rising to the surface mixing with the violent blue of the ocean. Below the water's surface, they could just make out the Fythi swimming without pattern and in such a violent way, the fear within them jumped to a much higher magnitude. There was no sign of Avador.

The little group strained to find the missing Elf amidst the water's chaos. They saw only the white-capped waves surrounding the deep red blood. It seemed the Fythi was coming their way, splitting the waters surface as it swam with great speed. But abruptly it changed direction and missed them altogether. Soon it was out of sight.

Falstaff raised his arms and ignored the shouts from his friends. He ignored the orders of Man-Poda as he shouted to his crew. He even ignored the pitching of the ship as it bobbed in the troubled ocean. The enigmatic words came to him with surprising ease and he released them towards the turbulent waters. The moments were going by and it seemed as though nothing was happening. He probed with his mind, tendrils of thought reaching into the depths of the very ocean, searching. Penetrating. The young mage felt them tugging and releasing all at once until…

"There!" Myia cried as she caught sight of Avador and pointed in a direction half a league away. A silhouette was levitated just above the water's surface. The form of a person could be made out, limp and motionless. Suddenly Falstaff dropped his arms and collapsed to one knee. The limp form of Avador fell back into the ocean. Everyone gasped.

"Hard over!" Man-Poda shouted and the helmsman turned the wheel as far as possible. "To the halyards!" Suddenly the lines used to haul up the sails were moving like serpents and the *Matheia* heaved in Avador's direction. The booming chant stirred the blood of the ship and pumped its heart drawing it closer to the floating Elf.

"Give me a line!" Stone shouted to Man-Poda as they neared Avador. The *Matheia's* captain blinked in stunned silence. "Now!" Stone shouted and yanked a long length of rope from a nearby Grayling. He quickly tied one end around his waist and the other to the ships railing. Without pausing to think about what he was doing, the Dwarf jumped feet first into the water next to Avador. Nearly losing his ability to move, Stone sank further than he anticipated. Tigran Eviathane grabbed immediately at his line. The rough rope burned into his palms as it slipped from his grip. Stone was sinking. Tigran grunted under the strain but managed to stop the ropes gradual descent. He pulled at the rope until Stone was visible above the water. The Dwarf had lost his helmet from the fall but right now he couldn't care less if *all* his clothing were missing.

Eviathane watched as Stone reached out towards Avador and put a strong arm around the Elf's chest. Satisfied the Dwarf had a secure grip, Tigran placed one foot firmly against the gunwales and yanked at the line that was attached to Stone. The big man heaved with all his strength and soon his friends were dangling above the water. In no time, a few of the Graylings were behind him and grabbed the remaining length of rope. Together they hoisted Avador and Stone up and over the railings. Avador was lowered gently to the wet decking of the ship. Myia brushed his soaked hair away from his face, Stone sitting with his back against a barrel breathing heavily. Avador was unconscious, the Wood Elf determined, her heart racing with relief. She looked over at the spent mage with tears in her eyes.

"You saved his life." She said with an uncontrollable smile. Falstaff said nothing merely nodding his acknowledgement.

"As did you," Eviathane put a strong hand on Stone's thick shoulder. The Dwarf remained staring at his wet boots until someone threw a dry blanket over his shoulders.

~****~

The moon was a razor-thin crescent, orange like a rusted sickle embedded into the blackened sky. It dangled silently just above the horizon; the waves seemed to reach up to it as they passed beneath in quiet worship. The *Matheia* held her course, despite listing drunkenly with the eerie presence of the moon at her right flank.

The little group huddled together within the ship's quarterdeck making a half circle around their sleeping leader. Avador had finally regained consciousness late that afternoon. But he did not avoid the consequence of diving into an unfamiliar situation to face a beast that was sure to kill him in an instant. The Elf had eaten nothing and spoke very little since his encounter. Something snapped inside the young Elf's mind. It wasn't the fact that he was in a life-threatening situation. No. He would do it again without thought if it were to save his friends. What occupied his mind was the fact that he is putting his friends in these situations and he really had no right. As a result, Avador chose to fall back within himself so he could make sense of it all. In a way he felt ashamed, mortified that everything is happening essentially because of *him*. The added weight of the horrifying fate of his father and the possibility of never seeing him or his mother again suddenly became too much for him to carry. His heart was breaking. Eventually, just as the sun was beginning to take its leave for the night, the troubled Elf decided, at least for the moment, to allow himself the luxury of sleep. In order to briefly escape the black thoughts that invaded his mind, he succumbed to the inviting verdict.

Stone was not much better than the Elf. Like Avador, he spoke very little and chose to stay within the privacy of his own mind. But when the Graylings prepared the afternoon meal, the Dwarf ate savagely as if it were his last serving of food. Now he crouched protectively along with the others over the Elf leader, his face overcast with both sternness and admiration. Stone Warhelm did not enjoy sailing whatsoever. In fact, it scared him to death. But looking at the sleeping Elven prince, he wouldn't be anywhere else but at his side. *My life is yours, Elfling.*

Tigran Eviathane stretched his entire height over his travel blanket. The hours stole away into the night yet he found it difficult, if not impossible to sleep. The floorboards beneath gave out a low creaking sound as he shifted his weight. His thoughts drifted now and again to various things, most of which jumped between his home and the journey ahead. He glanced over to his friends feeling the light swaying of the *Matheia* as it sailed through the night. All except Stone were fast asleep. He watched the Dwarf for a long moment as he sat with his back to the wood-panelled wall. The moonlight that oozed through the narrow slits for windows was weak but Tigran made no mistake of Stone's sombre expression. The big man sat up and shifted himself next to his sleepless friend.

"Do you think Avador will be okay?" Eviathane whispered wanting to keep Stone's mind away from the ocean. At first the Dwarf said nothing as if he wasn't even there.

"Yes lad." Stone said finally. "The heart of a king pumps the blood in *our* prince. He will overcome... he *must*." Eviathane nodded in agreement.

"Stone?" Tigran said after another moment of silence. "Do you believe that King Grandalimus' armies really turned and are now planning to attack us?" His words hurt Stone more than he will ever realize.

"I believe they have *not* turned and they never will. The men who swore their lives to the Elven king have proven themselves time after time. No lad, they were somehow *forced* to join the forces of Aonas and I regret to tell you, Grandalimus' army is the largest that ever existed. The men that have pledged their allegiances have completely devoted their lives for his name. They have no doubt in their hearts and minds of Grandalimus' virtue, for he has never led them astray." Stone's gaze lingered gracelessly towards his booted feet as though he knew which question was coming next.

"Why were *you* not 'taken' along with the rest of the army?" The Dwarf was right about the question. He shifted uneasily as if trying to hide shame.

"It is something that had plagued me ever since we discovered what happened to the Elf King's armies." Stone answered after a long moment of silence. "The best answer that I could provide myself is only this: My pledge of allegiance to Grandalimus is unspoken. The armies that have been taken..." *Entire armies.* Stone was shaking his head at the sound of what he had just said, "...are permanent soldiers that remain within designated barracks, quarters and training grounds. For me, that is too regimented, too structured. I remained a free agent but at the same time keeping my allegiance intact." *Just as it is now,* he thought pursing his lips. "I believe the answer lies somewhere within that philosophy."

There was a stirring to their right within the dimness of the room. Falstaff had sat up and had withdrawn the large volume from its pack. Apparently sleep was evasive to him as well. He opened the book and tilted it towards the weak moonlight that scarcely managed to enter through the quarterdecks narrow windows.

"It is getting increasingly difficult to keep our wits in one piece." The young mage whispered. He took a deep breath within his part of the gloom. "Avador needs us now more than ever." The *Matheia* groaned in the short silence that followed.

"Then we will let him know that we are still with him." Tigran Eviathane replied, his tone severe. Stone and Falstaff agreed silently. The hours marched through the night and soon enough sleep took over the weary company. It was as much needed, as it was deserved.

~****~

The days and nights that followed the dramatic attack of

the Fythi were gratefully uneventful. Avador Andor spent the first of those days mostly alone, retreated somewhere within his thoughts. No one intruded his privacy until they felt the timing was right. The sun was directly above them showing that it was midday, the sky was cloudless and the seas were tranquil. Stone, Myia and Nectario purposefully went below deck to meet with Man-Poda. Tigran and Falstaff approached the young Elf as he strolled the outskirts of the ship.

"We should come within reach of Gogatha in a couple of days." Tigran said almost offhandedly pretending his attention was drawn to the sea. "The captain just told me." Avador smiled and nodded.

"Avador." Falstaff moved in between the two friends and the young Elf stopped and rested his arms against the gunwales. The others did the same. "I know what is troubling you and believe me...*us*, we are all here because we *chose* to be."

"You do not understand entirely." Avador looked as if he would lose his composure. He released a sigh that seemed to have been under extreme pressure for too long. "I know that you are all here because you want to be. But that doesn't give me the right to accept the fact that I allowed you all to put your lives at risk. Who am *I* to permit this?"

"Avador." Tigran's tone was one of near anger. "Yes, it is true we came with you to find your father. It is also true that we continued on after we discovered that this is about much more than that. Our lives would have been threatened anyway. It makes *me* feel better just by knowing that we are doing something about it. Back home or *here*, we would not be anywhere else but next to you. Damn it Avador, you are my *brother*. And so is Falstaff. You would have done the same for us. There would have been no other option. Accept it." Tigran didn't realize it but he was breathing heavy and tears were threatening to spill out over his lower lids. Finally, the blur became too much and he wiped his eyes with his forearm. The Elf surprised him with an embrace that came out of nowhere. Then Tigran reached out with his massive arm and dragged Falstaff into the huddle.

"It is just as your father said: we are the *three sticks*... no one can break us."

I t was just as Man-Poda had told Eviathane: As the second day arrived with a magnificent sun peeking over the delicate line of the horizon, the *Matheia* neared its destination. The company had been awakened for the first time by a knock on the quarterdecks only door. They exited one by one to be welcomed by both Man-Poda and a subtle orange glow shooting forth from the morning sun. It washed their faces with its radiance and warmth as if trying to comfort them in light of the days ahead. The Graylings were nowhere in sight leaving a clear open deck. The captain of the *Matheia* asked everyone to group together.

"The crew is all below deck." Somehow Man-Poda's voice hinted severity in his tone, the usual sarcastic undercurrent gone. "We are half a day's distance from Gogatha. I have ordered the Graylings to douse the sails in order to move in slowly. I want as less movement showing from the ship as possible so that our chances of detection are minimized. Aonas' guards will not be able to see us as we approach but I am not taking any unnecessary risks." The captain's eyes roamed to each of the companion's. "This is our final leg of the journey to Gogatha and I want to prepare you as much as I can before we part."

Avador felt his heart flutter in his chest. His breathing became difficult to regulate. The reality of Aonas and the closeness of his proximity became an enormous weight on his confidence. The man responsible for his father's curse was on the island half a day away. The man that ordered the destruction of Feo-Dosia and the deaths and sufferings of innocent people suddenly became a dark and threatening nightmare about to come true. The man that is planning, even as the Elf contemplates, a mass destruction of all who refuse to bow down to his reign and possibly ruin everything Avador had known and loved, is closer than he would like to admit. *And it feels like that man is watching me.*

The Elf wrenched his gaze away from the taunting sea and turned his face back towards the quarterdeck. He suddenly wanted the ship to turn around so he could go back home. *They have gone well beyond safety. This is now foolishness.* His mind was screaming for him to stop this nonsense and turn around. But everything else he was made up of told him that he was not going back. Not yet.

Man-Poda caught Avador's reaction and stopped talking. The Elf didn't seem to notice. The huddled group took a moment to look at him. Without a word, he walked slowly towards the quarterdeck, climbed the rise and disappeared through the door.

Stone Warhelm walked in almost immediately after Avador with the *Matheia's* captain in tow. The Dwarf decided there was no time to spare with the young Elf, his morale was at an extreme low and Stone recognized it at once. They found Avador standing with his back to them and his head hung low.

"Look at me, Avador." Stone said sternly. The Elf raised his head. "*Look at me!*" Avador turned slowly and faced the waiting Dwarf, his violet eyes shimmering with dampness.

"I will be fine, Stone." Avador's voice was small as the Elf tried valiantly to sound convincing.

"I know you will." Stone said, his own voice softening. "I also know what you must be going through. You're young yet you endured much. You're afraid, but you are still moving on. *That's* what bravery is all about. If you were not afraid, then courage would have nothing to do with this, Elfling. You are doing everything right, more than anyone can expect from you. Do not second-guess yourself for that would be your downfall. Your instincts are second to none. You are more like your father than you will ever know." Stone closed the door and walked next to the troubled Elf. Man-Poda moved to Avador's left side and put an encouraging hand on his shoulder.

"I know your father, Avador." The captain's voice was quiet and solemn. The Elf showed no surprise, he was now accustomed to people knowing his father. "If he were here his heart would have already burst with pride. The people call him 'King of the Elves' but that is only because he is an *Elf.* In truth, those of your lands, whether Dwarf, Man, Elf and many of the other races look upon him as their leader. They chose it as such quite naturally."

"You see, Elfling," Stone cupped Avador's chin and gently turned his face to his own, "it is not the king's *title* the people follow... it is the *man* himself." The Dwarf gave Avador an unexpected wink.

"You have tramped a path of respect through your homeland, Avador. You sailed a course with the same magnitude on these waters." Man-Poda gave Avador's shoulder a squeeze. "Do the same on that island!" Avador smiled in spite of himself.

There was a sudden knock at the door. Everyone froze in place.

"Uh, I think the captain should come out and explain something." Tigran's voice seeped through the wood of the door. The others inside did not hesitate. They moved to the door as one and opened it. They found Eviathane on the other side pointing questioningly towards the bow of the ship. They saw Myia, Falstaff and Nectario standing at the railing as if something was interesting them greatly. Together they hurried to join them.

Avador took in a sharp breath. Stone stared in disbelief. Man-Poda merely nodded slowly as if he understood what lay in front of them. Not five hundred meters ahead and high in the heavens, the blue of the sky ended and a black began. A line as perfect as a razor's edge separated the two colours and it ran completely across the skies. Everything beyond the line was shrouded in murky darkness. The feeling it left was dismal yet fascinating. The small group turned to Man-Poda not really wanting to look away from the spectacle before them, but they needed an explanation.

"It is the reverberation of Skneeba's curse. Gogatha and its immediate surroundings are draped in continual night. No one within these waters has seen the sun in what seems like forever. Time is no longer measured for it became impossible to do so."

The company looked on as the *Matheia* kept its course towards the unnatural spectacle. The line above them advanced closer bringing the black side with it like a death veil. The effect made their skin crawl. Soon, the line was directly above them and they crossed beneath it and into the gloom beyond. The bright blue of the water and the vivid sky were left behind leaving them in bleak shadow. Eventually, everything that was normal and accepted by nature was out of sight.

~****~

The ship sailed on for what seemed like endless hours leaving the uncanny seam in the sky far behind it. The small company grew restless with the anticipation of what lay ahead.

The crossover into the bizarre territory left them on edge. The water itself a cheerless grey robbed of its colour. For a while it seemed as though all that was left was the water.

But after yet another hour they could make out clusters of tiny islands on either side of the *Matheia*. Some were nothing but jagged rocks thrusting upwards through the waters surface. Others were as large as two-story buildings; but they all housed some kind of ancient ruin be it simple stone arches or pillars of the finest black marble. Soon they were all around them, some miles away and some so close one would think you could reach out and touch them. Man-Poda, within the pilot box navigated the *Matheia* between them, easing her slowly on a path only he knew of. Avador found himself wondering how anything could be seen. With the absence of the sun, what caused the feeble presence of eerie light? Within moments, he got his answer: They sailed slowly past a small island though somewhat larger than most. It carried an ancient-looking stone structure silhouetted by something behind it that gave off a weak light. As they moved ahead and the structure moved behind them, the source of light came into view and made Avador's heart stop.

A misshapen moon appeared from behind the structure, pale and twisted. It brought the others to attention and they all gathered together as if their lives depended on it. The questions ran wild in their minds but a finger to Man-Poda's lips silenced them all. They sailed even further with the grotesque uneven thing that should have been a perfect sphere trailing next to them. It unnerved them that it was even around, so evil and unnatural looking.

After another incessant hour, they were free from the clusters of tiny islands and the captain of the *Matheia* emerged from the pilot box. Eviathane was back in full armour, the hilt of his long-sword gripped tightly in his hand. He was gazing ahead in the direction the ship was sailing. Miles away but drawing nearer, a long strip of land ran from west to east directly in front of them. Stone and Avador flanked either side of Tigran. Falstaff, Myia and Nectario drew closer. Together they watched the intimidating island ahead as it grew larger with each passing moment. The only one anticipating setting foot on that island was Stone... and that, was half-heartedly.

Chapter 22 - Tension

Simetra Andor sat at the table in the dining room of her now empty house. Though her home was warm and the fire she built in the fireplace blazed with lively flame within the stone and brick hearth, she could not shake the chill that ran deep into her very bones. She was alone and had never felt so much alone as she had at that moment.

The light that seeped through the windows from outdoors was fading into a dismal glow, mimicking, she thought bleakly, her hopes. Her son was out there somewhere. Dead? Alive? Her husband. What has become of him? She tried in vain to cast her thoughts aside. She was expecting visitors soon and it wouldn't do to allow her emotions to take over. They had, of course, countless times since Avador and his friends left all those weeks ago. She kept thinking of the day the Wood Elves showed up with the small gift of hope and the news that her son was still alive. Her thoughts naturally drifted to Myia, the Wood Elf that left in such a haste to find her son. Did she succeed in finding him? Was *she* even alive? There were just too many questions.

A sudden knock at the front door snapped her out of her deep contemplation. She knew who it should be but her breath involuntarily caught in her throat. Hastily, Simetra pulled back her crimson hair into a thin leather band, cleared her thoughts and walked to the door.

"My Lady, we are here." It was a female voice that Simetra knew extremely well. With a silent sigh she opened the door.

A tall, rather plump woman entered quickly followed by a

shorter, daintier one. After a hurried glance revealed no one else was around, the Queen of the Elves closed the door.

Within moments the three ladies were sitting at the table each with a spiced tea cupped in their hands. An awkward silence commanded the atmosphere until the dainty Human lady broke it.

"Are we ever going to receive word?" Her voice was a badly controlled whisper.

"We must remain calm, Rhya." Simetra's voice became instantly authoritative. "I know that Tigran is your only son and you have every right to worry. Do not forget, he was born a mere half hour after Avador, he too is like my son." Rhya pursed her lips and stared at her steaming tea. The Elf Queen directed her gaze at the other, quieter lady. She smiled in understanding.

"Our boys have been away for well over a month," the larger woman finally spoke, "I cannot sleep until I know they are safe and returning home." With great difficulty she suppressed her obvious pain and dabbed her eyes with an already damp cloth.

"Our *boys* are out there somewhere trying to correct some kind of wrong. Do not forget, Katia," Simetra said looking for the right words, "Falstaff has his grandfather's book and he has been studying it for many moons. Your father has told you that Falstaff will one-day command *magic*." The others looked at her as if she was trying to tell two grown women a fairy tale. They might have believed her if Myia's hasty departure hadn't prevented her from explaining the magic that Falstaff had actually used to save her people.

Simetra changed the subject.

"I am expecting a guest tonight." The two ladies looked up from their tea. "A Wood Elf from Myia's people will be here shortly." Before they could show any expression, a soft knock at the front door nearly made them drop their cups. Simetra stood slowly and moved silently to the door.

"Who is it?" She asked through the wood.

"It is I, Fallien." A firm, yet silk-like voice answered back. Simetra opened the door.

A tall slender Wood Elf with short-cropped dark hair stood with his head bowed, the hood of his brown hunting cloak lowered to reveal his face. Standing next to him at the height just below his hip, was a child; his head bowing in perfect imitation of the larger Elf.

"Please," Simetra said feeling the discomfort of someone bowing to her, "there is no need with such formalities. Come inside, both of you and sit with us."

The Wood Elf simply blinked his eyes, momentarily stunned by her response. Awkwardly he took the child's hand and did as he was told. The two ladies at the table watched in wonderment at the new guests.

This was the first time since Myia was given Master Wylme's horse that a Wood Elf entered the village. When they arrived with the news of their rescuers and of what happened to their homeland, Pelendria was shocked. The Wood Elves displayed their emotions for the sons of the village explaining with great respect and admiration what they have done for them. Their population was depleted drastically, they claimed, but they would do everything they can to protect the village. They passionately decreed their loyalties and merged into the Gwynfell Forest shortly after; it was as if they never were.

Now two have abruptly returned.

The uneasiness soon diminished. Simetra and the mothers of Falstaff and Eviathane grew increasingly comfortable with the sleek and rather charming Wood Elf. Though from an entirely different culture, Fallien showed no signs of discomfort as he sat at the table with the Elfling on his knee. The boy's name was Gallenot, or 'Gally' as the Wood Elf affectionately called him, and he was two years old. His mother was killed in the fire of Feo-Dosia and his father was brutally slaughtered by the Dark Dwarves. His grandfather, who was the Governor of Feo-Dosia died with the boy's father as they emerged from their catacomb-hiding place in the Plains of Paladin. They were attempting a search for food and water for the rest of the survivors when the Dark Dwarves ambushed them. Fallien and his family were close friends of the Feo-Dosia family. He lost his wife and daughter in the fire. Myia had entrusted Gallenot to him before she left.

The ladies listened intently at the fascinating, yet tragic story of the Wood Elf. Simetra offered more tea with biscuits and honey as the tale progressed. She became thoroughly proud of her son, as did the other mothers with theirs. But the pride did nothing to douse the fear that burned inside them.

"So Gally is to be the next Governor of Feo-Dosia." Simetra asked trying to keep the tension at a minimal.

"Thanks to his Aunt Myia and your sons." Fallien said managing a smile. He paused and then he added with a whisper, "One of your sons used magic to help save us."

Katia's eyes widened at the unexpected statement. She looked at each of the other ladies in turn to see their reaction. They too looked surprised. But Fallien ignored the expressions and continued.

"We have never seen magic actually used before this, in fact we were still within the catacombs when it was happening. Myia explained it all to us after the rescue." His attention went to Gallenot as Simetra took him onto her knee to feed him some porridge, another foreign food. The Elfling tested it with his tongue; decided he liked it and ate.

"Yes, Gallenot will be the next Governor," Fallien returned to Simetra's statement, "but Feo-Dosia is no more. Myia is the last of the Feo-Dosia lineage next to Gally and we do not know if she lives. Of course we will decide amongst us how we will continue until we learn about her circumstances. She would be more than glad to take over the title until Gally is old enough."

"There might no longer be a 'Feo-Dosia', Fallien," Simetra Andor looked intently into the Wood Elf's dark eyes, "but the *name* Feo-Dosia lives on. You and your people are most welcome here in our woodlands of Gwynfell." She absently stroked Gallenot's thick brown hair and gave her guest a sympathetic smile. "We have all seen enough suffering. The world changes every day whether we want it to or not. My son and my husband are out there in that ever-changing world and I cannot do a single thing about it. You have lost your family in the most brutal way and starting over seems impossible, I know. But you have the opportunity." Simetra tilted her head and gazed at Gally. "And besides," she added, "*Gwynfell* is only a name."

~ **** ~

Shrouded in Skneeba's concealing magic, Man-Poda edged his ship around the western flank of Gogatha. Avador took a stand with his company at his side along the starboard edge of the *Matheia*. Everything was oddly quiet. The closeness to the island did nothing to bring new sounds. The stillness was intense and they could almost *feel* the silence that seemed to brush against their skin. They shivered at the sensation.

The sandy beaches lined with tall slender palm trees stretched for miles along the coast. What would have been rich green undergrowth ran unevenly along and beyond the tree line. What lay beyond the line of palms was difficult to see, even with Avador's sharp eyesight. The only thing that was for certain, was somewhere miles deep into the island, was a mountain range that housed a barely visible silhouette of the most enormous mountain any of them had ever seen. Its top lifted away into obscurity high above the murky skies.

Still, they sailed on in a gradual arc around the island skimming past deadly reefs and jagged rocks. Man-Poda did not waver as the islands terrain shifted from smooth sand to rougher ground. Soon they were skirting giant cliffs and the island beyond them left their sight completely. Avador stared at the cliffs sheer face and marvelled at the natural defence it supplied for the island's western region. What could ever ascend over such heights? But the cliffs grew even higher the further they sailed.

The little group from another land was awestruck.

"We may converse *quietly*." Man-Poda spoke finally and stunned his passengers. He had left the pilot box and they hadn't even noticed. The ship sailed at a noticeably slower pace. "This piece of the island is called the *Gonda-Luda*, Gogathan for 'the Dive of Dreams'. In ancient times, the islands inhabitants once believed that when their lives went astray and out of control, or simply too horrible to endure, they would dive off these cliffs and their dreams would be fulfilled. Now most believe it to be a myth. Some, especially after the demise of King Jadonas, it had crossed their minds to jump, for never had they witnessed such troubled times as the present." The group dwelled on Man-Poda's words. What was waiting for them on this bizarre piece of landmass?

"Are you to come with us?" Avador asked after the short silence.

"I cannot, Master Elf. If I leave my ship and set foot on the island, Skneeba's spell will be contaminated and the *Matheia* will be revealed. It is too much of a risk. I will need to be here for your return. But you are right to need a guide."

Without another word, Man-Poda returned to the pilot box and took the controls. The cliff wall ended abruptly and he manoeuvred the sleek schooner around its sharp corner. To their left, another cliff appeared on the opposite side. It was the exact replica of the one whose corner they just rounded. Together, the two cliffs paralleled each other, both walls reaching high above the ship. The Matheia was a mere water bug, dwarfed by the size of the opposing walls.

A breeze channelled between the two cliffs swept passed them from behind, yet Man-Poda kept the sails doused. It seemed he preferred the Graylings to remain below deck and the *Matheia* to edge forward naturally. He was afraid to so much as reveal the ripples that would be generated by quicker motions of the ship.

Within moments the cliff walls grew noticeably closer to each other leaving the impression that they were in a giant funnel. Man-Poda kept his ship clear of both walls until it seemed it would eventually become wedged between them. The captain seemed unperturbed and continued. Once they thought they would scrape roughly against the right cliffs coarse face and reveal themselves with a crash. They held their breath and waited for the impact. Man-Poda surprised them once again with his navigational skills avoiding the wall by inches. Though essentially composed, sweat did appear in little beads on his forehead.

The *Matheia* slid through the slender tube of the 'funnel' and into an unruffled inlet where it floated unscathed.

"Any other ship would not fit," whispered Man-Poda with a wry grin. The others released their breaths.

"Don't be doing that *again*." Stone Warhelm was louder than he wanted to be. He then noticed the astounding heat. It enveloped him like a sticky shroud. "Is it always this hot here?"

"Master Dwarf," Man-Poda said sarcastically, "you *are* on an island. Stone said nothing. Instead, he began peeling off his leather vest. The humidity seemed to overwhelm him. It was an engulfing presence in the form of a perpetual haze in the air. To make matters worse, the wind was refused entrance into the inlet.

The rest of the company removed their cloaks and packed them away. Their gloves were removed with somewhat difficulty due to the astounding moisture. Sweat trickled over their skin in tickling rivulets. To them the cove might as well have been a giant oven.

Man-Poda steered them towards the opposite bank. The ship moved so slowly the group began to believe it was idle. The captain then released the lever that triggered the gradual descent of the anchor. It dropped slowly into the water without a splash. The only sound was a slight continuous clicking audible only from within the ship. It clicked for long moments and stopped abruptly. The anchor found the cove's bed. Man-Poda left his place within the helm and met with the waiting group.

"I'm afraid this is where we part, my friends." The captain of the *Matheia's* face developed a gloomy expression. The group felt as if a safety line has just been severed. Avador took a quick glance around. They faced a tiny landing of white sand that might fit ten people. Arcing around the piece of 'beach' at its far end was a cliff face that loomed high above them. The ship was still surrounded on three sides by the massive rock walls. The Elf wondered where they had to go and how they were to get there. There wasn't a single passage anywhere; everything was shear wall. And even though they were cloaked in a magic that concealed them, he still felt as if he was being watched.

Man-Poda understood his questioning look. "There *is* a pass Master Elf. You just have to know where it is. Wait one moment." The captain went below deck once again. After a few minutes he had returned, a Grayling at his side.

"This is Grynde. He is to accompany you on the island."

"But I thought..." Avador began.

"Only *I* am charged with remaining on this ship," Man-Poda swept his arm in a horizontal arc. "Me and the rest of the Graylings that have been my crew. Grynde was a stowaway who somehow managed to keep clear of Aonas' annihilation. He climbed aboard the *Matheia* as she embarked for the final time away from Gogatha."

The Grayling at Man-Poda's flank stepped forward. His face was one of grim determination. A long quiver was slung over his shoulder filled with the silvery harpoons. He was hunched slightly forward as were the rest of his kind, yet sleek and muscular. His body was naked save for the loose cloth about his waist and the quiver of sharp harpoons. His long white hair tied behind him in a long strip that brushed the decking.

"Grynde has been invaluable to me aboard my ship. He is trustworthy and brave and would like nothing more than to see the wrath of Aonas avenged." The captain paused; the sarcastic smile was back. "Much like yourselves."

Chapter 23 - Foreign Soil

Grynde stood with his back to the cove and the veiled *Matheia* that nested within it. His bare feet were firmly planted onto the shores he had left so long ago. He was staring straight up at the towering cliff wall ahead of him. Avador and his little group watched and waited. They had said their hurried goodbyes after Man-Poda had their packs filled with food and supplies. The captain was adamant as he shook Avador's hand in saying he will be here for his return. The Elf hoped his waiting would not be for nothing and wished he were armed with Man-Poda's confidence.

Now here they were, across the foreign waters and onto an even stranger land. Man-Poda had said Grynde would guide them to Vyn-Turion, the mountain that housed Sovereign's Reach. The company could not fathom a mountain so vast that it could carry an entire city. Avador had the image of Vor in his mind and tried without success to picture it on a mountain peek.

"What's he doing?" Stone Warhelm snapped Avador from his thoughts. The Dwarf was still pressing his feet onto the solid ground beneath them, his poise returning with each passing moment.

The Elf shook his head. "It has been a very long time for him to return here. I guess he needs some time to come to terms with everything."

The company took this moment to regroup.

"There is no way over the cliffs," Falstaff observed, colour returning to his face.

"There must be," Avador replied, "why would Man-Poda bring us here?" A short silence followed.

Tigran Eviathane, stripped of most of his armour due to the heat and humidity, crouched next to Nectario. "We have spent a great deal on the ship practicing and I truly hope you paid close attention to what I have showed you." He indicated to the bard's scimitar. Nectario's thoughts returned to the hasty lessons Tigran had been giving him aboard the *Matheia* and hoped they would suffice. He hoped even more that he would recall the developed skills in the heat of battle. The last thing he wanted was to freeze up and return to being a burden. He pursed his lips showing to the big fighter the resolve in his eyes. Eviathane, somewhat satisfied, returned his attention to the others.

"There is no way of knowing what we are up against," Avador was saying, "It will take everything we have to expect the unexpected. We must stay together and be each others eyes."

"I feel as though we are in the shadow of a mountain ready to collapse." Stone was breathing heavily, sweat glistening his entire body. "And Pike Dwarves were not built for this incessant *heat*." The Elf smiled comfortingly at Stone but there was not much else he could do. "Drink plenty of water."

The company turned their awareness to Grynde who had moved from his original position. He wanted them to follow. The huddle dispersed and they were quickly behind the Grayling. The grey-skinned man was walking the length of the cliff face with one hand brushing the rough texture. He stopped once, then continued and stopped a second time. His feet were nearly touching the still waters of the shore when he reached out with his left hand and grasped a crease in the wall about a meter over the water. An instant later he pulled and swung out over the shoreline and behind the crease without touching the water. He certainly was a nimble creature.

Avador followed until he too reached the water. He looked at the spot on the cliff where the Grayling grasped and noticed a slight scrape that wasn't there before. *The Graylings have sharp nails*, he thought. The Elf looked back at the waiting group and then for what he thought might be the last time, the *Matheia*. Man-Poda was nowhere on her deck. With a strong heave, he too swung around and disappeared behind the crease.

Myia was the only other member to swing over without touching the water. Tigran, Stone, Nectario and Falstaff had to wade the shallow distance and climb a ragged stone to meet the waiting Grayling. There was a tall protrusion flanging the right of the crease's wall that ran the entire distance to the top of the cliff. It allowed a thin pass and if one did not know the pass was there, it would have been missed entirely. Eviathane squeezed through with some difficulty and met with the rest of the group. What they saw before them left them in awe. The crease was deep on the other side of the tall protrusion and housed a lofty flight of steps that were carved into the very cliff. They were sturdy enough but extremely steep. The two walls of the crease squeezed the sides of the steps leaving nothing to hold on to. It was a high, near vertical climb that can only be accomplished in a single-file line. The Grayling urged them forward and they began the treacherous climb to the top of the cliff.

The ascent was slow; there was no other method. The company tried not to look down as they climbed. Eviathane was having the most difficulty, as in some place the crease walls were too tight together. He had to angle his shoulders to continue his climb and at the same time keep his balance. If they leaned too far back, they would fall. If they moved too fast or too slow they would bump into someone, and they would fall. Avador watched the Grayling ahead and tried to mimic his movements while keeping the pace for his group. If anyone had to stop for a much needed breath, they would do it as one. But rest was impossible. The shear angle did not allow for it. Their leg muscles were burning. They felt their hearts pounding in their chests and all they could do was concentrate on putting one foot above the other. They were forced into leaning forward the entire way.

Falstaff was sweating liberally beneath his robes. He had been praying for the top to appear a long time ago and more than once he thought he would not make it. He was just not physically equal to the rest of the company. The young mage tried to keep his thoughts away from the agonizing climb and onto other things. Once he dared a glance downwards and regretted it immediately. He was the last in the line and he thought at least if he fell he would not take anyone with him. But just when he thought he could go no further, he heard whispers above him. He looked up and saw his friends clambering over the top, one by one until he was next. His lungs were heaving and he felt as if he would faint. He pushed forward until his sight was turning black and his breathing was reduced to sharp hisses. He saw that the top was close when the dizziness took over. Then he felt himself fall.

Falstaff's chest was hurting so he knew he was still alive. He opened his eyes and saw the big smiling face of Tigran Eviathane.

"That was close brother." Tigran ruffled the mage's beard and Falstaff sat up with a violent jolt.

"What... what happened?"

"The big guy caught you by the scruff of yer *neck* is what

happened, Shortbeard." Stone was crouching next to him, his face still red from the gruelling climb.

The young mage looked around him. Everything was still bathed in the eerie moon's feigned glow. What should have been a coolness of the night was still hot and humid. Falstaff guessed by Stone's still flushed face and the continuing heat, little or no time had gone by since he blacked out.

They were gathered in the midst of a dense undergrowth that grew tall and thick. Sitting as they were, they were somewhat shielded from any curious eyes that might be wandering around the area. The cliff was behind them dropping off into the inlet far below. Ahead, the island of Gogatha waited like a giant beast ready to spring its trap.

~ **** ~

The pause was needed. But by the way Grynde was shifting uneasily, it was soon time to go. The wind blew stronger where they crouched at the peek of the cliff. It offered some relief to the heat and the humidity that seemed to strangle Stone Warhelm. The Dwarf had stripped almost every article of clothing that he claimed suffocated him. Sweat made his muscular body glisten even in the faint light of the warped moon. He even toyed with the idea of shaving his beard but abandoned the plan as soon as he had thought it; Shortbeard would never let him live it down.

Eviathane fought the urge to stand. He too was restless and needed to move on. Instead he glanced around him and shook his head subconsciously. Falstaff had looked up from his opened book and caught the expression.

"What are you thinking?" The mage whispered. Tigran pursed his lips as though in deep thought.

"Somehow when we were told we'd be on an island, I assumed we could see the ocean all around us from anywhere we stood." Falstaff followed the big man's gaze and smiled. From their position, they could see far off into the rest of the island with every side showing no end save for the cliff face where they stood.

Stone leaned close. "Most people imagine that, big man. Even I didn't expect it to be like this."

Within the short silence that followed, the little group stared in the direction of the giant mountain. Though shrouded in thick mist and roiling clouds and somewhat faded by distance, there was no doubt it was there. They all marvelled at the size of it and questioned if it was even *reachable* let alone possible to scale.

Avador stood slowly. There was no way of knowing unless they tried.

Grynde was quick but cautious. If he had forgotten anything about the island since he had left it so many years ago, he did not show it. His steps were smooth and deliberate, his eyes always knowing where to search. The Grayling had moved them from the bluffs and onto a rocky terrain dotted with large boulders and patchy grasses. They travelled for many hours without incident and the breeze no longer carried the scent of the salty sea air. Nor had they encountered a living person since they departed the *Matheia*.

But caution was always beside them.

Soon they were once again surrounded by land and there was no sign that they were even on an island. Avador had guessed that Man-Poda had known this part of the island was uninhabited. At least, he thought, back when the captain had left Gogatha it was uninhabited.

The Elf noticed that the Grayling needed little rest. Every time they had stopped for food and drink, Grynde was the first to rise and urge Avador to continue. He had been leading them in a somewhat easterly direction, almost as though he wanted to be centred on the island as much as possible.

Soon the heat gave little way to a coolness that came gradually and the Grayling stopped once again. Stone stopped next to Avador and the others circled around them.

"Night must have fallen, Elfling." The Dwarf seemed to some extent more comfortable.

"Yes," the Elf agreed, "the humidity has broken."

They camped near a small grove of olive trees surrounded by a thin scattering of evergreens. From what they could tell, the sparse growth of trees continued eastward until a bluff stopped them altogether. Avador moved towards the bluff while the others remained within the confines of their fireless campsite. He stayed low as he gazed over the embankment. He saw hundreds of tiny lights clustered in a valley below and strained his eyes to focus on what they were. It was a village, he concluded after his eyes adjusted. There was even a small amount of activity and a faint hum of voices. Avador stared a moment longer and returned to his friends.

Grynde waited in anticipation. He knew of the village; the Elf saw it in his eyes. He saw something else as well. There was a hint of both hatred and regret buried in the depths of the Grayling's silver eyes. The Elf looked at him quizzically.

"Me home."

Grynde shocked them all when he spoke. Avador nearly jumped out of his skin.

"Home... taken.... given." His use of the language of Man

was obviously limited and every word was pronounced with a strong accent. But there was no mistake at what he wanted to say. His voice was a whisper and not because they needed to be quiet. The group knew somehow that that was how Graylings spoke. It was too natural in the way he moved his mouth and the method in his expression.

"Aonas took your village and gave it to his people?" Avador had already moved next to the Grayling.

"No..." Grynde was shaking his head. "... Graylings killed... family *dead*!" Avador heard enough.

"Are we safe here?" Grynde stared at first as if he didn't understand what Avador had asked.

The Grayling looked around before returning his gaze to the Elf. "Safe... now." Then he shrugged. *Nothing is certain.*

Avador turned his attention to his group. They were all ready for sleep but remained standing.

"Stone. Take first watch. There is a small village below the embankment. I will go in and see what I could find."

"Yer *not* going in alone."

"I have to. Stealth and speed are needed. I will not be long." The others began to protest but were cut off by the Elf's defiant stare.

"Do not put yourself in any danger." Tigran spoke each word slowly and put a strong hand on Avador's shoulder. "If you sense it, retreat. We will not have enough time from up here to be of any help." Eviathane hated this. He hated another parting with his friend.

"I promise, brother. If I sense anything beyond my capabilities, I will retreat. Foremost is to keep us a secret. Besides, I do not plan on following trouble. Don't you think we are in enough of it as it is?"

Avador looked at his companions, each in turn.

"Rest, my friends. I won't be so long that you begin to worry."

Myia stepped forward. "I think I could speak for all of us when I say it is too late for that." Her chestnut eyes easily displayed her emotions. Avador returned a smile of understanding, his eyes locked onto hers for a moment longer before wrenching them free to look at the others.

"Trust me," was all he said before disappearing over the bluff. They stared after him knowing he was trying to protect them. They also knew that they were *not* going to rest until he returned.

~****~

Aonas moved towards Skneeba like a panther seizing upon its pray. The deformed mage shrank back until he felt his back touch the cool stone of a wall. A rage Skneeba could never shake built up within his heart once again. *So much power! Yet **he** uses it!* The king of Sovereign's Reach held the staff of Kara-Toh right up to Skneeba's face, the green vapour brushing against his skin.

The feeling was sickening.

"What happened to the Dark Dwarves?" Aonas' words echoed throughout the fountain chamber. Skneeba said nothing, his cheek pushing into the rough stone of the wall as if it would help him avoid the staff's revolting effect. He wanted to blend into the wall and never come out. His master held the staff there for what seemed like all eternity saying nothing more until at last he snatched it away. Skneeba dared to breathe once again, a slow trickle of cold sweat sliding down his spine. He watched Aonas turn his back and slowly walk away from him.

The ruler's mind was racing. A single thought could not remain inside his head for more than a moment. He knows something had gone wrong; his expression always betrayed his thoughts.

"Have they done what I have told them?" Aonas turned and fixed his stare directly into Skneeba's eyes. The mage nodded but the callous king remained suspicious. "Feo-Dosia *burned*?"

Another nod.

"Are the Wood Elves dead? *All* of them?"

A pause. It was a big mistake and it did not go unnoticed. Aonas smiled wickedly turning away from the mage as he did. Skneeba's heart sank for the millionth time as he watched his ruler walk to the large stone steps at the far end of the fountain hall and disappeared behind a curtain to the right of them. He knew what was behind that curtain.

"Come!" Aonas' booming voice shot forth from behind the black screen of the curtain. The mage did as he was told and walked his uneven steps through to the other side and met with Aonas.

They were in a short corridor, unlit and filled with the dust gathered from years of neglect. The deep green that the Sceptre of Kara-Toh's vapour emitted washed the hallway with an eerie light. Oh, how Skneeba wanted to rid Aonas of that thing. The king waited until Skneeba edged behind him before continuing to the end of the corridor that opened to the outdoors. Skneeba could smell putrid air as they walked closer to the exit.

They passed through the opening and were met with a deafening silence. The two were standing on a balcony that overlooked a massive courtyard. Aonas beckoned the disheartened magic user to the railing. Skneeba paused only momentarily. He had been on this balcony once before during Jadonas' reign. He closed his eyes and brought forth the vision of the beautiful square that seemed to go on without end hosting lush gardens and glimmering man-made ponds. He recalled the sounds of birds and small animals and the sweet smells of endless flowerbeds. Jadonas was a man who appreciated beauty.

The mage opened his eyes and looked at a nightmare turned reality. He wanted to jump over the railing and end his life but the bastard Aonas would not allow him even that. The green was gone, the ponds dried. Even the trees that flanked the outer rims of the courtyard he once remembered were uprooted and burned. In there place was an army so huge, it seemed to stretch out even beyond the great courtyard's borders and lost into the dismal grey of the land beyond. It was a sea of shifting people of every race standing in endless rows, eyes fierce and staring ahead. Skneeba dared a glance at Aonas. He was smiling as he turned his head to the awestruck mage.

"Beautiful, isn't it?" Aonas' voice was a scornful song. He looked back at the men below. "Grandalimus' Army."

~****~

The young Elf moved stealthily down the slope of the ridge. His thoughts were on his friends who he left under the canopy of evergreens. He knew they detested the fact that he left them to take cover while he went on alone towards another unknown. But he also knew that he was right. The activity he noticed from the village was more than enough to make him uncomfortable. Secrecy was key. And speed was essential.

Avador kept his eyes scanning the village and its perimeter.

It neared with every passing second. Soon the little points of light grew into the unmistakable forms of torches. The activity developed into the movement of people. There were more inhabitants than the Elf anticipated. He silently cursed the ongoing night and its strange illumination. The people must use torches all the time here.

He paused for a brief moment within the shadows of a large evergreen and pulled his cloak from his travel pack. Ignoring the heat, he threw it on to cover any sign of the glimmering chain mail beneath his tunic and pressed forward in a crouch. Within moments he reached the outskirts of the little village and stopped to gain sight of anything that moved.

Something was not right.

The Elf waited a moment longer until he was satisfied no one was around to spot him entering the village, then moved in with the stealth of a black cat. Pinning himself to the wall of the nearest building and sticking to the deep shadows, Avador slid towards the corner of the wooden structure. His keen ears picked up a sound that came from the other side of the building and he stopped instinctively. He scanned the area, his heart beating in his ears. Where were the villagers? The streets were empty and the windows of all the houses were dark. What of the torchlight he saw from the heights of the bluff?

Then he heard voices gathering together not far from the house he was blending into. They seemed to be coming from the opposite side from where he entered the village. Avador dared a silent glance passed the building's corner and saw the way was clear. He waited no longer and bound from house to house until what he heard came into sight. He stopped far enough away to get a clear view without being spotted himself. Just on the village's eastern fringe, there was a gathering of soldiers, all holding the torches that the Elf had spotted earlier. The soldiers seemed to be arguing about something. Avador glanced around the dimly lit area and noticed something that shocked him to his bones. The soldiers had left a rather large pile of dead bodies, their limbs dangling eerily just outside the glow of the torchlight. The Elf breathed in a long take of breath to calm himself and tried to measure the situation. There seemed to be a disagreement between the soldiers.

"Do it!" One hissed fearfully.

"Before it's too late." Added another.

Avador peered with more intent concentrating on the scene before him. There was a villager caked in blood lying unmoving in the midst of the soldiers. One soldier had his sword drawn and pointing to the villager's throat. The soldier's face was wet with streaks of tears. The scene baffled the Elf. Then, something darker than the gloom itself moved among the men. It was there and gone in the same instant and Avador would have missed it altogether if he blinked.

Without warning the soldier brandishing the sword swiped at the villager's neck and took his head clean off with a sickening wet sound. Avador gasped and darted his head back behind the building's wall. The soldiers looked over at once hearing the unexpected sound. Three broke away from the others and moved in the Elf's direction. But when they reached the house and peered around its corner, they found nothing that wasn't there before.

~****~

Myia Feo-Dosia kept her eyes to the village below as she hid within her own choice of shadows. The scattered torchlight below had at one point come together as if the bearers of the torches grouped together at the far end of the village. The Wood Elf found this perplexing. What was happening? A few times her keen eyes caught glimpses of the raiding Avador as he moved stealthily ahead. One moment he was there and another he was gone. Then he disappeared altogether and Myia realized that he had reached the village and went in. There were faint sounds coming from the far side of the village and the Wood Elf thought it might even be voices. But the wind had picked up in a steady rhythm up there on the crest of the tall bluff and she couldn't be sure.

Still, she waited. Myia refused to sleep as she was told to do. She wanted to wait and make sure Avador returns. The others did not argue for she had the sharpest eyes of all of them, yet they would keep one man on watch at all times while the others slept.

Avador had taken longer than anticipated. Myia even thought she caught a quick movement of the Elf fleeing the village and he should have been back by now. Maybe she was mistaken. Forcing down her apprehension, she crouched even lower and waited.

Avador Andor broke from the village outskirts and into the thin veil of the evergreens. He began climbing the bluff without looking behind him trying to remain as silent as possible. Fear almost betrayed him of even that. Once he stopped quickly to check for signs of pursuit. Finding there were none, he continued his steady climb within the deepest shadows he could find. Waking his friends and getting them away from here was the only thing on his mind.

"*Son.*"

The voice of Grandalimus Andor stopped Avador in his tracks.

H ow much longer can we wait here?" Stone Warhelm was more than a little annoyed by the Elf's delay. His watch had ended long ago but he refused to sleep disregarding Eviathane's urgings to do so. "Something has gone wrong!" He hissed the words in frustration.

"Calm yourself, Stone." Tigran tried his best to reason with the irritated Dwarf but his tactics were useless.

"I will *not* calm myself! It is just *wrong* for us to be sleeping while Avador is out there alone regardless of what he or *any* of you's are saying!"

"You have to trust him, Stone. He is a lot more resourceful than you give him credit for. Besides, if anything had happened to him, Myia would have spotted it." The two looked expectantly at the Wood Elf who was standing a few yards away. She said nothing but looked back with a hint of anxiousness in her eyes. Their hearts sank even further. That was it; every member of the little group was awake and packed. Even the tense Grynde was ready to go after the absent Elf. Without a word, Stone motioned to the Grayling to lead. One by one Avador's small group hastened as quietly as possible over the ridge and disappeared into the foliage.

~****~

Avador Andor slid the *Kingblade* from its scabbard and set its tip by his feet. The Elf lowered himself to one knee as if in prayer and touched his moist forehead to the cool steel of the hilt.

Father. He kept his words within the confines of his mind; he knew there was no need to speak them aloud. The wind seemed to die in response to Avador's thoughts leaving an eerie stillness within the evergreens scattered shadows. The sensation was as though nothing lived outside the boundaries of the Elf's darkened cover.

"*Avador,*" Grandalimus repeated, his voice the remnants of an echo, "*I sense the dilemma that even now lingers in your heart. My son, your compassion is divided into many portions and it is difficult, if not impossible to choose from those with the greatest significance.*" The young Elf swallowed hard at his father's words, afraid at what might be coming. "*Do not keep me at the foremost of your thoughts. You are not on a journey to save me from my fate. You are on a journey to do what I cannot. As King, it is my duty to protect our lands and its people.*" The Elf King paused to allow his words to sink into the mind of Avador who was already grinding his teeth in exasperation.

What are you saying? You cannot be saved? Avador faltered with the possibility of his words being true. The pause that followed wrenched his heart into one of complete and utter pain. *Father?*

And the tears flowed again.

"*My young boy,*" the hollow words returned with an unmistakable ache, "*my fate is sealed and must be accepted. As is yours. Our duty must remain clear. Do not allow your emotions to throw you from what you must do. It is a circumstance that I have faced countless times, each with great regret.*" Avador opened his eyes now and blinked back the tears. He drew in an uneven, choppy breath and searched for a resolve that would not come.

"*I have sensed what has happened to me back at the Kentro when we were all on the balcony. My first reaction* was to try and hide it from you. But it would have all been in vain. The curse was seeping through me in a slow trickle of changes. My insides were being altered even as we spoke. J felt the urge to cry but my tears were dry and gone. My insides were the first to change, to turn me into an empty shell of what J was." Avador was shaking his head at what he was hearing; a new surge of pain ripped through him at the thought of what his father must have went through. The young Elf could not fathom what it must have been like to feel a *curse* flow through you and in the end, eat you alive. The image of his father, of how he was once a powerful presence full of charisma and confidence came to mind but then stolen by the vision of what he saw back in Lord's Lair.

"Do not dishearten yourself, Avador," Grandalimus said as if reading the Elf's mind. "The curse has taken everything from me, everything except my heart. Jt is my core, my very essence that stopped the power from taking me completely." Avador believed this at once. A lesser man would have been taken over entirely. Like the other walking skeletons that attacked them in Lord's Lair, he thought grimly.

"Continue on to Vyn-Turion," Avador's father said before he could give the matter of the other skeletons another thought, "Lead as you were meant to lead, continue your task and finish it. The fate of our lands depends on what you do from here on. And do not despair. J am with you... J will always be with you..." Grandalimus' words trailed off into the nothingness that surrounded Avador. The Elf rose shakily to his feet and returned the *Kingblade* to its scabbard. When he turned to continue up the ridge to his friends, he found them all standing there watching with both patience and awe.

The little group had climbed back over the rise and rested.

Those who had already slept stood guard while the others lay in the deep foliage and closed their eyes. Only the restless Grynde crouched a little away from the group in anticipation of the journey ahead.

Stone sat with Tigran with their backs leaning against the trunk of a fallen tree. They watched their leader as he lay disquietly under his travel blanket. Something had troubled him greatly while he was gone on his trek to the village. In contrast, Myia slept somewhere to his right, her face more at peace now that Avador had returned safely.

"Something is happening on this island." Stone said as he stared out ahead at nothing in particular.

"What do you mean?" Eviathane asked turning to look at his friend. The Dwarf paused.

"Avador was affected by more than his encounter with his father below the ridge. When he awakes, he will tell us."

"Do you think he will be ok?"

"Hard to tell. But he will continue to lead us to where we must go, that is for certain." The Dwarf held his countenance in utmost determination.

"You have absolute belief in Avador, don't you?" Tigran asked smiling.

Stone nodded his head slowly. "Credibility, trust and respect are all virtues that must be earned. The Elfling is worthy of all three." He broke into silence thinking through the words to say. "Never in his life had he faced such dangers and impossible decision-making. Grandalimus himself would have been put through a difficult test to get us here. But Avador has made it this far even with the added weight of what's become of his father. Yes, young Eviathane, I have absolute belief in the Elfling."

Falstaff appeared from somewhere out of the darkness and

sat quietly next to Tigran. A sleepy Nectario followed the young mage and sat next to him. They all remained silent letting the distant sounds of the night take over the atmosphere. The five looked at the sleeping Elves before them, each man lost within their own separate thoughts. The wind picked up slightly and muffled any other noise as it swept past the nearby trees producing a low whistling sound. They seemed to be completely alone when the sound of a snapping twig barely reached the ears of Stone Warhelm. The Dwarf sat straight up and listened with more focus. The others looked at him questioningly and were about to ask what is wrong when the burly Dwarf grabbed for the first thing he could reach and swung it in a great arc behind him. There was a huge sound of breaking wood and a curious reverberation of slackened strings and the quiet of the night exploded into a deafening detonation of noise.

"We're ambushed!" Shouted Stone as everyone jumped to their feet. Avador and Myia were next to their companions in seconds, bows held nocked and ready to fire.

Stone dropped the splintered end of Nectario's lute and grasped the handle of his battle hammer that was still strapped to his back. The bard gasped in shock but there was no time for lamentation. A man lay unconscious before them with blood flowing freely from his forehead; a sword glinted dully next to him in the strange moonlight.

"A scout." Said the Dwarf raising his sight as at least a dozen soldiers materialized from the surrounding gloom moving around them in an attempt to encircle the surprised company.

Avador moved to the front of his group putting himself between them and the approaching men and pulled his arrow closer to his chin warning the soldiers that they were not to be taken without a fight. This seemed to work; the soldiers paused as one and stared in what seemed to be complete shock. One leaned closer to the man next to him and whispered something in his ear. Then they all turned their attention from Avador to Grynde who moved next to the Elf and slid a sleek harpoon from the quiver hanging on his back and held it in a throwing position. At once the dozen men replaced their weapons to their sheaths and held their hands to the sky. One of them dared a step closer and said something in a strange tongue. The company remained fixed in their position, live statues within the sparse trees.

"We mean no harm." The man tried again in the language of Man realizing the little group was not from Gogatha. This sparked a response.

"Who are you?" The man with the bow and the sharp ears asked suspiciously.

"I am Har-Kana, and these are my comrades." He indicated to the men standing next to him. "And *that*," he said pointing to the unconscious man at Stone's feet, "is our leader."

~****~

"That was my *father's* lute." Nectario shouted angrily at Stone Warhelm after the two companies settled into a less tense gathering.

"Remind me to thank him later." The Dwarf retorted and walked away leaving the bard standing with both fists clenched and mouth wide open. Stone walked to where Avador was talking with the leader of the other group, now recovered and a large bandage wrapped tightly about his head.

"Ours is among the last of the Gogathan villages," the man was saying to Avador as he approached. His skin was dark as were the rest of his company in typical style of the islands natives and his accent reminded the Dwarf of Man-Poda's. "In fact, we are not even soldiers. We are simple men who picked up arms to try and stop Aonas' soldiers from doing anymore harm to the island."

"Why do they even listen to Aonas?" Avador asked, horrified that the merciless *king* would even have followers.

"That, we do not know." The Gogathan was shaking his head as though the very thought disgusted him. "What we do know is that the kingdom has taken a turn for the worse. We hear that Aonas' mind is poisoned more and more with every passing day.

"Where will you go now?" Avador asked.

"Maybe to the next village. Maybe further south where Aonas has not yet attacked and warn its people of what is happening."

"That is a very good idea," replied Avador, "you do that while we make for Vyn-Turion."

The Gogathan shook his head once again. "Why you want to do that is a mystery to me. Why do you not go home?" Avador smiled. He did not tell the Gogathan everything deciding it was probably better not to.

"Many men have tried to enter the mountains surrounding Vyn-Turion. None have yet to return. Not as they once were anyway. They say Aonas has put a creature to guard his mountain fortress of any who try to pass. He calls it '*Gali-Gunzaro*'...Creature of the Night. It is a thing of great evil produced from the darkest form of unexplainable magic. It can only be harmed at night since its substance depends on it. And now, since night never leaves, we know it *can* be harmed."

The others were all gathered around now, including the Gogathans, hearing the leader's tale.

"The creature can only be seen when light touches it." Har-Kana added as he sat next to his leader. "Aonas has taken care of that, it seems."

"But how have you learned all that?" Avador was confused.

"Aonas first 'created' the Gali-Gunzaro when he took the throne. His people were leaving his fortress and city by the hundreds and coming to the island below to gather quickly diminishing supplies. They had every intention of returning to their families but Aonas had already lost his common sense by that time." Har-Kana paused to see if the Elf was following. Avador's face stared back attentively. "Once more, our *king* forced Skneeba, a truly powerful mage with little control over his actions, to draw from his lunar powers and created a guardian, a beast of the night to guard his mountain fortress. He did this purely on an impulse that told him those people were traitors and could never return. Many have tried but the creature slaughtered them all. One man had wounded it once, a veteran soldier that had gotten close enough when the sun's light was touching it. He waited bravely in the deep shadows for it to draw near and struck it valiantly with his sword but it was too quick for him in the end. He managed to call out to his followers and warned them of its weakness before it tore him apart with such cruelty and ferocity; he became unrecognizable as human.

The two companies parted ways with a renewed sense of duty, though with hearts somewhat heavier. The Gogathans moved south and Grynde took the little group northward. Avador marvelled at their bravery, a small band of vigilante villagers attempting to stand against impossible odds. He explained to his group what he witnessed in the village. They were just as mystified as the Elf at what was going on. All too soon, however, they were sure they were going to find out.

Grynde was relentless in his drive to move ahead; all the questions that puzzled the company seemed to not matter to the Grayling. His was a quest with only one goal: *retribution*.

"I am assuming, Elfling, we are moving towards the mountain range that houses Vyn-Turion?" Stone was speaking to Avador as they moved along a rugged landscape strewn with dry shrubbery and little cover.

"We are."

"And how do you intend on getting past that creature if we encounter it?"

"Haven't a clue."

"Right."

The warmth returned in a sudden wave that made it difficult to breathe. Sometime during the few hours the company had been travelling, day must have returned trailing a brutal afternoon heat behind it. But the lingering vision of night refused to give way. Everything was even now cast in gloomy shadow and the warped moon skulked unnervingly overhead refusing to shed more than a dull light. Whenever a stray cloud passed in front of the misshapen sphere, the land was shrouded in complete darkness and the company was forced to halt their progress until there was a break in the clouds. The result was maddening and did little to relieve their already breaking spirits.

Eventually the terrain grew more rugged and earthy changing from level ground to wild foothills. Grynde moved ahead as if possessed, stopping merely for short periods only to impatiently rise and beckon the tiring group to continue. Each time the little company would comply and allow themselves to be led over difficult terrain that hampered their progress and took a toll on their quickly diminishing energy. Finally

Avador took charge, realizing they would need their strength for what might lie ahead and called a halt. The group crowded together, breathing heavily and sweating freely.

"We will make camp by those boulders," Avador pointed to a cluster of large rocks the others would have otherwise missed. "They will provide both shade and cover from any wandering eyes." The others agreed vehemently and moved quietly to their leader's choice of rest.

"We must be in the foothills that base that mountain range." Stone was sitting with Tigran, Avador and Falstaff nodding northward to an ominous scene. The great mountain that housed Sovereign's Reach stood noticeably closer as a murky silhouette against a deep black backdrop. It stood unyielding and impenetrable against the obscure skies, an intimidating giant with the lesser summits of the mountain range that stood as its children far below its midsection. Even in these dark conditions it was unmistakable as to what it was. The scene teased at the very courage of the brave little group. The questions grew within their minds and the answers became more and more evasive. What were they to do when they reached the mountains? How were they to scale the impossible heights?

"The people of Sovereign's Reach must have a way to the city on top of that mountain." Avador was thinking more out loud than anything else.

"The people of Sovereign's Reach don't have a way into the mountain range at all, Elfling." Stone was quick to point out the obvious. "How can we fight a creature that cannot be seen in this relentless night?" The Dwarf was convinced, without the shadow of a doubt that the Gali-Gunzaro existed.

"Obviously, Aonas did not count on this 'night', this after-effect of the curse. He unwittingly created a way for us to harm the creature."

"But we can't *see* it, Elfling!" Stone was exasperated. "Once we enter the mountain range it will be able to see *us*! And that is not a sensation I want to feel any time soon." Avador was resting his chin in the cup of his hands looking somewhat like a little boy. His mind was searching for a plan but the plan was not coming very quickly. He too was rather lost. His eyes wandered over to where Falstaff was squinting through the pale light in an effort to study his great book. He had been doing that with every stop and Avador smiled at his friend's want to help in any way he can. It gave him more hope knowing that Falstaff was with them.

"Falstaff?" Avador moved closer and interrupted the young mage from his heavy scrutinizing of the books pages.

"Mmm?" Falstaff kept his eyes forward barely acknowledging his friend.

"Does it say anything in there about shedding light?"

At first, Falstaff did not reply. He just sat there thinking. Then a slow smile stretched across the mage's bearded features and the young Elf felt the beginnings of a plan form in his mind.

~****~

Once the incredible heat and the stifling humidity began to subside into a more comfortable atmosphere, Grynde was given the okay to lead. The company kept close to each other, their eyes straining continuously against the blackness that grew increasingly more impenetrable. Avador moved stealthily behind the Grayling, Falstaff and Nectario following only a few strides behind. Myia marched bravely behind the bard while Stone and Tigran took the rear guard. Each member of the group was immersed into their own thoughts but none kept their attention away from the task at hand. They felt as though they were marching to an undeniable death trap but their confidence in Avador prevailed over their fears. They moved ahead over the challenging terrain without any more doubt, their resolve placed forcibly intact.

The landscape changed progressively as the Grayling led them farther north. The low foothills grew ever more steeper and the soil more jagged. Even within the steady darkness the company could determine they were climbing in elevation. Eventually the air began to thin and breathing grew increasingly difficult. But along the incline of the slopes, the edge of a forest emerged from the obscurity beyond. No life was evident as they trudged on with minor difficulty. Once or twice Avador thought he spotted a flittering shadow within the vagueness of his surroundings as they broke the tree line. It could have been his imagination, he thought, but kept his senses sharp regardless.

The peeks loomed before them in the distance after many long hours of marching. They stopped only twice to rest and eat but each time was brief. The foothills were gradually left behind and the company found themselves on a continual angled climb over rough stone and loose rock that at times broke loose beneath their feet and forced them to come to a complete stop in order to keep from skidding backwards. They used the branches of the trees around them to support themselves in case they slipped and pull themselves up and forward. At times the terrain would level and they were given the chance to catch their breath but a climb like the one before always waited beyond each break.

Avador touched Grynde on the shoulder and gestured to him to stop. The others stopped abruptly and watched Avador put a finger to his lips. He then edged himself down the slanted rise until he reached Stone.

Putting his mouth to his ear, he whispered, "For the better part of an hour we were being followed." He watched the Dwarf's eyebrow rise in somewhat surprise.

"How do you..." he began but quickly stopped himself. Stone glanced around in nonchalant fashion.

"Whoever is out there has been keeping his distance. But now he's getting nearer.

"There's a trap waiting for us." Stone remarked almost inaudibly. "He's getting more confident."

"Whatever is waiting for us, it's over that ridge." Avador said keeping his voice at a whisper. "We'll make like we are setting camp so it doesn't seem like we caught on. I'll move ahead and investigate. You make sure our follower doesn't sound any alarms." But before Stone could respond, Grynde was already moving behind them, a quick shadow himself, wordless and silent. The group watched as a shiny harpoon appeared in his hand, glinting in the dull moonlight. Then, in one fluid motion the slender piece of steel flew through the gloom and the Grayling pounced after it. They heard a dull thud as the harpoon struck someone. Grynde was already on top of him with his clawed hand pressing roughly into his mouth blocking any sounds that might have emerged from his shock. Within moments, the group retraced their steps down the slope and stood behind the Grayling who still had his hand over his victim's mouth. It was a man wrapped in an old hunting cloak with the hood drawn to hide his features. He was embedded into a tree, the silver harpoon protruding from his left shoulder, blood spewing from the open wound.

Avador drew close and yanked the cowl away from his face. The man was bearded but young looking. His eyes were closed tight as he tried to ward off the pain, his teeth clenching beneath the Grayling's firm grip. Tears of agony flowed freely down his face.

"Gag him," Avador said. "I'll move ahead and see what's waiting for us beyond that ridge. The Elf never made five steps when the man pinned to the tree bit savagely into Grynde's hand. The Grayling released his grip only for a moment but it was enough to allow the man a brief scream. The sound was like an explosion after the lengthy quiet of the night. Grynde struck him hard with his elbow across the temple, and the man went limp.

But it was too late.

They could already hear the silence of the forest ahead come to life with shouts of astonishment and rage. Then, the ridge exploded as dozens of heavily armed men in black cloaks burst over the crest and charged the company that stood in shock only fifty yards below. Their rush was swift as they took the downhill and the group took a defensive stand. There were too many. There was no way they could hold them for more than a few minutes. Myia and Avador fired off two arrows each and the Grayling released as many harpoons. Six men dropped and rolled crashing into the trees but the rest seemed not to notice and drove on relentlessly. The sudden attack allowed only the smallest glimpse of what was coming. They were basically human in appearance but madness reflected unmistakably in their eyes. Long, sharp tongues hung grotesquely from yawning mouths. The sight was horrifying and they were immediately on top of the little group.

Tigran Eviathane unleashed his long-sword and let it fly in arcs of lightning. His scream was a long howl almost as if he was anxious for this fight. Men were cut down before him as though they were nothing but a mild hindrance. But the rush was long and men kept coming without slowing down.

Avador forced the group in a circle, the *Kingblade's* silvery blade glinting wildly as the Elf swung his sword to hold off the attack as much as he could. Tigran was at his right and he could hear the clang of the big man's sword ring loudly in his ears. *There's too many*, he thought frantically. Then, to Tigran's right, Falstaff went down in a heap beneath his robes, a stray mace smashing into his shoulder shattering the bones. Eviathane dropped his shield. He leaned down and hefted the mage over his shoulder with one hand using the other to parry off relentless attacks. He was cut and bleeding in at least a dozen places and his strength was beginning to fail.

Stone held his powerful hammer with both hands. Already he was looking towards the next man's skull, which he crushed with another wild swing. His battle cry surged through him as if it were the very strength that kept him alive. For him, this was normal: A battleground in which every second might be your last. But he had an army with him to repel the numerous attacks from every side. His company was no more than a handful and they were greatly outnumbered.

"Grynde!" Avador screamed from one side of their circle. The Grayling moved swiftly next to the desperate Elf. "We need to get out of here... *now!*"

No one was sure if the Grayling understood but he moved frantically away from them slashing at two of the black cloaked men and motioned at what seemed to be an escape eastward. Avador did not hesitate. Before the opening was closed off again, he thrust Myia and Nectario roughly towards the Grayling and they fled. Myia was unwilling to leave them behind but the look from Avador showed he wasn't accepting anything else.

Stone, Eviathane and Avador moved backwards barely holding the attackers at bay while trying desperately to keep their wits. All three knew they could do nothing against the dozens of men that remained in the fight, a fight that was undeniably theirs. The three fighters broke for the forest eastward and they were followed immediately, the surge of frantic men creeping behind them. They ran like hunted animals discovered without warning. They ran, and they did not turn to look at what was breathing down their necks.

~ **** ~

"Okay! Okay! Put me down! I can run!" Falstaff was screaming over Tigran's shoulder as the big man drove through the crowded undergrowth that grew above his knees jostling the wounded mage and making the pain in his shoulder almost too much to bear. Eviathane would have refused to put his friend down under normal circumstances. But now things were far from normal. He was losing blood from many places and with it his strength. They were being chased by dozens of grotesque lunatics that desperately wanted to kill them and were gaining by the second.

The big man strained to see what was happening ahead. Sweat flowed into his eyes and it stung painfully. Wiping them frantically with his free arm he thought he caught a glimpse of a bridge spanning a huge chasm; but he couldn't be sure. Avador was shouting something at his group behind him but the rush of wind carried his words away. Finally Tigran slowed briefly to ease Falstaff down and together they ran on.

Suddenly a rush of spears and arrows whipped passed them and into the surrounding trees. Eviathane felt helplessness begin to sink in. His skin crawled knowing he was left fully exposed from behind. And now they were shooting *projectiles* at them. He wished he still had his shield strapped to his back but it was too late for wishes. Knowing he was slowing, he fought to regain his resolve and pressed forward. Abruptly they emerged from the short run of forest and very nearly dropped off a deep chasm. But Tigran was right. There *was* a bridge, narrow and spanning an abyss hundreds of feet wide.

Avador was shouting for everyone to move across. Nectario was looking after the Grayling who was already crossing in a series of pounces that rocked the slender roping of the bridge. The bard hesitated as he looked down.

"Move, you fool!" Stone heaved Nectario and forced him onto the narrow wooden floor of the swaying bridge. Then they ran in a forced single-file line across the treacherous heights as another shower of spears and arrows rained all around them, some embedding into the wood of the bridge, some dropping uselessly into the chasm striking the rock hundreds of meters below. It seemed the end of the bridge would never come. The little group, breathing heavily and sweating freely, forced themselves to run even faster. When they neared the end a sudden jolt dangerously shook the swinging bridge below their feet. They each dropped to their knees to keep from falling. The crazed pursuers reached the bridge and were trampling it with enormous force. The company thought they were in the middle of an earthquake. They forced themselves to their feet and ran the remaining length.

All except Tigran.

The struggling fighter collapsed about forty feet from their destination, his strength completely drained. Avador saw this at once. The crazed humans, unhindered by fatigue, were drawing closer to the fallen companion. Avador bound back onto the narrow bridge, an arrow already nocked to his bow. He saw the enemies were almost on top of his friend and fired the arrow into the first as he raised his sword to finish off the unfortunate man who failed to cross the chasm. He gave a painful grunt and fell over the side screaming all the way until he hit the jagged rocks below. The others behind kept coming, one by one and maddened beyond rage. But the Elf was relentless in his strive to save his friend. He advanced across the swaying bridge caring nothing of what happens to himself thinking only of the infuriated beasts that wanted to kill Tigran. One at a time Avador took them down with his arrows all the while advancing closer to his friend. He ignored the spears that flew at him and let them fly at times so closed he felt the rush of the wind they created. He ignored the shouts of his friends on the other side of the chasm. The wind blew hard and harsh whipping his cloak in every direction but he ignored that too trying to keep his stability in check. An arrow grazed his thigh but he didn't slow. Many men fell over the bridge as Avador struck again and again. Many clung to the rope railings even in death. Their entry towards Eviathane was soon congested with the bodies of their own and they began climbing furiously over one another to get to him. But they were too late. Avador fired his last arrow and unleashed the *Kingblade*. The fury built within the Elf was the fire that fuelled him. He stood over his friend's fallen form and dared them all to try and take him. Those who tried soon discovered the young Elf was a force to be reckoned with. Limbs were lost in a spray of blood; Avador was soon drenched with it, his own mixing with that of his attackers. At one point the maddened humans were even forced to back off in a short retreat. That's when Avador reached down with strength he thought he never had, and yanked the big Eviathane to his feet.

"Avador..." Tigran began. He wanted to tell his friend to run. He wanted him to escape. But he stopped himself, thinking if he stays and dies, Avador would have sacrificed himself for nothing. Tigran found his strength somewhere in the depths of his core and released a scream so loud it left both parties stunned. Then, shocking Avador with another feat of strength, he shoved the Elf ahead and began to run. The pause from their pursuers gave them enough gap to get away but within seconds they were after them again causing the bridge to jerk violently. After what seemed like eternity, the friends were across to the other side but the enemies were nearing as well.

Stone was waiting for them.

While Avador struggled on the bridge, he had Nectario ready with a long dagger to cut the thick roping that was attached to large solid pins buried into the earth. The Dwarf braced himself on powerful legs and swung his battle hammer at the first hapless man to reach the other side. He crumpled in a heap on the wooden flooring of the bridge.

"Now!" He shouted at the hysterical bard. Nectario cut frantically at the substantial ropes as Stone took out as many men as he could. But not all were stopped by the valiant Dwarf. A handful made it across and attacked at once. Nectario cut through the first set of ropes and the bridge angled dangerously to one side. Stone fought off madmen trying to kill Nectario who in turn fought to topple the bridge and be rid of the incessant attackers.

Myia let her arrows fly, dropping as many men as possible before they could do any more harm. Avador was up and fighting those that made it across, striking menacingly with his father's sword. Grynde was a whirlwind of arms and legs as he smashed into the oncoming men clawing the flesh from their very bones.

"Hurry up, *bard*!" Shouted Stone Warhelm his back to Nectario as he swung his deadly hammer at their pursuers.

Finally the last of the roping was severed and the shouts of those still atop the bridge could be heard from miles around. The bard drew his scimitar and swung it wildly in a clash of steel against the bizarre savages that threatened to kill them all.

But the handful that made it across, though frantic to slaughter their hunt, died at the hands of Avador's little band.

They died without knowing why they even attacked this insubstantial group. They were once men that reasoned and thought. They were at one point a logical race that cared for others and fought only to protect. But that time might as well have been centuries ago. Though they did not remember, Aonas very recently had them transformed into what they are now. Their morals were stripped from them and they were turned into animalistic carnivores. Their past was soon forgotten and the only thing left was an unquenchable hunger to kill. They still maintained the human ability to think, but for them, that was only a tool to help with the hunt.

~****~

"The Prince of the Elves is alive." Aonas might have been talking to himself but Skneeba wasn't sure. What he knew for certain is that something new snapped inside the madman's head. Something broke and it was beyond repair. He now struck out at the inhabitants of Gogatha. He forced the powerful mage to change them; to mutate their very being into something even wolves would look at as savage. Hundreds of them from strategically placed sectors of the island. Soon they would begin their slaughter of the rest of the population. *Sooner or later*, he thought dismally, *Avador would run into one of these packs.*

"How he survived the Ecliptic Wraiths is a mystery." Aonas cut into Skneeba's thoughts. "All this time I thought they had taken him out of my game. But that is not the case, *is it*, Skneeba?" The dark magic-user turned to face away from Aonas. "No matter. What can one man do to me? He has no army. I have taken it. All his men are at my disposal. And soon they will attack their own country and give that to me as well."

The two were back in Aonas' private chambers. The king of Sovereign's Reach sat at his writing desk, the staff of Kara-Toh resting crossways in his lap.

"He thinks he can reach me." Aonas paused a moment to collect his thoughts. "How did he know to find this island?" He swivelled his head ever so slowly in Skneeba's direction until his eyes found the mage's. For a moment Skneeba thought the king would stand up and kill him. But he did not do that. Instead he released a laugh so loud and long that it went on forever. It became nerve-racking and almost hostile. It seemed to Skneeba that his master would never stop laughing. He preferred, now more than ever, to be dead.

E viathane stared at his arms and legs. And then down at his chest. Blood began to once again blossom beneath the white bandages that Myia had already changed twice before. His cuts were deep and many and it was difficult to keep them all from seeping. Pain ratcheted his entire body in excruciating stings and sores that he never felt before.

They were crowding a large crevice near the ruined bridge. The lip of the chasm on this side ran along a mountain wall made of bare rock hugging it in a huge arc. The elevation was high and they knew now they faced directly north at the mountain range housing the great mountain Vyn-Turion. They saw it clearly. It emerged before them, a giant naked rock spire penetrating the sky high above. The very sight of it left them in awe for they knew that at the very top sat an entire city. Even though they were staring at the colossal mountain, they could not envision what the city might be like.

"Here," Stone was saying to Tigran, "have another swig." The Dwarf handed the big man his flask full of warm ale in an attempt to help numb the pain. The air at this height was bitter and dry and it chilled the little company right down to its very bones. Tigran accepted it without a word. Avador moved to kneel next to his friend, his own body wrapped in bandages beneath his heavy cloak, which he held tightly enfolded about him.

Falstaff sat a few feet away; his arm suspended in a makeshift sling, his mood one of obvious melancholy. The pain in his shoulder hurt more than the mere pain of crushed bone.

It was the reality that someone tried to kill him, to end his life like it was nothing more than a passing thought. He understood now more than ever that evil was a force to be deemed genuine and it enraged him. He felt violated and he could only imagine how the others were suffering. What was Eviathane, his friend from childhood, feeling, his brother who sustained so many wounds to protect him? And what of the others before him? The ones who went to war knowing that the other side would undoubtedly try to kill them? It was true that this journey brought on many circumstances that threatened his life but now it has gone too far. The young mage was at the point of bursting with anger.

Falstaff's thoughts were interrupted when Stone Warhelm moved next to him and handed him the flask of ale. He took it wordlessly and sighed heavily.

"Try not to move your shoulder too much Shortbeard." The Dwarf attempted a smile. "The damage will take long to heal as it is."

The mage nodded. "Can you help me with my pack?" Falstaff shifted uncomfortably, his pack was heavy with the giant book and something sharp was digging into his back.

"That book of yours is hindering your movements, Shortbeard." Stone said silently noticing Falstaff's beard had actually grown during this quest. "I told you that long ago."

"That book saved us more than once, Stone." Falstaff was immediately annoyed. "Can you just help me take off my pack so I could try and rest?"

Stone fought back the urge to taunt Falstaff further and reached behind his back. The Dwarf paused suddenly before continuing to slide the pack over the mage's tender shoulder. When he brought it around, there was a long arrow embedded into it. The Dwarf cleared his throat and walked away without another word. Trying not to laugh was suddenly an impossible feat for the young mage as he slowly lay down across his travel blankets and waited for sleep to arrive.

After the group were sufficiently rested, Avador motioned to Grynde that they were ready to continue. Eviathane had vehemently denied any disability caused by the wounds he sustained and truly, he seemed his strong self again. The cuts had finally stopped bleeding and he was dressed and packed before any of the others. Falstaff's spirits also seemed to rise after the much-needed rest and he stood waiting and ready to go. Nectario finally felt like he belonged with the group. Avador and the others, Stone included, praised him for his bravery at a time when nothing less would do. Tigran even mentioned he took out dozens of men single-handedly and saved all of their lives. The bard could not stop grinning even after the Grayling led them around the narrow lip of the bare-rock mountainside and toward a tricky climb down where a pass into the mountains awaited them.

~****~

It took the company the better part of three hours to reach the bottom of the high rise that faced the central mountain range of Gogatha. To the west was the base of the chasm they crossed only a few hours before. The remains of the ruined bridge dangled high above. To the east was a long stretch of rock-strewn foothills that spanned so distantly that their horizon disappeared into the continuous gloom. To their backs was the near vertical cliff they had just come down from. But it was what lay directly ahead that the little group was concerned with. The mountain range housing Vyn-Turion began with a heavy mist that seemed to slither in long white streams before the pass. The pass itself was a huge gash that cut into the mountains from base to peaks. Avador stared passed Grynde towards their destination. He looked directly at the pass as if he would find some answers to his many questions somewhere within the gliding mist. Then he looked at the others trying to determine what they must be feeling. But he did not have to ask. He already knew. The pass was the only way in to reach Vyn-Turion. And from there, Sovereign's Reach. The Gali-Gunzaro skulked somewhere in that pass.

Avador took the front of the little procession as they neared the massive empty space between two forbidding cliffs. The wind howled from within as if it was the solemn cry from the mouth of a giant. The Elf stopped them once to make sure they knew what to do. His plan he had was simple at best but it was the only one he could come up with in these circumstances. The group nodded wordlessly that they understood and he led them forward into the haze before them.

The wind died abruptly within the open maw of the pass leaving only the heavy mist that lurked inside. The only sound was the quiet footfalls of the little company as they edged themselves further into the giant crevice. Everyone depended on Avador's ability to penetrate the darkness and even he was having difficulty. The warped moon was blocked by the giant peeks before them and they were robbed of its muted light. The Elf glanced back once to Grynde to make sure they were heading in the right direction. The Grayling nodded and they continued on. The stillness became nerve-racking. Nothing was moving all around them. There was no sign of danger or creature, nothing to warn them of any threat. The only thing that was attacked was their imaginations. Each visualized the Gali-Gunzaro within the privacy of their minds. No one knew what this creature looked like or what form it would show itself as. Some saw it as a huge figure, dark with deadly claws and fangs. Others saw it as snakelike with scales as thick as armour. It was long and powerful, it walked on two legs and it walked on four. It spit venom and it breathed fire. It hissed and moaned and killed for pleasure. Whatever it was, they all agreed on one thing: it was their most horrible nightmare.

The group pushed on trying not to think about where they were. Avador told them to stay quiet and they intended to do just that. Time stopped entirely as they moved ahead trying to keep their wits about them. They expected to be killed at any second. Which corner hid the Gali-Gunzaro? Who would be slaughtered first? How many more steps were they to take before meeting their most feared death? These thoughts teased their sanity as they walked in the dark.

Somewhere near the end of the line Nectario began to whimper, his fear beginning to overcome him. The rest of the group stopped as one and held their breath. Myia reached out instinctively and clutched the bard's shoulder in an attempt to steady him. Panic began to set in. At first they thought it was over. It was hard enough trying to stay calm in the midst of all this anxiety. Now they worried about the bard too. Amazingly, he calmed. Myia kept her hand on his shoulder a moment longer until she was sure he would stay that way. Nectario's handsome face was beaded with sweat, his eyes wide. But he nodded that he will be okay. The Wood Elf gave him a reassuring squeeze and they continued on. The quiet remained persistent until even their breathing seemed loud. They began to feel like they were not alone. Something was watching them. The little hairs on their skin rose and sweat slid down their backs in cold rivulets.

They have never been so terrified...

The silence was violently disrupted by the wail of the hideous creature called the *Gali-Gunzaro*; it was directly in front of them. The group stopped in their tracks. They could not move. They could hear the way its claws scraped the hard mountain rock beneath it. Its ragged breathing came in quick spurts of shrill gasps. The company was instantly unnerved.

And it was all Falstaff could do to maintain the cloaking spell that saved the lives of the little group.

The creature knew they were there, just as they knew that *it* was there. The two faced each other down in blind confrontation. They heard its breath blow in raspy hisses and it heard the muffled breathing as the petrified group fought to remain still. But neither one could see the other.

Falstaff was struggling brutally to uphold his spell. He knew that if they moved too much they would be detected, for the spell acts along the lines of a chameleon blending into its surroundings. The mage would have preferred invisibility but two things prevented that. The first is the fact that it was beyond his capabilities. The second, he needed a lesser spell such as the one he was casting, for him to do what he was planning next.

Avador assembled his nerve and slowly put a finger to his lips. Facing his panic-stricken group, he mouthed the words 'trust me'. This seemed to help. They began to gain control of themselves and the overpowering urge to run began to subside enough for them to hold their ground. The Elf was on edge but with a great effort he did not show it. He knew if he panicked and lost control, so would the others. And that would be the end for them. With long unhurried gestures, Avador motioned for them to fall back. They did so trying to avoid quick and sudden moves that would give them away. They saw only each other; the creature remained beyond their sight. It prowled somewhere in their vicinity, hungry for the blood it knew was near.

The Gali-Gunzaro moved in a large circle around the terrified group as if it was deciding with frustration where to pounce first. It let out a sudden raspy howl, high-pitched and heart stopping; it's aggravation peaking. Avador began his gamble with Falstaff's abilities. Motioning to the mage that he was ready, he held his bow tightly and drew an arrow from the quiver Myia had given him earlier, his own emptied on the bridge over the chasm. Falstaff took in a long slow breath until his lungs were filled with the cool air of the mountain pass. He released it gradually, thinking that Avador had more faith in his skills than *he* did.

But there was no time to dwell on these thoughts.

The young mage blocked out anything that was happening around him and focused only on the words, the words that he had etched into his memory. He could not fail Avador. He *will* not fail any of them. Slowly his good arm raised and pointed to the young Elf that did not fall back but stood apart from them only a few steps ahead. Enigmatic words seeped from the mage's lips in a soundless whisper. Falstaff exerted every ounce of his efforts to concentrate, to put aside a fear that kept threatening to overcome his determination. He will not allow it. Sweat soaked his robes where they touched his skin but the words continued to flow in perfect archaic intonation, the accent flawless and clear. The minutes crawled by and Falstaff did not waver. The horrifying sounds of the night creature were cast from his ears and ignored until finally the new spell fused with that of the cloaking spell and he sent it in Avador's direction.

The Elf took in a sharp breath as the rush of magic flowed through him. He shut his eyes at the bizarre sensation that threatened to overpower his senses. His head was spinning as though he was dizzy and he fought back the urge to retch. He wasn't sure how long the feeling lasted but when he opened his eyes again he knew that Falstaff was succeeding. Avador was levitating twenty feet off the ground. He braced himself as best he could without the feel of earth beneath his feet and tried to concentrate on the task at hand. He hung in the darkness with a sapphire-tipped arrow ready to fire at the unseen enemy. Abruptly there was a flash of light and it burned into his eyes that were adjusted to the near blackness. The light was gone as fast as it appeared but he saw the Gali-Gunzaro... they all did. It was *exactly* how each of their imaginations had conjured it. It was pure evil personified. It stood on two gangly legs, long-limbed and clawed. Its face was elongated and its mouth was a stretched gap that allowed a slender tongue to hang loosely from between two rows of pointed teeth. A thin black tail was moving from side to side in anticipation for the kill. That is how Avador saw it.

Someone screamed below him and the Gali-Gunzaro advanced toward the sound without pause. But Avador had already shot the arrow and it buried itself into the creature's arm. The beast screamed in fury and slashed out finding nothing but air. The little group below tried frantically to stay away from it. It was almost impossible without making quick movements that would give them away.

Falstaff was struggling the most. When the creature attacked he very nearly lost his focus. He had summoned the light spell that gave Avador the opportunity to see his target. Almost at once the light was doused and the creature was vulnerable once again. The Gali-Gunzaro was hissing with frustration.

Someone was beating it at its own game.

It went suddenly on all fours, its fury and lust for death swelled deep within its black heart. Uncontrollably it lunged forward toward the midst of heavy breathing. The pitiful group before it heard the movement but saw nothing. A claw found Stone's shoulder. One instant he was standing at the forefront of the group and in the next he was sent spinning into the cold rock of the cliff wall. Everyone froze where they stood; the Gali-Gunzaro was somewhere in their midst. Stone clenched his teeth at the burning pain in his shoulder trying to keep the creature from finding him. It crept closer to the fallen Dwarf, anticipation for the kill before it.

A thunderous scream, desperate and angry, came suddenly from somewhere above them. It was Avador trying frantically to draw the Gali-Gunzaro's attention. The creature paused and turned his interest towards the sound of the Elf's voice. Then suddenly, Falstaff faltered. *This is too much for me*, the mage was thinking, and Avador shimmered into view. The creature saw the Elf immediately and howled hysterically. Falstaff nearly panicked and came close to letting go of the levitation spell that suspended Avador in the air. But he held on as the creature abruptly bounded from cliff wall to cliff wall grasping frantically to outstretched landings and climbing higher towards the unguarded Elf. It was almost on top of him when Falstaff released another flash of light. Avador caught a glimpse of it pouncing from the last ledge and loosed an arrow when the light disappeared. There was a *dull* thud and a loud screech. Avador hit his mark but he was too late. The creature's momentum carried it into the Elf and it wrapped its gangly arms around him in an effort to take him down with it. The two dropped like a stone in a tangle of limbs. The beast hit first with Avador landing on top of it. The Elf felt himself slowly begin to lose consciousness, pain racking his entire body. The Gali-Gunzaro was writhing under him, it too in utter pain. Avador summoned the last of his strength. With the wind still knocked out of him, he rose above the Gali-Gunzaro. There was a piercing ring within the darkness as Avador unsheathed the

Kingblade. In one swift motion the Elf's sword hacked at the creature beneath him. It released a final howl grasping at the Elf's ankles in a clawed death-grip, and its life drained from it completely. Avador then dropped onto the dead Gali-Gunzaro and everything went black.

Chapter 26 - Sovereign's Reach

Vyn-Turion was a giant spire of rock that broke away from a clinging forest that tried futilely to grow higher up its elevation. The receding clusters of trees were already at such a high altitude that the air about them was thin and icy. The massive girth of the mountain that stood within its lesser peaks covered the entire central region of Gogatha. Even within the haziness of the continuous night the colossal mountain can be seen from almost anywhere on the island.

Somewhere on its southern face huddled seven tiny travellers: Two Elves, three Humans, a Dwarf and a Grayling. The wind blew bitterly at them and they were forced to tighten their hold on their cloaks. They had spent the last two hours hiking through the isolated mountain pass that led them to this mountain. It was a long and strenuous trek along jagged rocks and narrow passages. Their leader had been unconscious the entire way and he had to be carried. Sometimes the large, powerfully built Human cradled him in his arms and when he grew tired, the burly Dwarf would take over the burden.

Now, after the better part of two hours, Vyn-Turion loomed before them. The less significant peaks seemed to move apart as they advanced toward the 'King of Mountains' leaving it in clear view to stand like a giant sentry protecting the very skies behind it.

"I'm okay, Shortbeard." Stone spoke loudly to penetrate the sound of the rushing wind. Falstaff was trying to put more of his salve on the Dwarf's wounded shoulder. "I see a crease in the mountain wall straight ahead. We'll go there to rest, hopefully it will get us out of this wind."

The little company followed the brawny Dwarf towards the large crease in which they entered one at a time. The fold in the rock was tall and deep, but very narrow. With a little effort they managed to move inside and the wind was blocked completely. They moved in a single file line within the crevice and to their relief it opened somewhat so they could gather together in a knot.

Resting the unconscious Avador gently on his back, Eviathane rolled up his cloak and tucked it under the Elf's head. Stone immediately began to start a fire and soon the company prepared to eat their first hot meal in what seemed like a lifetime ago.

"That was amazing what you did back there." Nectario's voice merged with the crackling of the fire. He was talking to Falstaff who was placing a dampened cloth on Avador's forehead.

The mage's thoughts were far away. "I nearly failed us all." He said quietly after a time.

"No one could blame you," said the bard with enthusiasm in his voice, "if it wasn't for you, we would never have made it through the pass."

"He's right, Falstaff." Tigran Eviathane broke into the conversation. "What you accomplished, what you *did*, I never would have believed it if I wasn't there." The big man put a strong hand on the mage's shoulder, a huge smile crossing his face. Then he turned to Avador's limp form next to the fire. The firelight washed the Elf's sharp features in a deep orange glow. He seemed strangely at peace laying within the midst of his little company.

"Nothing seems broken," Falstaff said finally. "But we won't know for sure until he wakes up." He stared at his friend's bruised body until something averted his attention. From the shadows, Myia came into view.

"You should all eat something," she said softly. "I'll tend to Avador." The friends paused for a moment and then agreed shifting to take some warm dry beef from the extended hand of Stone Warhelm.

~****~

The company slept then, still unaware of what time of day or night it was. But it didn't matter. The weariness that had built within them was so much that sleep came almost immediately. The wind became a steady hum just outside the opening of the crevice, a rhythmic strum of an unseen instrument that brought on a hypnotic daze. Inside, beyond its bitter touch, it was a welcoming sound for the seven weary travellers. Not long after, the rains came. At first it was the melodic patter of icy drops on the cold rock beyond. But before long, it came in steady sheets that sent bitter spray into the breach of the crevice. Soon the company huddled closer to the fire and each other in an effort to keep warm, their breath coming out in white gusts.

Tigran Eviathane pulled his cloak tighter about his shoulders, the steel of his armour beneath conducting the surrounding cold. He stood just inside the crevice opening and stared out at the rain that fell just beyond his reach. Now and then a light spray so cold it burned whipped at his face. But he didn't seem to notice, his gaze fixed into the depths of the torrential downpour. He had slept for a while, but he couldn't be sure how long his eyes were closed. Nothing specific had woken him, his eyes merely opened and he wanted to sleep no more.

He turned back towards the warmth of Stone's crackling fire and sat down with his arms resting on his knees. He looked at his companions and noticed for the first time how haggard and battered everyone was. Their clothing was torn in many places and stained darkly with blood. How many times had they nearly lost their lives? What keeps them going regardless? Tigran never thought about it until now. It just never occurred to him that quitting was an option. He gave out a long sigh and decided that it wasn't and it won't ever be.

The better part of four hours went by before the company began to stir. Stone had been up first and stoked the fire with large chunks of a fallen pine he had rounded up before the group fell asleep. The cold didn't seem to bother the burly Pike Dwarf. In fact, it seemed as though he was right at home within the chilly climate. The rain outside subsided into a slow drizzle leaving the outdoors with an extra layer of haze to the gloom beyond. Everyone was awake when a meal of simmering meat and toasted bread was prepared by the versatile Dwarf. Each took turns watching over Avador as he slept fitfully beneath a heavy travel blanket. The Elf's erratic movements while he slept showed that he was haunted by terrible dreams that provided no comfort. At times he spoke incomprehensible words that caused his little group to worry for his sanity.

Falstaff was dabbing a moistened cloth on his friend's sweating brow when the Elf showed signs of recovery. His eyes opened just a sliver before shutting them tight against the brightness of the fire. His head was throbbing and his eyes burned painfully beneath their lids. Avador took a moment to get his bearings before attempting to open his eyes again. First one and then the other opened to find dark hazy silhouettes crowded above him. He blinked away the stinging sensation until his vision cleared. His friends were all there before him, relief emanating from their faces. Avador realized all at once that everyone was still alive and abruptly sat up, his body rebelling against uncountable sores and aches.

"Hold on, Elfling." Stone's voice was a booming drum in his ears, "Lie back down before you hurt yerself even more."

"Wh-What happened?" Avador managed to gasp.

"You killed the Gali-whatever-that-thing-was-called, is what happened. Damn near killed you, too." The Dwarf couldn't hide his enthusiasm even though his shoulder still burned from the creature's claws.

"We made it through the mountain pass because of you," Falstaff said to his friend.

The Elf raised a weak arm and rested it on the young mage's shoulder, a smile forming with great effort on his lips.

"No," said Avador, "because of *us*."

The rains gradually died back into the soft patter they had begun as only to diminish completely. If there had been a sun it might have shown itself then but as everything bright in this light-forsaken land, it did not come. Stone peered out into the gloom beyond the light of his fire as if judging the safety of venturing out again. He turned back to his group and decided they had rested enough, but how much time had they lost in doing so? Avador had managed to stand on his own claiming his fall was mostly broken by the bulk of the night creature and he will be fine. His claim was returned with unconvinced glances but they said nothing to dispute him; the quest must continue, they all knew that.

After Stone put out the fire, and the last bit of warmth they might see for days, the company drew their tattered cloaks tighter and stepped out into dreariness. The rocky ground beneath their feet shimmered with the wetness left by the rain. The contrast between the climate of the island below and the mountain range was startling. Almost at once the company lost their footing and fell. Slowly and carefully they climbed to their feet sliding and slipping the entire time.

"Black ice!" Grumbled Stone Warhelm. "I've seen it during the long winters of Pathen. Rain so cold that it freezes upon reaching the ground. It has the look of mere wetness, I should have checked." The group glanced around uneasily. What now?

"Grynde?" Asked Avador. The Grayling skittered closer to the Elf. "How do we get to the city up there?" He pointed skyward to the unseen peek of Vyn-Turion.

The Grayling stood there, unaffected by the frigid temperatures. At first he said nothing as though he did not understand what the Elf was asking. Then he tightened the strap that held his quiver of harpoons and beckoned them to follow. Slowly, cautiously, the little group followed after the bent form of the powerful Grynde as he edged closer to the mountain wall. He stopped there as if deciding. It has been a long time since he was forced from the island that was once his home. But once again, his memory had not failed him.

They crept guardedly around the vast base of Mount Vyn-Turion for long minutes. The Grayling stopped a few times as if testing the walls for some kind of sign only to continue on for even longer minutes. Finally he stopped and straightened his bent frame, towering over the others as he did so. The group stared at his back as he peered into another crevice opening, the long white hair sweeping below his knees. *In there*, he pointed. Quickly Avador moved ahead careful not to slide along the frozen earth and looked to where the Grayling was pointing. The open maw of a giant split in the rock stared back. Inside was blackness.

"In there?" The Elf asked pointing. Grynde nodded once and stepped back. Avador frowned and looked at his group.

Then he shrugged and crept forward into the utter blackness, his hand gripping firmly the hilt of his father's blade.

There was a sharp strike of steel against flint. Once, twice, and a torch held in Stone Warhelm's hand ignited to life. The little company from a distant land were gathered together in a tight huddle within the bright yellow glow of the solitary torch. Quickly he lit a second and handed it to Avador's waiting hand.

"These are the last two, Elfling," cautioned the Dwarf. Avador nodded and swept his torch forward. They were standing in the crevice that gradually formed into a man-made corridor that wound ahead beyond the glow of the torches. The walls on either side of them rose upward only to also disappear into blackness. The sudden uneasy feeling that they were standing at the base of countless of tons of rock began to work on their nerve.

Grynde's face appeared abruptly into Avador's torchlight.

"In... out...stone...air...in... out... stone... air..." He said in his heavy accent. The Elf stared back at him not fully understanding what he was trying to say. The Grayling gave him an agitated look and tugged on his wrist to follow. The corridor went on for long minutes winding left and right until reaching a wide staircase. Avador raised his torch and saw that at the top of the stairs was an arched wooden door braced by wrought-iron diagrams and hinges. He moved slowly up the staircase and put his ear to the cool wood. The sound of wind came to his ears. This perplexed the Elf. Moving the light away from the door, he tried the iron handle and it gave easily. The door pushed open just a crack with a low creak. Avador peered through until his eyes adjusted to the gloom beyond. Another corridor.

Silently he led his friends into a wide hallway and a rush

of cold wind blew past them. The corridor seemed to have angled upward beneath their feet. They climbed the inclined floor and followed it as it too wound unevenly forward. It stretched on for a long time, the feel of the chilly wind still brushing past them as they marched ahead. Suddenly the darkness broke and a grey haze could be seen ahead. They followed it to the end of the hallway and discovered an opening that led outside. The group was astounded. One by one they stepped out into the open air. Behind them now was merely a crevice opening untouched by human hands.

They were on a landing that was dotted here and there with old benches and what must have been fountains at one time. The fountains were built of thick grey blocks of stone along the wall of the mountain. It seemed that once, pure mountain water poured into these fountains to cascade into naturally formed channels that grooved along the mountain rock and to flow over the cliff edge beyond. The rim of the cliff was arched with a railing built along its edge.

Avador glanced around, amazed. This must have been a rest spot for travellers leaving and going to Sovereign's Reach. How many of these are there along the rise of the mountain. How beautiful it must have been when the water still flowed over this mountain and into the waiting island below. The effect must have been one of endless waterfalls decorating the cliff faces of this great mountain they called *Vyn-Turion*.

The Grayling's words returned to the young Elf... *in, out, stone, air*. He repeated them to himself silently until he realized what Grynde had meant.

"This is one of many landings." Avador said suddenly. The group caught on immediately. "The tunnels wind in and out of the mountain at selected elevations entering and exiting the mountain at fixed positions." *Brilliant*. The Elf took a final look at what must have been a beautiful resting spot. With a deep sigh he followed Grynde around the arc of the landing where another crevice opened to yet another corridor within. This is going to be a long trip, he thought dismally.

And so they climbed, the small company of seven, upwards through winding corridors and once-beautiful landings along the great outer walls of Mount Vyn-Turion. No traveller crossed the little group's path. None would dare leave anymore. The passages and the gloom within were theirs alone. The twisting corridors were always wide, apparently so they could accommodate horses and wagons. Each time they exited one of these hallways they appeared on a different side of the mountain, winding around the vast circumference of the giant rock, each time cautious of unwanted eyes.

The hours grew long and the group began to tire. Avador called for a halt announcing they will camp at the next resting spot. After a few brief moments to drink water from their provisions, they hiked the last hour to the next exit. Once outside, the air seemed to have cooled somewhat. The landing they found themselves on was slightly different than the previous ones below. It was equipped with fire pits and wood that must have been kept at a constant supply. This slight change must be due to the fact that the temperature was even colder at this altitude.

The company took a moment to gaze out at the island below. No one really knew which side of Gogatha they were looking at. The forests and valleys and rivers spanned for many miles below. The coastline appeared vaguely miles away through the dim haze of the warped moon's light, a steady build-up of wispy clouds just beneath them helped to obscure the view.

"By the looks of things," Avador said thoughtfully, wrapping his cloak tighter about his shoulders to ward off the chill, "we should reach the city after another day's travelling up these caverns." The Elf glanced at each member of the little party separately. No one had anything to say, their bodies in need of rest. Grynde merely stood there neither agreeing nor disputing Avador.

The watch was set and the company wrapped themselves with their travel blankets and were asleep instantly. Although the firewood looked alluring to the little group, no fire was made, Avador stating that they were too close to the city to risk sending the smoke skyward... a sure sign that someone escaped the Gali-Gunzaro.

And so they endured the bitter chill of the higher elevations keeping close to each other to draw whatever warmth they could. The face of the mountain provided many jagged folds in the rock that could be used as shelter against the wind. Avador stood first watch. The young Elf placed himself in the midst of a gentle wind, his cloak fluttering behind him as he stood in the shadow of an outcropping of rock. He gazed in every direction, the violet in his eyes so deep they were almost black. Nothing stirred beyond the vicinity of the plateau where the group had camped. No sounds or voices could be heard from the city miles above them. Was it really there? Was there in fact a city on the apex of this mountain? Avador's pulse quickened at the thought of nearing Sovereign's Reach. Aonas was there as well... the man he had grown to hate more and more with the passing of every moment. He hated also the reality of not knowing what to expect once they make it to the city. His little group depended on him. He knew that whatever must be done to see them through this safely, *he* would do. Even if it meant that he would lose his life.

The echoing cry of a night bird broke the Elf's contemplation. Someone within the sleeping company stirred and rose. Avador glanced over and saw Myia Feo-Dosia walking to where he stood.

"I couldn't sleep." She said matter-of-factly. Avador gave her a knowing smile.

"It isn't a good idea not to rest, Myia." He said screwing up his face to show feigned condescension.

"I know," she replied with a quiet laugh, "but the truth is, I wanted to talk to you." Avador smiled and gestured to one of the benches near the cliffs railing. They sat for a few minutes listening to the sound of the soft wind. For a while, neither spoke; they simply gazed at the few speckles of light that suggested life many miles below.

"What's on your mind?" Avador broke the quiet between them and moved his eyes upon the Wood Elf.

Myia sighed. "Young Andor. I want you to know that I never met anyone such as you." Myia ignored the reddening of Avador's cheeks. "Nor will I ever. I know that you must be under an immense amount of stress. You try not to show it but you cannot hide it from me. You are a great leader, and I want you to know that when things start to get bad again. We are all with you because of you. I also know that much of that pressure is in keeping us safe." Avador thought Myia was reading his mind.

"Myia. I never would have made it this far without all of you. You are all just as important on this quest as I am. You yourself have saved all our lives. Do not think I will forget that easily." The Wood Elf shivered and Avador put an arm around her slender shoulders pulling her closer to him. For an instant she tensed at the gesture. Slowly she allowed herself to relax and rested her head on his strong shoulder. For many warm moments they said nothing else. They simply sat together on the bench overlooking the island that was now blanketed with billowy white clouds that shifted slowly below the landing.

Before long, the clouds swirled all about them and the world ceased to exist.

"We'll get through this." She whispered from somewhere within the mist.

"We'll get through this." Avador repeated. And for the first time on this adventure, he had absolutely no doubts.

C ities are built in many ways. Their histories vary from one to the next. Some chronicles are legendary while others merely grow to become the city that now is through a gradual expansion as time moves on. But not one member of the tiny group was ready to behold the city that waited slightly beyond their grasp. After all the watches were made and the company took the greatly needed rest, they set out once again. They travelled all of the next day winding through the great caverns and making there way upward through Mount Vyn-Turion. They took fewer breaks with the anticipation of the last leg of their journey coming to an end. They knew with each passing moment, they were getting closer to Sovereign's Reach. They wanted nothing more than to leave these caves and finish this quest and go home.

Avador Andor slowed to a crawl. The corridor they were hiking through was coming to an end. The sound of voices and shouts and the squealing of wagon wheels reached their ears. A hazy grey light brightened the end of the passage with the promise of an exit. The beating of his heart quickened and his mind was racing. They were just below the city streets of Sovereign's Reach. The Elf kept just ahead of his group while the others fanned out behind him.

"Everybody, wait here just for a moment." The Elf's whisper barely contained the anticipation in his words and the others grew tense. "I am going on ahead to see the situation so I could decide the best way to get up there." He pulled the cowl of his cloak over his head and disappeared into the shadows of the cavern walls leaving the anxious group without waiting for a reply. Eviathane started forward but stopped when Grynde raised a warning hand.

With quick, cautious steps, Avador moved towards the brightening grey light. The sounds of the city only metres above reached his ears with an increasing intensity, his heart responding as if echoing the very streets. The corridor ended and he peered around a flanged wall that hid him in its shadows. Another landing waited ahead, only this one was within the mountain. Light poured down a flight of steps accompanied by a large ramp to their right. The Elf was amazed at the amount of work it must have taken to build these passages that led all the way to the base of the mountain.

He forced his thoughts aside concentrating on the task at hand. More slowly now, he stepped away from his hiding place and onto the final landing. He felt suddenly naked and vulnerable but he forced his feet to move him towards the stairs. Choosing the ramp on the right to approach the entryway onto the streets above, he inched closer one small step at a time until he was able to peer out at the city of Sovereign's Reach.

"I don't like this!" Tigran muttered for what must have been the tenth time since Avador left them.

"I told you already," Stone snapped at him, already stressed himself at both the waiting and not knowing what was happening. "We can't just jump into the city and announce our arrival! The Elfling is right to scout ahead. He'll be back!"

Eviathane forced himself to sit back to the quiet wait that the others accepted grudgingly. The minutes passed by at an agonizing rate almost as if they were taunting them. What was Avador doing and he's been gone for so long? They began to grow fidgety and their patients faded to almost nothing.

Abruptly Avador appeared from the shadows and they jumped in spite of themselves. He was carrying a rather large bundle of clothing.

"Do you *have* to be so damn *quiet* Elfling?" Stone Warhelm lowered his raised hammer.

"Sorry, habit." Replied Avador. The group crowded around the Elf who was breathing heavy, his face glossy with sweat. "Put these on." He gave each member of his group a long, beige-coloured robe. "We are going to be priests for a while."

Avador made them wait an entire two hours in the caverns with the hopes that the street's activity would lessen. In the end, he was right. After the long wait, people began to leave the streets paying no attention to the underground entryway long since abandoned, and made their way home. Soon, the loud raucous of the city people lessened and the sounds of activity dissipated to almost nothing. Then, after peering cautiously out the entryway one last time, the Elf led his disguised group onto the waiting streets of Sovereign's Reach.

~****~

Gan-Potou sat at the edge of his narrow bed with hands clasping each side of his face. The captain of Aonas' private guard stifled a scream for the millionth time. Sweat glistened his entire body regardless of the room's chill. His dark skin soaked through to the bone; he was left with an uncontrollable shiver. His thoughts were many and scattered. He couldn't force a single one to remain for more than a few seconds. Like Skneeba... no, *worse* than Skneeba, he belonged to Aonas. His king, he thought briefly, had a very cruel imagination.

When was the last time he slept peacefully? He could not

remember. His eyes were puffy and red and he felt his sanity drift farther away. Soon, he thought, it would be beyond his reach. Again he suppressed a scream. He must get *some* kind of rest. Tomorrow he is to be on duty for Aonas' every impulse.

Slowly, forcibly, he swung his legs back onto the bed and stared at what lay hidden in the shadows of each corner of the ceiling. Hours later, when he really had no other choice, his body finally gave in and a sleep filled with hideous nightmares of his own death many times over took him for what remained of the night.

~****~

Robed and hooded in their priest's garb and hidden surreptitiously in a dark alley, the company all stared at Grynde and at how ridiculous he looked. Avador had tried in vain to keep him from hunching but it was hopeless. He succumbed to the fact that the Grayling's natural make-up always returned him to a stooped position.

When they climbed into Sovereign's Reach, it was all that they could do to keep from staring in utter shock. The streets were mostly cleared and Avador barely managed to get them fifty metres to the alley they now took shelter in. A patrol of ten guards rounded a corner just as they ducked behind the length of a gaping lane. The Elf buried the group and himself deep into the shadows of an alley he noted beforehand. Avador's objective was to get above ground without being seen exiting the caverns. It would have provoked too many questions. The flight was swift and quiet but they managed to get a glimpse of the city. A great wall towering higher than the city's lofty buildings arced left and right and continued until it disappeared from view in both directions. The wall, it seemed, stood at the edges of Vyn-Turion and encircled the entire city with its stone embrace. The city itself was vast beyond description, easily three times the size of Vor, the city of cutthroats. In its centre, perfectly ringed by the great expanse of the metropolis, was the stronghold of King Aonas, huge and grey with its spires reaching skyward like the fingers of a desperate hand.

"He can't come with us." Avador said conclusively. His words were spoken with a natural finality as if there just wasn't any other way. The group stood in silence hating the fact that they were to lose their only guide but knowing that their leader was right.

"Elfling," Stone spoke first after the uncomfortable silence," we can do this. We'll head towards the stronghold; under these disguises we should make our way with less hindrance." It was obvious that the Dwarf was embarrassed with Avador's choice of profession as a cover but he also knew that time was keeping its incessant pressure upon them leaving the Elf with little choices. He had already cut the bottoms of his robe to adjust for his shorter height.

Avador turned to Grynde and put his hand on his sturdy shoulder.

"This is where we part, my friend," the Elf was hoping that his words were being understood." Make your way back to the Matheia and we will meet you there."

The Grayling did not move an inch.

"You have done more for us than we could ever ask of you; it is up to us now to finish this."

The Grayling kept his ground.

It wasn't simply that Grynde did not understand; the

Grayling was refusing to leave them. The others stood staring not knowing what to do.

Avador did.

"Aonas." He said, his voice firm. Then he raised a hand to his throat and made a gesture of a knife slicing sideways. The Grayling clenched his jaw and took a step back. He then raised a long arm and placed a clawed hand on the Elf's shoulder. Grynde glanced at each member of the group and tilted his head forward. They bowed in return. Then, without another word he tore the robes from his body and thrust them into a corner of the alley. Smiling once, the Grayling turned and disappeared back towards the entrance of the alley, checked the streets and broke for the fifty metres that led him to the tunnels of Vyn-Turion.

"Through us," Avador said after a moment of stillness, "he will get his retribution."

Sovereign's Reach sprawled out in every direction in a bulk of countless buildings large and small, tall and low. At one point the population was vast and thriving and activity was intense. Some sections were open and spacious allowing for farming of land amazingly fertile. Industries were plentiful with fabrication establishments and profitable markets. Every nature of trades and crafts were present at each corner. An entire section of the city was reserved for smiths and their forges; their furnaces were kept continuously hot to prepare steel and weapons of every form. Now they remain cold, the fuel that kept them burning lay as useless piles of coal. No one remembers the last time they were used.

The city had people designated to certain sections to light huge oil lamps on tall poles that spanned throughout its entirety. It was a remarkable setting: A long time ago, one could have had the impression of a tiny slice of the galaxy sitting at the top of this mountain. But now the lights were few and scattered and lit only out of necessity leaving scores of black patches throughout the city.

In the midst of all this was a tiny group of six guised in priest's robes, and the lack of light suited them just fine. Hiding the weapons strapped beneath their heavy garb, they walked through the streets as if they belonged there. They were making their way in the general direction of Aonas' stronghold, each passing moment edging them closer. But with each of those moments, their uneasiness increased accordingly. Along every length of street and around every corner, skulked a heavy patrol of guards. Not a single citizen walked along the roads.

So far, no one had given much notice to the six clerics that made their way through the all too quiet streets. It seemed as though no one paid much attention to religion or to those that followed it. The hours marched on without incident but sooner or later, the company thought bleakly, their luck would run out.

"The stronghold lies a few miles ahead of us, Elfling." Stone turned to Avador as they paused in yet another alley. The Elf nodded in agreement. The others waited in the blanket of darkness for the next command to enter the streets. Avador peered from behind the wall and motioned for the others to remain where they were.

"We need to rest," he said finally. "Down this street I see an abandoned shack. We'll make our way there and rest for a few hours before continuing." He paused for any objections. None came. Avador was ready to lead them out when he stopped unexpectedly.

"What is it?"

"Ssh!"

The sound of booted feet scraping the stone along the

streets reached their ears. And by the sound they generated, it was obvious that there were many. The Elf motioned the frozen group deeper into the shadows when the noise stopped suddenly. Perplexed, Avador held his breath and waited.

A scream shattered the stillness and the company instinctively put their hands to their weapons, but Avador shot his hand up to stay them.

"I will not *do* this anymore!" A cry came out mournfully. Avador gazed cautiously from behind the wall. A patrol of at least thirty men stood staring in utter shock at one of their own, their faces ashen with fear. The one screaming drew his sword and hurled it to the ground.

"You *fool!*" One hissed at him. Then the unthinkable happened.

Something peeled itself from the man's very shadow.

A thing murkier than the night, all claws and teeth with gangly arms that reached the ground seized the poor soul's head and bit into it. Blood sprayed everywhere drenching his companions. The man screamed endlessly, terror and pain overwhelming him, his pleading doing nothing to stop the creature from hideously killing him. The guard was begging for it to stop for what seemed like all eternity, begging his companions to help him. But they did not. Instead they watched in utter horror at what was happening to him. His screams were horrifying and they curdled the blood. The thing was merciless, without pity. And the man suffered continuously until his death, which came gratefully as the echoes of his screams reverberated momentarily and disappeared. Then the thing simply vanished; its purpose completed. All that remained was blood and body parts that lay scattered everywhere about the large patrol.

Stone Warhelm was pressing a gloved hand over Nectario's mouth as he gasped in terror. A blanket of silence drew over the unnerved group hiding in the alleyway only metres away from what had just happened to the wretched guard. Just beyond the entrance to the alley, the rest of the guards were trying frantically to keep their nerves together, some allowed muffled sobs to escape their lips. The minutes crept by agonizingly slow until finally their leader took control.

"That is enough!" He shouted at his men. "Enough!" The men of the patrol composed themselves just enough to listen.

"Just make your rounds like you're supposed to and ignore it. It is not really there. It is *not* a part of us!" The leader was valiant but he himself did not sound convinced by his words. But that was all he could offer for now. Slowly, grudgingly, they moved passed the alleyway and continued down the darkened streets. Avador waited until the sounds of their steps and the clanging of their weapons disappeared completely before turning to his group, his face livid with pure anger.

"*That* is how Aonas gained control of my father's armies." The Elf was speaking through clenched teeth. The others stood there uncomprehendingly. Stone was the only one that seemed to understand.

"Yes, Elfling," The Dwarf's countenance mirrored Avador's rage. "Each man has one of those *things* watching from his shadow." Stone was shaking his head at the very thought. "I can't imagine how they keep their sanity."

"Let's move." Avador said forbidding himself to think about it any longer than he has to. "We'll make our way to that shack, we can't stay here."

The company began to exit the alley when Eviathane put a hand on Stone's shoulder.

"Uh, Stone?"

"What?"

"*You* don't have one of those things in *your* shadow, do you?"

"Shut up!" Stone's anger was rekindled. How ludicrous, he thought as Tigran turned his grin to hide it from him. But as they entered the streets, the Dwarf couldn't help but throw a nervous glance at the long shadow at his side.

~****~

The shack was indeed abandoned but it offered adequate cover and warmth though a slight putrid smell lingered within. Behind two large shelving units was a short entryway that led to a second room somewhat hidden from those not doing a thorough search. But Avador had acquired by now a sort of 'second-nature' habit for exploring what is unknown to him, and the Elf had ultimately found it. Choosing the second room to camp the night, and with the help of Eviathane, they pulled the shelves closer to the entry for it lacked a door. The little company laid out their blankets and prepared to rest their weary bodies.

"We don't have much time for a rest, I'm afraid." Avador said quietly. "I want to resume again before the streets fill with people. Rest now, my friends. In a few hours we'll set out. If something goes wrong, or if we get separated, we will make our way back here." He stopped to look at each of their faces. They were all in agreement.

They slept soundly with Avador Andor keeping watch. Someone must do so and the Elf refused to allow any one else to stay awake. They made no sound within the shack but from time to time, the thud of booted feet would pass by only to recede further away.

Avador's mind raced the entire time his friends slept. He could not sleep even if he wanted to. They were so close to

Aonas now that his pulse quickened involuntarily. He could almost feel nothing.

He sat for a while in silent numbness, but his senses curiously sharp. So much could happen from here on, he thought. So much could be happening even now. Aonas is nothing less than a madman; his twisted mind would take him anywhere. Avador thought back to his father's words when he spoke of his armies. *It is up to you to free them.* But how was he to do that? What can he do against the awesome power that holds them trapped? Who is *he* next to the evil that waits in the form of hideous sentinels in their very shadows with orders to kill if they disobey? Avador's mind ventured to when they were back in Pathen and sleeping in Stone Warhelm's cottage. Two of those things had attacked them there... *Ecliptic Wraiths*, his father had called them. And the *Kingblade* has the power to destroy them. But how can one sword annihilate so many? There would be a slaughter before he could kill even a handful. The Elf was at a loss. Sighing, he sat back and waited for the time he would wake his friends.

The people of Sovereign's Reach were still in their homes when the Elf led his group of five through their streets. As they moved on, Avador kept a mental note of the location of the shack in case it would be needed. The minutes moved on and still the patrols did not seem concerned with their presence whenever they were forced away from the cover of shadows. They were beginning to think their disguises were perfect for their situation. No one cared about the priests. What harm can they do? They rounded another corner as they edged towards the stronghold when their luck ran out.

"Stop!" A shout came from their left. They froze as one and turned to meet whomever it was that yelled out to them. A sentry broke from a rather large patrol and marched towards them in almost lazy strides. Avador put himself between him and his group, his heart pounding savagely in his chest. The sentry stopped and stared at him for long moments before speaking, as though studying something that wasn't quite right.

"Remove your hood." He said calmly. Avador paused and then did as he was told. Long locks of sweat-dampened hair fell about his face and shoulders. The patrol inched closer to their captain. Nothing good can become of this.

"You are Clerics of the Celestial Order?" The man asked, his voice elevating a decibel. The group nodded within their hoods. Avador kept his eyes on those of the guard's.

"Then why is it you all have *hair*?" He looked at Stone... "And *beards*? The Celestial Order are priests who are shaven, it is against their faith to have hair!"

The little company stood at a frightened loss without an answer... until Stone thought of one: He walked up to the guard and withdrew his hammer. The guard's eyes went wide as the Dwarf heaved his weapon in a great arc smashing it into the jaw of the bewildered man. He went down in a heap.

"Run!" Avador shouted during the stunned pause of the rest of the patrol. They rounded a corner and soon the chase was on.

The Elf moved them around the bulks of the giant buildings in a desperate attempt to lose them. Frantically he summoned the location of the shack and did his best to manoeuvre towards it. It was a good spot and with two exits if another was required. He cursed at his misfortune and the lack of a better plan. But what else could he do under such circumstances? The best he could hope for is that the squad that was now fanning out somewhere behind them would eventually lose interest and move on. He lost them momentarily as they fled behind a jumble of large warehouses and the shack was in his sights. Quickly, stealthily, he led his group to the shack and through the open doorway. They slid behind the shelving units and through the second entry that led them to the room beyond. With great effort, Eviathane pulled the wooden unit against the entryway and they all backed into the darkness, their weapons drawn and their hearts beating wildly in their ears.

There was a long moment of silence. They waited holding their breaths as if they could hear better if they didn't breathe. The distant sound of pursuit faded into another direction and they allowed themselves to release the air in their lungs. Slowly their eyes adjusted to the dark and they turned to each other to make sure everyone was all right. Everyone was, relief beginning to set in. Then, with a startled realization, Avador gasped. Stone was at his side, he too realizing what was wrong.

His whisper was a sudden hiss. "Where's the *bard*?"

Chapter 28 - Too Far

The chase was a blur. Nectario was racing after his group through alleyways and warehouses, sprinting through the thick smog and hazy night. But somehow, no matter how much he tried to stay with them or how fast he ran, he managed to take a wrong turn. He almost ran directly into a stone-built wall skidding to a halt with arms flailing.

What was once fear of getting captured quickly became utter horror when he realized he was alone. At first he was exactly that. Alone. But the brief silence exploded when a surge of guards poured into the alleyway shouting at his discovery. Sweat enveloped him entirely, his scimitar flashing in the pale light. The guards were on top of him at once. They were not about to lose this opportunity; a pack of wolves had just cornered their rabbit.

Nectario dropped his weapon; he knew he stood no chance. Within seconds the guards seized him and threw him roughly to the cold stone street disregarding completely the fact that he was unarmed. The shouting intensified all around him. He was more than scared. He was petrified. He did not fight, would not even if he could. He simply gave in to the mass of weapons and arms that threw him around like a shabby doll.

Nectario wasn't sure how many times he blacked out. The bard was dizzy with fear; eyes closed shut to whatever fate was to come. Abruptly the commotion stopped and he found himself pushed up against a wall, a blade digging painfully at his throat.

"Do not resist." A hoarse voice reached through the

pounding in his ears. "We cannot do anything but kill you if you do." The warning was severe and honest with a hint of remorse. Nectario tried to speak but his voice was lodged in his throat inches away from the blade.

"Your friends are hiding and you know where they are. Bring us to them." Nectario's eyes shot open, his head shaking.

"You *must!*" The man who held the blade was desperate; sweat moistening his face.

"No!" Nectario's voice returned, loud and harsh.

"We cannot let you live, don't you *understand?*" The guard's voice cracked with fear. The bard saw it in his eyes. He was losing a battle within; he was readying himself to kill him. Nectario's fear intensified. He did not want his throat cut. He did not want to die.

"Okay!" He shouted as the pressure of the blade increased, blood trickling from an opening wound. Tears filled his eyes and streaked down his face as his captor withdrew the long knife. Then slowly, bitterly, he led the entire sentry to the old shack they had used as a hideout.

~****~

"Not *this* time Elfling! You can let all of damnation come after me; you are *not* going out there alone." Stone Warhelm was immovable. "If yer goin' out there then *I'm* comin' with you." The others had drawn close, already decided that they were not staying behind either. Avador looked at his friends who had already drawn their weapons. The looks on their faces told the Elf that there was no chance that they were going to leave him alone again. He sighed and pursed his lips in thought.

A noise interrupted them and they turned their heads towards the doorway. Then, without warning the sounds of booted feet drew closer with a deep rumble. The company froze where they were. The sounds were suddenly all around them.

"*Elfling!*" Stone hissed. "We've just been surrounded." The group moved together in a tight circle, their backs to each other.

A resounding crash made them jump as one. The door was violently smashed in from the other side of the darkened room and dozens of guards burst through the opening. Avador looked to the second exit at once but it was useless. Armed sentries were already beginning to fill in. The company was caught off guard and were forced to stand and fight. They were seriously outnumbered; the guards were everywhere.

Stone's hammer was already swinging. Three of the men went down from his blows. Avador and Eviathane stood back to back their blades slicing wildly. Blood sprayed everywhere, the screams of the dieing loud in their ears. Falstaff summoned a giant ball of flame and hurled it forward. A handful of men shrieked and ran from the shack as they burned alive, a trail of fire flapping behind them.

The guards did not stop coming; they did not hesitate. Soon the entire shack was filled with them. They grasped Falstaff by the wrists and struck his head with a heavy cudgel. The mage was immediately knocked unconscious. The rest were thrown forcibly to the hardwood flooring of the shack, their weapons taken away. The Dwarf was howling with rage, Eviathane his echo. Avador looked to each, his face remorseful, unable to save them this time. Myia was trying vehemently to break free but the hands of the guards were the stronger. Before long, the little company was captured and brought outside. A convoy of three cages drawn by horses waited for them. The company was soon tied firmly and thrown into these cages. Myia was shoved into one with Avador. Eviathane was forced into another with the unconscious Falstaff, and the fuming Stone was by himself.

The horses grunted in the darkness, their breath coming out in white puffs. No one moved for long moments. Stone moved to the bars of the cage and peered outside. One man was standing alone, his head bent in shame. Then a guard moved towards him and grabbed his arm to guide him forward. He whispered something to him before leading him closer to the Dwarf's cage. Stone's eyes went wide. *The bard.*

Then, abruptly, the guard opened the door to the cage and threw a tied Nectario inside with Stone. Within seconds they lurched forward. The cages groaned and creaked and soon they were rolling ahead as the horses started walking, the cages flanked by hordes of guards.

They travelled for the better part of two hours, winding through streets and avenues. The clomping of the horse's hooves and the squeaking of the wheels were the only sound throughout the journey. The company sat within their cages chained to the very bars. Weaponless and sore, escape was impossible. They simply stared out from between the bars and watched as the monstrous stronghold neared with every passing moment.

The buildings ended abruptly, the streets opened to roads that ran through once colourful gardens. The road ahead was choking with overgrown weeds and wild plantation that grew sporadically along its route. Arched bridges spanned over dried ponds. The towers and spires of Aonas' fortress loomed above them, giant sentinels that towered over everything. No banners were flown along the walls. No standards decorated the entire bulk of the stronghold.

They crossed a final bridge that went on for at least a mile over what was once a small but beautiful lake. They continued on afterwards down another street flanked by closed-down shops and what might have been guesthouses at one time. Large gates stood open before them and they passed through to a courtyard waiting beyond. The courtyard was vast and looked as if it were trampled by thousands of feet, the dirt forming many loose clumps over a span of hundreds of meters.

No one stopped them to ask questions or check for recognition or credentials. They just rolled on by with no hindrance of any kind. Soon they moved along a giant ramp- way and into the giant keep. There the horses were stopped and guards swarmed all about the cages. The doors were opened and the company was pulled out. Every part of their bodies was sore and numb from the long, uncomfortable ride. They tried to stretch but before anybody could move anymore, a group of guards came forward holding thick strips of heavy black cloth. They pressed the cloth roughly over everybody's mouth and nose. They discovered that the cloth was dampened with something oily, and it burned. The little group fought feebly but after a few short moments, everything went black...

Aonas moved along his fountain chamber with grim purpose. Too many things have occurred that the big king did not anticipate. He was right in using his guard to keep a watch for the Elf Prince, though he did not expect him to find his way to the city let alone get passed the Gali-Gunzaro. Skneeba was now almost useless to him. He had ordered him to curse the Elfling as he had with his father. But certain events had denied him that indulgence. The curse, his captain of the guard had translated, was cast only by a series of chants, verses spoken and sung. In fact, by removing Skneeba's tongue, he had also removed the ability for most of his spells. No matter. The dark mage is no longer needed; he is disposable. Indeed, he thought distastefully, the little Elf is a formidable foe. He stopped in his tracks… *was* a formidable foe.

Aonas strode to the end of the chamber where the steps started their incline at the rear and ended at a dais that housed his throne. He halted there and looked up the rise, the Sceptre of Kara-Toh gripped firmly in his hands. The king of Sovereign's Reach struggled to gather his thoughts. His armies were practically ready. The warships were being loaded and supplied. The siege machines were assembled and rolling towards the great ships even as he considered his next approach.

But what did he have to consider? There is no one to stand against him. The lands beyond have no army. The greatest force belonged now to him. *What* did he have left to consider? Only that Sovereign's Reach, Vyn-Turion, and Gogatha were not enough for him. The people do not view him as an exalted ruler? He laughed to himself. They did not deem him their *true* King? They won't have a choice. He will take until there is nothing left to take. He will speak and they will obey. Everything he desires will be his. How much more powerful than *that* can a King be? A smile stretched across his rust-coloured beard, his heart ready to burst with excitement. He was going to climb the steps of his empty chamber to his throne but then he remembered something else. A little visit to his captives might allow for some entertainment…

Stone Warhelm had his eyes fixed on Nectario as the bard hung from his chains across from the Dwarf. Stone was conscious for the better part of an hour and waiting for the bard to awaken. His anger had boiled within, only to increase and threaten to overflow. The Dwarf could not accept a traitor. How many times have they saved each other's lives? Stone

Warhelm would not have done it. He *could* not have done it. He lives by another code; he would have taken death before revealing the location of his friends. He would have tried to escape in *any* way possible even if he died in the attempt. He would have died so the world could have a chance. Why did he allow this weak fool to come with them? He knew it was a mistake from the start. He had warned them all...

Nectario stirred where he hung limply by the chains that held him to the wall. He blinked at the light of a single torch burning in a rack next to a door made of steel. His eyes stung as he opened them slowly against the orange glow. The cell came into view, painfully, gradually. The grimy walls, the cold rock, dark stains of blood left over form years of disregard. With his mind still hazy, Nectario's eyes scanned the tiny room until they fell upon another person chained to the wall across from him. A Dwarf, and his eyes were burning through him... the bard gasped. It was Stone Warhelm.

The very silence was brushing against Nectario's skin. The Dwarf did not take his eyes off him. The bard wished he was back in the alley dealing with the swarm of guards.

Suddenly Stone released a roar and lunged forward, the bard flinched regardless of the chains that bound the Dwarf. Abruptly the chains went taut and Stone's legs were taken from under him and he dropped heavily to the soiled floor. Nectario stared in shock, his eyes wide. For long moments the Dwarf did not move, he stayed sitting on the floor, his arms raised to the tension of the chains. The only sound was the ragged breathing of Nectario as he tried to hold himself together.

The uneasiness went on forever. Nectario was numb all over. The lack of sensation could have been from a number of things. It could have been from the beating he endured from the guards. It could have been the fact that his arms were raised above his head for so long. Finally the bard gathered his composure and tested his voice against his shame.

"I... I did not want this." He said feebly. Stone did not respond; he merely sat there with his head lowered as he tried to bring together his own thoughts. "I wish now more than ever that I had been killed." The bard tried again. The anger in Stone's eyes did not subside. The hush between them grew long and nerve-racking.

"I don't want to kill you." The Dwarf said after a while, his voice surprisingly low. "I will simply never trust you again." Nectario sighed and looked away trying to keep his mind away from the discomfort. Then something caught his eye. The bracket pinned to the wall that held the chains to Stones right arm had come loose. It was obvious that it happened when Stone ran at Nectario; but the Dwarf hadn't noticed. The bard's breath caught in his throat and he debated whether he should tell him or not. He stared at the slumped form of Stone Warhelm sitting on the cold floor. Then he looked at the loosened pin to make sure he wasn't seeing things. Finally he decided to chance it. Slowly, reluctantly, Nectario told Stone that he could free his right hand if he wanted to.

~****~

Down the long length of a connecting corridor, Avador Andor was chained within another cell. The Elf had been beaten, for he fought savagely upon waking from the drug-induced sleep. He had awakened even before being chained and brawled with the guards that were holding him. In the end, they were too many and he was forced into the cell he was in now and chained. He watched as they brought the still unconscious Myia Feo-Dosia into the cold room and chained her as she was to the wall across from him. Their disguises had been torn off them, their weapons confiscated. A strange altar stood exactly between them, the rock withered and faded.

The Elf felt the shame return in a slow trickle of pain. He had failed them all. Where *were* the others? Were they still alive? He detested not knowing. They had come so far, trusted him completely, only to end up here in these cold cells on an island they wanted no part of.

"Are you okay?" A frail voice startled the Elf from his thoughts. Myia Feo-Dosia had come awake and he hadn't even noticed.

"I am fine. You?"

"I have been in better circumstances."

The two went silent for a while letting the stillness settle around them like a shroud.

"I hear something." Avador whispered suddenly. Myia raised her head to hear. Footsteps were coming from a long way off but they were growing louder without any attempt to hide their approach. The two Elves stared at each other questioningly. Then, the rattle of a large ring of keys sounded clearly through the metal door. One was chosen and slid into the keyhole. After the low *snick* of the release mechanism was heard, the door creaked open.

Tigran Eviathane watched as Falstaff regained consciousness. The mage flinched at the light of the solitary torch that burned into his eyes. His head was pounding and his muscles were aching. His wrists, he noticed, were raw and stinging. It took him a while but he managed to come to his senses and found that Eviathane was staring at him from across the room. His arms were chained to a wall, he was bleeding from the mouth and there was a big old smile across his face.

"Why, are you *smiling*?"

"We're *alive*, aren't we?"

"Alive but chained to this filthy cell."

"*Exactly.*" The smile was still there.

Falstaff hesitated. He stared at his friend as if he had extra limbs. "How could…"

"You mean to tell me, that the Great Falstaff can't get us out of here?"

The mage went livid. "Sure. I'll just conjure up the keys and get us out of here!" There. His point was made.

"*That's* the spirit!"

Falstaff went slack. He was not going to give Tigran any more satisfaction. He changed the subject.

"So we made it inside the stronghold of Aonas."

"I would have preferred to have made it inside under *our* terms." The big man's smile finally went away and he found himself staring at his prison for the hundredth time.

"Did you see Aonas?" Falstaff asked.

"No more than *you* did." The young mage realized that Eviathane woke up and found himself in this cell.

"So you *can't* get us out of here?"

"No more than *you* could." The two sighed simultaneously. What else could they do now besides wait for an outcome?

Stone Warhelm gripped the wrought iron pin that held the chains to his right wrist. The chains were long enough to allow for movement but they didn't allow him to turn completely around to face the wall. He just managed to reach far enough so that he could grasp the head of the pin. He tested it and found that it *was* loose; there was some play between the steel and the rock in which it was embedded.

"You're right bard. It's come unfastened. But I will still need time to break it free."

"I *am* sorry Stone." Nectario apologized again.

The Dwarf paused in his attempts at freeing the pin. "If you break a glass, and put all the pieces back together... is it the same glass?"

Nectario sighed. It was hopeless. He did manage to get back on the Dwarf's good side by telling him about the pin and he was hoping that with time, things would get better between them... *if* they manage to get out of this cell, that is.

Aonas stood at the entry of the cell staring at the little Elf that hung before him. He was a huge man, bigger even than Tigran Eviathane. A long king's robe was draped across his broad shoulders, tattered and filthy. A tall slender sceptre was held loosely in one hand, deep green vapour emitting from a small black sphere flanked by two crescents at its tip. The man was grinning beneath a red beard streaked with grey. At his side was a soldier, dark-skinned and fit. The soldier had a short-sword strapped to his waist along with a wicked-looking dagger. His head was held high, proud. But there was something about his eyes that betrayed his stance.

Avador's eyes never left those of Aonas' since the moment he walked into his prison. He knew this man immediately and the hate for him burned white-hot beneath his chest. There was a moment of silence and it was long and lethal. Elf and king stared each other down letting the other know their worth just by their glare.

Ultimately, Aonas spoke. "Take the bitch down and bring her to me." The soldier never hesitated. He moved towards Myia with the ring of keys and unlocked the shackles from her wrists. He then brought her forward effortlessly, the Elf too weak to struggle. Aonas kept his gaze on Avador, the smirk widening. He quickly grabbed Myia by the wrist and forced her hand onto the altar. The man's grip was made of iron.

"This is the Wood Elf with the sapphire tipped arrows." It wasn't a question; it was a statement of fact. "A descendant of Feo-Dosia." Aonas' countenance taunted the very fact that Myia's family were dead. Tears welled up in the Wood Elf's eyes and she looked to Avador.

"Gan-Potou. Hold her hands." The dark soldier did so at once. The king reached into his robes and withdrew a heavy wooden mallet.

Avador spoke, his voice laced with gravel. "Aonas. You better kill me now or this will be the end for you." The Elf felt a thread of sanity begin to fray.

"No!" The king's shout was thunderous. "You *will* die *Prince* of the Elves but you will suffer on the road to your death... just as your father suffers even now." Avador nearly fainted, tidal waves of emotion hammering at him from every side. But he held his poise; he refused to show weakness before this madman that has caused him so much pain and suffering.

Aonas held his gaze and his grin on the Elf as he motioned his guard to break Myia's hand.

The Wood Elf's scream began even before the hammer fell...

Stone Warhelm was soaked through with sweat when he heard the long length of the pin drop heavily to his feet, the chain attached rattling noisily. He had been shaking the head of the pin in all directions simultaneously inching it outward for long and demanding moments. It took a great effort and the Dwarf was beginning to think that it would never come out.

Nectario took in a sharp breath from across the cell. "You *did* it!" He exclaimed.

"Not yet bard. Not yet." Earlier on, the Dwarf had been afraid that his efforts would have been wasted when he heard the muffled sounds of footsteps just beyond the metal door. But they did not stop; they moved on until he could hear them no more. Then sometime later he heard them coming back, only this time someone was laughing hideously. Still, they did not stop when they reached his prison door but moved passed without slowing. They mean to leave us hear to die slowly, Stone had been thinking.

The Dwarf took this chance to work on the other pin. First he tried wrenching it by its chain but this one held fast. Then he tried another approach.

"You better pray that whoever's out there is long gone." He said to Nectario sardonically. He then reached down and lifted the heavy pin. Without caution he gripped its shaft and brought it smashing into the chain attached to the other pin. Bright orange sparks flew where it struck and Nectario flinched as steel struck steel. Again and again the Dwarf hammered at the chain. The head of the pin warped and chipped as it struck the chain blow after blow. The result was noisy but Stone Warhelm was not one to be taken prisoner.

Soon, the Dwarf began to tire. The chain was sturdy but the pin was thicker, heavier. The link was bending and twisting with every hit and Stone refused to stop, growling now with every effort. The sweat poured down his face and into his beard, his arm muscles were burning painfully when finally the chain gave and flew off its pin in a shower of sparks.

Stone Warhelm was loose.

N ectario waited in the silence that followed Stone's escape. He wasn't sure what he was waiting for because the Dwarf did nothing but wait by the thick metal door with his ear to the cold steel. The wait was an aggravatingly long one.

"What are you doing?" He asked finally, unable to contain his impatience any longer.

"Waiting for a chance to take," was his answer. So the bard settled back against the wall and resumed watching Stone do nothing.

Abruptly Stone stepped back dragging both lengths of chain with him. He heard something, a devious grin forming on his lips.

"Hey! Idiots!" He screamed at the top of his lungs. "I'm free! I broke my chains!" The Dwarf was taking an obvious gamble. Then Nectario heard a noise, an abrupt stopping of footsteps, then the jangling of keys.

Stone gripped the heavy pin; his pulse quickened when he heard the door unlock. And then it opened. The Dwarf did not hesitate. He reached out with his free hand and yanked whoever was out there inside the cell with him. There was only time for a yelp before Stone smashed the pin against the man's head. He went down at once.

"Didn't expect me to be tellin' the *truth*, did ya?" Hurriedly the Dwarf peered out into the corridor and found that it was empty... just as he assumed by the amount of noise he heard beyond the door. He shook his head at the sheer stupidity of Aonas. He had in his possession the little party that defied all odds to get here, and he never thought to multiply the guard?

He gave it no more thought. Hastily he snatched the guard's keys and brought them over to Nectario.

"Find the key that unlocks your wrists. I'll listen for anyone else coming." Stone moved to the fallen man and dragged him away from the entrance and closed the door just enough that it remained a hair's-width ajar. "Make it fast!" He said and looked down at the unconscious soldier noting a short-sword and dagger.

"Can't disobey while yer knocked out, my friend. Yer safe for now." The Dwarf reached down and unsheathed the man's weapons. By this time Nectario found the right key and freed his wrists; the chains dropped uselessly to the floor. He then made a motion to find the key to Stone's chains but the Dwarf waved him off.

"No time for that," he said and handed him the dagger. "Don't hurt yourself."

The two left the cell and closed the door. They found themselves in a long cold hallway that ran in two directions. Torches ran along both walls leaving the corridor well lit. Stone chose to go right since that was the direction he heard the footsteps going the first time. Avador must be that way. The hallway continued a long ways. Soon other doors to cells came into view on both sides of the corridor. Their hinges were still sealed over with rust indicating that they have not been opened for years. Stone pressed on dragging his chains behind him.

Finally, the end of the hallway came into view. There were two doors in this section that had evidence of recent use. The Dwarf did not hesitate. He pushed his ear to the door on his right and put a finger to his lips. The bard made no sound. After a brief moment, Stone nodded in approval. He then retrieved the ring of keys from Nectario and tried them one at a time into the keyhole.

Avador Andor stopped breathing when he heard someone trying to unlock the door. This took longer than the first time and it puzzled him. Still, his fear returned with full intensity. Finally he heard the familiar *snick* and the door swung open creaking all the way. The Elf was so shocked to see Stone Warhelm that at first he thought he was hallucinating with fever.

"*Elfling!*" Stone could barely contain himself. He ran inside with the bard, their hearts hammering. The Dwarf could not keep his hands from shaking as he tried key after key to the Elf's shackles. Finally one worked and Avador was free and fell into Stone's arms, weakened by the many hours of hanging off the ground.

"Look to Myia," Avador gasped as the Dwarf helped him to a kneeling position and moved quickly to Myia's side. The Wood Elf was chained as he and Nectario were. Aonas must have hung Avador in a different way on purpose. But Myia was not moving, nor was she conscious. Then Stone saw her hands. They were broken and coloured a grotesque purple. Rage seized the Dwarf anew but he held himself intact.

"Yer safe now, girl," he said even though she couldn't hear it. Hastily he found the right key and with the aid of Nectario, helped the little Wood Elf next to the waiting Avador who stood valiantly against his dizziness. Then he rushed to the opposite cell and tried the keys. He shook his head again at the frustration but in the end this door as well opened inward to where Falstaff and Tigran stared in astonishment. They were chained to walls across from each other seemingly unhurt but for a huge welt on the side of the mage's head.

"*Now* can I smile?" Eviathane asked the still stunned Falstaff.

~****~

The little company was back together and they were making their way down the corridor. Eviathane carried Myia gingerly in his arms while they pushed ahead through the torch-lit hallway. None of them knew where they were going but at least for now there was only one possible direction.

The corridor of cells went on for countless meters. They had passed the cell that Stone and Nectario were in and continued on. After long moments, they found themselves at the foot of a winding staircase that coiled upwards into the rock. They moved onto the steps without hesitating. Upward they climbed all the while wondering what they will find when the steps end. Moments later they got their answer. An arched doorway stood open and they slowed their approach.

Aonas sat thoughtfully on his throne, his eyes glossed over completely. He shifted his big frame, fidgety with anticipation. He reveled in what Gan-Potou must be doing to the wretched Wood Elf before the eyes of the Elf Prince. He reveled at the very thought of his warships that had already departed Gogatha. And there was one more thing he reveled in: he took great pleasure at how successful his scheme had become. Every man that had once pledged his 'iron-clad' allegiance to the 'Great' Grandalimus Andor was now his to control. Every soldier that served his weak brother was under his command. *Every single man that walked with a cursed shadow beneath his feet obeyed Aonas...* and they had boarded the ships that were on their way to make him the most powerful man alive. Except for *one*, he thought sadistically. And he was wreaking havoc in the dungeons.

But Aonas had others beneath his heel: assassins, thugs, and corrupt soldiers. All of them paid generously; all of the wealth attained by his father and forefathers had been depleted upon these men whose hearts were as twisted as his own. The king could still not believe an entire army was attained in such a way. Warriors from Gogatha and the lands, which he will soon take, have come to his side by the mere influence of the golden coin and manipulation by promised lands in which they may pillage and claim as their own.

These men were to board a second fleet of warships very soon, save but a modest hundred or so who were kept behind as a private guard led by Gan-Potou.

Now what is taking the ever-faithful captain so long?

"Where are we?" Myia Feo-Dosia asked weakly after the company stopped in a large room that might have been a cellar at one time. Her hands were throbbing with pain, tiny gnarled things, and their bones broken and useless. She remembered what had happened, the memory returned like the outburst of a storm.

"We're lookin' for our weapons, girl." Stone answered as he peered out a heavy wooden door. "How're ya feelin'?"

The Wood Elf glanced sadly at her hands. "Like I am of no help."

A hand went to her shoulder and she looked over, dizzy still but strengthening. The pain in her hands was nearly unbearable. Avador was next to her.

"We will find a place in here to provide for your hands." The Elf's heart hurt for Myia. He wanted to find help for her desperately.

Quickly the Elf moved to where Stone was standing.

"Any idea where we are?" He asked without hope. But the Dwarf seemed to actually have a clue.

"By the layout of the fortress, we are still some levels below where we came in. There are no windows anywhere; we must still be beneath ground." Stone looked back to the group. Falstaff stood next to Tigran and Nectario; Avador remained close to Myia. They were all keen on moving ahead.

"There's a chamber down the hallway, the door is open wide. It seems to be empty. It's strange to me that it would be even down here."

"We move as one." Added Avador. A quick look into the corridor showed that it was empty and the Elf moved them all into it and towards the chamber. Before the end of the corridor, they fanned out and divided themselves cautiously to either side of the open doorway. The Elf and the Dwarf peered in from opposite sides. It must be a sleeping chamber of some kind. No movement came from within and the company went inside.

The room was large but nearly empty. A single bed was pushed to one side against a wall, yellowed stains dotting its solitary sheet. A tall wooden wardrobe stood shut alongside the connecting wall near the bed. But instead of a fourth wall on the right, a large archway opened to an adjoining room.

The group moved in, curious and cautious. In the exact centre of this slightly smaller room was a podium; a large volume lay opened upon it. Nothing else was in this room apart from the dust that covered everything and developed into small puffs beneath the feet of the intruders.

Falstaff moved forward, his friends flanking him on all sides. He reached the book and looked down. It was archaic and the words were of a race and time unknown to him. He stood before it in utter awe, the pages so old it seemed as though they might crumble at his touch. The others moved closer, one eye on their surroundings. The young mage ached to discover what is told within the book's pages, what secrets it keeps. The others just wanted to leave.

"*Do you want to read it?*" The voice came out of nowhere and they jumped out of their skins.

Standing at the archway was a tall gangly man, robed and hooded in black. Where did he come from?

"*Put away the blades,*" the voice said, "*there is no need for them here.*" The black-robed man stepped closer, his movement's jerky as if one leg was shorter than the other. Slowly he removed his cowl and the group froze in recognition.

Skneeba!

"*I am very pleased that you made it out of those dungeons,*" he said letting the words exit his mind and enter theirs. "*Because now... we again have a chance.*"

~****~

Skneeba stayed close to Falstaff. The others moved back to give them space. They were told that even though they were given this unlikely stroke of luck, there was extremely little time to put it to good use. Typical, thought Avador, it has been that way since they started this journey. They were told of the men that remained on Gogatha and how dangerous these men were under the control of Aonas, and that they patrolled the halls above. They were warned that at any given time the dark mage might have to leave without notice in answer to Aonas' call.

Skneeba drew his words away from the minds of the others focussing only on Falstaff. The young mage, dumbfounded from the beginning was trying vainly to learn what Skneeba was attempting to teach him. The minutes crawled by, the others watching for the approach of others. Still, Falstaff could not comprehend what the dark mage was trying to show him.

"It's hopeless." Falstaff said more than once. And every

time he would get the same reply: *you can do this... concentrate!* Giving up was not an option for the young mage. They have been given a chance, miniscule as it might be, and they were not about to give it up. The minutes seemed like hours. No one moved from his or her positions but they were getting restless... especially Avador, yet he remained as tolerant as possible.

Abruptly Skneeba's face jerked up. *"I must leave."* He said suddenly. *"Aonas calls."* Everyone stood in awkward indecision.

Falstaff gritted his teeth. "Go." He said simply. With a final glance at the little group, Skneeba replaced his cowl and vanished through a hidden door.

The little group waited motionless for long moments. They looked at Falstaff and he looked back almost apologetically. But he was determined.

"Let's go." The mage said finally. "Skneeba told me where our weapons are."

For the first time, Falstaff led the group. Through twisting corridors and up winding staircases they followed the young mage. Falstaff was once again under great pressure. A spell was just given to him by Skneeba but he felt incompetent, untrained to cast it. He was afraid, nervous beyond anything he had ever felt before. Skneeba explained a great many things in the use of the magic in such a short time but Falstaff knew he had only soaked in a fraction. The dark magic-user described how if he were to increase his level of efficiency, he must be able to conjure the power under the most stressful of situations. He told Falstaff that he too was once a novice, an apprentice that invoked the simplest of spells only to have them disappear from memory once cast.

But all that changes, he assured him. Like a fighter using

a sword, a mage uses magic. His ability to wield it enhances with practice.

Finally Falstaff stopped before another door at the end of a torch-lit corridor. He seemed to be searching for something in the very grain of its wood.

He turned around slowly. "In here." He said hopefully and the door creaked open at his touch.

The room beyond was small but there was another door at its opposite side. Shelves and cupboards lined the wall to the left and right but they were all empty of anything.

"Are you *sure*, Shortbeard?" Stone sounded disappointed. The young mage said nothing in reply. He walked to the left side of the room and examined a tall shelving unit.

"Help me with this," he said to no one in particular. Tigran and Avador stepped forward and together they hauled back the empty shelves. Sure enough, an opening in the wall was revealed. And in another room beyond, in a pile on the floor, were a scimitar, two bows, a quiver of sapphire-tipped arrows, a long-sword, a heavy war hammer... and a *Kingblade*.

~****~

Skneeba moved through a crowd of armed men, struggling to get to Aonas. The king waited on the small balcony beyond the steps to his throne. He was looking out at the empty courtyard below in anticipation of what he planned next when he heard the familiar scuffling of Skneeba's feet in the short hallway leading to the balcony. He did not even turn when the dark mage stopped behind him.

"My army of paid assassins," he said wickedly, "near the warships." Skneeba took in a ragged breath.

"No, I will not join them in battle," Aonas answered an unasked question. "I will take their lands when they are mine."

The king of Sovereign's Reach turned then, slowly, and looked down at the cowering Skneeba. "Have you studied what I asked of you?" Aonas asked already knowing the answer. The dark mage nodded sadly and this made the king smile with delight. Aonas had ordered Skneeba to find a curse that required no voice, a horrible and grisly curse to use on the Elf Prince and his friends. He was finished toying with them. It is time to give them real misery.

Avador and his friends had reached the upper levels of Aonas' fortress and were making their way under Falstaff's directions. The young mage had led them without slowing save for a few wrong turns, which he quickly corrected. They had stopped at the end of a massive atrium and deciding their next advance when they heard voices approaching from the opposite direction. The voices came and went and after a few moments, the group stepped into the large hall.

The atrium had once been ceremonial and formal. Chandeliers hung from its high ceilings and tapestries decorated the massive walls but they were torn and ugly now, along with a gray carpet that ran from end to end down the hall's center.

The company reached the middle of the atrium when four guards entered abruptly from the other side. They stopped in shock but drew their weapons.

Tigran Eviathane was already running at them, sword in hand and a need to battle rising in his chest. He never slowed. The big man attacked the leader, who was huge and powerfully built. But the guard never even defended himself when Eviathane took his head clean off his shoulders with a great swipe of his sword. The little group stood stunned, mirrored by the remaining three guards who dropped their swords at once and inched backwards. The little group instantly surrounded them.

Tigran looked at Nectario, the grin was back. "Always take out the biggest first," he said brightly.

But the moment of triumph ended abruptly when one of the guards suddenly panicked and pushed through Falstaff and the weakened hands of Myia Feo-Dosia. He was faster than anyone anticipated and was already running and screaming down the adjoining corridor.

The alarm was sounded.

Almost at once, the not-too-distant shouting of others erupted beyond the halls. The little group stood frozen in the atrium. There was nowhere to hide. If they retreated back from where they came, they would be trapped in the dungeons.

"Well," Stone said suddenly, almost grinning, "we're already wet, might as well jump in the water." And with that said, the little group from another land gripped their weapons and roared down the corridor howling at the fight that was charging at them from the other direction.

Aonas heard the shouting, burst into the fountain chamber with Skneeba in tow, and found utter chaos amongst his men. Many were emptying out into the halls beyond the double doors. Others stayed where they were unsure of what to do.

"My king!" One shouted finally. "The prisoners have escaped!"

Impossible! Aonas' eyes widened.

"Find them and kill them!" The king bellowed above the turmoil and the dozens of men began to push through the heavy double doors to where the sound of a massive struggle was taking place.

Aonas stood with Skneeba at his side, the Scepter of Kara-Toh in his vice-like grip, and his back to the steps to his throne. The two-dozen men he had held back stood before him in a protective arc. He stood listening to the shouting beyond. He could hear an approaching clash of steel and a peculiar crackle of fire that puzzled him. Flashes of intense blue light lit the seams of the now closed doors in sporadic rhythm. This left him gob smacked. But he was not afraid. *Let them come,* he thought evilly. *Let them come and feel what it is like to be cursed.*

The doors burst open and six figures rushed in. A Dwarf slammed it shut again and wedged the handle of a giant hammer into the handles of both doors and unsheathed a short-sword. At once, the doors were forced but the hammer held. Then the little group, cut and bleeding but seemingly oblivious of their wounds, charged again.

They opened out at the rushing soldiers. Falstaff went left with Eviathane, Nectario and Stone went right. Avador Andor ran straight ahead, the *Kingblade* flashing where it wasn't stained with blood. The little company of friends received the onslaught of the paid assassins as if the guards were mere babies and howled their separate battle cries. Amazingly, they held their ground against the greater numbers and cut down many before breaking through completely. Then the soldiers simply stopped fighting and drew away from the infuriated group pushing back to either side until there was nothing between Avador's little group and Aonas.

The ear-splitting silence that followed was unbearable. Even the hammering of the great double doors ceased suddenly. Avador stared directly at Aonas, fury reflecting from his eyes as he struggled unsuccessfully to tame his adrenalin.

The Elf took a step towards Aonas; the king took a pace back. Falstaff and Eviathane flanked Avador at once. A smile stretched across Aonas' bearded face and he raised the long length of his scepter above his head, the vapor swirling as if it were alive.

"SKNEEBA!" The name reverberated all across the chamber. Immediately the dark mage dropped to one knee and made a motion with his hands as if pushing at an imaginary wall. A sound a lot like the clap of thunder exploded in everyone's ears and they stepped back guardedly.

All except for Falstaff.

The young mage was waiting and he too dropped to one knee as the echo of thunder faded completely and he made a motion with his hands as if he were catching a large imaginary ball in both arms. And that is how he remained, unmoving. Nothing else happened. Aonas stood perplexed, refusing to let his anticipation fade.

Then, unexpectedly, the Scepter of Kara-Toh swung wide in a great arc and found Skneeba full on the mouth.

"*Fool!*" Aonas shouted at the dark mage that was now laying sprawled on his back. "Have you *failed* me?" Skneeba was shaking his head *no*. He has done what was commanded of him.

Aonas turned his attention to the kneeling Falstaff.

"So. A magic-user has come out to play." The king was scornful, the smile reforming. Skneeba was horrified at what Falstaff was in danger of. A sudden vision came to mind of everything he endured happening now to the young innocent mage. But there was absolutely nothing else he could do about it. The tears flowed freely down his dark face in utter despair.

But as Aonas pointed the staff in Falstaff's direction, Avador was already bounding towards the steps, the *Kingblade* swinging in a desperate sweep. It found the scepter dead on its black sphere and the impact sent a powerful jolt down the blade and into the hilt. The sword flew from the Elf's grip and arced all the way back to where the stunned soldiers stood. It hit with a resounding clang. But Avador did not stop. He moved forward unsheathing his fathers jagged dagger. Aonas was waiting for him, the ruined end of his scepter swinging desperately at the advancing Elf. Avador dropped to a crouch as the length of the staff swung harmlessly above his head, and pounced with a maddened growl. The thrust carried him up and into the towering Aonas and he grabbed the king by the throat. The smaller Elf, in complete control, forced the giant Aonas on his back and pushed him painfully against the stone steps. The dagger was at his throat.

"No Elf Prince!" Aonas gasped. Tears were flowing down his cheeks and into his beard. "I have not been able to control what I do, another force guides my hand!"

"He *lies!*" Avador barely heard Stone Warhelm shouting but he knew it anyways. "He's in a river and it's pulling him. Elfling, he's using you as a branch to hold on to!" Avador was in his own world.

"You are no *king!*" The Elf's voice was almost inaudible. Everything he and his friends endured to get here, Feo-Dosia burning, thousands of innocent people dieing, the ill-fated soldiers taken over horrifyingly and forced to attack their own lands... *the curse thrust onto his father*, it all flowed mercilessly into his heart.

"Just *kill* me!" Aonas shouted at the shaking Elf, the Scepter of Kara-Toh ruined, his control gone. What was left for him?

Avador inched his face so close to Aonas' he could smell rotten breath. "You don't *deserve* to die." His whisper was deep and raspy. In the next instant, Falstaff stood from his crouch and thrust his arms forward. There was the sound of an eerie wind that turned abruptly to a high-pitched wail, and nothing else. And it stopped almost at once. Everyone stood in the silence. Aonas was shivering in a cold sweat.

"A king stands with his people." Avador straightened and stepped roughly on Aonas chest with one foot. "A king goes into battle *with* his soldiers and at the forefront. A king is *chosen* and honors his duties until he dies. A king looks after the *many* before himself! Aonas." The Elf pointed a finger right at him; it may as well have been a blade. "Aonas," he repeated, "*you* are no king! And I will take blood from my very heart and use it to sign my name!"

A roar broke out among the men still alive within the chamber followed by one beyond the doors. Avador stepped off Aonas in disgust and walked down the steps. A soldier rushed before him and stopped. Bowing suddenly, he raised a sword horizontally with both hands.

The *Kingblade.*

Avador accepted it and thrust it high above his head. The roar returned with greater intensity.

Skneeba stood with the help of Falstaff. Myia joined Avador alongside Stone Warhelm, Tigran Eviathane, and Nectario. The commotion continued for a few minutes more until the dark mage stood shakily before the man that was once his master and raised his arms. Tears streaked his face as the reality of being free overwhelmed him.

"*Aonas!*" Skneeba cast Aonas a dark glance sending his telepathy into his mind and into those standing expectantly in the fountain chamber. Aonas lay where Avador left him, powerless.

"*The evil and destruction you have commanded will not go unpunished!*" Skneeba paused to watch Aonas cringe before him. Then he looked at Falstaff who was standing slightly behind him. "*You have done well young mage.*" He said to him and touched him playfully on the nose. *"You mastered the spell under the most stressful of situations. You have warded the curse perfectly."* Skneeba paused again to look at Aonas whose eyes went wide with a sudden and horrifying realization. Abruptly something crept from his very shadow, something sinister, dark, and terrifying.

*"I give you **Móa-meth**, the weeping demon! Rooted into your shadow, he will follow you wherever you go. He is the curse you forced me to send onto these people, these heroes! Instead, he is yours to suffer. No more will you cause pain onto others. No more shall an evil thought be turned into a reality simply by your twisted command. For if you do, Móa-meth will be watching and you will suffer... you will suffer!"*

Chapter 30 - Legend

Avador sheathed his sword and moved closer to Sknee-ba. His friends were overwhelmed with admiration, their hearts filled to capacity for his very being. They stood waiting in anticipation.

"Skneeba!" The Elf said abruptly. The dark mage seemed to read his thought and was nodding his head. The soldiers were relieved of their duties leaving the little group, Skneeba, and a whimpering Aonas to occupy the chamber.

"*The army of Grandalimus sails on.*" Skneeba confirmed the Elf's fears. "*They remain with the Ecliptic Wraiths in their shadows. I am sorry Avador; the curse is irreversible.*" The mage shook his head at yet another thought. "*The army that is not cursed but paid must have set off recently. If they have not they will before long. They are under orders to destroy your lands at any cost, to let nothing stand in their way. Their reward is doubled once completing their task.*"

Stone Warhelm stepped forward, his anger rekindled. "And there is no doubt that neither army is aware of what happened here." It was not a question but a statement of fact.

A horrible laugh resounded from the steps leading to the dais. "You have lost Elf *Prince!*" Aonas was spitting as he spoke, his glee sadistic. The lunacy in his eyes intensified to the farthest extreme. He looked both excited and terrified all at once. "Release me of my curse you pathetic, deformed *beast!*" Aonas felt the paranoia begin to strangle him. He felt what so many have felt because of him. He laughed hysterically and he cried pathetically; his mind found a place in which it could never leave again. But he also had the sense to know that he could not live like this. He shocked the others when he turned suddenly and broke for the curtained hallway that led to the balcony. He ran and never slowed. He thrust the curtain aside tearing it completely from its brass rod and burst down the short length of the corridor. Still, he did not stop until he thrust himself from the balcony and dropped to his death on the courtyard far below. He never screamed once.

Something happened immediately after. The warped moon began to shimmer and then fade completely. The frenzied clouds vanished as if they never were. The gray skies began to clear and brighten until the light became almost unbearable. A sun beamed from the skies high above and forced the incessant night to flee from the lands. Color returned with vivid sharpness and the people that remained on Sovereign's Reach and all of Gogatha stopped what they were doing and laughed and cried and froze in disbelief.

The fountain chamber brightened instantly, the people within squinting at the suddenness. It was all as if they were waking from a nightmare and the picture of reality came into clear vibrant view. After the short and stunned silence, shouts of exhilaration broke out all around.

The origin of the curse is dead. Skneeba smiled in spite of himself.

The enthusiasm of the little company intensified with the greatest of passions. Everyone hugged each other uncontrollably. The roar of Sovereign's Reach's people became deafening mixed with the now audible gleeful cries of the Gogathans far below.

Avador waited for the noise to settle down into excited murmurs. Then he gathered his friends closer to him.

"We must leave at once!" He said sternly. The others were in full agreement.

"*You will need me.*" Skneeba declared suddenly. When the others hesitated, he repeated his words. "*You will need me!*" His expression was almost desperate.

"There is one other thing, Elfling." Stone pushed forward. There is a guard that I locked into my cell. He must be freed."

"*Gan-Potou!*" Skneeba came to a sudden recollection. "*He is still trapped with an Ecliptic Wraith!*"

"Show me where he is!" Avador was already moving. The group left the fountain chamber and broke for the dungeons.

Stone Warhelm fumbled excitedly with the large ring of keys that he still had in his possession. They stood before the cell door that Stone was locked in. Avador Andor stood at his side, the *Kingblade* gripped in both hands. Gan-Potou was on the other side of the cell door and they were praying that it was not too late. Within seconds, the Dwarf found the key and unlocked the door. Avador threw it open and sprang inside. Gan-Potou reacted instantly. The captain of Aonas' guard thrust himself onto the Elf and wrestled him to the cold filthy floor. There was a clatter of steel as the two struggled to overpower each other.

"*Do not resist!*" Skneeba burst into the cell but Gan-Potou was not listening. The dark-skinned guard was indeed a seasoned fighter. He was already striking Avador in the ribs with his knee. The Elf struggled to keep from getting the wind knocked out of him and to maintain his hold on the *Kingblade*. He did not want to kill this man.

"*Trust in the Elf Prince!*" The dark mage tried again.

"Ignore the wraith!" Avador gasped. "I have the power to destroy it!"

Gan-Potou's eyes went suddenly wide, but a hint of disbelief remained within. He was still afraid.

But what have I got to lose? He thought grimly. The captain of the guard released his grip on the Elf and stepped back, arms raised in submission.

The Ecliptic Wraith stripped itself from Gan-Potou's shadow at once, its gangly outline tall, lean and menacing with claws ready to strike. Avador howled at its dark hideous form and pounced forward, the *Kingblade's* steel cutting through the creature as if it were nothing but air. There was a momentary wail and then the creature vanished. The only other sound came from Gan-Potou. He had fallen to his knees and was left sobbing uncontrollably with his face buried in his hands.

~****~

Sovereign's Reach was a plethora of colours and euphoria. Its remaining people had begun celebrating almost at once. The streets became choked with crowds and flowing banners. Whether one person knew the other was not a factor; children and grown-ups alike danced and embraced one another in utter glee. The day had returned and the ceaseless night was gone.

Their heroes wound through those streets unnoticed. Gan-Potou and Skneeba led the way until they found the great walls at the very outskirts. There they paused in a huddle within its enormous shadow. The trek was long but they made it without hindrance.

Skneeba moved next to Myia and tenderly took her broken hands in his own. *"You will feel some pain."* He said with sadness in his steel grey eyes. She nodded bravely. The dark mage took in a long breath through his nose and shut his eyes.

The others encircled them, watching. Skneeba loosened his grip and allowed the Wood Elf's hands to simply rest on his palms. Suddenly she winced, a great pain causing her to grit her teeth. The bones in her hands began to reform and take the shape they once had. But she did not lift her hands free of Skneeba's; she waited valiantly for him to finish. The process was slow but necessary. The group stood next to her, hands on her shoulders in support. And finally, it was finished. Myia opened her eyes, her brow glistening with perspiration as she released a long slow breath. The others waited with eagerness. Then the Wood Elf lifted her hands and wiggled her fingers; a huge smile was on her lips. She hugged Skneeba at once, the others laughing joyfully.

~****~

"If you want to catch the ships, you cannot do it if you climb down Vyn-Turion and hike through Gogatha." Gan-Potou was talking with Avador.

"Is there another way?" The Elf was asking. The others stood there in doubt of their chances.

"There *is*," the captain of the guard said almost too quickly, "but I am not sure what you will think of it."

"Whatever it is, we have no other choice." Avador said thinking of how many times he had already said that on this hazardous quest.

"Then follow me." Gan-Potou smiled and walked through a door in the giant wall before them.

The company went after the captain and found him climbing a long staircase that ran up through the great wall. They followed obediently wondering at the same time what Gan-Potou has in mind. When they reached the top of the great wall, their collective breaths caught in their throats.

Gogatha sprawled out before then in every direction. The island was far beneath them but radiant in every way beneath a blazing sun. The sea was a gleaming blue that sparkled and glittered all around and beyond the island that was suddenly tiny, a single pebble in comparison.

Stone turned to Tigran. "Now you see what you thought originally: you can see the water all around the island," The big man raised his eyebrows, smirking and nodding at once. His breath was still caught in his throat.

Gan-Potou led the little group about fifty meters from where they stood around the great length of the giant wall. They passed watchtowers and battlements where soldiers had once observed from for any attacking ships. He stopped at a point that had a break in the parapets.

"This way." He said excitedly and went through the break where a ladder waited. The others followed the captain down the length of the ladder to where a secondary wall clung to the one they had just climbed down from. This wall was smaller and did not go all the way around the length of the larger but stopped suddenly in either direction. The wind flowed freely against their skin, for there was nothing here to block it. The wall was more of a landing that dropped off along every edge. Strange contraptions, all frame and canvas, were lined along the rim, locked to chains embedded to the floor. The company edged closer to examine these curious pieces of equipment but wary of the sudden drop beyond.

"Sky Catchers!" Gan-Potou declared proudly.

Stone moved over to the captain of the guard, gripped his shoulder and pulled him close to his face. "What do you *mean?*"

Gan-Potou tried to hold his smile. "These are what we use

to surprise attack an assaulting army." Still in Stone's steel grip, he looked at the others, "This landing is one of many that encircle the entire wall. There is also one below us and below all the others. We dive off the walls, thousands of us, using the Sky Catchers to fall upon the unsuspecting army."

The group crowded around these strange flying apparatuses in utter awe. The things were equipped with two long pikes pointing forward and metal rams and shields in their midsections. Straps hung unused by solid frames that were also used to mount the long sleek canvases that were of beige colour and spread out to either side like wings.

"Brilliant!" Tigran Eviathane shouted excitedly.

"What do you mean, *brilliant*, you savage?" Stone was appalled. Eviathane ignored him completely already anxious to try one out. The others were a little less enthusiastic.

"They are really quite safe," Gan-Potou spoke up as if reading their minds. After all, we will not be flying into the midst of an army. And there is a strong wind; we should be able to clear most of the island. Just do what I say and you should be fine.

But moments later, the group realizing there really was no other way to even have a chance of gaining the warships, they allowed Gan-Potou to instruct them of how to fly these things.

"Now they don't actually fly... they *glide*. Eventually you *will* reach the point where it will become impossible to gain height and you will descend to the ground. I will jump ahead and you will follow my *every* move... my every move." He looked at the others as if he were a condescending teacher. "The two handles at the front are for ascending and descending. Push up *gently* and you will go up or slow your descent. Pull gently towards you, and I stress the word 'gently', and you will glide downwards.

"The straps behind, which will be attached to each of your ankles, are for steering. Pull down with your left foot and you will turn left. Pull down with your right and you will turn right. When we near the ground, push hard on the forward handles just before landing and the nose of the Sky Catcher will spring upwards and you will be placed in a vertical position and will be able to land on your feet. That's it." Gan-Potou looked at the little group as if he just explained how to go swimming in a peaceful lake.

After adjusting the Sky Catchers in accordance to the groups weight and height, Gan-Potou strapped himself into his own harness. He took them through a dry run and they followed dutifully getting the feel for each lever. The captain shouted each command for every control over and over until they moved as one with the correct motion. Their hearts were pounding rapidly against their chests at what they were about to do, mostly; they tried not to think about it. Gan-Potou ran through the commands again and again until he was satisfied that they were as ready as they will ever be.

Suddenly, the captain of the guard reached up and released the pins that held the chains to his Sky Catcher. The two lengths dropped noisily to the floor and Gan-Potou stood up effortlessly. The little group could not believe they were actually going to do this.

Tigran Eviathane was the first among them to release the chains and he stood excitedly. Avador came next, then Myia, Nectario, Skneeba, and Falstaff. Fear and adrenalin coursed through them at the same time. Avador looked over at Stone who had not moved yet, his eyes wide and staring straight ahead.

"Scared but doing it means *brave*, remember?"

"Don't *talk* to me Elf!" With that, the Dwarf released the chains and stood with the rest of them.

The company of eight, Sky Catchers at their backs, stared out into the endless sweep of sky before them. The ground and sea far below were suddenly blurry, a melded mass of indistinct haze. They fought back the dizziness and replaced it with resolve. They used their own separate thoughts to psychologically prepare themselves. The seconds were endless.

And then they jumped.

From that moment, and for years after, none of them would be able to describe what they felt; a mixture of freedom, fear, and an out of control exuberance swept through them as they caught the very wind and sailed over everything below the horizon. They howled for long moments trying to suppress the commanding thrill that overwhelmed all other emotions as they hung suspended in the skies that now belonged to them. The rush of having miles and miles of open air between them and the ground far below assailed them to the point of near-numbness. Through the chill wind they flew and they tried in vain not to look down. They caught glimpses of each other as they struggled with the onslaught of sensations. They tested the controls as much as they dared, inching left and right, getting the feel of this new and unrivalled experience. It was a long time before they remembered that they had to follow Gan-Potou's every move.

The captain took them over the island's eastern shoreline sweeping it in a great arc equalled only by a rainbow. They followed dutifully, fearful of going off course and losing him completely. The great mountain, Vyn-Turion was far behind them, lost within a cluster of cloud and they left it as it was: a bad and distant memory.

They continued on, gliding fluently through the ample

winds. So many miles were covered in such a short time that it left them in utter disbelief. Countless forms of terrain moved beneath them: hills, valleys, rivers and lakes. They were all there one moment and gone the next... one dream fading, another appearing.

The shore became clearer now with the sea's white-capped waves flowing onto the beaches only to even out and recede back to where they came from. The forests were on their right, the trees becoming more distinct as Gan-Potou carried on with a slow and gradual descent. Soon the beach was rising up to meet them and they fumbled to bring to mind the proper instructions to land. The ground then became a blur as it rushed beneath them in an indistinct sweep of sand. The captain, some distance ahead of the others, suddenly pushed forward on his levers and his Sky Catcher slowed and swung upward. Gan-Potou then dropped harmlessly to his feet. The others followed his movements and they were surprised at how easily they landed. Their legs were unexpectedly numb as though they were made of jelly and their blood flowed faster than normal, but they were back on solid ground, safe and unharmed.

A blood-chilling scream came suddenly from their left. Stone Warhelm was sailing past them and above the water, skimming over it until he landed face-first meters away from the shoreline. Gan-Potou released his harness and ran to the aid of the Dwarf. He reached down and quickly hauled him to his feet shouting and cursing at whoever was unfortunate to be in his vicinity. He was yelling something about drowning when they all realized that the water was knee-deep. Laughter broke out then, but the Dwarf failed to see what was so funny.

The little company carried their Sky Catchers to a stand

of palm trees to their right and set them in a cluster atop one another. Then they readjusted their weapons and huddled together. The heat and humidity were back and it did not take Stone long to dry off, though that did not stop him from grumbling about his dislike for the hot temperatures.

"The cliffs you spoke of are only a few miles west of here." Gan-Potou said when they all gathered together. "I chose this spot because there are stables with horses hidden in the forests beyond these palm trees. We'll make for the stables on foot, it is only a short trek, and from there we should make better time with the horses." Everyone was in agreement and they wasted no time. Avador motioned for Gan-Potou to lead and the group followed eagerly and broke through the tree line.

They hiked through the lush green of the forest taking in its sweet smells and clean air. Small streams flowed sluggishly in many places and tiny waterfalls could be seen from a distance. Myia was suddenly reminded of her old home and a memory pang wrenched at her heart. But she forced it away and carried on.

Within moments they reached the stables. If not for his keen eyes, Avador would have missed it entirely it was so well hidden and camouflaged with its surroundings. Gan-Potou did not hesitate. He took them inside where a man who was seeing to the horses stopped what he was doing, shocked to see anyone approach unexpectedly. But he soon realized who it was and welcomed the captain of the guard with open arms.

"Gan-Potou!" he declared animatedly. He was dark-skinned and bearded in the style of Stone Warhelm but greying with age. "Can you believe what has happened?" His blue eyes were glittering. "We have back the *sun!*"

Gan-Potou smiled. "You can thank these people for that." The captain stepped aside and allowed the stable keeper a good look at the little party.

"My friends," Gan-Potou said to Avador's group, "this is my old comrade, Tyk-Mada. He was once my superior officer." The captain was beaming with pride.

"Gan-Potou is being delusional," Tyk-Mada said shrewdly, "I am *still* his superior!" They all laughed while the captain of the guard shook his head smiling.

The group ate a brief meal of fruit, cheese, and dried beef provided by Tyk-Mada. They were surprised at how famished they were not remembering when it was that they ate last. The stableman was a hearty host and could not offer the little company enough. The horses, he had said, were the least he could provide for the people who had taken care of Aonas and freed his friend, and the rest of Gogatha. Regardless, Avador could not keep from thanking Tyk-Mada for his generosity.

Before long, the little party were on horseback and the stableman was readying his own mount and beaming with pride.

"Just leave the horses tied at the cliffs and I will be there shortly to round them up. You will be riding harder than my old bones can take." He gave Gan-Potou a knowing nudge with his elbow. The captain of the guard smiled in return.

Tyk-Mada gave the group a final farewell and wished them good fortune and greater results for their journey across the ocean. Gan-Potou embraced the old man, held him momentarily at arm's length, and climbed atop his horse. With a final wave, the group steered their horses west and broke for the cliffs where at their base far below, waited the *Matheia*.

The trek to the cliffs took the little company through a dense forest where Gan-Potou led them carefully but quickly on a well-used trail safe enough for a horse to gallop over. The trees of the forest soon thinned out and the smell of the sea came out to meet them with a promise that they were nearing. Eventually, the trees ended completely and Gan-Potou was leading them over green fields that surprised the group at how vibrant it's colours were. When they arrived on the island, it had been grey and dismal, an extreme contrast to what it is now. They almost did not recognize that they have been here before.

After only a mere hour, the cliffs were looming before them, sheer drops that overlooked the endless sea beyond. The little company on horseback slowed their mounts at a small stand of stray pine where they stopped and dismounted.

"We'll tie the horses here." Gan-Potou instructed. "Tyk-Mada will be here shortly to water them and bring them home."

"The stairs are further ahead," Avador said to Gan-Potou, excitement coursing through him at getting back on the ship and reuniting with its captain. They left their horses and moved cautiously towards the area where Avador remembered the hidden steps.

"You going to be okay, Falstaff?" Tigran said almost sarcastically.

"Do you want to go ahead of me?" The young mage replied. "That way, you could catch me if I fall."

It took the Elf a little bit of time to search out the exact location of the steps for if one did not know they existed, they would appear simply as an ordinary surface of the precipice. But before long, he found them. Avador looked at the members of his group with an expression that asked if they are ready. They nodded at once. Without another moment's hesitation, the Elf sat on the cliff's edge and put his foot on the first step of many that led to the little alcove housing Man-Poda's ship.

Going down was considerably easier than climbing up. The group followed Avador's method of keeping his back to the stairs and leaning towards them as he lowered one foot after another onto the declining steps. Before long, the entire company was standing on the small patch of beach that fronted the water.

"Where is the ship?" Gan-Potou asked, panic beginning to set in. The others were staring right at it and had forgotten that it was cloaked from the island's inhabitants.

"*It is there, Gan-Potou.*" Skneeba entered his thoughts at once. "*I have originally kept it hidden to allow safe passage for the Graylings who were missed during Aonas' annihilation of their race. It turned out that it was also useful to get this party of heroes safely onto Gogatha.*"

Gan-Potou, regardless of how many times he had witnessed Skneeba's power, was amazed once again.

The well-defined sound of a chain being reeled in carried itself across the smooth glass-like waters of the inlet. Man-Poda had seen the group standing on the tiny piece of beach and ordered to be taken closer. The collective hearts of the small company beat faster as the ship drew nearer. Stone Warhelm and Falstaff, on the other hand, were not so enthused.

The *Matheia* glided before them. What was once a shabby craft unfit to sail the seas, was now, to them, a mythical vessel that would carry them away from this land they simply want to forget.

Man-Poda stood at the bow, a grin so big split his face almost in half. When the crew inched the ship as close to shore as they would dare, a rope ladder was thrown over the hull and splashed into the salty water.

"Will you come with us?" Avador asked Gan-Potou.

"I would want nothing more, my Prince." The captain of the guard looked sad all of a sudden. "But I believe someone must stay behind and begin the clean-up of Aonas' aftermath."

"That is what I thought," answered the Elf, disappointed yet understanding. The company said their goodbyes to Gan-Potou and in return received many words of gratitude for saving his life. Then, one by one, the members of the little group waded the short distance to the ladder and climbed it to the main deck. Man-Poda was waiting, the grin still huge.

"Avador Andor!" He proclaimed enthusiastically in his raspy accent. And then turned to the rest of the group as they climbed aboard, drenched from their swim. "All of you, *heroes!*"

"You and the Graylings are free to occupy your island." The Elf said happily.

"I have come to that assumption when the wicked moon vanished and the sun returned to take its place." Man-Poda was overcome with both relief and euphoria.

A lone Grayling, tall, muscular and grinning, broke from the rest that waited for their next instructions.

"Grynde!" Exclaimed Avador. The Grayling walked proudly towards the Elf, straightened, and towered over him with a smile. He then returned to his hunched posture, took the other's hand and bowed. Avador hugged him in response.

"You are a good man." He said; the Grayling was beaming.

~****~

After the *Matheia* squeezed through the two lengths of rock that was the precipice-funnel leading into the inlet and sailed past the cluster of islands that fronted Gogatha, the sleek schooner was soon drifting back into the deepest waters.

The little group took up their accustomed positions. Avador helped with minor repairs not quite completed during the wait for their return, Tigran helping Nectario with his sword skills, Myia enjoying the view and laughing at the two 'combatants', and Falstaff and Stone disappearing into the quarterdeck not willing to come out just yet. Skneeba had joined the Captain of the ship in the pilot-box offering insight of what has happened on Gogatha since he was away and how Avador's little band helped to put an end to all of it. Man-Poda could not help but be amazed at the accomplishment despite all the odds thrown against them. He was very proud indeed to know them.

Avador walked into the control room and joined Skneeba and Man-Poda, his brow glistening from the repair work and warm weather.

"Man-Poda," the Elf said enquiringly, "do you have any idea how much further ahead the warships are?"

The Captain's lip curled at one corner. "Doesn't matter. We will catch them." Avador felt the beginnings of a pout. Man-Poda laughed jovially. "My crew members on the crow's nests all marked a long line of ships many miles behind us. Those are the second wave of ships you have told me about. They are slow and cumbersome. The ships with your father's armies are at a greater distance ahead and are not yet visible. We have *days* ahead of us before we reach your lands." Man-Poda saw the worry on the Elf's face. "The winds are on our side, young Prince; my ship is much faster than the others. We *will* catch them." The Captain slapped a hand on Avador's shoulder. "Now stop worrying and trust your Captain." The three in the pilot-box laughed and exited onto the main deck where the salty winds brushed passed them and filled the numerous sails of the *Matheia*.

"You look more concerned than even *I*, Elfling." Stone Warhelm said to Avador as he entered the quarterdeck. The Elf shut the door and joined him on the blankets strewn across the wooden floorboards.

"I *am* worried, Stone." Avador answered honestly. "I do not know what to do once we gain the ships and dock at Land's End."

"*That* is what troubles you?" The Dwarf almost chuckled. "I have seen you conquer immeasurable odds. I have faith you will do so again."

Avador was shaking his head. "It is an enormous weight..."

"You are your father's son!" Stone cut him short, "you think it has been easy for him all these years?" Avador was suddenly embarrassed. He did not know exactly what his father has been through. The Elf King has kept from him his journeys and battles deliberately... but *why*?

"Before the time of your father," Stone continued, "the races have been scattered throughout the lands claiming territories and believing they must be detached from one another in order to prosper. Grandalimus managed to gain the respect of each race simply by standing by what he believes in. They saw that he was right. After all, I was among the first to pledge my allegiance to him. I have been at his side at every war, every battle. He has gained the loyalty of the Dwarves and they stand with him without question, as do the Humans. Before you were born, Elfling, before your father became king in the eyes of all the races, the races were scattered. Now they are happily mixing and watching each other's backs. *That* is the army we'll be facing, *that* is what we are up against." Avador had a sudden idea of what was required of him.

"War." Stone said after the brief silence. "It is something I was born to do. I have seen too many of them, but I was younger then. In times of war, when my enemy stood before me, my sole thought was 'it's better that *his* mother cries'. But wars are senseless; your father knows that." The Dwarf paused to see the effect in the Elf's eyes. "He also knows that it's impossible to try and convince that to an invading army. Even after each victory, in the filth-strewn soil... when the dust faded he would say, 'no one wins'."

A hush spread out before them when Stone finished speaking. They sat in the silence and felt the tranquil swaying of the ship as it moved along its ocean path. The minutes turned to hours and eventually the steady hum of the busy Graylings began to silence. In time, all the members of the little group entered the quarterdeck, weariness finally getting the better of them as the sun began its descent into the western horizon.

Skneeba entered a few moments after as the company prepared to climb into their blankets, his silhouette framed in the doorway against the fading light. He said nothing at first; he simply stared at each face one by one. Then, with his jerky movements, entered and closed the door behind him. The dark mage moved next to Falstaff, something bulky in his hands came into view as he neared.

"*I believe you lost something?*" Skneeba said to Falstaff, though the others could hear as well. Falstaff sat up, alert at once, yet speechless. The dark mage moved the object into the final rays of light and revealed a large backpack, torn yet intact.

"My book!" Falstaff declared.

"*I recognized the dangers of allowing Aonas to discover it and took it when you were brought into the stronghold and stripped of your weapons.*" Skneeba handed the book to Falstaff's waiting hands. "*Your grandfather was wise to give it to you.*"

Falstaff was stunned. "How did you know about my grandfather?"

"*There are extremely few in this world such as we, Falstaff... such as you and I.*" The younger mage's heart swelled suddenly with pride. "*Your grandfather left your village long ago after the passing of his wife. He left in search of the knowledge we know so little of. We met on your lands by chance. I was whole then.*" Skneeba sat next to Falstaff, his face saddened by the reminiscence. "*He was older than I and he recognized my abilities at once, astounded by my talent to control them at such a young age. The magic you create, young Falstaff, comes from his book. But the book is for the novice magic-user. I think maybe he has known that you would follow in his footsteps and left the book for you.*

"*But do not think it has been easy for him. He has grown restless in your village; some people even began to distrust and fear him. They did not know that the power of the arcane is something a magic-user is born with. Most people are not even able to become magic-users; some can but do not know it. It is something that your grandfather discovered during his travels before finding your village and settled there.*"

"I do not know my grandfather," Falstaff said quietly, "I have not been told much of him."

"*Oh, he is a good man, Falstaff. Regrettably, I have lost contact with him when I returned to Gogatha. He may return one day to your village; one never knows. Yes, he is a good man. And you, young mage, have been given his name.*" Falstaff's eyes went wide and Skneeba smiled shrewdly beneath his hooded robes.

The *Matheia* sailed through the night and many nights after, the ships holding Grandalimus' armies coming into view on the tenth day of travel. Unfortunately, the good weather did not hold longer than that. The line of warships appeared on the grey horizon as storm clouds formed their ranks in a slow yet intentional procedure and invaded the sun until it was taken over completely. The winds intensified almost at once as the brightness of the day turned into a dreary grey and rain beat down on the creaking wood of the schooner.

But the Graylings were ready.

The booming chant began abruptly sending excitement throughout the struggling ship. Sails were doused and lines were drawn, the crew's movements the echo of their Captain's bellowed orders.

Avador stood on deck next to Man-Poda, the rain soaking them both to the bone.

"The ships ahead have slowed, Avador!" Shouted Man-Poda above the wind's howl. "We are trying now to keep from being thrown into their midst. The warships behind have entered the storm but they are huge and powerful, more capable of meeting its rush!" Avador took a moment to soak in what this meant.

"We have only a day's worth of sailing left before we reach Land's End," the Captain continued, "if we can manage to keep ahead of those ships, we'll ride out the storm before them and reach shore without being discovered!" Avador didn't like the odds.

The Elf entered the quarterdeck where the others waited, water pouring off him and onto the floor.

"Did ya get more *ale*?" Shouted Stone in annoyance. Falstaff was lying in his blankets, once again trying to keep from retching.

Avador ignored the Dwarf and let them know what was happening as he removed his wet cloak. The others decided to just be patient and wait, realizing there really was not much else to do.

Outdoors, the *Matheia* struggled on. Rain and wind struck at her from every side, but her crew was among the best and were managing to keep the ship upright, though one would not imagine it was so by the endless creaking that drove Stone Warhelm to the edge of panic.

The hours moved on and it seemed as though the storm would never end. Night took over the seas and a huge bright moon struggled within its own turbulent ocean of cloud, sending its light only when it was permitted. On the *Matheia* fought in the roiling ocean, tossed and shoved effortlessly, wedged between two fleets of soldier-packed warships.

~****~

Slowly, yet inevitably, the night emptied its hours into the waiting lap of dawn. Only then did the storm show signs of fading. The ship began to bob less and less and the creaking weakened almost completely. It wasn't until these hours that the group managed to sleep, when the *Matheia* began to rock them gently into a peaceful slumber.

Badom's eyes were watchful in the dim light. He had awakened early so he could be alone for a few moments. He was keeping one eye out for Bogdan as he was filling his pipe, and one eye towards the sea when the Gnome saw the giant warships climb over the horizon. Hastily, he dropped everything and ran to where his friend still lay beneath a tattered blanket.

"Bogdan!" He shouted breathlessly. "Bogdan wake up, something's happening!"

"Something's *always* happening!" Bogdan shouted back.

"Now let me sleep, the sun hasn't even woke up yet, for Shah's sake!"

~

Avador was the first to awaken when daybreak was still only an orange line splitting the horizon. The Elf moved wearily through the calm patter of fading raindrops along the deck, his cloak wrapped tightly about him. He stopped when he reached the bow, alone and curiously at peace. He let the breeze caress him as he looked ahead and gazed at the warships that were preparing to dock at Land's End. *This is it.* He thought coolly. This was the moment he must do what is needed; the answer to what that was, remained evasive. He stopped looking ahead and walked to the ship's stern and gazed out behind them. The warships have broken through the storm and somehow gained quite the distance. The Elf remained calm when the ships revealed themselves with greater detail, nearer now than throughout the journey. The Graylings on deck were fewer than when the storm was at its full intensity and Man-Poda was nowhere in sight. Avador walked back to the quarterdeck and decided to wake his friends. Today, something was going to happen.

The sun climbed timidly into the eastern sky, barely hovering over the water line as if reluctant to allow this day to carry on. The army marched as one. They drew their ranks with the same discipline and obedience inspired by their true King. Their march was point-blank thunder and it instilled instant fear into any creature alive to hear it. They marched onto the vast land before them, a country that was once their own. Now they will destroy it. The lands before them, great cliffs that shuddered at their approach and the plains beyond felt the tremor of their advance. An army of every race, every type of warrior, their loyalty intact yet unable to control what they were about to do, flooded the edge of land and fanned out in two directions. The docks, long abandoned as a consequence of the raiding warships were empty of their usual life. There was nothing to stand against this massive juggernaut that was ready to destroy anything unfortunate enough to be caught in its midst.

Stone Warhelm, sleepy-eyed and awestruck by what was happening before him, gazed helplessly at the army that he had once fought at the side of. It was all he could do not to break down on the *Matheia's* very deck.

"I have awakened to a nightmare." The Dwarf's words were practically inaudible. But Avador heard him and could not help but agree. The little company stared despairingly at the sight before them as the ship neared the emptied-out warships. Behind them, the second fleet, just as massive as the first, approached like death itself and were beginning to spread out to flank their preceding comrades.

Avador's jaw was hurting from long moments of gritting his teeth. The *Matheia* slipped between two massive warships in an attempt to claim a small piece of the docks. The walls of their hulls towered high above and blocked out the sun leaving the slender schooner in their colossal shadows. Man-Poda had taken over the controls in the pilot-box and eased his ship closer to Land's End. The deafening march of the army rang loud and clear and shuddered their very hearts as it broke free of the shoreline and moved onto higher ground. The distinct clang of weapons and armour demonstrated its unrivalled power.

The Prince of the Elves watched his father's army with a growing resolve. His mind raced as he tried to contain the right memory, the correct decision to make the necessary move. The second fleet of warships were nearing the docks now, the shouts of the men aboard a clear promise that the taste of death was already on their lips.

When the *Matheia* docked, he had his answer.

The army of Grandalimus fought a war that was happening inside their hearts. Tears were falling like rivers. Dark thoughts entered their brains as a new war inside their very minds began to take place. They did not want to do this. They had family here, friends from childhood and memories of another time. The very peace they once fought to keep became the destruction they were about to commit. And they wanted no part of it. They would rather die in the name of Grandalimus than serve under Aonas. One by one, the soldiers let this thought linger in their minds as a grim possibility. The march began to slow its booming tempo and go completely off time, the hands of the soldiers inching to their blades. And finally, the marching stopped altogether and there was silence save for the passing of the gentle wind that snaked through the ranks of soldiers like an unseen spectre.

Avador Andor flew off the ramp of the *Matheia* and landed on the shores of Land's End. The *Kingblade* was unsheathed and his cloak flying as he raced for the very heart of his father's army. He heard the shouts of his friends but they were bluntly ignored. One man put himself in the biggest gamble of his life, one man against thousands.

The Elf reached the rear lines of the soldiers and did not slow. He ran straight into their midst, rushing passed weapons and armour and astonished gasps. No one knew what this blur of deep violet and green was, catching only a glimpse of a movement that disappeared the next second.

Avador reached beneath his shirt of chain-mail as he ran, nearing the very centre of the massive army. The Elf was swallowed whole within the sea of soldiers, a tiny speck among the stars. And then he stopped abruptly and drew forth the amulet sent to him by his mother. The mass around him drew back and he was standing on his own ground. He gripped its silver chain and dropped to one knee, the *Kingblade* digging into the dirt before him. *With this*, his father's words re-entered his mind in complete vividness, *I summon my soldiers to attention!*

Avador raised the amulet high above his head and began to spin it on its chain. A piercing whistle shredded the air around the Elf and intensified as he spun it with greater force. The amulet sang its song in a single note.

"ANDOR!" The army howled as one and it thundered across the plains and over the very ocean. Avador stood and raised the *Kingblade*; it's silvery steel gleaming in the rising sun.

"Andor!" He repeated, adrenalin overpowering him completely. Suddenly, Skneeba was at his side. He did not know how he got there. Then Falstaff, Stone, Eviathane, Nectario and Myia came after.

"ANDOR!" Skneeba raised his arms and the blade of Avador's sword brightened even more. It flared to a blinding level and its power split into thousands of directions.

"ANDOR!" The weapons of Grandalimus' army began to glow with the same intensity. The Ecliptic Wraiths came out at once. But the army was no longer afraid. They knew what was happening and they howled anew. Avador kneeled as the last of the *Kingblade's* power drained into the weapons of the soldiers.

Then, the massacre began.

The weapons of their captives cut down thousands of

Ecliptic Wraiths in a single blow. The army's roar mixed ominously with the shrieks of the Ecliptic Wraiths. The men were howling, as the vision of their freedom became a truth before their very eyes. Gone were the keepers in their shadows. Gone was the fear of making a small mistake only to be killed by their captors. Gone was the ungodly command to destroy the people of their own lands. The men of Grandalimus and the combined men of Jadonas were free to fight for what *they* believed.

Aonas' true followers spilled out of their warships and surged onto the edge of land as if they were an extension of the sea itself, and crashed like a torrential wave onto the earth. Their battle cries resounded before them, reverberating into the newly freed army that stood in their way. *Destroy the lands at **any** cost!*

Avador Andor turned to face the army that broke from the shoreline and formed their ranks. *War is senseless. But try telling that to an invading army.* The Elf threw off his cloak and the chain-mail beneath gleamed in the strengthening sunlight.

Then he sent himself howling into his first war, his father's army a deafening roar at his heals.

The armies were like two swarms of giant insects, clashing ferociously into each other with a deafening clatter of weapons, armour, and battle cries. There was no time to shape formations or plan strategies; these were two armies bluntly attacking each other with the sole purpose of surviving.

Avador Andor fought by the side of his friends, indomitable in their own right. They acted as his shield and he as there's. Stone Warhelm was home, surrounded and outnumbered. The mages sent bursts of flame and lightning into the masses of malicious soldiers, defending their own in waves of heat and thunder. The fighting was tremendous, more than any of them had ever seen. Tigran Eviathane was unconquerable, his sword a weapon to be reckoned with in his able hand. Nectario was always there, braver now than he had ever been, a cavalier in the midst of chaos and death. His scimitar flashed wildly cutting down those that broke through the defences of his friends. Myia was in their centre, a fallen short-sword in her hands, valiant within the pandemonium that was the heart of battle. Time stood still. The little party, engulfed by the protecting army of Grandalimus as it tore ferociously at the onslaught of the enemy, became its smallest unit.

The King's men fought with a vigour they never before had, spilling the blood of challenger after challenger. This was a war they must not lose; so much was at stake. The shores of Land's End, once a port and docks for ships coming and going became a battleground, bloodied and soiled with fallen men from both sides.

The army of Aonas was of lesser soldiers next to the fearless men who had more at stake than the simple loss of money. Steadily they were pushed back to the very waters and the warships that brought them and forced to spread out into a long, thick line of bewildered soldiers. The men of Grandalimus continued their onslaught, splitting its ranks in three. Two masses flanked the enemy army on both sides while the central bulk shoved ahead.

But Aonas' men refused to surrender; it was fight or die. In a desperate attempt to push back the overpowering assault, the foot soldiers dropped to their knees to allow archers and spearmen clear shots at their enemy. Their first volley was an arc of raining arrows that struck many of the charging men and downed them where they stood. This bought them some time and the spearmen thrust their missiles before the confusion was over. But Grandalimus' men were seasoned and ready for it. The front lines dropped to a crouch as one and locked shields in one swift motion. Most of the spears were wasted as the army returned to its fighting stance and surged forward.

Avador was among these men. His body, soaked in the blood of his enemies, he fought with an unexplainable inner rage. He shouted orders bringing the ranks of his men forward and into formations that were utterly impenetrable, and the men obeyed without question. His friends, all of them, were still at his side, the fighters cutting men down with their weapons, the magic-users shocking them with power they had never seen before in any war... nor will they ever see again.

Finally, Aonas' army fought no more. There was nowhere left to retreat. Many of its men were already floating lifelessly in the very sea. The flanking sides of Grandalimus' men had the warships blocked against any escape. The enemy laid down their weapons and surrendered.

"That was *it*?" Stone's shout echoed throughout the beachfront; his adrenalin was left unquenched. A roar of victory followed and the remaining men of Aonas were left to decide where to go and what to do next.

Chapter 31 - Home

Pelendria was shrouded in darkness. Midnight came and went and Simetra Andor placed another chunk of deadwood into the fireplace. She could not sleep this night, even more so than the previous nights. The rumours were eating her up inside. The villagers that returned from travels had arrived with many tales. Some brought her hope while others seemed too far-fetched to be true. The one that remained a constant was the one that said a war had taken place, quick but fierce. Some said Grandalimus was at the head of his army once again. Some spoke of a young Elf becoming a legend at the war's conclusion. But every report said that the war would be etched in history, a war with magic and steel working as one. Simetra was not sure if she was to be afraid of the latter.

Snow had fallen across the lands surrounding the village nearly a week ago. The rumours began a week before that. The trees of Gwynfell were transformed into a white, mythical forest and Simetra Andor felt the pang of heartache. She used to venture the forest with her son when it snowed; it was her favourite time of year.

A sound drew her away from her thoughts. She sat up in her chair and listened beyond the crackle of the fire. Voices. They were coming from Gwynfell, low and hushed but definitely there. The voices grew louder as they neared. Simetra stood almost fearfully. This was a strange hour for any sort of activity in a village. She moved to the window of her bedroom and cautiously peered out. The darkness beyond hindered her sight but her vision was still sharp and it adjusted quickly. A company of men appeared through the break in the trees, their silhouettes unmistakable. They paused briefly at the edge of the tree line, exchanged words, and split into separate directions.

Simetra heard the sound of booted feet crunching the snow beneath them and they were working their way to the front entrance of her home. They reached the door and one of them tapped lightly on its burnished wood. Simetra walked gingerly to the door, unsure of what to do. Someone tapped again and she opened the door. Outside stood a Dwarf, a human, a Wood Elf and...

"Avador." Simetra breathed her son's name in disbelief.

~****~

The Kentro was once more a bustle of activity. The tables were set up again and the kitchen was alight with cooks and servants rushing to finish up the preparations for the night's activities. Drinks were served fervently as the night progressed and the village hall filled steadily.

Combat Master Wylme Tagom was the one who set everything up. He hustled almost as much as the servants trying to keep up with everything. He wanted this night to be perfect. At times he shouted above the noise level for certain tables to be taken care of, his big frame held in his always-intimidating stance. Tonight was a night for celebration; Pelendria's heroes were home.

Falstaff, Tigran, Avador, Myia, Nectario and Stone had politely refused the table that was set for their honour. Instead, they preferred a table outdoors on the terrace where the noise level was less. Out there, they watched the soft flakes of snow fall all around them and listened to the Cerulean River rush in the ravine beneath them. Stone rather enjoyed the view of his Trood Mountain home from the balcony.

The little group was still trying to come to terms with the fact that they were home, a place that was not so long ago, just a distant memory. It was as if they were watching themselves in a dream. At times they were distant, their thoughts distracted by the ordeal and the events that were still as fresh as their healing wounds. The parents were proud and they did absolutely nothing to hide it, making it a point to never leave their side. After all, they too, could not believe their son's are home.

Skneeba was with them as well, a silent shadow at their side, taking in the enjoyment just as much as they, though keeping his emotions in check. But amidst the merriment was another shadow, another wraith that refused to go away: The haunting thought of Grandalimus. Skneeba explained to them that the Elf King was indeed cursed to walk the earth as a creature neither alive nor dead. Aonas chose his curse wisely, selecting one that was irreparable. But the dark mage swore he would seek the answers that remained hidden from them. What he cannot undo now, he will find a way to do so or die in the attempt. As great as his power is, he still has much to learn... the answers are out there, he *will* find them.

The Wood Elves of Feo-Dosia were present as well. Though unaccustomed to wine and ale, they were indeed enjoying the celebration for the return of one of there own and the heroes she fought by. The people of Pelendria accepted them with open arms, and they could not be more grateful. If anything good became of the destruction caused by Aonas, it was the joining of these two civilizations.

Simetra Andor watched her son as he laughed and conversed with his friends. His boyish face was back every time he laughed, but at times, the evidence of something forever changed within him was present as well. The three friends, brothers in their own right, shared a strengthened bond that was indestructible. Her son was *home*. She still could not believe it. How long has it been since he left so hastily and with little explanation to search out his father and bring him home? She sighed and almost wept. Her son brought back a part of his father, and that part was within him. His virtues, his strength, they were among the many parts. His leadership, charisma and love... his flair at being a *King*.

Simetra muted her pain and shelved it deep inside her heart where she could bring it out later. She looked again to Avador. And then she looked at his friends. The same pain she felt was evident on their faces as well. Tonight, they were present yet far away. They wanted this time to get together alone and speak of everything that happened. They wanted to get together with their parents and talk about their quest, what it has done for them, and about what to do for the future. Later, she guessed, they would get their chance. She turned her attention back to her son and at that moment, she knew that this wasn't finished for him.

Epilogue

P ale moonlight spilled out of its surrounding clouds and poured over the landscape that housed the tombs. The light washed the earth beneath it in its white shine and gave the deceiving effect of the land being covered with an eerie blanket of snow.

The prince that can never be king stood before the bone structure that was Lord's Lair. Strange, he thought. What was once frightening to him now seemed almost ridiculous to have been so. A sudden gust of wind swept by and the Elf tightened his cloak about his shoulders.

All else was quiet.

The Prince of Elvenkind moved closer to the entrance, his heart beating faster, the bright, and full moon hanging high above him. He was alone... but not for long.

Avador entered Lord's Lair, lit a torch, and walked the length of the long corridor, his head held high. When he reached the arched doorway at the end, he pushed it open and it swung in effortlessly at his touch. The chill swept through him at once as if warning him that only those that are not completely alive are permitted to enter. He shrugged the feeling off and entered.

The room was exactly as he remembered it when he first came here with his friends. A veil of dust had gathered over their footsteps where they had trampled before. The crumpled heaps of bone that were the animate skeleton men that had attacked, lay scattered where the group destroyed them. Nothing else had changed. Everything was black as ink beyond the torch's reach; the Elf was the only thing visible. But he pressed forward, relaxed and steady, until he found the steps that lead to the landing. Taking in a long breath, Avador began to climb.

Defiant like a slumped snow-covered rose refusing to die, Grandalimus stood on his platform, his head bowed. If he knew of his son's approach, he did not show it. The minutes crept by adding to the anticipation. It was not until the distinct *ring* of the *Kingblade* being released from its scabbard that the King's head jerked up as if in response.

"Father." Avador whispered in the faint, orange light of his torch. The Elf brought up the blade and held it before him. Grandalimus' face reflected perfectly in its silvery surface, firm, strong, and as he was.

"*Hello, Avador.*" The Elf King spoke as if nothing was wrong, as if a proud father was simply speaking to his son. In fact, that is how it was.

"I could not stay away." Avador continued.

"*J know.*" Grandalimus was smiling in his reflection. Avador was oddly calm, at peace considering where he was.

The Elf King looked away for a moment and then returned his gaze. "*J am willing to believe that there is no father alive as proud of his son as J am of mine.*" Avador blushed, unable to contain a smile.

"I want you back, Father."

"*J know, Son.*"

"Skneeba has promised he will find a way."

"Skneeba…" Grandalimus was nodding his head, a sad smile on his lips.

"He *will* find a way." Avador was convinced.

"*One day, perhaps.*" The Elf King seemed unconcerned.

"*But for now, brave Avador, there is something you must know.*" A silence followed then, a hush that stressed the importance of what was to come. Father and son stared at each other in the deep orange glow; the rest of the world did not exist.

"*You may be a prince in the view of the laws that state you are. You may be the son of a king. But know this: I have become a king, not because my father was one, but because the nations wanted it that way. In fact, I still do not consider myself one.*" Avador was waiting patiently. "*I am just a man; my blood flows as any other. And you are just a man. What makes men different from one another is the way they perform and act on the responsibilities that must be accepted. Most wait in the darkness in hopes that someone would do something. Who is that someone? Who stands out above the rest?*" The Elf King paused and looked down at his son with more intent.

"*Twenty years ago, I was standing by a lake, at the moment of your birth. I was praying, whomever you are, that you would be a man that stands out.*" Grandalimus paused again. "*Avador. It made me proud that you acted so instinctively to come after me. Yet your friends were right in holding you back. If you would have seen me changing, no one knows what that would have done to you. It is bad enough that you have to bear it as it is.*" Avador was about to say something but his father waved him off.

"*Time is life's greatest luxury. When one sees that he is about to die, nothing in the world matters at that moment... except time. You have learned that you have to make due with what you have, even if the only ground you have to fight on is the bit beneath your feet. Never make your life pointless, my son. I have faith that you will not. No matter what happens, know that I will always be with you.*" Grandalimus touched the point of the

Kingblade meaningfully. Avador fought back the urge to tell his father again that that is not enough; the knowledge of it need not be brought up again. It was time now to accept and carry on. Avador allowed his tears to flow freely. Through the blurriness of his vision, in the blade of his sword, Grandalimus' own tears were flowing. The two men faced each other for a moment more. The price that was paid must be worth the future. They both knew this. Hope will always be their shadow, the little bit of strength needed to carry on. Love will always be their bond, indestructible and eternal.

Grandalimus Andor, *the King of the Elves*, stepped forward and embraced his son. His son embraced him back with arms that promised he would be the man he was meant to be. It was hours after when they parted. Avador Andor, the *Prince of the Elves*, drew in his resolve like a cloak, and started his journey home.

The End

ARMIDA PUBLICATIONS LTD
(member of the Association of Cypriot Book Publishers - SEKYVI)
office | 36a valesta str, 2370 ayios dhometios, nicosia, cyprus
mailing address | p.o.box 27717, 2432 engomi, nicosia, cyprus
tel: +357 22 35 80 28 | fax: +357 22 35 11 16
email: info@armidapublications.com
www.armidapublications.com